KT-373-611

Unbecoming

Jenny Downham

David Fickling Books

31 Beaumont Street
Oxford OX1 2NP, UK

Unbecoming
is a
DAVID FICKLING BOOK

First published in Great Britain by
David Fickling Books,
31 Beaumont Street,
Oxford, OX1 2NP

www.davidficklingbooks.com

Hardback edition published 2015
This edition published 2016

Text © Jenny Downham, 2015

978-1-910989-02-9

1 3 5 7 9 10 8 6 4 2

The right of Jenny Downham to be identified as the author of this work has been
asserted in accordance with the Copyright, Designs and Patents Act 1988.

A CIP catalogue record for this book is available from the British Library.

Typeset in Frutiger Light by Falcon Oast Graphic Art Ltd.
Printed and bound in Great Britain by Clays Ltd, St Ives plc.

For the Erbe women
For Andrew, Jack, his brothers and the others

PART ONE

One

It was like an alien had landed. Really, it was that weird. Like an ancient creature from another planet had crashed into Katie's day. She should have been at home studying, not sitting on a plastic chair in a hospital corridor trying to make conversation. And there were only so many times you could ask someone if they wanted anything from the drinks machine and not feel like an idiot when they refused to acknowledge you.

'Hot chocolate?'

Silence.

'How about a cappuccino?'

More silence.

Even ET had a wider vocabulary.

Katie didn't know what to call her either. She'd tried 'Nan' earlier, but that sounded strange and got zero response. Mrs Todd? Grandma? There were no rules.

What was good was that you could stare at her and she didn't seem to mind. She was quite pretty actually, had a soft lined face and her cheeks were all rosy with the fading light.

What was *bad* was that she smelled (bread left to fester in a plastic bag was Katie's closest approximation) and she was also really thin. You could actually see her collarbone pushing up from the top of her cardigan, like it wanted to escape, and the skin at

3

her neck was so transparent you could see her pulse quivering.

At the end of the row of chairs (was that supposed to be discreet?), the social worker was asking Mum endless questions. *Did Mrs Todd have any medical conditions? Was she usually so confused? Was her late husband her carer?*

'I'm not sure how far we're going to get with this,' Mum said. 'As I keep telling you, I haven't seen her for years.'

'You're named as emergency contact on her husband's medical bracelet,' the social worker said. 'That seems strange if you were out of communication.'

'Well, I assure you I'm not making it up!' Poor Mum was getting increasingly stressed. 'And he'd have been a boyfriend, not a husband. She wasn't a fan of commitment.'

'She *is* your mother though?'

'I'm not sure she qualifies for that role. Look, surely she's better off staying here? Can't you find her a bed somewhere?'

The social worker looked mildly shocked. 'Your mother isn't a patient. She arrived with her partner in the ambulance and there are no medical reasons to admit her. Are you telling me you're unwilling to take her?'

If Mum had an answer to that, she managed to keep it down, and her silence was clearly taken for compliance, because the social worker smiled and turned back to her paperwork.

The old woman just sat there, eyes shut now. She wasn't asleep though – you could tell by the tip of her chin. Maybe it was a trick? Maybe she wanted them to think she was napping, so she could scarper when no one was looking? Her boyfriend was dead, the doctors thought she was too vulnerable to go home and her daughter didn't want her. Why not escape and start a new life somewhere else?

Chris appeared back from his trip to the toilet. He stood in front of them grinning and jiggling his feet, clearly buzzing with the strangeness of it all. 'There's a café.'

Mum shook her head. 'Not now.'

'I'm hungry.'

'I said not now.'

He hopped from foot to foot and back again. 'Why not?'

'You want to sit here?' Katie tapped the chair next to her. 'Come and say hello?'

He shook his head, feigned sudden fascination with his shoes. 'I'm quite thirsty as well.'

The social worker stared at him. She was probably thinking, What's the matter with this one? Why's a hulking teenager acting like a kid? How many things can go wrong in one family?

'Welcome to my life,' Katie wanted to say. But instead, she stared back, because that's what always worked best. You let them know you'd noticed and they looked away.

'The café's not a bad idea,' the social worker said, avoiding Katie's eyes as she turned to Mum. 'This may take a while.'

Mum sighed as she opened her purse and handed Katie a ten-pound note. 'Stay together. And come back as soon as you're done.'

Katie nodded. 'Anyone else want anything?'

Mum shook her head. The social worker didn't even bother replying. Katie looked at the old woman. Maybe she'd like a meat pie or a sausage roll – something traditional and bulky to feed her up. Katie leaned in and whispered, 'Do you want anything to eat, Gran?'

No answer. No movement. And 'Gran' didn't sound right either.

The queue in the café was ridiculous and there was hardly anything left when they got to the front. They bought a packet of

5

cheese sandwiches and two boxes of orange juice, and because the café was closing and Mum was bound to be ages they sat on the wall outside to eat. The sun had sunk beyond the horizon completely now and it was cold. Chris huddled next to Katie and rested his head on her shoulder. She didn't stop him because it was dark and no one would see.

Over the road was a kebab shop. It had a sign in the window that advertised 'shish, doner, falafel'. The smell of frying onions was delicious. They should have come out here in the first place and got kebabs for supper. Would Mum have minded? Yes. She'd be worried about food poisoning from spit-roasted meat and additives in the chilli sauce. Also, since it looked a bit run-down, she'd probably think they'd be offered drugs alongside the kebab. Katie sighed. Mum was very predictable.

Wednesday evening's family plan had been: two hours' revision (Katie), make supper (Mum), homework (Chris), eat supper (all of them). Then Chris would be allowed an hour's Xbox while Katie did a practice maths paper and Mum trawled the exam board's website for mark schemes and examiners' reports so that when Katie finished they could go over the paper together to see where improvements could be made. After that, it would be bedtime. Katie would have her usual chamomile drink (Restful Nights), so she got plenty of sleep and woke up refreshed for tomorrow's study session at school.

But none of that had happened. Instead, they were at a hospital miles from home – no revision, no supper, and the very real possibility of a total stranger coming to stay with them. Katie felt an odd sense of lightness. Because if predictable evenings could be turned upside down with a phone call, then maybe anything could be flipped on its head? Even the worst things in the world. She got out her mobile and dared one more text to Esme: PLSE LETS TALK.

6

Chris sat up suddenly. 'Where's the dead husband?'

'Boyfriend,' Katie said. 'Apparently, she didn't believe in commitment. And I expect he's in the morgue.'

'He might be a zombie.'

'I doubt it.'

'That can happen.'

'Only if you play too much Xbox.'

He stuck his tongue out. 'You don't know. That woman might be one as well.'

'Let's hope not. And "that woman" is your grandmother, who might be coming to stay with us.'

He blinked at her. 'Where's she going to sleep?'

Excellent question. Why hadn't that crossed Katie's mind? They only had a three-bedroom flat.

'Katie?'

'I don't know. Stop asking me stuff.'

'Will it be my room?'

'Yes.'

'Serious?'

'Yeah, and the zombie boyfriend's going to live under your bed.'

Chris gave her a V-sign and shuffled along the wall.

She didn't care. Let him get angry. She shoved her own V-sign at his big face and another at his little eyes and a third at the general bulk of him and the way his body seemed to take up more space in the world than hers was ever allowed. It *wouldn't* be his room, would it? It'd be hers and she'd be expected to bunk in with Mum. And Mum would be stressed, which meant she'd demand Katie's help and attention even more than usual. *Thank goodness for you, Katie, always so reliable.*

She leaned back and stared at the sky. It was grey and heavy with cloud. Any vague optimism she'd felt leaked away. In fact, she hoped a giant storm was coming – something that would rupture the fabric of the earth. Because her life had just got worse. First Dad. Then Esme. Now this.

A bus stopped in front of them. It was going to a place Katie had never heard of. That was the third bus in ten minutes and they all had different destinations on the front.

'Hey, Chris, you fancy hopping on that bus and seeing where we end up?'

'No!' He looked terrified.

Only two people got off – a girl, who walked past them, talking into her mobile: 'I might see you later. I'm not sure what I'm doing yet.' And a man, who stopped just in front of them holding a can of beer. 'Hello,' he said, and then he looked at Chris while pointing his beer at Katie. 'Is she with you?'

They didn't say anything and the man walked away.

Chris said, 'We should go inside.' He said it gently, like it mattered to him. 'We shouldn't be out here now.'

Katie shook her head. 'I don't want to.'

'It's dangerous.'

'Not everywhere's dangerous. It's statistically impossible.'

'Why are you getting down, then? Where are you going?'

'Nowhere. My legs have gone to sleep. Stay there.'

She walked a little way along the pavement. Across the road, three men came out of the kebab shop. They unwrapped their food and took great steaming bites. I don't know any of you, Katie thought. I will never know your names or see you again. It felt so liberating. To be away from the claustrophobia of the town where they lived – the dull streets, the unexciting shops and cafés, the tiny arts centre, the one school. A place where once rumours began, they easily spread.

8

Breathe, breathe. Don't think about that now . . .

If she lived in this city, no one would know her. She'd reinvent herself. New clothes, new hair, maybe a piercing or a tattoo. She'd get a job, take a gap year instead of going straight to uni. She'd be like that girl getting off the bus. *I'm not sure what I'm doing yet.*

Imagine that.

Katie licked her dry lips and closed her eyes. When she opened them, only a few seconds later, Chris was jumping off the wall.

'It's Mum!' he cried.

'What on earth are you two doing out here?' Mum pulled Chris to her as if she hadn't seen him for months. 'I've been looking everywhere. I thought you'd been kidnapped.'

'Kidnapped?' Katie said. 'That's ridiculous!'

Mum frowned at her. 'Terrible things happen in the blink of an eye.'

Old men die. Old women get abandoned. Hospitals phone up out of the blue.

And that was just today.

Chris was crying. A great sob welled up from deep inside him. 'I don't like it here.'

'Oh, sweetheart,' Mum said, 'it'll be all right. We just need to get you home and safe. Don't worry, we're leaving now.'

Across the car park, arm in arm with the social worker, the old woman appeared. She looked totally bewildered.

'The four of us?' Katie asked.

Mum nodded, all the light squeezed from her face. 'The four of us.'

Two

Mary had a blanket over her knees, and she was clutching her handbag tight and she didn't know where she was, but she wasn't at home and that was reason enough to be wary. Was she supposed to be working? No, this wasn't a theatre, it was too domestic for that. Here was a sofa, a television, a lamp on a corner table, a little column of drawers and a carpet. Here was a girl setting down a tea tray.

Was this a hotel, perhaps?

'Here you go, Grandma, a nice cup of tea. Shall I put it on this table for you?'

Who?

'It's Katie, remember?'

The girl was staring, expecting an answer. To distract herself from the unease growing in her belly, Mary picked up the cup and took a sip, held the liquid in her mouth and swallowed. She took a breath, did it again. See? Everything normal, nothing to look at here!

'I wasn't sure if you took sugar,' the girl said. 'But we don't actually have any, so is it OK like that?'

Mary wiped her mouth with the hankie she kept up her sleeve and tried to think of a suitable sentence to pacify the girl. *What charming windows you have. How lovely the sky.*

The girl leaned against the balcony door, watching her. She

looked upset. Or maybe it was a trick of the light. 'I thought I didn't have grandparents,' she said eventually. 'And now it turns out you were there all along.'

She had no idea what this child was talking about. Her heart gave a little leap of fear.

'We're the smallest family ever now Dad's gone, not even any cousins or aunties. We're like three sides of a triangle holding each other up.'

Mary struggled to sit taller, snatching at the girl's mention of family, afraid the meaning would disappear like things sometimes did when she concentrated too hard. But then she heard a noise. That was something, that noise. That sounded like a door, like someone breezing in from outside.

'It's Chris,' the girl said. 'He finds it hard to be quiet.'

And then there were two children standing in front of her. Two. And still no clue who they were.

Unimportant questions were asked, like: Are you warm enough? And, Do you need more milk in that tea? Mary was told their mother was upstairs rearranging beds and soon they could all get to sleep and wouldn't that be nice?

It was the girl doing the talking. The boy gawped, gimlet-eyed. Something was wrong with him, staring at her so unnervingly.

'He's shy,' the girl said, as if she could read minds. 'He'll speak when he gets to know you.' She turned to the boy, grinning. 'And after that, he won't shut up.'

The boy laughed, which made the girl laugh too. Something stirred in Mary, watching her do that.

Think woman, think. Who are these people?

Air filled her lungs. Her lungs expanded. Oxygen whizzed around her body. Air came out again in a rush of warmth and a soft, 'Oh,' escaped her lips.

11

'You OK, Granny?'

No, she was not! Because she'd remembered suddenly and precisely, as she had at least twenty times that day already, exactly what was happening. She'd gone with Jack in an ambulance to the hospital. The doctors were terribly sorry, but they couldn't save him. They also couldn't allow her to go home. Instead, they'd located a daughter.

Caroline.

Then these two children must be . . .

Caroline's children.

It rendered her speechless. Just the thought. After all these years.

Three

Katie couldn't sleep. She lay in the Z-bed next to Mum and tried to relax, tried to breathe into her toes and think of nothing except the present moment and her own body. But she kept thinking of the old woman across the landing instead. Why did Mum never talk about her? How did you keep your own mother hidden? Why would you? Even people who hated their families still managed Christmas and birthdays.

Katie leaned on one elbow and looked at the dark shape of her mother in the bed. *Who are you?* she thought. Because it felt like everything had shifted and nothing was quite to be trusted any more.

The curtains were slightly open, and through their gap the sky was darkest blue. Katie pushed off the duvet and crept quietly across the room, eased the window open and leaned out to smell the air. It had stopped raining and a gentle breeze stirred the leaves. The air smelled different from earlier – fresh and cold. As she leaned out, she saw a cat dash under a parked car, heard footsteps and laughter and watched a group of people cross the patch of green in front of the flats and go out through the gate. Beyond the estate were the streets and houses of North Bisham. Katie could send semaphore from here . . .

Flash, *did you get my text?* Flash, flash, *please let's talk about what happened.* Flash, *it's doing my head in.*

'What's going on?' Mum said. 'Why are you standing there?'

Katie turned as her mum struggled to sit up. 'Sorry, I couldn't sleep.'

'Aren't you well?'

'It's stuffy in here, that's all.'

'And now it's freezing.'

Katie pulled the window shut and stood with her back against the ledge.

'Did you hear a noise?' Mum said. 'Is that what woke you? Do you think she's wandering about?'

'I didn't hear anything, I was just hot.'

Mum dragged the duvet up to her neck and leaned back against the pillows. She looked vulnerable, as if there was something wrong with her and Katie had come to visit. 'What do you reckon that social worker would have done if I'd refused to take her?'

'Stuck her in some emergency place, I guess.'

'I should have let her do that.' Mum ran a hand down her neck and rubbed at her shoulder. 'I felt completely pressurized.'

'It must be scary being handed over to a bunch of strangers.'

'Strangers?'

'Well, she doesn't recognize you after all these years. That's the same thing.'

Mum sighed and nestled back into the pillows. 'So, she's a poor old woman and I'm cruel and heartless?'

'I'm not saying that. It's just . . . well, it's weird for everyone, I guess. She's bereaved. You're freaked out. Me and Chris know nothing about her.'

'You know she walked out the door when I was born.' Mum's voice was low, hardly more than a whisper. 'You know she didn't show her face again for years.'

'But you lived with her when you were older. That's what you

14

said in the car. So, why have we never met her? Why have we never had a birthday present or pocket money or been invited to tea?'

Mum frowned. 'Is that all you think about – the things you've missed out on?'

It did sound like that, but Katie hadn't meant it that way. 'It's strange, that's all. She's your mum and you never talk about her.'

'I don't consider her my mum, that's why. She didn't feed or clothe me or make sure I went to school or look after me when I got sick. Her sister, Pat, did all that. As far as I'm concerned, Pat was my mother. The woman who gave birth to me was another person entirely.'

'And Pat's not about to appear out of the woodwork, is she? She's definitely dead?'

'You know she is.' Mum pulled the duvet higher. 'It takes more than biology to be a parent, it takes sacrifice. You can't just run about doing what you like.'

Katie felt something shift and tighten in her stomach because those were the exact words Mum yelled at Dad all those months ago. It made it difficult to breathe, so Katie turned back to the window and pressed her cheek against the cold glass.

'First thing tomorrow,' Mum said, 'I'll pop into work and let them know what's going on. After that, I'll call the hospital and get a list of nursing homes. Somewhere must have a space.'

Over there, beyond the trees, were the big houses with gardens and gates, where kids probably had two parents and didn't have to share a bedroom with one of them. Ordinary families.

'Chris can have the day off school to sit with her. He's had a late night as it is. Your maths session's at eleven, isn't it?'

Katie's family used to be ordinary. Before Dad got a girlfriend and Mum got a skip and chucked Dad's stuff in it. Before Mum declared their family home was tainted and dragged them to this town. Before Esme. And now Katie could add a secret grandmother and an ancient family rift to the ranks of unordinary things.

'Are you listening to me, Katie?'

'I can miss maths.'

'No, you can't.'

'I'm on study leave, remember? None of the school sessions are statutory.'

'Well, they should be.' Mum patted the bed beside her. 'Come here.'

Katie didn't want to be touched, but Mum was holding her hand out, so Katie went slowly over and sat beside her.

'Your future's a very important part of this family's equation and nothing's going to jeopardize it.'

She leaned over and ruffled Katie's hair, which Katie didn't remember her ever doing before. It was all a bit awkward.

'Smoke alarms!'

'What?'

Mum threw the duvet off. 'I'll check the batteries.'

'You think she'll set the flat alight?'

'I wouldn't put it past her.' Mum grabbed her dressing gown from the chair and pulled it on. 'I'll hide the front door key as well.'

Katie laughed, she couldn't help it. 'You don't want her here, but you don't want her escaping?'

'I don't want her causing chaos.' Mum shoved her feet into slippers. 'She might look harmless, but she's capable of anything.'

Four

'Sure I can't tempt you onto the balcony?'

The old woman shook her head and curled her fingers tightly round her bag. Katie unfolded a deckchair and turned it to the sun. She put up the umbrella for shade and plumped one of the cushions and put it on the chair. 'It's a good view and you'll be able to see Mum come back across the grass.'

More head shaking.

And where was Mum anyway? She'd been gone far longer than the half hour she promised. And Katie had to get to school soon, which felt like just another disaster waiting to happen – not just maths revision, but the inevitable stares, the whispers, the feeling that her legs were too short and her arms too long and her walk too weird and her clothes not right.

Oh, God!

The balcony suddenly felt very exposing.

She closed the doors and sat on the carpet at the old woman's feet. Maybe she should call Mum and *insist* on missing maths? Mum could stay out and Katie could sit right here keeping an eye on things. It made total sense. She could think of some old lady activities, like knitting or macramé and look them up on YouTube. It might be fun being a carer. She might even be good at it. If she found the right name (and she hadn't tried *Nana* or *Grams* yet), it might be like a magic key that opened the old woman up to communication. Maybe when you got to know her, she'd be like one of those wise women in fairy tales, full of advice and wisdom. She might even have potion-making skills and Katie could get her to make some kind of 'forgetting serum' and get Esme to drink it.

Katie sighed. First of all, Mum would never let her skip a revision class so close to the exam. *An investment in knowledge pays the best interest* was her favourite quote in the world. Second of all, this grandmother sitting in front of her was clearly incapable of intelligent transaction. She'd spent last night looking terrified and this morning looking confused and now she had her eyes shut again. She was clearly not going to do or say anything of merit, so instead of fantasizing about magic potions, Katie should encourage the poor thing to eat and help her feel comfortable.

'How about some breakfast? We don't usually have anything exciting in the house, but Chris sounds like he's raiding the freezer, so we might get lucky. You fancy something to eat?'

No response.

'Actually, it's not a house, it's a flat. Maybe you remember coming up in the lift last night?' God, now she sounded patronizing. 'We're on the top floor,' she added. 'It's a great view. If you were to come out on the balcony right now, you'd be able to see the whole of North Bisham shining away in the sun.'

The old woman opened one eye – seamlessly, without letting the closed one even flicker. It made Katie smile because this was something she thought only she could do. She'd never met anyone who'd been able to replicate the exact spookiness of it. No frowning. No screwing up your face. Just one eye closed and the other open. Like you were half sleeping. Or only half alive.

'Bisham?'

She spoke! Katie was almost too shocked to reply. 'Yes, do you know it?

'Victory Avenue?'

'Um, no. Is that round here? You want me to Google it?'

The old woman snapped the other eye open. 'What?'

Of course! This poor woman probably didn't even know computers were invented. Google it? What was she thinking? She was an idiot!

'It's like a map. I can look it up. You want me to?'

Katie was elated. They'd had a conversation! A whole one and it made sense! They sat in silence looking at each other. It went on for ages. It made Katie think of zoos and how weird it was when a caged animal came up close and studied you as intently as you were studying them.

Eventually, the old woman said, 'Caroline lives in Bisham.'

'Yeah, she'll be back soon. She just popped to work.'

'Work?'

'At the estate agent's. She had to hand some keys in.'

Katie watched her absorb this. 'You're Caroline's daughter.'

'That's right.'

The old woman shook her head as if she couldn't believe it. 'You're all grown up.'

'Well, we missed out on seventeen years together, didn't we?'

And that's when Chris came in with a chocolate cake. He'd cut it into pieces, which meant he'd taken the opportunity to eat at least one slice out in the kitchen. He'd remembered plates and napkins though, which surprised her. Katie took the cake from him and held it out. 'Would you like some?'

A small smile. 'You're very kind.'

'Hey, she talks!' Chris said.

Katie glared at him. 'Don't be rude.' She held the plate nearer.

'Which piece do you want, Mary? I expect you're hungry, aren't you?'

'Mary' sounded right, seemed to work too, since her smile widened.

'Mary,' Katie said again, enjoying the sound. She didn't know a single other human being with that name. 'I'm going to put the biggest piece on this plate for you, look.'

Chris got himself a slice and sat on the carpet at Mary's feet. 'Can you believe Mum didn't make me breakfast? She never forgets stuff like that. Not ever.'

Mary peered down at him. 'I have absolutely no idea who you are.'

'I'm Chris!' He banged his head with his fist to prove it. 'Hear that? That's me.'

'You live here?'

'Where else would I live?' He spiralled a finger at his temple, meaning *crazy*.

Katie rammed her foot at him because he hated it when people made that gesture at him, but he just laughed and slid out of reach.

Mary looked from Chris to Katie and back to Chris. 'You two have exactly the same colour hair.'

Katie smiled. 'Titian.'

'Either of you get called Copper Top?'

'Dad calls me Agent Orange,' Chris said. 'Well, he would if he was here . . .'

'What does your girlfriend call you?'

He laughed. 'I haven't got one. Mum would go nuts.'

She turned to Katie. 'What about you? Are you courting?'

A memory of a kiss, like a grainy black-and-white dream, drifted across Katie's mind. She pushed it solidly away. 'No, I'm not.'

'Pretty thing like you. No suitors bashing at the door?'

'That definitely doesn't happen.'

'When I was a girl I used to climb out my bedroom window and down the drainpipe to go dancing.' She leaned forward conspiratorially. 'Every week a different boy walked me home. Once they knew where I lived, they couldn't keep away. Boys everywhere! Can you imagine? My father used to go mad. He said it was unbecoming for a young lady to enjoy so much attention.'

Katie didn't know what to say. It was all getting a bit odd. How could someone refuse to talk for hours and then suddenly have the capacity to launch into erotic memories with total eloquence? Katie took a bite of cake so that she wouldn't have to say anything. It was pretty good for something Chris found lurking in the freezer and she discovered she was starving. She polished her piece off in silence.

She was so busy licking each finger clean that she didn't notice Mum arrive. It was as if she'd apparated in the doorway and was suddenly standing there leaning on the doorframe watching them all. 'Everyone all right?'

'She talks,' Chris said, wiping his mouth with his sleeve. 'She was only pretending she couldn't.'

'Is that right?'

'And she's eating.'

Mary looked up at Mum, chewing thoughtfully. 'Where did you come from?'

'I had to let work know I wasn't coming in.'

'What's your name?'

Mum didn't answer, didn't move from the doorway, like her legs were stuck to the carpet. The only thing that moved was a finger that scratched at the seam of her trouser pocket. She looked exhausted and furious all at once. She looked as if she wanted to

21

scratch away at that pocket until there was a hole big enough to climb inside.

Seeing them both together in daylight, Katie could see the resemblance. Mary's hair was mostly white, but there was auburn in it too and Mum's was the opposite – mostly auburn, with streaks of grey shot through. Mary had an old woman's hands – the skin veiny, the fingers gnarled. Mum's had a spattering of brown age spots on the back and Katie knew she felt the first nags of arthritis in the mornings. They had the same blue eyes, the same slim build, even the same heart-shaped faces. *This is how it will be for me*, Katie thought. *I'm going to look like the two of you*. One day her legs would thicken, her hair would whiten, her skin would sag and she'd wither and grow old. It was like seeing the stages of her life laid out.

Mary was still gazing at Mum. 'I'm absolutely sure I know you from somewhere.'

Chris jumped to his feet. 'I'll do introductions.'

'Don't,' Mum said.

But he was wired from the cake and ignored her.

'Mrs Todd,' Chris said, standing in front of Mary. 'Please meet Mrs Baxter.' He waved his arms in Mum's direction as if he was a game show host. 'Mum, this is your mother, Mrs Todd.'

'Sit down, Chris,' Mum said, glaring at him. 'You're being ridiculous.'

But Chris didn't sit. He held out his hand to Mary instead. 'And my name's Christopher.'

Mary smiled graciously and took his hand. 'A pleasure.'

Mum looked as if she was about to stride over and tear them apart.

Chris was pumping Mary's hand up and down as if he'd never let go. Both of them were laughing. Mum took a step forward, as if this was just what she'd dreaded. 'For goodness sake!'

'Chris,' Katie said frantically, 'why don't you offer the cake round again?' She leaped up and dragged him by his arm and pointed to the table. 'Quickly now. It's over there, look.'

Mum frowned and Katie knew she was wondering where they'd got it from.

'Freezer,' she explained. 'It's a welcome cake.'

Mum shook her head disapprovingly. She probably expected Katie to have cooked a saucepan of porridge and certainly wouldn't like them having chocolate gateau for breakfast. She waved Chris away when he held out the plate. 'Not for me.'

Katie declined as well, though she would have liked some more. Things were hard enough for Mum already. Solidarity was required. Mary and Chris each took another piece.

Katie patted the chair next to her. She'd never seen her mother look so uncomfortable. 'You want to sit down?'

Mum shook her head. 'I've got to make some calls.'

The clock ticked. Chris and Mary chomped. Mum fiddled with her pocket.

'So,' Mum said eventually. 'Since you've decided to communicate, perhaps I can ask if you'd like a bath? I think it's probably a while since you had one of those, isn't it?'

'A bath?' Mary huffed. She turned to Mum as if she was trying to work out who was giving her such ridiculous instructions. 'I'm off to visit my daughter actually.'

Mum avoided eye contact, shuffled her feet.

'She *is* your daughter,' Katie said gently.

Mary shook her head. 'My daughter's a lot younger.'

'Charming.' Mum brought her hand out of her pocket and uncurled her fist, examined her fingernails as if they were intriguing, as if she'd never really noticed them before. Katie felt so sorry for her. All these years without a mother and now one had turned up and it was the saddest reunion ever.

'She's your daughter, all grown up,' Katie said. 'She's Caroline.'

Mary stared at Katie, her eyes searching. 'She is?'

'I promise you.'

'I sent a man out to find her. He didn't say anything about her being grown up.'

'Well, this is all very awkward,' Mum said. 'So, if it's all right with everyone, I think we'll get on with what we're all supposed to be doing. Katie, you need to get to school. Chris, you keep an eye on things here.' She turned to Mary. 'You might like to listen to the radio? Chris will sort that out for you. I'm going upstairs to phone the hospital.'

Mary looked alarmed. 'Hospital?'

'You can't stay here.' Mum sounded very sure of this. 'I'd say they've been negligent.'

Chris reached out for another piece of cake. Mum shook her head. 'No more.'

'But I'm hungry.'

'Then have a banana.'

She frowned at him. She meant it. Chris sat on his hands and stuck out his bottom lip. Mum stomped off up the stairs.

Mary looked at Chris, bemused. 'Well,' she said. 'She's not very nice, is she?'

Five

Here's what happened, exactly how it went.

Three weeks ago, Esme had been sitting on the edge of her bed making a joint. Right at the edge, her bare toes dabbling at the carpet, and every now and then she'd flicked Katie a look.

'Biggest fantasy,' she said. 'You go first.'

'I don't have one.'

'You do. Of course you do.'

But Katie wasn't going to say. She knew what that would do.

'The first thing that comes into your head,' Esme said. 'How hard can it be?'

'I should probably go.'

'You only just got here.'

'My mum keeps texting.'

'Sod your mum. You're seventeen.'

But if she continued to ignore the texts, if she didn't go home soon, Mum would do something mad like call the police to report Katie missing. *She's never late, she's a good girl, she never breaks the rules. She must have been abducted.* Abducted by Esme, her one and only friend, who just lately had been ignoring her, moving away, hanging out with other girls. But who today had said, 'Come back to mine, you want to?'

25

And Katie had felt two things at exactly the same time. One – excitement. Two – fear.

'Come on, Katie. How hard can it be to say one measly fantasy out loud?'

'All right, how about my dad announcing it's all a joke and he loves my mum after all?'

'Not that kind of fantasy, you doughnut! A proper one. A sexy one, you know. I've got tons.'

'Have you?'

Esme crossed her legs on the bed like a storyteller in for the long haul. 'Hundreds.'

She really did. They mostly involved werewolves or vampires falling instantly in love with her, but she also had one about a boy at the tech college who had a car and had gone round a friend of Esme's house and chucked stuff at her window and then, when she opened it, whisked her off to some field where they made 'sweet love under the stars' (Esme's words) and she'd quite like that to happen to her (though not with that particular boy). She rattled off a few more about doing it in public and some steam punk weirdness to do with an automaton coming to life, and just as Katie was beginning to wonder if they'd drifted apart so much they literally had nothing in common any more, Esme mentioned Simona Williams from the year above (who everyone knew the rumours about).

'Sometimes I imagine the stuff she gets up to,' Esme said, 'and I think how she seems so confident, almost cool, you know. She looks like a boy with that haircut. She could actually *be* a boy in a certain light, and sometimes I look at her in the canteen or wherever and I wonder what it would be like to have her do that stuff to me.' She looked at Katie. 'You ever wonder that?'

Katie was shivering. She had so much fear in her guts her fingers were in knots. She shook her head, blushing. 'I don't know.'

They didn't talk for a while and Katie wondered what that meant. Was Esme leaving a space on purpose? Was Katie supposed to fill it?

Esme scooted up the bed, opened the window and leaned out. She waved the joint. 'Sure I can't tempt you?'

'No thanks.'

Esme sighed. 'Such a good girl.'

And maybe it was that. Because that's what Mum always said and Katie didn't want to be someone who was always so predictable and boring.

Or maybe it was watching Esme with the joint – the way she kneeled there, her elbows on the window ledge, taking long drags and blowing smoke into the garden where it danced off into the trees and got all mixed up with the branches. She looked so far away, like nothing could reach her.

But mostly it was what she'd said about Simona. Because why would she say stuff like that?

'I do have a fantasy,' Katie said.

Esme turned from the window. 'Yeah?'

It was like standing on a high building and looking down and being crazily attracted to the idea of falling. No, it was like knowing you were already falling, that you were tipping over the edge and it was too late to even think about clawing your way back up. It made Katie's heart race, her nerves scramble as she moved closer to Esme on the bed, so close she could run a finger down Esme's arm, down to her hand until their fingers brushed.

And then . . . Katie leaned in and kissed her.

No! She couldn't think about it now. Remembering would have to wait, because now (oh God!) she was walking through the school gates and there she was – Esme, sitting on one of the benches near the main path with all four of her ridiculous friends.

These were the girls Esme had been in primary school with. *They're like my sisters*, she used to say, although she'd been perfectly happy to drop them when Katie arrived at the school. 'You know so much more about so much stuff than they do, Katie.'

Not stuff about clothes or boys though, or stuff about music or what was cool or not. Or where the best parties were, or which bars or shops served you alcohol without asking for ID. And, slowly, Esme decided it was dull to have a friend who was never allowed out, who didn't have a Smartphone or a Facebook page, who was always looking after her brother or spending time with her mum.

Esme had new trousers – blue with white polka dots and a tie belt and a white blouse with little capped sleeves. She looked amazing. Katie had never seen any of these clothes before.

A couple of the other girls had taken their shoes off and hitched their skirts up to expose their legs to the sun. They were talking way too loudly about some gig over at the tech college and how it was a fiver to get in, and how someone's brother worked the bar, so maybe they'd get in for free.

The world seemed to pulse as Katie got closer, like she could hear her own blood.

You just have to walk past. They might not even see you.

She breathed her mantra – *fire, earth, water, air* – and told herself that the elements were older and stronger than any human and that these girls were insignificant, and one day they'd all be dust.

Keep walking. Soon it will be over.

'Look who it is.'

The mouthiest of the group, Amy, had a sixth sense for sure, sniffing the air like a pack animal who could smell fear approaching. And now she'd spoken, Esme turned and for a moment it was as if she forgot to be appalled, because there was a flash of warmth in her eyes before she leaned back on the bench in disgust. The others

28

looked over slowly, one at a time, and something rippled through them.

Amy shielded her eyes with her hand from the sun's glare. 'Hey, I like your cardigan.'

Katie ignored her, kept on walking.

'Very unusual.'

It helped to pretend she was foreign and didn't speak their language or understand sarcasm.

'But then you've got unusual taste,' Amy said. 'Or, at least, that's what I heard.' She shot a knowing look at the others. 'Any of you heard that?'

And there it was again. Proof Esme had told them. Proof Esme had betrayed her.

They giggled like children who'd been told a filthy joke. One of them even bothered to fall off the bench with merriment.

Go up to them, Katie willed herself. *Go up and stamp on their stupid feet.* But instead, she found herself trying to look smaller, found herself walking past as if she was insignificant, worthless and might as well be ignored. It was a way of walking that felt familiar. Despite his weight in the world, she'd seen Chris shrink into himself when people stared at him, and it shocked her to realize that walking past these girls made her feel like her brother.

The maths room was empty except for Ms Nayyar, who looked up from her desk and gave Katie a broad grin as she walked in. 'Ah, my most reliable student.'

'No one else here?'

'Too hot for them, perhaps?' She wiped her brow with a dramatic sweep.

Katie got out her maths stuff. Yes, she agreed, it was a heatwave and yes, it was surprising after last night's rain and yes, it probably *was* hotter than Delhi, where Ms Nayyar's brother had taken his kids to visit their grandparents. Katie tried to be interested in the details, tried to nod and smile in the right places, but all she could think was – *Esme, why did you tell them?*

All the way through the study session she felt anger build inside her. She was an idiot for trusting anyone. She was also an idiot for coming to maths – the hottest day for ages and she was the only one who'd bothered. What a fool! By the time the class was over, the anger began to feel like something alight. She was *so* predictable. She hated it about herself, and yet the only unpredictable thing she'd ever done had gone horribly wrong. Even now, she knew that she'd walk across the playground, and if Esme and that lot were still there, she'd hang her head and slink past them. Then she'd walk home in twenty minutes (she'd once been dull enough to time it) and then up to the flat to do more studying.

The girls had gone. The twenty-minute walk took exactly that, even though fury should have made it quicker, so to make some-thing different happen before a predictable afternoon set in, she went to the shop and bought a box of strawberry Cornettos.

Mum was at the kitchen table when Katie got in and Mary was in the lounge, which meant they probably hadn't been in the same room since she left for school. The whole world was at war.

'What's this?' Mum said. 'More sugar?'

Katie ignored her, tore open the box and handed two to Chris, handed Mum hers and sat at the table to open her own.

'Am I allowed?' Chris was clearly gobsmacked.

'Live a little,' Katie told him. 'Take the other one to Mary.'

Mum raised an eyebrow. 'Mary?'

Katie gave her a long look. 'We have to call her something. What do you suggest?'

She knew she was spreading the anger. It was stuck to her like tar and the only way to get it off was to rub it onto other people.

She ripped the cardboard disc from the top of her ice cream and exposed the white chocolate curls and strawberry sauce. She peeled back the red shiny paper. It made her feel about six years old.

Chris came back and shoved one of the Cornettos in the freezer. 'She's asleep.'

They sat in silence, licking their ice creams.

'How was school?' Mum asked eventually.

'Fine.'

'Maths went OK?'

'Yep.'

'You'll do some practice papers tonight?'

'Sure.'

Mum sighed. 'For goodness sake, Katie, don't go all monosyllabic on me. I'm having a hard enough day as it is! I only asked a simple question.'

But it wasn't simple. *How was school?* It was a more complex question than Mum could ever imagine. Should Katie say, *I kissed my best friend and now I'm a social pariah?* No, she could never in a million years tell Mum that. What then? News of the gig at the tech college? No, none of that either. *They'll need fake IDs for that*, Mum would say. *Where are their parents, that's what I want to know? I don't want you hanging around with girls like that, they're a bad influence, blah, blah.*

Katie decided all Mum wanted was a distraction, so she told her that school was pretty quiet now exams were in full swing, maths had been empty, the teacher had been sweet and it was definitely useful to look at stuff one-to-one.

'That's what university will be like,' Mum said. 'Just you and a tutor going over mathematical theories together.'

Katie didn't think of maths when she thought of university.

31

Instead, she imagined a place where she could reinvent herself, a place where nothing had gone horribly wrong yet.

She crumpled her ice-cream wrapper, tossed it in the bin and took a breath. 'So, how did the phone calls go?'

Mum looked instantly exhausted. 'I've had enough of it, stuck upstairs in this weather. I've been passed from department to department and absolutely no one wants to take responsibility.' She slid a notebook across the table. 'Look at this. I've spoken to every one of those people. Seems you can only be given help once you're in the system, and to get in the system you need to be assessed, and to be assessed you need a doctor's referral, and to get one of those you need a doctor and a permanent address.' She laughed with no humour. 'I managed to get her an appointment with my own doctor, but not until Tuesday, so what are we supposed to do with her until then?'

Katie scanned the notes, pages of scrawl with numbers and names and random sentences. *Can she manage personal care? Does she have wide-ranging medical and social needs? Mini mental health exam? Adult Care Team referral?*

The anger slid out of her. Poor Mum. Poor Mary.

She passed the notebook to Chris, but he ignored it, was tracing patterns on his ice cream with his tongue and pretending to be stupid. She passed it back to Mum.

'I'm sorry,' she said.

Mum smiled wearily. She read and reread the notebook, like picking at a scab.

1954 – the promise

Mary leans over the side of the bed and clutches at her sister, because surely this can't, surely no one can be expected . . . Another one, already another one, like a great wave coming from afar. Mary's back arches against it as it comes closer, like a belt tightening – pulling every ligament, wrenching muscles into tension, straining each vertebra so that her spine will surely snap. She's turning inside out with it. She's going to burst, wet and violent, across the bedroom walls.

'I can't do this.' Her voice is smaller, seems to come from far away. 'It hurts, Pat. Please make it stop.'

'There's nothing to be done,' Pat says. 'It's too late for anything.'

Mary closes herself to Pat then, because what does she know? Even now, in the heat and terror of it, Pat's determined to be right. They should call an ambulance, shouldn't they? Get a midwife to come?

Out there, beyond the window, Saturday night is happening. Out there, girls are putting on lipstick, spraying perfume at their throats, walking to the Roxy, their heels click-clicking, their breath like smoke in the frosty air. Mary envies them with all her being. She'd trade anything to be out there instead of in here, with this . . . oh . . . this awful inevitability. There's no escape, that's the worst thing. And it's going on for ever and . . . ahh! here comes another one!

'They're getting closer, aren't they?' she gasps. 'That was sooner than before.'

'It's all right,' Pat says. 'It means it's nearly over.'

'But this is already more than I can bear.' She can hear herself moaning, low moaning, pushing into screams.

'Quiet!' Pat hisses. 'You want the neighbours to hear?'

'The neighbours can go to hell!'

Mary knows she's desperate. She sees herself as Pat sees her, desperate and so afraid and she doesn't care. See me like this. This is me. Did you know this was me? All these years you envied me, big sister, but I reckon you don't envy me now! The peak arrives more quickly, takes her more completely than before.

'Breathe,' Pat says. 'I read it somewhere. Like blowing smoke.'

And Mary blows, blows until she's giddy . . .

And then something amazing. There's suddenly distance and over there, far away, she sees herself as a child sitting in the arms of the cherry tree. It crosses Mary's mind that perhaps she's dying, which seems a shame, but at least there's no pain here for an instant. Here's the day the sun shone ladders down the side of the house and she spied Norman, the boy next door, cleaning his bike. She wanted to secretly throw something at him, but the cherries weren't grown yet, and apart from branches and leaves there wasn't anything. Here was the day she smeared her lips crimson and smacked them together, enjoying the strange taste of stolen lipstick as she clambered swiftly down the tree, crossed the grass, slid silently over the wall and tapped Norman on his shoulder. 'You want a kiss?'

And now this – oh, again, oh, not again! Will this last for ever? She wants to push. She's losing it, completely. This will never end

34

and she hears herself screaming. She really can't stand any more. All moments of peace are ended, all memories have gone, and she's back in her bedroom with these walls and her sister flapping about like a lunatic and this unavoidable need to push. It's like puking. Urgent and ridiculous.

How can she still be alive and feel this much agony? She actually feels the baby as, 'Oww!' as its head presses against her, opening her, stretching her so wide it burns. It has to stop, she has to make it stop. It's like being eaten by fire. She scrabbles with her hand, reaches down to put an end to this, to do something, anything that will make it go away. But her fingers meet the baby's head – and it's so entirely shocking to touch her unborn child, that the room goes still. She is touching her daughter. She is the first person in the world to touch her. For the rest of Caroline's life, that will always be true. The baby's head is convoluted like a soft mountain range. Her hair is wet fluff, the curve of her skull so tender as she, as Mary, pushes her out and there's a face between her legs. For an instant, for a completely odd and confusing second, it's her being born, she thinks, and she lies blinking between her own mother's legs with the pressure of the world across her shoulders and she knows above all things that this child must be loved. *If I can give you nothing else, I promise you that.* Pat's fumbling with hot water and towels and saying, 'Pant, don't push!' when there's nothing Mary can do to avoid it, nothing, no panting in the world is stopping this.

It takes three pushes (only three! Pat will recount later, as if even in the process of giving birth to an illegitimate child, Mary is blessed with good fortune) and the baby lies on the bed slippery as a mackerel and Mary is a mother.

She's done it. She's survived, and so has the baby and so has Pat and all three of them are crying.

'It's relief,' Pat says. But then she looks at her watch, so maybe it's fear, because their father's at the pub and he'll be home soon and how the heck are they going to explain away a baby?

Six

'"Slut" was a word I was familiar with,' Mary told the girl who came running up. 'But from my father's lips it made me feel terribly exposed. Can you imagine?'

'I'd say Houdini was a more appropriate term,' the girl said, grabbing her arm and steering her back across the street. 'Mum's freaking out.'

'I had errands.'

'What errands?'

'A place I needed to go.'

'Just ask me if you need anything.' The girl chivvied her along a stretch of pavement. 'Come on, we have to hurry.'

'Where's the fire?'

'Sorry, but Mum's pretty stressed. Also, you've still got your nightie on, which is kind of mortifying.'

And then they were hurrying through a gate, across a courtyard, through some doors and into a lift. The girl said, 'I won't tell her you made it all the way to the main road, if that's all right with you?'

Out of the lift and into a hallway and Mary was struck by a blankness, by the hollow sound the girl's knuckles made as she rapped at a door.

A woman flung it open. 'Thank goodness. Where was she?'

'By the gate. Not far.'

Mary was pulled inside. There was a coat rack, a fish tank, a pile of boots and shoes. The door was shut behind her. The world got smaller.

'Kitchen,' the woman said, pointing the way.

Mary was invited to sit. The girl was invited to leave. The woman sat behind a table strewn with papers and put her fingers in a pyramid under her chin. 'Where were you going?'

'I needed something.'

'What?'

'I needed . . .'

But it had gone. It was like trying to catch light in her fist. Damn!

The woman frowned. 'I know being under the same roof is uncomfortable for both of us, but you can't run off. There are roads and cars out there. It's dangerous. Also, my daughter's got better things to do than chase after you.'

They gazed at each other in silence. Mary had no clue what was expected of her.

The woman said, 'You never could stay in one place longer than five minutes, so I don't know why I'm surprised.' Then she said, 'When that social worker told me you'd been at the same address with Jack for thirteen years, I thought you might have changed.'

Jack? The name hurt. Mary shrugged it away.

'That's a world record for you,' the woman said. 'Thirteen whole years.'

Was this an interview? It was most disconcerting.

The woman said, 'Yesterday, you said you sent a man out to find me. Why did you say that?'

Mary thought about that. It certainly had the ring of truth. 'Perhaps you were lost?'

The woman sighed. 'Never mind.'

Mary was taken to the lounge and put in a chair by the window. She was ordered to, 'Stay there.' She was commanded not to 'even think about moving'. A boy was set up as a guard. The girl was instructed to go upstairs and look over some blinking maths papers. The woman went away.

It was just a few minutes later when Mary sat up with the shock of remembering. So stupid to have forgotten, when it was as sharp and clean as a knife to her now. Victory Avenue. That was it. It's *all* that she wanted. Number twenty-three – with its blue gate, its neat front garden, the tiled steps leading up to the door. She'd count them as she crept up to the window to peek in and count them again as she tiptoed away. Eight steps in all. Each one embedded in her brain.

She got out of the chair and walked to the door. She wouldn't forget this time. She'd say it over and over until she got there. But the boy who took her arm said she'd better sit back down or she'd be in trouble.

'I have to go.'

'You're not allowed.'

Allowed? Was this child in charge? He was young, with red hair and pyjamas. He stood there with his hands on his hips and insisted she sit.

'Please get me a paper and pen most urgently,' she told him.

'You want to write a letter?'

'Never mind what I want,' Mary said. 'Just get me a pen.'

He picked up a little black bag with a zip and handed it to her. 'Here. I have to go to my room to get paper though.' He jogged to the door. 'Don't go away,' he called over his shoulder, 'or I'll get bollocked.'

Mary wrote *23* on the sofa and drew a line underneath it. Then she drew another line under the first one and ran her finger along them. They were like two golden streams of water – one going forwards and the other back. When she pushed them, they came together and intertwined, and when she took her finger away, they sprang apart. It was entrancing. She did it several times. She didn't know they made golden ink. Had they always done that? Was it real gold? Such a thing must be expensive, surely?

The boy who appeared in front of her said, 'Mum's going to go nuts when she sees that.'

Mary smiled up at him. Such a fierce and lovely face he had. 'Hello,' she said. 'Where did you come from?'

He stepped closer. 'Serious. You're going to be in real trouble.'

'Stop worrying!' She tapped the seat next to her. 'Sit here next to me and we'll have a cigarette together.'

'I'm a child!'

'Are you sure? You're pretty big for a child.'

'I have a thyroid complaint.'

'Perhaps you eat too much?'

'It's nothing to do with eating, it's to do with my metabolic rate.' He folded his arms at her. 'I have special needs.'

'We all have those. I *especially* need to leave, for instance, but you're not letting me.'

He frowned at her. 'That's my pencil case. Can I have it back, please?'

He held out his hand. She wasn't quite ready to give it up, but he snatched it from her anyway.

'Manners!' she said.

He stuck his tongue out, squatted on the carpet with his back to her and emptied pens onto the floor.

Mary turned her attention to the window. Ragged clouds shifted above the tops of two trees – an ash and a sycamore by the look of their leaves. Beyond them was the pointy tip of a tower with ropes stretched tight from its ramparts and dozens of flags flapping in the wind. Had they just appeared? Her heart thrilled.

'Is that a boat?'

The boy didn't look up.

She struggled to stand, but the chair was deep and her legs didn't obey her. She slumped back down exasperated. 'Please could you answer me. There's a mast and rigging out there. Are we near the sea?'

He shrugged. 'It's just buildings.'

'Why does it look like water rippling?'

The boy stood up and pressed his nose against the window. 'It does a bit.'

'But is it?'

'It's the sky and the flats opposite and a bit of the church behind that, nothing else.'

'What about the flags?'

'They're for decoration.' The boy craned his neck. 'I wish it was the sea though, that'd be cool.' He turned to her. 'Mum said this town would make us happy. She said when she lived here it was brilliant, but me and Katie think it's rubbish. It was better living with Dad.'

Mary swallowed her disappointment. No sea then. And she'd been so certain of it. 'Tell me,' she said. 'What exactly should I be doing?'

'No idea.' He stared at her, unblinking. 'Mum said it was only for one night.'

'What was?'

'You being here. But it's been two nights already because there's nowhere else for you to go. Do you know all this?'

'Of course.' She peered at him. 'What's your name?'

41

'Chris.'

'How old are you?'

'Fourteen.'

'That's a good age.'

He smiled. 'Is it? Why?'

'It's the age of adventure.' She returned his smile, feeling suddenly fond of him. 'I always wanted a brother. I would've called him Nemo.'

'That's the name of my goldfish.'

Which is, she realized, where she'd got the name from, because hadn't she been introduced to some creature in a tank? The simplicity of her imagination shamed her. There was no stretch to it any more, it had become domestic, parochial. But the boy didn't seem to notice, was back counting his pens, putting them into colour-matched piles.

Someone else used to do that. Some other child. Ah, how slow her brain was. Think now, think. Not pens but buttons – poured onto newspaper from Pat's jar and picked out one by one – the biggest, the smallest, the prettiest – each held to the window by a child with red, red hair.

Caroline!

She was startled to find the word laid out in the real world. Startled to find a girl kneeling in front of her.

'She's making phone calls,' the girl said. 'Would you like a cup of tea?'

'She drew on the sofa,' the boy said.

'Serious?'

The boy pointed. 'There, look! And Mum's going to think it was me because she used my pen.'

The girl peered over to see. 'Twenty-three?'

Mary slapped her hand over it, suddenly ashamed. She'd done

42

this! What had she been thinking? She pulled her hankie from her sleeve and gave the sofa a rub.

'It won't come off,' the boy said. 'It's a permanent marker.'

She licked her hankie, dabbed more vigorously. 'Don't worry. I'll explain it. I know the people who run the place.'

The girl said soothing things about Googling a cure instead, which was kind of her. She got a gadget from her pocket and slid it open. She sat opposite Mary in the armchair, her hair shining copper.

'You look like someone,' she told the girl.

'Do I?'

'She went missing, so I hired a fellow to find her.'

The boy sat up. 'A detective?'

'Charged a fortune. I had to take a smaller room just to pay the fees.'

The boy looked thrilled. 'We could hire a detective to find Dad.'

'He's not lost,' the girl said. 'We know exactly where he is – playing happy families in our old house.'

'But a detective would make him talk to us.'

'That's not what detectives do, Chris.'

'They might. You don't know.'

'Just leave it,' the girl warned.

'The detective would go to our old house and knock on the door and find out Dad's desperate to talk to us, but his girlfriend won't let him.'

'Christopher Baxter!' the girl snapped. 'Would you just stop!'

He jabbed his foot at her and she slapped it away.

'Get dressed,' the girl said. 'You're going to the shop. We need hairspray or insect repellent to clean the sofa.' She switched her gadget off and pocketed it. 'So, you better hurry up, before Mum sees it and blames you.'

43

'I'm not allowed to the shop on my own. And anyway, I'm on guard duty.'

'I'm taking over.'

The boy shook his head very slowly. 'You're not the boss of me.'

'I'll go,' Mary said. 'It's too hot in here anyway. Just point me in the right direction.'

The children exchanged glances and Mary understood exactly what they meant. They meant: *No, Never, No Way!* They meant: *You're crazy and you'd get it all wrong and why would we ever let you?*

The girl said, 'Mum doesn't want you to go out.'

'Do we have to tell her?'

The girl looked at her long and hard, as if working out the right answer. Finally, 'I think she might notice.'

'She could come too. We could all go. We could have a little sit somewhere and watch the world go by.'

'Mum's busy,' the boy said as he stuffed his pens back into their case. 'And Katie's got to go to school, even though no one's talking to her.'

'Shut up, Chris,' the girl said. 'You don't know anything.'

'You told me that!'

'Well, I'm untelling you. And anyway, I'm on study leave. What's your excuse? How come you get another day off?'

He paused in his pen stuffing and grinned at the girl. 'I've got a headache.'

'Mum fell for that?'

'We could drive!' Mary said.

Both children laughed again. The girl was extraordinarily pretty suddenly. It was quite shocking. Mary wanted to tell her that happiness suited her, but was dazzled by how this girl stirred

44

memories in her. It was as if electrons in her head were firing for the first time in ages, light jumping into dark and making tentative connection.

'Neither of us know how to drive, Mary.'

Mary rootled about on the floor for her handbag because *she* certainly knew how, and adventure was calling. 'I have keys somewhere, and a driving qualification. We'll zoom right past your school and cock a snook at the lot of them, eh?'

The boy looked delighted. 'How do we do that?'

Mary showed him by thumbing her nose, wiggling her fingers and sticking her tongue out. 'Like this. It's a derisive gesture, as you can see.'

The boy fell backwards on the carpet and stuck his feet in the air. 'Can we drive past my school and do it too?'

'One may also cross one's eyes,' Mary said. 'If one really wants to make a point. The trick is never to let them know you're afraid.'

The boy laughed even harder, but the girl stood up and looked disdainfully down at him. 'I'm going upstairs to do a practice paper,' she said. 'Don't let Mum see the sofa and I'll get stuff to clean it later.'

1948 – how it began

Clamped under her father's arm, Mary's dragged sideways along the garden path. She slaps at his thighs to be let go. She pummels at his hip, his arm, but he takes no notice. Norman comes trotting behind, his eyes wide with fear.

'What are you going to do to her?'

'Scram,' Dad tells him, 'if you know what's good for you.'

Norman backs away as Dad kicks the door. It swings on its hinges. Mary grabs the frame with both hands, but her fingers slide off with the force of her father's stride.

Pat, writing her diary at the kitchen table, looks up, dismayed. 'What's happened? What did she do?'

Mary twists and pushes at her father, but his grip only tightens as he hauls her across to the sink. 'Now wash your face,' he roars.

It's like looking at a stranger. A stranger with eyes the colour of stone. Mary wonders where the laughing father of that morning has gone, for she can't see any trace of him. This can't be my father, she thinks. I helped him bank the fire. He told me I was an angel. He had a smile that loved me. Now here is a man whose eyes are cold.

'Use soap,' he snaps. 'And a cloth. Or should I do it for you?'

Mary picks up the flannel and dabs at her face.

'Kissing boys,' shouts this strange father. 'Wearing lipstick! You're twelve years old!'

'Nearly thirteen,' Mary whispers.

'I swear if I *ever* see you near that lad next door again, I'll knock you into Kingdom Come.'

'Daddy,' Pat says, putting a hand on his arm. 'You're frightening her.'

He pushes Pat off, his eyes furious. 'Did *you* know what she was up to out there? Bold as brass the two of them.'

'She didn't mean it,' Pat says. 'She doesn't understand. It'll be Norman chasing *her*. Let me speak to his mother.'

But Mary can't let Norman be blamed for what she'd begun. 'I dared him.'

Dad glares at her. 'To kiss you?'

She nods very slowly. 'I was up the tree spying and he was fixing his bike and I wanted to know what it felt like.'

Dad shakes his head as if trying to make the picture disappear. Then he tells her that she's cheapened herself, that there are names for girls like her, that from now on she's banned from talking to Norman and banned from climbing trees, and that unless she's running an errand, she's to stay indoors. Pat will find her jobs to do, starting with polishing everyone's shoes.

Pat quietly offers Dad some tea, but he ignores her and goes back outside, slamming the door behind him.

Mary leans against the sink as air from outside shifts the air inside, stirring the heat from the oven.

Pat turns to her. 'Now look what you've done.'

A small sound escapes from the back of Mary's throat. It's odd because it seems not to come from her at all. 'I didn't mean to.'

'You never do.'

'It was only Norman. Why's he so furious?'

'Because you're his precious girl. He wants to keep you safe.'

Mary closes her eyes because she wants Pat to go away. She

47

wants the whole house to go away, in fact. The street can go too if it wants. And the town and all of the people. She knows what Pat means by 'safe' and she doesn't want it. 'Safe' means spending her life doing nothing but going to school and then, when school's done, doing nothing but typing and shorthand lessons, just so she can work in an office and stay living at home. Then it means finding a nice man to marry and having his babies and doing his washing and ironing and scrubbing his steps and polishing his banisters. Mary shivers at the horror of it. 'You know,' she says, opening her eyes. 'As soon as I get my school certificate, I'm off to London.'

Pat actually laughs. 'Don't be ridiculous.'

'I'm being perfectly serious.'

'You're not going anywhere. When you finish school, you'll be fifteen and still a child and you'll do what Dad tells you. What on earth do you want to go to London for? Most of it's bombed out.'

'I want to get into acting. All the top producers are in London.'

'Is that why you've been copying silly accents from the wireless? You plan to be a movie star?' Pat's still chuckling as she scoops her cigarettes from the counter. Her fingers are yellow. Dad told her about it yesterday, said she shouldn't serve food like that because it put him off, made her go to the bathroom and scrape at her skin with a pumice stone.

'I was in the school play. The teacher said I had perfect diction.'

'You think that counts? Don't be silly. Everything's just a fad with you. You like the thrill of saying ridiculous things out loud and seeing the shock on people's faces.' Pat inhaled deeply and blew the smoke right at Mary. 'You'll grow out of it one day, I expect.'

Mary's belly churns with something deep and furious. 'Stop it, Pat. Stop taking all my possibilities away. Why do you always make everything sound so dreary?'

48

'I'm going to ignore that comment, Mary Todd.' Pat brings the cigarette to her lips and takes a long pull. All the skin around her mouth wrinkles like a drawstring on a purse. 'Now, how about you stop being such a drama queen and get on with polishing those shoes?'

Two days later, Dad comes back from work with a length of silk – dark as thunder and shot through with emerald green. As he flutters it from the paper, it's as if he's smuggled an exotic bird home and set it free in the dining room.

'For you,' he says as he settles it on Mary's lap.

Mary strokes the material in awe. 'Where did you get it?'

'Never you mind.'

No one has silk any more. Not new at least and never so much of it. 'It must've cost a fortune!'

'Don't you worry about that.'

Pat comes in from the kitchen, teapot in hand. She stops, open-mouthed, by Mary's chair and stares at the material draped across her sister's knees. 'Whatever's that?'

'It's for me,' Mary says. She can't believe it. She looks up at her father, amazed. 'Was it more than five pounds?'

He taps his nose. 'Ask me no questions and I'll tell you no lies.'

Pat sets the teapot on the table. 'We've still to pay this month's bills.' Her voice has a brittle edge to it and Mary feels an increasingly familiar stab of guilt. Dad's apologies are becoming more extravagant. He bought her a pair of kid gloves only last week and a box of hankies the week before – hand-embroidered and all the way from China. Mary loved the surprise and exotica of them, but Pat thought them 'wasteful', dragging Mary into the hallway to tell her that if she'd only stop being so wilful there'd be no need for Dad's reckless spending.

49

'I don't ask for presents,' Mary had hissed back at her. 'He's making up for his bad temper!'

'And why does he manage to keep his temper with me?'

'Because you're so well-behaved.'

Pat was pleased with that answer. Being 'good' was her small delight – to be the one who could predict Dad, who could tell the difference between 'tight-but-good-spirited' and 'drunk-and-grief-stricken', who knew from the way he shut the door after coming in from the pub if he needed his pipe and slippers and her company by the fire, or if he'd rather be alone in the sitting room with the photograph album and his whisky.

'It's not his fault,' Pat said. 'It's the sorrow.'

And because Pat had been twelve when Mum died, she understood how that felt. And because Mary had only been three days old, she wasn't supposed to understand it at all.

But sometimes Mary dared to creep into Dad's bedroom to look at the wedding photo and touch Mum's face through the glass. Here was a mother who had lost son after son at birth, who had been warned by a doctor never to have more children, but who had refused to listen. Here was a mother who said, 'I'm having one more and this last one will be the best of the bunch!'

And when she got pregnant with Mary, all her hair fell out, and when the doctor told her the baby was going to fall out too, she lay on the sofa and didn't move for months. And when Mary was born, she looked just like her. *Copper Top*, Dad called Mary sometimes, *my beautiful Copper Top*.

Pat didn't look anything like their mother. Pat had mouse-brown hair and was the recipient of rare and sober parcels from their father – a cotton apron with pockets, a case of peaches from some fellow at the yard, a sturdy brush for the steps. She seemed pleased with these things, but Mary thought them dull.

50

Pat never got anything so lovely as yards of beautiful silk.

'We'll share it,' Mary tells her sister. 'There's plenty. It'll make two dresses.'

Pat rams a cosy on the pot and turns to their father. 'Where exactly do you imagine her wearing such a dress?'

Dad shrugs amiably. 'She can wear it round the house, can't she?'

'A silk dress, for round the house?' Pat juts her chin at him. 'Do you not see how this encourages her?'

He gives her no answer as he reaches for a slice of bread and butter. He searches the table for the jam pot.

Pat plonks herself opposite him. 'When I was growing up I was never allowed fripperies.'

'When you were growing up, there was a war on.'

'And I had to keep house for the two of you! I had to count the pennies and queue at the grocer's and get tea on the table and generally make do and mend. No one ever bought me presents.'

Mary doesn't want this gift to cause a rift. She stands up and holds the shortest edge of silk under her chin, lets the length of it tumble to her ankles, hoping to distract them. She twists her hips and watches the material ripple. 'There's magic in it, look. Like Cinderella's ball gown.'

Dad chuckles. 'And Pat will be a fairy godmother and turn it into something for you.'

Pat's scowl deepens. 'And when will I have time to do that?'

'You'll find time.' Dad reaches for his knife as if it were settled. 'And if there's any spare, you can make something for yourself.'

'Spare?' Pat says. 'I get the spare?'

He gazes at her curiously as he spreads jam on his bread. 'You don't like dressing up. You've never shown the slightest interest in dancing or music.'

'I don't like noise and drunkenness, but I like a fiesta.'

'When was the last time you took up an invitation?'

'When was the last time I *had* an invitation?'

Dad's face darkens. Pat's never this forceful with him. What's wrong with her? 'When that lad next door hauled his mother's piano out into the street, I didn't see you joining in.' He chinks his knife against the jam pot as if he's won a point and there's nothing more to be said. 'Let the girl who has the fire have the dress.'

Fire. It's a word he's used before. A word Mary clings to. She has it and Pat doesn't. She knows it too, has always known it. It's something hot and wild, and sometimes it makes her want to walk out the door and off down the road and not stop. A straight road holds the promise of something – a milkshake in the Corner Café, a bus ride to Tiffany's on Marine Parade to watch the dancers going in, or even (when she's older, she's promised herself this), a trip to London.

Imagine a night out at the Empire Rooms or the Lyceum? There'd be a big band raising the roof and hundreds of people. Strangers might stop and talk to her, she might be asked to dance. She'd definitely have some kind of adventure.

'You're a home body,' Dad tells Pat as she sullenly pours the tea. 'No use denying it.'

'And what am I?' Mary asks, kneeling beside her father. 'Am I a world body?'

'You're trouble,' he tells her sadly. 'That's what you are.'

Seven

Katie had imagined a country cottage with roses blooming round the door – isn't that where grandmothers were supposed to live? But Mary's house was a terraced council place, bleakly identical to all the others in the street. There was a frenzied section of motorway above their heads and, as they got out of the car, the sky seemed low and moody and the air thick with exhaust fumes.

'I know the people here,' Mary said, gazing up at the house.

'You live here,' Mum told her.

'I do not. What utter rubbish.'

Mum pulled out the envelope the hospital had given her and waved it at Mary. 'Then how come I've got your door keys?'

But Mary wasn't interested. She walked briskly up the path and rapped on the door.

'No one's going to answer,' Mum told her.

'Jack might,' Chris said.

Mum glared at him. 'That's enough.' Then she glared at Katie. 'Keep an eye on your brother.'

Katie dragged Chris to sit down with her on the wall while Mum fiddled with keys.

'What's it like to be dead?' he whispered.

'How should I know?'

'Do you think it's dark?'

'Probably.'

'Do you think other dead people are scary?'

Katie told him to count the paving stones in an attempt to distract him. He usually did stuff like that without prompting, but this time he ignored her and stared at Mary instead.

She was peering through the window. 'Such a lonely place to sit,' she said sadly, to no one in particular.

'Here we go,' Mum said. 'Door open. Everyone in.'

Mary went first, bustling past Mum and straight down the hallway. The rest of them stood in a huddle at the bottom of the stairs. It smelled weird – hot and sweet. Katie wondered if this was what death smelled like and swallowed hard.

'Come in,' Mary called. 'Come and look at all the lovely things.'

'Can we put the lights on?' Chris whispered.

Mum shook her head. 'Don't touch anything electrical at all.'

It was difficult to see in the gloom. The three of them crept down the hallway and peered into what seemed to be a lounge. There was a sofa, a fireplace, a hard-backed chair under the window, an old-fashioned TV on a stand. But as Katie's eyes adjusted to the half-light, she saw floor to ceiling shelves crammed with books, piles of magazines stacked on several coffee tables, a glass-fronted cabinet heaving with paraphernalia – masks and carvings and brightly coloured statues. It was like a charity shop. The mantelpiece was covered in ornaments, the window ledges piled with paperwork and baskets of knick-knacks. There were feathers tacked to the walls, cushions on the floor, articles torn from newspapers randomly sellotaped to the back of the door. It was hot, difficult to breathe. Even the carpet and curtains were stifling.

Mum obviously thought so too. 'I'll open some windows, shall I?'

Mary walked about, touching things as if she'd never seen them before. She ran a finger gently along the top of a clock, used cupped hands to pick up and cradle a china dog, before placing it gently down again; she tinkled the glass beads on the chandelier above her head.

'Would you look at this!' she breathed as she opened some kind of musical box. An old-fashioned tune piped thinly at them, while a plastic ballerina did a three hundred and sixty degree turn on her pedestal.

Mary sat down on the sofa and sighed with pleasure, the music box on her lap. It was as if she'd come to a particularly wonderful gallery where she had special permission to handle the exhibits.

Mum clearly had no such thoughts. Now the curtains were open, she looked positively shaken, standing there with one hand to her cheek as if she'd walked into a horror film.

'It's filthy,' she mouthed to Katie from the window.

Katie nodded, but she didn't really agree. The room was certainly messy, but nothing was damp or rotting, there weren't mice or cockroaches scurrying for cover. It was lived in, that was all. Maybe it was part of Mary's illness that she forgot to tidy up, and maybe Jack was too busy looking after her to do it himself.

Mary had picked up a cushion and was stroking it as if the texture and feel were deeply comforting.

'You want to bring that with you?' Mum asked her. 'You want to put it in the bag?' She pointed to the suitcase she'd wheeled in from the car.

'Am I going somewhere?' Mary asked brightly.

Mum frowned. 'We've come to collect some bits and pieces, remember? Enough for a day or two – a couple of nighties, some changes of clothes, a few toiletries perhaps?'

Mary didn't look as if she was going to be looking for clothes or her toothbrush, or anything useful. She was stroking the cushion and gazing contentedly over Mum's shoulder at the view through the window – another road, more houses and cars, a sprawl of shops. Everything about this place was crammed with life.

Chris had edged in from the doorway to examine what looked like a range of plastic mountains glued to a board. He touched it with a finger. 'What's this do?'

'Don't touch,' Mum snapped. 'Leave things alone.'

Mary turned to see what he was looking at. 'That's Wolf Mountain,' she smiled. 'Bring it here and I'll show you.'

But Mum shook her head vehemently, mouthed at Chris that it was dirty and not to touch it. She also whispered under her breath, 'How can anyone live like this?' as she picked her way across the carpet. She squatted down at Mary's feet. 'Do you have a place where you keep important documents? A drawer or a file somewhere? I don't want to go nosing through your stuff, but we need Jack's birth certificate and bank details. Also, your medical cards and national insurance numbers. Do you know where those things might be?'

Mary shrugged. 'Jack deals with all that.'

Katie watched her mother take a deep breath. Mary had said exactly the same thing at the breakfast table earlier when she was asked if there were any milk or newspaper deliveries that needed to be cancelled.

'I'm so sorry,' Mum said. 'But Jack's not here. Jack had a heart attack and he died.'

Mary looked at her with a mixture of disbelief and alarm. 'When?'

'Three days ago now. You went to the hospital in the ambulance with him, do you remember?'

'No, because nobody told me!'

56

'They did. But you've forgotten.'

Mary looked at Katie for a moment, then at Chris and then back to Mum, as if she was searching for an explanation.

'I saw him through the window,' she whispered.

'You didn't. It's just that your memory's gone bad.'

'Are you telling me I don't know what I saw? You think I could forget a thing like that?' She waved Mum away. 'You talk a load of nonsense.'

Funny how Katie had been looking forward to this – it had seemed dramatic, the idea of going to Mary's place. She'd imagined neighbours flocking to greet them with sympathy and pots of tea. She'd imagined a whole crowd of people chatting together in a sunny garden, telling stories, filling in the blanks. Mum would relax for once in her life, perhaps even melt a little towards Mary. Katie had even gone so far as to imagine that Mum would announce they'd all be better off moving into Mary's place together. A chance to get out of that flat and away from school and the humiliation of Esme. A chance of a new life!

It seemed a ridiculous fantasy now. In fact, looking at Mary sitting on the sofa staring at the empty fireplace as if she could see flames leaping in the grate, when there was only soot, it seemed like a very bad idea to bring her back at all. Jack had a heart attack in this place and being here might send Mary crazier than she already was. Perhaps Mum thought so too, because she unzipped the suitcase and yanked out a roll of bin liners and a bulky carrier bag.

'Let's get a move on.' She beckoned Chris to sit next to Mary on the sofa. 'Look after her. Don't move and don't touch anything. Katie, come with me.'

Katie shot her brother a puzzled glance. He shrugged back from the sofa, his hands on his lap. He looked awkward, as if he'd found himself unexpectedly in a doctor's waiting room.

Out in the hallway, Mum issued instructions. Katie was to empty the fridge of all perishables. If there was any washing up to be done, she was to do it, but she was to use gloves. She passed Katie the bin liners and the carrier bag. 'Everything you need is here, including spray and surface wipes. Clean up anything particularly disgusting, but don't touch a thing with bare hands.'

Katie was also to check the cupboards for medicines (list of potential medicines, courtesy of Google, provided) and then make everyone a cup of tea (milk, biscuits and a Tupperware of tea bags also provided).

Mum thought of everything. Always. Except she was clearly relaxing the 'no sugar' rule of her own volition now.

'The meds might not exist, but have a quick look anyway,' she said. 'If she's on Doxazosin, then that's important. The other ones aren't so urgent. Oh, and check for Aricept. That's a drug for dementia. You never know . . .'

'Dementia?'

'Seems highly likely to me. She's absolutely all over the place with her memory.' She took a breath. 'Right, call me when the tea's ready and make sure the cups are clean.'

'Where are you going?'

'Upstairs, to see what the situation is. The council are going to want this place back. We can't have them knowing she lived like this.' She checked her watch. 'Let's get this over with.'

The kitchen was small and dark and smelled stale, as if someone had been cooking chips for years and hadn't bothered ventilating. Katie switched on the light and unlocked the outside door, surprised to find a tangled little garden. Daylight made things worse though, because now she could see how yellow the muslin hanging at the window was and how grimy the floor looked. She felt like a forensic officer at the scene of a crime as she donned gloves to open the fridge. She half expected a severed head on a plate, but it was remarkably ordinary inside – a scrap of cheese, a jar of pickle, a few shrivelled carrots and sprouting potatoes and an old tub of marge. She poured milk down the sink (holding her nose, because it had clotted), followed by the dregs of an orange juice carton. She kept watching the door, hoping Mary didn't come in. Shouldn't they have asked her if this was OK? Maybe she wanted the pickle. Maybe it was Jack's pickle?

She boiled a kettle (trusted the electrics for five minutes) and looked out at the garden while she waited. It was overgrown, but rather beautiful in its wildness. All sorts of colours and textures were weaving together. When the kettle was ready she washed up the few cups and plates she found festering in the sink. But the simple act of washing up felt wrong. This might have been the plate Jack ate his last meal from. She might be washing him away.

Now for the medicine list. *Tolterodine, Lisinopril, Doxazosin*. The top one had an asterisk next to it. Mum had written, *withdrawal of bladder meds possibly increasing confusion?* Everything about Mary seemed to have a question mark next to it.

She tentatively opened a cupboard above the sink. It was packed with cereal boxes. Damn! Did they count as perishable? Probably, since no one was going to be eating them now. Which meant she had more stuff to throw away. She hauled them out, but on each and every one was a Post-it Note: *If it's dark, come back to bed*.

God, that was so sad! It must be Jack's writing. Jack keeping Mary safe, guiding her back to their bed in the night when she wandered off and thought it was time for breakfast. Katie couldn't throw those stickers away. She peeled them off and put them carefully in her pocket before chucking the cereal in the bin bag. In the next cupboard – no medicine, but coffee, tea, cups and plates. On the inside door: *Only one teaspoon of sugar, you're sweet enough!*

59

Katie peeled that off too. Perhaps Mary would like to have the stickers at the flat to make her feel at home. Now Katie was looking for them, she found several more: *The kettle is hot, like you. You set my heart on fire, but don't touch these matches.*

By the door to the garden: *If you want to go outside, please take me with you.*

They were everywhere. They were so, so beautiful. And here, on a corkboard, was an actual drawing. And it hurt to look, because it was a stick-figure man with 'Jack' written above in the same handwriting as the post-its. He was holding hands with a stick-figure woman, 'Mary', and underneath were four more stick figures with names scrawled above their heads – 'Caroline, Steve, Katie, Chris'.

Here was Katie's family drawn by a dead man and here was Dad holding hands with Mum and it was all so perfect, like reading a really romantic book or watching a movie. Katie pulled the picture from the board and rammed it in her pocket. She grabbed the biscuits and went into the lounge. Mum could find the medicine. Mum could make the tea.

Chris was clearly disobeying instructions too, since Wolf Mountain was plugged in and fully operative. Plastic wolves with blue metallic eyes stood on a plateau. Lights glistened in the snow at their feet. Their white fur stood up in frozen peaks. Chris bent his ear to them, listening.

'Hear them howl?' Mary said. 'They're guarding things, that's why.'

Chris nodded. 'I'll put them in the suitcase.'

'That's it. Bring the wolves.'

Katie hoped they weren't serious. Mum would hate having anything electrical from Mary's house in the flat. She'd think it would start a fire or, at the very least, blow all the fuses.

'Here,' Katie said, hoping to distract Chris, 'biscuits.'

He took the packet with a grin, but it didn't deter him. He placed the wolves carefully in the case. 'Aren't they great?'

'Lovely,' Katie said, as she ran a finger through the glass beads of the chandelier and watched rainbows shimmer across the room.

'These are Jack's souvenir smoking pipes,' Mary said, waggling a handful at Katie. 'Wherever we went he'd pick a new one up. This one is from Austria and splits into three. I always rather liked the Tyrolean picture.'

'She really did see him through the window,' Chris said, pointing to one of the chairs with the biscuits. 'He was sitting right there.'

'I see him all the time,' Mary said. 'Why wouldn't I?'

Chris eyed her curiously. 'Does he ever look dangerously hungry?'

Katie frowned at him, but he took no notice. If he wanted to scare himself thinking Jack was a zombie, that was fair enough, but he should leave Mary out of it. She didn't need reminding Jack was dead. Mum had already upset her with it.

'Jack was a great collector of things,' Mary said, holding out what looked like a bunch of sticks. 'These are porcupine quills. He used them for fishing.'

She showed them a miniature sailing boat made from a Dutch clog, with golden thread for rigging and parchment sails, some nautical coasters, a rotring pen set, a perfume bottle with a black balloon pump.

'All the way from Paris.' Mary gave the pump a delighted squeeze against her throat. 'It's hand-cut lead crystal with a silver tassel for added elegance.'

How could she snap out the names for things so readily? How

could she remember what they were for and the places she'd got them? Maybe it was something to do with being here, in the home she'd shared with Jack. Maybe memories came back if she was in the right place for long enough?

'I'm sure he'd like you both to take something as a gift,' she told them. 'What would you like? What about this shoehorn? You want this? Always useful to have a shoehorn. This one's from Freeman's, celebrated purveyor of footwear in Lavender Hill. Have you ever been to London?'

Chris shook his head. 'We haven't been anywhere, not even abroad. Mum's scared of flying.'

'Is she? Shame. There's so much to see. Still, you're young. There's plenty of time.'

She smiled happily as she passed more things to put in the case. Still nothing useful by the look of it, but it was lovely the three of them looking through her stuff together. The curtains billowed like white summer dresses in and out of the windows as all the detail flowed from Mary's lips – a Sparklets soda syphon, a resin rocket lamp, a sun clock by Anstey and Wilson, a Meakin coffee set. Mary was like a presenter on *Antiques Roadshow* teaching them about ancient objects.

Mum came striding in with an armful of clothes. 'I've found blouses and skirts and underwear. I couldn't find any vests or socks and I wasn't sure about these trousers.' She held them up to show Mary. 'They've still got the label on. If I bring them, will you actually wear them?'

Mary shrugged, told Mum to ask Jack, who she thought was probably upstairs.

Mum gave an exasperated sigh and turned to the suitcase. 'What's all this?'

'Stuff we're bringing,' Chris said.

'No, no, absolutely not.' Mum put the clothes on a chair. 'We can't take all this.' She reached down to the case. 'Why the heck do you need a plastic pineapple?'

Mary scowled at her. 'That's an ice bucket! What are you doing? Put that back!'

'Maybe the clock,' Mum said, 'but not newspapers or ornaments.' She reached down again. 'What's this? A pipe?'

Mary snatched it back. 'These aren't your things! You think you can rootle through them? Who said you could do that?' She put the pipe back in the suitcase, added a stack of what looked like old theatrical programmes and put her hand out to Mum. 'Give me the pineapple.'

Mum passed it over. She looked furious as she turned back to the clothes. 'Well, these will have to squash on top, so don't blame me when they're creased!'

Katie glanced at Chris. He was busy eating a biscuit and pretending not to notice, which meant he probably felt as guilty as she did. They hadn't stopped Mary being ridiculous with her packing and now trouble was brewing again. There'd been a similar encounter the previous evening when Mary had wanted to go for a walk after supper. Mum had patiently explained that it was late, that the streets were dangerous at night, that it was nearly time for bed, but Mary'd put her coat on and insisted. Katie had offered to take her for a stroll round the block because she wanted a break from revision, but Mum had said she wasn't risking both of them and locked the door and put the key in her pocket. Mary had stood in the hallway demanding to be let out. She couldn't stand locked doors. *Was this a jail? Was Mum going to slam them all in the coal hole?*

Mum had insisted they didn't have a coal hole and no one was being slammed anywhere, but she wasn't going to unlock the door because it was dark outside. Mary'd lost her temper, 'How about unlocking your heart?' she'd yelled rather spectacularly before stomping off to the balcony to smoke a furious cigarette.

Now, a whole new day had arrived and Mary was in trouble again. Different house, different argument. Same impasse.

Mum squashed the clothes in the case and forced the lid shut. 'No more,' she said. 'I was imagining photos or a couple of Jack's things, not all this. You can't bring everything.'

Mary shook her head. 'Open that case. I haven't checked upstairs yet.'

'What do you need from up there?'

'My shoes. My dresses and things.'

'I've collected your clothes already and you've got shoes on your feet. There's no point bringing more.'

'My father bought me reams of glorious silk,' Mary said airily, 'and my sister made it into a dress. Every time I wore it, I got kissed. I'm not going anywhere without it.'

'There isn't room.' Mum said, desperately zipping the case. 'We'll have a much clearer idea of how long you'll be with us after seeing the doctor. But until then, all your other things need to stay here.'

'Doctor?' Mary said. 'What doctor?'

'The one we discussed yesterday.'

Mary folded her arms. 'I'm sorry to disappoint you, but I don't recall any such discussion and I'm afraid I have plans tomorrow.'

'Tomorrow's Sunday. The appointment's on Tuesday.'

'Unfortunately, I have plans on Tuesday as well.'

Mum turned suddenly from the suitcase. She looked furious, strange and determined. 'We discussed this. You agreed to see the doctor and so I made an appointment. Your plans will have to wait.'

Mary stepped forward to challenge her, gripping the edge of the sofa for support. 'I don't think so.'

Mum was exasperated now, her face flushed with it. 'You're not well. We won't get any support from social services until you're in the system and no support means no specialist help.'

'Specialist help?' Mary hissed. 'What on earth are you talking about?'

'A nursing home,' Chris told her through a mouthful of biscuit.

Mum turned on him. 'For goodness sake, Chris! Would you just stay out of this?'

Chris shrugged. 'I'm only saying what you told me.'

'Well, don't!'

Mary looked horrified. 'You're making me leave?'

'No one's making anyone do anything,' Mum said. 'Not until we've seen the doctor.'

'I don't want that to happen,' Mary said, fumbling at her pockets. 'I don't like the sound of that at all.'

Mum unhooked Mary's handbag from the back of a chair and passed it to her. 'Is this what you're looking for?'

'Thank you,' Mary said. 'Now if you'll excuse me, I'm going out for a smoke.'

Katie held her breath as Mary left the lounge, waiting for a door to slam, waiting for a yell over the shoulder, but neither came. Instead, Katie heard the kitchen door open and gently close again. Then silence.

Chris helped himself to another biscuit. 'She'll hate it in a home,' he said. 'Even if it's a nice one.'

Mum gave him a fierce look. 'No, she won't.'

'What if she does?'

'Well, she can't stay here, can she? This place is a death trap.' Mum flapped her arms to show them all the deadly things. It included the lounge and everything in it, all the rooms upstairs, Katie, Chris, Mum and everything beyond the window. 'She'll be happier in a home. It's the best way I can care for her.'

'But *you* won't be there,' Chris said.

'That's right.' Mum nodded her head very slowly at him. 'You're going to have to trust me on this one, Chris.' She turned back to the suitcase and yanked it upright.

'I like having her around,' Chris said. 'She makes me laugh.'

'Well, I'm very glad about that,' Mum said, 'but perhaps that's because you don't have to do any of the work.'

Eight

The intoxicating sound of a gull brought Mary to stillness. She sat on a handy bench opposite a church and watched the bird dip and soar, its white wings outstretched. She experienced a moment of such unadulterated pleasure that she imagined she really may have been happier than she'd ever been before. But almost as soon as she thought that, a whiff of hot pastry caught her nostrils and she realized she could be happier still if she had something warm and delicious to eat. Like a magic trick, there was the girl. Today, despite the heat, she was wearing trousers and a jumper. Foolish child. However, she was also holding out a brown paper bag from which the delicious smell was coming.

'Here you go, Mrs Runaway,' she said. 'One microwaved croissant.'

Mary took the bag and pointed to the sky with it. 'Seagull,' she said.

'Yes,' the girl agreed, sitting down beside her. 'It must be lost.'

The cake was delicious. Mary crammed it into her mouth in only four bites, could really have done with another one besides. She licked the butter from her fingers and wiped them on her skirt.

'When I was young,' she told the girl, 'I could fit five cherries in my mouth at once. I'd burst them with my tongue and spit the stones across the garden.'

The girl laughed, then leaned over and patted Mary's hand. 'I'll buy you a big bag of cherries on the way back from my exam this afternoon. We'll get Mum to pay. She won't mind. She'll be feeling guilty about getting cross at us. You wait and see.'

'Cross?' Mary said. 'Was she? I don't remember.'

'She's mad at me for chatting with you instead of revising, she's mad at Chris for talking about Dad, and mad at you for listing your boyfriends at the breakfast table.'

Mary felt the stirring of panic that came with a blank memory. 'I did that? I'm usually very discreet. Why did I do that?'

'Chris wanted to know who Mum's father is.'

'Did I know?'

The girl pulled a scrap of paper from her pocket and unfolded it. 'Robert Gibson, you said. Is that right?'

'Ah, Robert.' Mary pressed a hand to her cheek. 'Oh, he was marvellous.'

The girl smiled. 'Yes, that's what you told us. Anyway, Mum went crazy. Mostly because Chris got it into his head that she should let us see our dad now she had one of her own. She won't though, cause Dad's living with his girlfriend in our old house and they've had a baby, which is a pretty unforgiveable offence.'

'I don't remember anyone going crazy.'

'Well, it's all relative, I guess. She doesn't really do yelling. More quiet fury, you know?'

'And I was there? Are you sure?'

The girl looked awkward and . . . was that pity in her eyes? 'Sorry, shouldn't I remind you of these things?'

It was like walking the edge of a precipice. No, it was like waking up and discovering a toe had come off in the night, or a finger was missing. She had no recollection of an argument at all. Essential parts of her were falling away and not coming back. What was it that doctor had told her the other day? 'I'm suspecting you have tangles in your brain, Mrs Todd.' Stupid bloody woman. Why couldn't that be a blank memory? Why did she get no choice in what she remembered and what she forgot?

'People can only do their best,' she whispered to the girl beside her.

'Yes,' the girl agreed.

'We should try not to judge them too harshly.'

'Are you talking about you and Mum?'

'I'm talking about everyone I ever knew.'

The girl looked at her unblinking. 'Why did you and Mum fall out, do you remember?'

'Perhaps you could ask her?'

'I have. She won't talk about it. Pat's a saint and you're a sinner and that's all we're getting. But nothing's ever that simple, is it? I mean, you lived with each other in London when Mum was a teenager, didn't you? Was it terrible? Did you hate each other?'

'That's a lot of questions.'

'I want to understand.'

'Well, if you ever find out, would you be kind enough to let me know?'

The girl laughed. 'Maybe we should hire that detective after all?'

This girl was young and lovely and clearly trying her best and all Mary could do was smile as she tried to push the panic back down. She wanted to say, *I'm forgetting so much. Please help me. I think my heart is breaking.*

But what she actually said was, 'Why are we sitting here?'

'Because you ran away again.'

A thrill filled her. 'Did I get far?'

'Every morning you get a bit further. You really would make an excellent escape artist.'

Mary chuckled. 'I wonder where I'm going?'

Something about the weather being mild, was it? Or something about needing to fetch something? See someone? Whatever it was that had brought her to this bench, she was glad of it. She sat, her hands slack in her lap and let the sun warm her face.

'Vitamin D is absorbed through the eyelids,' she told the girl. 'Did you know?'

The girl didn't reply.

'Did you hear me?'

It wasn't often that Mary attempted to impart wisdom, but when she did, surely the child could have the courtesy of listening?

'I'm talking to you, Copper Top!'

But the girl was looking away across the road, biting her lip. A terrible habit that only showed the world you were afraid and was generally to be avoided at all costs. What was she gawping at? Mary shaded her eyes and strained to see. A group of girls had appeared over there outside a shop. They were all legs and bare arms, tapping into their gadgets and jabbering nonsense far too loudly.

The girl said, 'Can we go now?'

'Because of them?'

'Not really.'

Mmm, well, you never find out anything from the young if you go at them directly. She knew that from her years evading Pat's rules. She surveyed the young women and tried to assess the possibilities. They were clearly confident sorts, taking up lots of room on the pavement, wanting people to notice.

'Do you know them?' Mary asked.

'I know her.' She nodded towards one of the girls. 'I used to be friends with her.'

The girl she referred to was blonde, her hair laced with sunshine.

'I bet they're buying booze,' the girl said. 'Some people have got their last exam today, so they'll be planning something for later.'

'They didn't invite you?'

'Esme used to get me invited to stuff, but not any more.'

'Did you have a row?' Mary asked.

'Kind of.'

'Why don't you go over and make it up?'

'Not when the others are there.' The girl turned to her, eyes shining. 'They think I'm a freak.'

Mary was shocked to feel a sudden rush of love. Why did this child move her so much? Perhaps because she was capable of putting her heart on a plate for the world to see. 'Some things are worth pursuing.'

'They'll say stuff.'

'So what if they do? Words never killed anyone.' Mary crept her hand onto the girl's knee. 'Don't be like Pat, always hiding away, thinking you're never enough.'

The girl looked at her with serious eyes. 'I didn't know Pat was like that.'

'Risk your heart,' Mary said. 'It makes things happen. You see if I'm right.'

But then the group gathered themselves to move off, so none of it mattered anyway. And was it Mary's imagination, or did the girl shuffle closer, try and make herself smaller as they walked by?

Mary really must remember to teach her about courage in the face of adversity. A subject at which she was expert.

Nine

Maybe the sun bleaching through the exam room window messed with Katie's head, because time definitely slowed down. She could actually feel the dull thump of each passing moment. Never had vectors or Newton's laws of motion felt so torturous and even though there were only two questions she struggled with, it felt as if days had passed when Mechanics was finally over.

She was going to slink away as quickly as possible, but a couple of the boys said they were going to get a Coke from the machine by the common room and was she coming or what? This was so entirely weird, that she tagged after them. They sat on the wall outside and went over questions they remembered.

She'd mucked up coefficients of friction big time, but she'd remembered to convert to radians per second when working out linear speed round a circle and yes, she'd used Newton's Second Law to find the equation of motion in the radial direction. Not too bad . . .

The boys even told her about some party a friend of theirs was having after exams were over and she put the details on her phone. Why not? If she studied really hard, Mum might let her go.

It was so nice to be included that Katie felt herself relax for the first time in days. The breeze ruffled her hair. Birds twittered over-head and it was so hot it looked as if water beamed at her from the walls of the main school buildings across the playground. They actually looked rather beautiful, as if waterfalls swept their sides.

Another exam done and a whole week of half term coming up. Only one more exam after that and now a party to look forward to. She was lucky. She must keep thinking this. She was not Mum making difficult phone calls. She was not Chris. She was not poor dead Jack. She was not Mary, trapped in the flat with no choice about anything. She was Katie Baxter – blessed to be alive and healthy on such a sunny day.

She felt positively optimistic as she threw the empty can in the bin, said goodbye to the boys and picked up her bag. So optimistic, that when she saw Esme and her friends over on the grass by the drama block she made a decision.

She'd casually walk up and ask how exams were going. Then she'd ask if they had any plans for the afternoon. She didn't want to hide away like Pat. She wanted to risk her heart like Mary.

The girls would admire her courage and include her again. Simple.

When there's a collision between two objects, Newton's Third Law states that the force on one of the bodies is equal and opposite to the force on the other body. But there weren't two bodies, there were five of them and only one of her and how could she ever have thought they'd be inclusive or that things would be equal?

She knew it as soon as she veered off the path towards them.

'Hey,' one of them said, nudging Esme, 'here comes your friend.'

Ex-friend. Which is why Esme looked so horrified. Which is why she did a backwards collapse on the grass, like a sniper had got her. Katie felt a fierce burning flood her face. How could a friendship go from something to nothing? More than nothing, in fact – a negative, because they'd lost the thing they had.

It was palpable the way the others judged Katie as she got close – their eyes flicking up and down, checking out her complete lack of tan or makeup, her inability to do anything with her hair apart from shove it in a ponytail. But if she turned round and walked away she'd look a total loser and make everything worse. She had to go through with this, had to make them change their minds about her. She'd keep it short, not say anything too mad and pretend she hadn't noticed Esme blanking her.

But maybe Esme ignoring her gave the other girls permission to be meaner, because there was a certain electric energy in their eyes as they shushed each other, like they were in a play and the main actor had just arrived and clearly didn't know her words.

Imagine them on the toilet. Imagine them slipping on banana skins.

'Hi,' Katie said. 'I thought I'd come over and see how you were.'

'All of us?' Amy said. 'Or just one of us?'

'All of you.'

'Interesting decision.' Amy smirked. 'But then I heard you're good at those.'

'Could we just drop this now?'

'Drop it? Why? It's fascinating.'

'Actually, it's getting kind of tedious.'

'You think?' She turned to the others. 'But we want to know all about your unusual tendencies, don't we?'

Heat amplified across Katie's chest and face. 'Never mind. Just forget it.'

'Don't be like that. We're curious, that's all.'

One of the other girls laughed. 'Three-way curious, Amy?'

Amy wagged a finger. 'Funny!'

Katie's heart was clanging, banging in her chest. *Esme, Esme, say something!* But no, she lay on the grass with her golden hair spread about her as if she was dead.

A third girl eyed Katie enquiringly. 'So, what *did* actually happen?'

Sunlight flickered through the trees overhead and splashed all their keen and upright faces. Katie felt as if she was watching herself, seeing them laugh at her, listening to herself unable to speak, because what could she say? *I'm confused? I'm an idiot? I wish I could turn all the clocks back?*

'Anything you can remember would be fine,' the girl said, 'like, exactly what you were thinking when you jumped your only friend?'

'I didn't jump her.'

'Oh, she was up for it, was she?'

And Esme – finally! – sat up and scraped the hair from her face and said, 'Just give it a break, you lot, will you?'

Which Katie appreciated. Although really, there had to be rules in the universe and one of them had to surely be that if you betrayed someone absolutely, you weren't allowed to keep doing it and you definitely weren't allowed to feign death when they got attacked.

Amy was still eyeing her up and down. She said, 'You must be boiling in those jeans.'

One of the others said, 'She likes it hot though, doesn't she?'

They all laughed like drains again. Except for Esme. She wasn't laughing.

'So, you just had an exam?' Esme said. And although she avoided eye contact, it was definitely a question levelled at Katie, and it sounded like a serious question, not a piss take. And it was the first time Esme had spoken to her in over a month.

Katie tried to get her heart under control. 'Mechanics.'

Amy sniggered. 'You're doing an A level in fixing cars?'

'It's maths.'

'So, now you're showing off?'

'I'm just telling you what it is.'

'All right, keep calm!'

Katie ignored her. 'Did you get your art coursework done, Esme?' Because how was she supposed to find stuff out if Esme wouldn't talk to her?

Maybe it was using her name, just chucking it out as if she had the right to say it, but Esme's eyes flickered to Katie's briefly and then away. And was that a hint of a smile?

'Yeah, all handed in.'

She'd dyed her hair again, made it blonder and her fingernails were painted blue, green, yellow. Once, Esme had painted Katie's nails. Not that long ago – autumn in fact, just after Katie arrived at the school and Esme had befriended her, just after they started walking to school together, when they still hung out.

'You had the written exam yet?' Katie asked.

'Just finished.'

'How did it go?'

'Not sure.'

I see you, thought Katie. You know exactly, but you don't want to let your guard down in front of these girls. 'I've got English in a week, then I'm done,' Katie said. 'What about you?'

Amy faked a massive yawn. 'Could this get any more interesting?'

'Shush, shush!' One of the others pointed across the grass. 'Here comes the other one.'

Katie turned and there was Simona Williams (who everyone knew the rumours about) crossing the grass.

'Hey,' Amy called. 'Can I ask you something?'

Simona stopped and looked at them all with such condescension that Katie could barely breathe. 'What?'

'Do you want to come on a picnic?'

'Not if you held a gun to my head.'

'But I heard you like eating out.'

Simona narrowed her eyes. 'Is that supposed to be funny?'

'It *is* funny actually.'

'Only if you're small-minded, bigoted and stupid.'

Amy started laughing, a snorting, hiding kind of laugh. It was the kind of laugh that's supposed to show everyone you're nice and don't really mean to be such a cow. Her shoulders were shaking with it, and maybe it was contagious because Esme caught it and the others followed, one by one. And it was such a relief that this terror wasn't hers that Katie began to laugh too. Someone else could take the flak for a change. Someone else could be the geek, the odd one out. It was delicious. It felt like belonging. Katie Baxter was part of this group of giggling girls and it was better than not being, better than being Simona Williams, who was shaking her head at them as if they were idiots, who was telling them all to grow up as she stalked away.

It was hilarious.

For about twenty seconds.

As soon as Simona disappeared into the drama block, Amy turned on Katie, wanting to know why she was laughing, what was so amusing, did she think mocking a poor innocent lesbian was cool? Esme sighed and lay back on the grass, an arm slung across her face.

Don't leave me, Katie thought. *Don't disappear again. Why are you letting this happen?*

Amy saw her looking, said, 'Christ! Just give it up, will you?'

And the others all giggled again.

Despite the sun, despite her jeans and sweater, Katie was cold, really shivery cold. She'd actually thought for the briefest moment that today might be different. The world had seemed momentarily pleased with her. She'd been lulled by sunshine.

Stupid! Stupid to think it could ever be all right.

She grabbed her bag. 'I'm going.'

Amy tutted. 'That's not very friendly, is it?'

'I don't want to be friendly.'

'Not what I heard. I heard you're *very* friendly.' There was something vicious in her voice now. 'Or maybe I'm not your type.'

Esme stirred on the grass. This had gone too far for her perhaps.

'You're surrounded by morons,' Katie told her. 'Get out while you can.'

She wanted bombs to fall from the frigging sky. Right on the heads of these stupid girls. She had fury in her again, mad fury surging up from her feet to her gut, and maybe they knew, maybe they thought *that's enough*, or maybe they were bored of it, or maybe they were trying to mess with her head, because they didn't say a word as she walked away.

Ten

It was strange how different Katie's bedroom looked – not just the unmade bed or the things Mary brought back from her house piled all over the floor, but the curtains tied with a scarf and the window wide open. Katie always worried about people looking in from the flats opposite, but it was quite nice having light streaming into the room.

She went to her desk and pulled out a handful of blank revision books from the drawer. The best one was slim and hard-backed with an elastic to keep it closed – that'd do. She grabbed her pencil case and ran back downstairs, pretending not to notice Mum's questioning look as she jogged past the kitchen to the lounge and out to the balcony.

'Right,' she told Mary. 'This is going to be *your* book. I'm putting your name in the front and we're going to write all your important things in it. Like a memory book, you know?'

Mary smiled politely, but didn't say anything.

'We're going to start with a family tree – see how many names we know between us.'

Mary was looking at Katie as if she had absolutely no idea what she was talking about.

Katie reached for her arm and stroked it. 'What's the matter?'

'I'm not myself.' Mary rubbed the back of her neck with the

palm of her hand as if she had a headache. 'Every morning I think I can do things, and by the afternoon it turns out I can't.'

'Did you do anything this afternoon with Mum? Do you remember?'

'Not really.'

'She said you ran off again – you almost got to the high street, I hear. That's an achievement.'

Mary shook her head. 'There was a party. Fireworks and bonfires and dancing. Pat wanted everyone to line up for a photo, but people were so busy getting riffy-raffy, they ignored her. Was that today?'

How could a whole day slide away? How could memories from years back be clear, and stuff from hours ago be lost in fog? Katie stroked her arm. She hoped that being stuck in the past wasn't like being dragged down by anaesthetic, unable to wake up, sinking despite yourself. She hoped there were plenty of good memories inside Mary's head to explore. She kept quiet, kept stroking Mary's arm until, finally, she closed her eyes. Katie wished her sweet dreams and opened the book. She'd just have to start it by herself.

In primary school, each child drew their family tree. When Katie showed hers to the teacher, she was told off for not making an effort. *But there's only four of us*, she said. She was instructed to ask her parents for help. Her dad – an only child – said his own parents had died when he was a young man and told her their names. It was like having ghosts on her poster. He said Mum was an orphan too and showed her a photo of Pat that Mum kept in her purse. He said Pat had never learned to swim and should never have gone in the sea. She looked very strict in the photo. But not half as strict as Mum when she came in and saw them looking at it. She snatched it back. She said some things were private. She wrote a note for the teacher saying such a project shouldn't be statutory.

She said, *Schools should check with parents before they go stirring things up*, and refused to talk about it again. For the first time Katie realized adults had secrets and it made her afraid. Perhaps the world was full of unspeakable horror and when she was old enough, she'd be told. She also began to worry that her parents would die like her grandparents and that Chris and she would be alone.

This new family tree was different. It had Mary Todd at its centre. Katie drew a vertical line to show she had a daughter, Caroline, in 1954. Mum wouldn't thank Katie for putting her date of birth down in black and white, but maybe she didn't ever need to see?

Katie drew a horizontal line and wrote Jack's name next to Mary's. Poor dead Jack. Was it possible to miss someone you didn't know? Because she did, especially when Mary claimed to see him about the place. It felt like a weight in Katie's chest – thinking of him lying in a mortuary waiting to be buried.

She added Mary's sister, Pat, to the tree and wrote *adopted* between her name and Mum's. She wondered briefly if that was the right word. Should it be *fostered* instead? Or *surrogate*? What was the word for a woman who brought up a child when the child's real mother had run off? Mmm, she'd have to give that some thought . . .

Above the two sisters, Katie left a gap for their unnamed parents. She put Dad next to Mum (another thing Mum would find hard) and wrote *separated* in a bracket between them. She put Dad's dead parents above him. Then she put Chris and herself.

Already, the page was looking crowded. By the time she found out about Mary's parents and dared to add Dad's girlfriend and the baby (a half-sister!), she'd have a massive family. Instead of a triangle, she'd be part of a new shape, one with branches and roots. She almost wanted to seek out that old primary teacher and tell her all about it, which was weird.

She headed the next page of the book – *Facts*. Mary was seventeen when she gave birth to Mum in 1954. Katie had watched enough episodes of *Mad Men* and *Call the Midwife* to know that being pregnant and unmarried in the fifties was a massive deal. No legal abortion, no government hand-outs, no council housing, just shame and stigma. Nightmare! And if Mary's dad really had called her a slut, then he sounded pretty strict, so maybe he'd thrown her out and that's why she'd gone missing for years?

Katie headed the next page *Things Mum says*, because on the way home from Mary's house she'd said she'd never been happier than when she lived in Bisham as a girl (funny – Katie had never been *un*happier!). Chris had piped up with, 'So why did you leave?' And Mum had looked at Mary in the rear-view mirror and said, 'Someone turned up on my doorstep.' Nine years old and you discover your mum is your aunt and your real mum is a total stranger. No wonder Mum never wanted to talk about it.

This was a good idea. A book!

Every morning when Mary was brightest, Katie would ask her questions and discover all sorts of juicy secrets. She'd have to try and differentiate between crap and truth, of course. Mmm, that might be difficult. Had Mary really shinned down the drainpipe to go dancing, or did she just wish that happened? Anyway, before too long, the puzzle of the past would be resolved and Mary and Mum would patch things up. Mum would stop thinking everyone was about to abandon her and mellow out. She'd forgive Dad. She'd let Katie drop an A level next year, because only nutters took four. She'd also let her have a gap year abroad and . . . oh yes, if Mum ever got wind of any rumours regarding Katie and Esme – well, maybe she'd be so chilled out by that point the horror wouldn't actually kill her.

So, Katie had a plan – but the only way for it to work was if

Mum had no idea. She'd hate all this prying into the past. She already felt uncomfortable with Jack's Post-it Notes on Mary's bedroom wall, so a secret book would be even more distressing. Here she came now, tapping on the window and pointing to her watch. That gesture meant, could Katie please lay the table and sort out drinks. Katie felt a stab of irritation. It was nice sitting out here huddled in a chair watching light fade from the sky. Did they always have to eat at exactly half seven? Mary was asleep, for goodness sake! Mum tapped again, louder now. This probably meant – I've been on my feet all day, I've had no time for myself, I've made hundreds of phone calls, kept Mary safe and catered to her every whim, policed Chris on his Xbox and made supper and all you're doing is sitting on your backside watching the sun set, so will you please help me out here because I shouldn't have to ask twice!

Katie snapped the book shut.

Supper was horrible. Not the food, which was pasta and pesto – the atmosphere. Mary barely ate. She seemed so different – sort of deflated, like her air had come out. Her eyes kept searching the room, searching faces, as if she was trying to work out where she was and why. At one point she grabbed Mum's hand and whispered, 'Pat? Is that you?'

Mum shook her head. 'I'm Caroline.'

'Are you sure?'

'Sun downing,' Mum whispered to Katie later. She'd gone straight to her laptop while Katie cleared the table and looked up symptoms on some dementia website. 'Late afternoon and evening, she'll lose energy and be prone to restless and impulsive behaviour. Her concentration will lapse and she's likely to do things which may endanger herself or others.' Mum reeled them off as if they were certainties, slapped the laptop shut and slumped back in her chair

83

to gaze hopelessly at the ceiling. 'Brilliant. Doesn't life just get better by the hour?'

Mary was watching TV with Chris at the other end of the room. She didn't appear to have heard. Katie went to sit with them. It seemed wrong to talk about that stuff in front of them and Katie didn't know what to do about it.

'Shove up,' she told her brother. He huffed, but moved over and she sat between them on the sofa. They were watching some detective programme about a psychic who knew what people were thinking and could tell the cops where bodies were hidden.

'I'm going to learn to read people's minds,' Chris said.

'You can read mine if you like,' Mary laughed. 'Let me know what you find.'

Katie leaned in to her. Her grandmother was warm and solid.

Eleven

Mary played the memory game as she walked. Today's category was: love.

She is twelve years old sitting in a cherry tree and spies a boy cleaning his bike. Blossom falls into her hair and down the back of her dress. Sunlight climbs the side of the house as she smears her lips crimson.

She is fifteen and has permission to stay at the street party until midnight. It's not as glamorous as being allowed into London to the Festival Pleasure Gardens, but it's better than nothing at all. A man clutches her round the waist and spins her. He demands a kiss and she proffers her cheek, but Pat pushes him off and brushes down the place on Mary's dress where his hands have been.

'What are you like?' Pat admonishes.

'You tell me!' Mary demands, standing with her hands on her hips and her chin tipped at her sister.

What *was* she like? It became a phrase, asked of her for years.

She would never come to any good, that seemed to be generally agreed upon. She was too encouraging of male attention, too bold, too opinionated. She couldn't be trusted with any domestic task. She broke things. Couldn't cook for toffee. She had no control of herself. Don't put a baby in her arms – she'll drop it. Not a motherly instinct in her.

And the ridiculous notions she came up with! The Royal Academy of Dramatic Art? She'd clearly lost her mind if she was still on about acting. Dad would rather she dug fish from the sand every day than have his baby girl leave him. She was the apple of his eye, his treasure. Pat was very sure about Dad's opinion on this, and when he wavered she wagged her finger and told him that being an actress was only one step away from prostitution.

What picture is this now? Ah yes, Mary's on her way to secretarial school and a young man winks at her as he swings onto the bus. She knows she's supposed to smile coyly at the floor, but she smiles into his eyes instead and neither of them look away. He's there again at the bus stop the next day. Same wink, same smile. They get talking, she tells him where she's going and that evening he's outside the gates, *just happened to be passing, what a coincidence!* His eyes are full of something and she knows what it is – desire. When he asks if she'd like to go dancing on Saturday night, it makes her heart sing.

Is it just her? Do all women and girls possess this gift – something hot and quick that draws men to them? Has she always had it? Should she love it as much as she does? It feels like a spark that keeps tipping into flame. And it's freedom of sorts, isn't it? It's something that belongs to her, that Pat and Dad can never take away. If she's to be trapped in this little town, then why not make life a bit more interesting?

She studies other women – the angle of their necks as they sew and knit, her own sister's tired eyes as she goes through the household accounts. She dares to ask how it is for married women, in their opinion. What are men like to live with in that way? Jean next door says, *It's two minutes of pleasure and a lifetime of pain.* Pat says, *That sounds about right.*

She confides in a girl at the typing pool, who laughs and says, 'I should think men do gawp at you, Mary, with that trim little figure of yours.'

She asks her friend Audrey while they stand in the queue for the Roxy. 'Do you think there's something wrong with me? It feels like a sickness to be thinking of love all the time.'

Audrey frowns and says, 'You better be careful. You're getting a terrible reputation.'

Mary ended up at an intersection. A bigger, busier road crossed the quiet one she'd walked down. Here, the world was full of traffic. Light bounced off metal, engines hummed. She seemed to recognize this place. Had she been here before?

There was a wonderful smell of coffee coming from somewhere, ah, yes – that café was open. She rather fancied sitting at one of those outside tables and ordering something to drink. But no, to stall was to forget and there was a place she needed to go. She'd woken with such certainty and already it was slipping away. She'd know it when she got there, of course, but all she had right now was the ache of it. It was like having your hands tied when you wanted to scratch. It was like seeing a man you wanted to kiss and standing next to him was his wife.

She walked on a little way. She'd definitely been here before. That tree over the road looked very familiar. Was she being ridiculous? Didn't all trees look the same? The angle of that roof struck a chord too. So did the queue at the bus stop and the buildings over there that sparkled and winked as if they knew something.

She crossed the street and that's when she saw the number twenty-three glistening in sunshine on a gate. That's when she noticed a neat front garden and tiled steps leading up to the door. Eight steps in all.

'It's here,' she shouted. 'I found it.'

For a brief moment she swung, one hand strapped to the gate, the other grasping air. She stepped badly, her foot at an odd angle.

Someone said, 'Hey, love, are you all right?'

Her foot hurt. She tried to rub it, reached towards it, but it was too far away.

'You knock yourself?' The same voice, a man's voice.

There were a small group of people at the bus stop. This man was one of them. They were all looking at her.

'She by herself?' one of them said.

'You cold, love?' the man said. 'You're shivering.'

The world shifted from dream to reality and back again. As Mary opened the gate it was as if everything thickened, as if the air had density and texture.

When the man comes up behind her and asks if she lives here, she shakes her head. 'My sister does.'

He looks pleased, asks if he might take her arm and help her up the remaining steps. It will get embarrassing when they get to the door because Pat will be furious. But never mind that. She's going to knock, and when Pat answers Mary will take whatever consequences come her way. Even if the damn place falls down about their ears.

She glances at the man who has linked arms with her. She'll have to get rid of him before things get tricky.

'You OK?' he says. 'Am I going too fast?'

'You can go now.'

He raps on the door. 'I'll just wait until someone comes.'

'I'll be fine.'

'I'm not leaving until I know you're safe.'

A woman answers. A woman Mary's never seen before. She stands blinking down at them, says, 'Can I help?'

'This lady says her sister lives here,' the man says.

'No, love. Wrong address.'

'Well, that's what she says. She pointed me here.'

The woman frowns. 'Never seen her before.'

'So, what do I do now?' says the man. 'I've left my missus at the bus stop.'

'You should call the police, shouldn't you? If she's lost.'

The man looks at his watch. 'I'm already late.'

'Well, you can't leave her with me.'

They both look at Mary, assessing the possibilities. This is ridiculous! Do they think she's a robber? Do they think she's one half of Bonnie and Clyde? She smiles her sweetest smile. 'If Pat's not here, would it be all right if I came inside and had a little peek? I'd love to see the bedrooms.'

The man says, 'My mother-in-law's like this. Wears a bracelet with her address on. You reckon she's got something like that?'

The woman's eyes soften. 'What's your name, darling, do you remember? Where have you come from, eh?'

This really is none of their business. Mary tries to draw the appropriate words together. 'I'm currently living in London. I caught the train and walked here from the station. I stopped off for refreshments at the coffee bar.'

The woman shakes her head, looks doubtful.

The man says, 'You mean the café?'

'If you like. There's a particular seat near the window. I watch this place from there.'

The woman frowns. 'You watch my flat?'

'Just to make sure everything's the same, you know – the mantelpiece and the neatness. I have to know she's being looked after properly, you see. Now, I'd appreciate it if you'd let me come inside.'

89

The woman's eyes fill with something. Pity? Boredom? She turns to the man. 'Why don't you try the café? That's probably where she came from.'

'I'm late for work already. How about you call the police instead?'

'Not the police,' Mary says. 'That really won't be necessary.'

The woman looks sorry. 'But you don't seem to know where you are.'

'I'm at Pat's house.'

'No one called Pat lives here, darling. And it's not a house, it's a block of flats.'

The panic builds slowly. It's as if the world widens out to include things that don't belong – this woman's bare shoulders, the ring through her nose, the man tapping away at some gadget, a car alarm blaring, the sound of traffic building up on the road behind them.

Where is she? What year is it?

The hands are the best clue. Folded like origami round her handbag. She lifts them in front of her face to look. They are lined and dry.

She is ancient.

The world shifts once more.

The woman suggested she walk Mary back to the café. She said this was a less alarming solution than calling the police.

The man rubbed Mary's arm in a friendly fashion. 'Cheerio then. Best of luck.'

Mary stalled at the gate to look back at the house. It was all wrong. The window frames were some sort of white plastic and it never used to stretch so high or wide and there never used to be balconies or quite so many doors.

The woman said, 'These flats were built years ago. Maybe

it's a block of flats like this? Down a similar road perhaps?'

'Did you ever find a suitcase?'

'No, darling, I'm sorry. What was in it? Something valuable?'

But Mary couldn't remember, so she smiled instead and they continued a slow path out the gate and along the street. Daisies were scattered on the verge. Had they been there earlier? The bus stop certainly looked familiar. Mary yearned to sit there and let the sun warm her, but the woman had her firmly by the elbow and was chivvying her along.

'Don't worry,' the woman said. 'I'll walk you to the café and hopefully someone will recognize you.'

'I know her.' Mary waved at the girl who came running up. 'She's a bit of a relative.'

'Thank goodness,' the woman said.

The girl was out of breath, her hair wild, her eyes brimming with tears. 'I've been looking everywhere! You've never gone this far before.' She turned to the woman, 'I'm so sorry. She let herself out the flat before anyone was awake.'

The woman handed Mary over, told the girl she really should keep a better eye. The girl apologized many times. The woman mentioned Pat, told the girl about the coffee bar. They all shook hands. They waved goodbye. They smiled and wished each other luck.

'Why didn't you wake me up?' the girl said. 'I would've come with you.'

'I didn't want to disturb you.'

The girl gave her an old-fashioned look. 'It's a heck of a lot more disturbing having you disappear. You're lucky that woman found you.'

'I found *her* actually.'

'Well, whichever way round it was, you completely freaked

91

everyone out. I'll call Mum, let her know we're on our way home.'

'Let's not hurry.' Mary clutched the girl, relieved to have a familiar arm to hold. 'I quite fancy a coffee if you want to know the truth. How about a little sit-down before we go anywhere? I could murder a cake.'

The girl laughed. Her face lit up with it. 'I'm so glad to see you, Mary. I've never been so glad to see anyone in all my life.'

Twelve

'So, Mrs Todd,' the man said, 'do you know why you're here?'

Mary looked down at her feet and silently named her bones. She started with her metatarsals and intended going up in size until she got to her femur, but was interrupted by the woman sitting next to her, who leaned over and patted her hand. Mary could feel her own body trembling through the woman's fingers.

'Did you hear?' the woman said. 'You need to tell the doctor if you remember why we came.'

The room grew pale. *If you do crosswords, if you read books, if you avoid aluminium saucepans, if you extract all metal fillings, if you . . .*

Mary swallowed the panic and examined the woman's face for clues. She looked very stern – all that hair tied up so tight. It looked like a snake was sleeping on top of her head.

'You need to answer the doctor's question,' the woman said.

'Why don't *you* answer?' Mary suggested.

The woman frowned. 'I think he wants to hear it from you.'

Something terrible had happened, Mary knew that. A scream had shot out of her like liquid. There had been people staring, a blue light flashing.

And now she was in a room with a man and a woman and a desk. It was a small room, bright with sunshine. Through the window there were trees with leaves as wide as open hands. Summer then.

The man said, 'Perhaps you remember the journey here, Mrs Todd? Did you come by car or public transport?'

And over there, on a chair beneath the window, was a girl. Nothing too terrible could have happened if they were allowing a child to be here. Mary relaxed a little. She recognized this girl. She had her feet on the chair with her knees tucked up and was wearing those galumphing boots of hers. Mary gave her a friendly wave. At least she was something cheery to look at.

The girl waved in reply, said, 'We came in the car, remember? Mum drove and you and me sat in the back.'

The man wagged a finger. 'It'd be better if we let your grand-mother answer.'

No getting out of it then. 'Well,' Mary began, 'what precisely is it you would like to know, young man? Why we are here, or how we all got here?'

The man looked as if he was thinking about that. He eyed Mary steadily. 'This is a memory clinic, Mrs Todd.'

'Of course it is,' Mary said, 'which explains why nobody's got a clue what's going on!'

The girl by the window laughed. It was infectious. The woman caught it and smiled. Even the man behind the desk twinkled.

'Let me explain,' the man said. 'Your daughter's doctor got in touch with us because she's concerned that you might be having a bit of trouble remembering things.'

Blood knocked at Mary's temples. 'Caroline's doctor?'

'Yes,' the woman said. 'I'm Caroline and you came with me to meet my doctor, remember?'

This was Caroline! How strange not to have recognized her.

94

The man said, 'Would you say you've been having problems with your memory, Mrs Todd?'

'Not at all.'

He nodded. 'Well, let's consider the next half an hour an MOT test, shall we? We'll just run through a few things and check everything's in working order.' He opened a file and flicked through it, pulled out a piece of paper and read it up and down. 'So,' he said, 'can you tell me a bit about yourself, Mrs Todd?'

'What would you like to know?'

'Perhaps a bit about your childhood? Do you have any brothers or sisters, for instance?'

'I have a sister.' Mary shot a look at Caroline. She was cross with her for talking to doctors behind her back. '*She* can tell you about Pat. They got to know each other *very* well.'

'She's referring to the fact her sister brought me up,' Caroline said. 'My mother was very young when she had me, so my aunt and uncle looked after me instead. They didn't have any other children.'

'Of course they didn't,' Mary said. 'It was a marriage of convenience, that's why.'

Caroline reddened from ear to ear. Ha! Serve her right. 'I actually thought they *were* my parents. No one told me any different.'

The man wagged his finger again, this time bringing it to rest on his lips. Shut up, that meant! That told her. Treacherous woman.

'And where were you born?' the man asked.

Ah, now – that was an easy one. 'I was born,' Mary said, with absolute certainty, 'by the sea.'

Every day the wincing pain of sharp shells beneath her toes as she made her way to the water's edge. Every day the knowledge that there was more to life than sweeping and scrubbing and counting pennies, more to the world than her father's house and the little town with its twitching curtains and inflexible rules. On the beach was so much water, stretching against the line of the sky. The numb fury of it kept her alive.

'The sea was delicious,' she said. 'Looking at the horizon made every day possible.'

'Which part of the country?'

'The wet and salty part.' Again, the girl laughed and Mary smiled over at her. 'I'll take you one day if you like.'

She meant it too. They could go on the train, take a picnic, kick off their shoes, run to the water, get in a boat. They could light candles and float them on the waves like they did all those years ago after the tragedy with Pat.

The man behind the desk coughed and shuffled his papers about. 'Do you know the date today, Mrs Todd?'

'No,' she said. 'Do you?'

He met her gaze, his eyes still twinkling. That was a very good sign. 'Not without looking at my watch.'

'Exactly! You young people and your gadgets!'

She was flattering him, she knew. She guessed his age at sixty. The lines on his brow suggested too much worry and the shadows under his eyes hinted at either a love of wine or a capacity to stay up late reading by bad light. A good-looking man though, still had plenty of hair . . .

'What about your date of birth, Mrs Todd. Could you tell me what that is please?'

'Which one?'

Confusion crossed his face.

'I've had two,' Mary said, hoping to clarify. 'The first, there was a terrible storm above the house.' *Boom!* She clapped her hands together to show how loud Pat made the thunder whenever she told the story of Mary's birth. 'The second, it was night – perfectly clear, no rain at all. Although, as soon as my father got back from the pub and discovered a baby in his house, the storm clouds gathered – I'll tell you that for free!'

The man wrote that down on his sheet of paper.

'It wasn't his fault,' she went on. 'He had such high hopes for me, that was the trouble, and he didn't know what to do. You can't lock a mother and baby in the coal hole to punish them, can you? It's not that sort of misdemeanour. So, after he finished calling me every name under the sun, he stopped talking to me at all. Not a single word. Not ever again. How's that for stubborn? He had to leave me little notes to communicate.' She turned to Caroline. 'You remember those notes?'

Caroline shook her head. 'I don't think the doctor wants to hear about that. He just wants you to answer his questions.'

The man nodded briefly. 'Right, I'm going to say three words to you now, Mrs Todd, and I would like you to say them back when I've finished. Ready? Here they are . . . apple, penny, table. Now repeat those words back to me.'

Ridiculous. 'Apple, penny, table.'

'Very good. Now, can you tell me what this is please?' He held up the thing he'd been writing with.

'It's an instrument for writing.'

'Do you know what it's called?'

'A writing instrument.'

'How about this?'

Mary's stomach churned with the tea and chocolate biscuits she'd been given earlier. How easily she'd been bribed. Damn that daughter of hers! Divert this man, that was the trick.

'Tell me, young man,' she said, leaning forward to get a closer look, 'where did you get that lovely tie?'

* * *

It was so sad! But also ridiculous and humiliating. The doctor was treating Mary like a child, holding up pens and pencils and watching her squirm. She was pretty good at parrying, but it was totally obvious she was stressed.

The doctor held up more random objects and asked Mary what they were. She was very inventive – a stapler became a snatcher, a ruler was a sovereign (that one made Katie laugh again because it was just so clever), pens and pencils were described as implements for composing, scribbling, jotting. She wasn't wrong about any of them, but you needed to look sideways at her answers to see the truth. Katie sighed louder than she meant to when the doctor asked Mary who the Prime Minister was. Such a cliché. Didn't that only happen on TV?

'That,' Mary humphed, 'is a moveable feast.'

'I agree,' the doctor said. 'It's got very confusing lately. Would you like to hazard a guess though?'

'It depends *when* you mean.'

'I mean now. Who's the Prime Minister today.'

Bloody politics! Who cared? Half the kids in Katie's school wouldn't know the answer. More than half, in fact. Katie slid her feet off the chair and let them thud to the floor, pretended not to notice when Mum gave her a warning look. She stared down at her feet instead and tried not to feel guilty at the reddish mud that still caked the sides of her boots from when Mary knocked on that woman's door and they'd walked the 'long way back' from town.

Katie had been so relieved to find Mary safe that she'd abdicated responsibility for what happened next. She'd rung Mum, told her they were on their way home, but instead, they'd gone for lattes in a rather nice café and then embarked on a 'morning promenade' at Mary's instigation.

She'd been like a dog off a lead, following scents, having

occasional convictions about directions and then being distracted by things – pigeons squabbling outside the bakery, cakes in the window (her love of sweet things was crazy), a kid's scooter tied to a lamppost, hundreds of poppies dropping petals onto some bloke's lawn. Katie took loads of photos. Everyday things seemed special viewed through Mary's eyes and Katie didn't want to forget it. It was such a relief not to think about exams or Esme or any of that stuff. They'd hung out by the river for ages (hence the mud), got a hot dog from a van, fed the ducks and ended up outside the primary school. That's when it went wrong. It was as if spectres dragged Mary down, because she literally sank onto a bench and refused to move.

'Totally irresponsible!' Mum said when Katie finally dared to call her. 'You said you were coming home. What on earth are you doing two miles from the flat?'

'It's such a lovely day,' Katie told her. 'Surely walking's good for her?' But Mum was only interested in being furious.

No studying had been done and Mary was over-tired and didn't want lunch because she was full of hot dog. Didn't Katie know that routine was what old people needed and that when she'd been sent to find Mary that morning, Mum had expected them to come straight back, not go gallivanting off on some madcap adventure?

It probably hadn't been the best idea to mention the party at that point.

'Absolutely no way,' Mum said.

'It's after exams. Everyone's going.'

'At some boy's house? Anything could happen!'

Some hope.

Over the rest of the week, Katie hadn't gone anywhere or done anything much except study. Mary had seemed quieter, more tired, less up for adventure, and although she still wanted to walk each morning, Katie was under strict instructions not to let her further than the gate. Once, she'd disobeyed and taken Mary as far as the high street and let her have a ten-minute sit in the café again, but that was it. She wished now she'd been braver about it, fought for Mary's rights somehow. She thought Mary might be getting worse and she wondered if they'd ever find out where it was she wanted to get to every day. Because soon she might forget she even wanted to go.

The doctor was repeating the stupid word test. Mary had got it right the first time, but now got it dramatically wrong – snake, shilling, stable. But at least these were more interesting words than the original ones and had a satisfying alliteration. Katie must remember to point that out to Mum later – it'd be proof that Katie had actually done enough revision for English, despite turning down Mum's nightly offers of help.

It's hot and monotonous in this office (assonance). *My grandmother is lost in the past* (consonance). *Do I miss Esme? Let me count the ways* (caesura).

'Last thing,' the doctor said.

About time.

He produced a pen and paper and asked Mary to draw a clock face. But Mary was tired now, put the paper on her lap and sucked the end of the pen like a kid.

'I'd quite like to go,' she said.

In the chair next to her, Mum sighed. 'She keeps saying that.'

The doctor nodded. 'Almost done.'

'She doesn't mean home with me. In fact, she means anywhere *but* with me. This is one of the problems I'm having. She's always running off.'

The doctor pursed his mouth. 'Itchy feet, eh?'

'It's dangerous, isn't it? Her wandering about.'

'It's not uncommon. Maybe get her a pendant with her name and address on it?'

Mum looked dismayed. 'That's it? That's your advice?'

The doctor leaned back in his chair and studied Mum for a moment. Katie held her breath. 'I'm afraid there's not much else I can suggest. She's possibly disoriented in a new environment, or she might be searching for something related to her past. Try distracting her, perhaps? Or get someone to go with her?'

'My daughter fetches her. But she's got studying to do. It's terribly disruptive.'

He nodded, was clearly choosing his words carefully. 'Generally speaking, people only become more agitated if you try and limit their freedom. My best advice is to ensure she's safe and let her get on with it. Now, I'd like to send your mother for a CT scan, that should give us a bit more information.' He turned to Mary. 'How about you stay with your daughter for a few more days? Try not to give her too much trouble, eh?'

'What might happen if she went back to her own place to live by herself?' Mum said. 'What's the worst thing?'

The doctor blinked at Mum as if he couldn't quite believe she'd asked. 'It's pretty clear that there's some alteration in intellectual and emotional background.' He glanced at Mary, as if checking just how offended she might be if she understood what he meant. Katie wanted to cover her ears and lead her away. 'A CT in conjunction with these cognitive tests and recent medical history will provide a pretty accurate diagnosis. At that stage we can discuss prescribing an inhibitor, a drug that promotes communication between nerve cells. We may see some stabilizing of your mother's condition at that point, but ultimately, this is a progressive condition, Mrs Baxter, and I really don't think your mother will be living independently again.'

Katie stared at the doctor's mouth, at the way it moved as he spoke, like some awful fortune teller who knew the end of every story. Mum would feel crap listening to this. It meant she had to keep being responsible.

'Couldn't we get some help for her in her own home?' Mum asked. 'Some people have live-in carers, don't they?'

The doctor shook his head. 'I'm really not the man to be asking. You need to sort this out through social services. Although I don't think live-in care will be one of the options, not in the current financial climate, I'm afraid.'

Mum leaned forward, as if getting close to him meant Katie and Mary weren't in the room and couldn't hear. Katie watched with dismay. 'This has all happened so suddenly,' Mum said, her voice low and confidential, 'and there's absolutely no support in place. I know we were lucky to get this cancellation today, and I'm grateful, but it took me hours of negotiating. You wouldn't believe the hoops I had to jump through.'

The doctor laughed softly through his nose. 'I would, actually.'

This seemed to encourage Mum – she leaned nearer, spoke more rapidly, words falling out of her. On and on about how difficult it had been, how Mary might seem OK for a while, but it didn't last, how she was definitely getting confused and tired earlier each day, how sometimes she got anxious and woke in the night, how she kept thinking Jack was alive, how Mum was a single parent with a full-time job and one of her kids had special needs and the other one (glancing at Katie briefly) had her English AS level tomorrow and university applications and personal statements to get on with after that. It was horrible, like Mum was chucking up on the man's carpet. And all the while, Mary sat there listening.

'I can't get an appointment from the mental health team or the DWP for love nor money,' Mum went on. 'Social services are digging their heels in, telling me they can't get involved until she's been diagnosed. I'm pretty suspicious it suits everyone to let me get on with it. It takes a massive financial and logistical burden away from the state if I blunder on, doesn't it? Everyone just passing the buck.'

Including us, thought Katie.

Beyond the window, past the hospital gates, cars were crawling by with their windows down. Drivers had their elbows out, and even from here Katie could hear the pulse of music from countless stereos. Over the road, nestled in the middle of some houses was a playground. A woman was pushing her kid on a swing. Outside the playground was an ice-cream van.

If Katie was brave, she'd take Mary's hand and say, 'Fancy getting out of here?'

She'd have a go at Mum on the way out: *You shouldn't talk about people in front of them. You do it to Chris as well, and he hates it*. Then she'd lead Mary out of the room and into the lift and over to the park and she'd buy her a 99 with a chocolate flake and sprinkles. They'd sit on a bench and watch the kid on the swing and the sun would shine down on them.

But that was what would happen in a perfect world. And this was clearly not one. And Katie wasn't brave, as almost everyone knew. And anyway, it was too late because Mary was crying. She'd cried last night as well – Katie had heard her on the landing and gone out to lead her back to bed. She'd seemed in a daze.

'Oh dear,' Mum said now. 'You're getting upset.'

'This isn't where I'm meant to be,' Mary whispered. 'This isn't what's supposed to be happening at all.'

Mum hesitated for only a second. 'What's supposed to be happening is that you come home with me. The doctor thinks that's best for the moment.'

'But you don't want me.'

'Well, I don't have a choice right now. I have to do what the doctor says.'

Mary wiped her tears away with her fingers. It was shocking – something intimate and private about it, like no one should be looking. The doctor shuffled his papers. Mum reached out a tentative hand to Mary's arm. Katie sat on her chair, feeling utterly useless.

Twenty, thirty seconds went by before Mary stopped crying very suddenly, almost as if she'd forgotten why she was doing it, which maybe she had. She brushed Mum off and looked around the room – at the doctor and his desk, the chairs and carpet, at Katie by the window.

'Well, this is nice,' she said, 'isn't it? They've done it up nice.'

'Very nice,' Mum said. 'Aren't we lucky?'

Thirteen

Katie stood outside the bedroom door and leaned her ear against the cold wood. Inside the room, Mum was on the phone *again*.

'I see that, yes,' Katie heard her say, 'but surely you can see my predicament? I was told *one* night by that social worker, *one*. It's been well over two weeks now and no end in sight. She's got an appointment for a CT scan in another fortnight. That'll be over a month I've had her. A month! And goodness knows how long the results from the scan will take to appear. I'm having to arrange a funeral on top of everything else.'

There was silence then, or actually no – a tapping sound, a soft rhythmic thud. A pen against a knee? A finger on the table?

'So what if I told you I could no longer manage?' Mum said. 'What would you do then?' More tapping. A sound that expressed increasing stress. Katie had watched it building for days. 'So the state is forced to step in and make emergency arrangements only if I threaten to dump her? No, I'm not having a go at you, I'm stating the facts. It becomes all about me and my failings, rather than what's best for her, doesn't it? I become the evil daughter who abandons her mother and you all get to tut at me. Oh, I don't care if that's not how you see it, it's how it looks from here. Yes, I do have a pen. Right, well I appreciate that. Please go ahead.' More silence now – she was clearly writing something down. 'OK, so I

105

ring this number and ask for Eileen Thomas. She's the manager of the care home, is she?'

A sigh. A brusque thank you. The chair sliding back on the carpet.

'What?' Mum hissed and Katie knew this was aimed at her, although how her mother knew she was there was beyond her.

'Didn't want to disturb you,' Katie said as she opened the door.

'Then why were you eavesdropping?'

Katie felt herself blush. She wanted to say, *This is my room too now, remember? I have a right to loiter!* But then Mum would say she didn't find it easy sharing either and weren't they all making sacrifices and couldn't she just have a moment's peace?

'I just thought I'd come and let you know how my last exam went.'

'Oh, Katie, I'm sorry.' Mum took off her glasses and rubbed her eyes. 'I hadn't forgotten, really. I've been thinking about you all day.' She put her glasses back on and smiled wearily. 'So, tell me all about it, every detail please.'

Katie gave her what she wanted – told her the questions she'd chosen and why and how many pages she'd written and the fact she'd checked her work and finished in plenty of time (but not too soon because then Mum would think she could have written more) and yes, she felt confident and yes, very definitely relieved that exams were finally over.

'What did the others say?' Mum asked. 'Did everyone find it so manageable?'

'What others?'

'Well, you're quite late back. I'm assuming you hung about and discussed the paper?'

Katie nodded. 'Yeah, I did for a bit. Most people thought it was fine.'

She was too ashamed to admit the truth – that she'd spoken to no one after the exam. She'd come walking out into sunshine, feeling relieved and eager to celebrate. She'd dared a text to Esme, asking if she wanted to meet, but got no reply. Determined not to let it deflate her, Katie went to the shopping centre, bought herself a double chocolate muffin and a large mocha latte and sat on a bench to celebrate by herself. It was only when a woman with a little kid in a buggy came and sat next to her and started making small talk about the under-fives club at the arts centre that Katie had a wave of feeling so pathetic that she had to leave. Everyone else was probably at a pub or in the park and she hadn't been invited. Instead, she was in a shopping centre cramming sugar in her face and talking to a total stranger about rubbish.

And it was walking home that decided her. Courtesy of the maths boys, Katie had all the details for Saturday's party on her phone. Esme never missed a party. If Katie's life was going to improve, she had to get her best friend back. A relaxed and happy environment with free-flowing alcohol to steady the nerves was the perfect opportunity.

Katie sat at the edge of the bed and folded the corner of the duvet into a triangle and smoothed it flat. 'I have a proposition.'

'Oh yes?'

'Now my exams are finished, why don't I look after Mary for a few days?'

Mum frowned suspiciously. 'Why would you want to do that?'

'Because you can't stay off work for ever and I don't mind hanging out with her. I'll just follow her about and see where we end up.'

'What on earth for?'

'You heard what the doctor at the memory clinic said about letting her wander. He thought she might be looking for something from her past. If I go with her, it might help her remember stuff. It'd be like an experiment, like Pavlov, you know – see if a stimulus promotes a response. It'll be very educational.' Katie smiled to lighten the mood, but Mum wasn't going for it. She was positively glowering, in fact. 'Maybe she's trying to get to the seaside.'

'The seaside!' Mum made it sound like the worst place on earth.

'Well, she did grow up near the sea. I could take her on the bus. I talked to her about it a couple of times and she was really up for it. You can make all your calls in peace or go back to work or whatever and I can take her out, and in return you'll let me go to the party I told you about.'

'Just because exams are over, doesn't mean everything collapses, Katie. You've got open days and summer courses to apply for. We need to begin work on your personal statement.'

'I'm supposed to write that myself.'

'And work experience? Is that finalized?'

'Well, I was thinking I could look after Mary for work experience. I already asked school and they said it was OK.'

'That's ridiculous. You can't put looking after your granny on your CV! All you do is sit around talking for hours.'

'I like talking to her.'

'Think what a difference professional work experience could make to your university application.'

'I might not go straight to university. I might take a gap year.'

'And do what in it?'

'I don't know. Travel the world?'

'What? No! God, this is a nightmare.' Mum stood up, walked past Katie to the door, yanked it open and marched downstairs. Katie pelted after her.

Mary was at the window looking down at the courtyard. She

turned round expectantly as they came into the lounge. 'Lovely day out there.'

'The seaside?'

Mary beamed at her. 'Oh, yes. Shall I get my coat?'

'You're not going now!'

'It's rather pressing.'

Mum shook her head, exasperated. 'Of course it isn't. The only thing that's pressing round here is you!' Mum yanked her glasses off and rubbed both eyes, a fist balled in each. She looked like a child silently crying. 'No one's going to the seaside. No one's travelling the world. Now, I'm going to make some more phone calls, so will you please both sit yourselves down and stop being so relentless.'

Katie took Mary to sit on the balcony. Mum stayed inside and Katie shut the door on her.

'What did she call us?' Mary said as Katie opened a deck chair.

'Relentless.'

'What did she mean by it, do you think?'

'I think she means we both want something and she doesn't want us to have it and it's annoying her.'

'I *do* want something,' Mary agreed, smiling sadly. 'Trouble is, I keep forgetting what.'

It must be terrifying having your memories drift out of your head, yet Mary still managed to find humour in it. Katie felt a rush of fondness for her and an interesting opposite rush of fury towards Mum.

'Let's do some writing in your book, Mary. Let's write down every name of every boyfriend you ever had. And then let's write down all the places you went with them and all the windows you climbed out of and every country you ever visited in your life and then, if you ever forget, I can tell it all back to you.'

It was fun for a while, but Mary tired easily in the afternoons and she soon fell asleep. Katie sneaked upstairs so she didn't get roped into any more conversations about summer courses.

Her bedroom was beginning to look like a gallery with the pictures of old movie stars she'd stuck on the wall. She'd been hoping to detract attention from Jack's Post-it Notes, which Mum seemed to hate.

'Sorry, ladies,' she said as she unstuck the pictures from their central position and moved them to the edge. She didn't want to get rid of them completely – she loved their vulnerable but determined eyes.

She got Blu-Tack from the drawer and several sheets of A4 and wrote one giant letter on each page and coloured them in. *Mary's Family.* She tacked them across the top of the wall like a banner and moved the Post-It notes directly underneath – all the messages from Jack, including the little stick figure picture. They could have centre space. She didn't care what Mum thought of them any more.

It still looked a bit empty, so she got out the photo album Dad made for her tenth birthday and chose one photo for each of them and stuck herself, Chris, Mum and Dad in a little row. She'd have to take a photo of Mary and get one of Jack from somewhere if she was going to replicate Jack's drawing, but this would do for now.

Katie spent the next half hour choosing photos from her phone, printing them out and sticking them to the wall – the block of flats where Mary knocked on the door, the poppies, the primary school, the tables outside the café Mary liked so much. If Mum was going to limit Mary to the flat, then Katie would bring the world to her.

It was only half an hour later when Mum came tapping on the door. She sidled in and shut the door behind her, leaning on it and biting her lip.

110

'What's going on, Mum?'

'I just got a call from work. They want me to meet a client tomorrow.'

'That's fine. I'll look after Mary. I said I would.'

'But I don't want you taking her anywhere. I won't be able to concentrate if I'm worrying about you all the time.'

Typical Mum. She wanted help, but on her terms. 'Well, I'm not staying in all day. You can't expect that.'

'No, I thought you could sit outside on one of the benches or take her to the local shops. Would that be OK? No buses or trains, though. No leaving Bisham.'

For a second, Katie told herself to say no, because those options were rubbish. She wanted to find out where Mary was trying to get to every morning and it certainly wasn't the nearest bench. Hadn't the doctor at the memory clinic said people got agitated if you stopped them going where they wanted?

But Katie didn't say any of that because there was a deal being offered here. 'So, can I go to the party?'

Mum sighed. 'I'll need to speak to the boy's parents.'

'No way! No one does that.'

'I want to know they'll be there. I also need to ask about alcohol.'

'What about it?'

'Will there be any?'

'Of course there will, but that doesn't mean I'll be drinking it.'

'Well, those are my terms. Like it or lump it.'

'I'm going to look like a total idiot if you call the parents. I guarantee no one else will do that.'

'Well, maybe other people don't care about their kids the way I care about you.'

Katie felt a thrill of anger – it wasn't so much caring as

111

suffocating! 'Actually, you know what, never mind. I can't look after Mary tomorrow anyway – I've got plans.'

Mum frowned. 'What plans?'

And because it was a total lie, Katie said nothing, shrugged instead.

'I'll pay you. I wasn't expecting you to do it for nothing. Twenty pounds, I was thinking. Does that seem fair?'

Katie tasted the words in her mouth. It was a game she played sometimes – daring to see how it would feel to say certain things out loud. Words like, No and Can't and Don't you see? Money didn't make claustrophobia a more attractive prospect.

'Don't look at me like that,' Mum said. 'Come on, you were the one who offered in the first place.' She went across the landing to her room and came back with her handbag and fumbled around in it. Katie felt a bit strange as Mum took out her purse and scrabbled for notes – sorry for her, or something. She looked desperate. 'Here you go – payment in advance.'

For a millisecond, their fingers touched.

'You were right, I do need to get back to work. I was a bit harsh earlier and I'm sorry. I've got viewings to sort, appointments to make, and even if I don't manage to catch up, it won't do any harm to show my face. I don't want my colleagues stealing clients in my absence!' She laughed and leaned in, nestling her head on Katie's shoulder for a second. It was such a remarkable thing for her to do, that Katie was silenced by it. 'If tomorrow goes OK, maybe you can do Thursday and Friday, possibly even a couple of days next week?' Mum sat on the bed. 'She'll be gone after that, I promise, and then we can all get back to normal.'

Fourteen

Today's category for the memory game was: men.

As Mary walked she got to twelve, which wasn't bad, because she was sure she'd repeated none except for Robert, who deserved to be repeated, because he'd been her first. But thinking of men brought her to the baby. And thinking of the baby brought her to Pat. She tried to keep within category, but could only remember censure – her sister's breath in her face as she hissed her disapproval. *You've done it now, Mary. Nearly full term and not a word to anyone. There'll be no bringing Dad round this time.*

Pat picks up a cup and sloshes it over to the draining board. She comes back for a plate and strides over to the bin with it. She puts both plate and untouched sandwich in the bin and lets the lid drop with a thud. She turns to Mary, her eyes furious, 'Look what you did.'

'What did I do?' Mary sits on her hands to stop them shaking. 'Everything isn't my fault.'

'No. But this is your fault.' Pat says it quietly, like there's no disputing it. She crouches down by Mary's chair. 'Who's the father?'

Mary shakes her head.

'It'll be all right,' Pat says. 'Tell me his name.'

'No.'

'Do we know him? What's his job? Will he make an honest woman of you?' Pat's eyes clutch at her. 'Mary, I'm your sister. You can tell me anything. We should be friends.'

'Friends? That's a laugh. You don't even like me.'

'I gave up everything for you, everything that I was going to be.'

Yes, thought Mary. *And don't I know it.*

Tears spill. Splish, splash onto the kitchen floor. It surprises Mary that this is how it is. She thought she was stronger than this.

Pat relents, kneels by the chair and strokes Mary's back, describing slow circles. Mary doesn't want her to stop. Maybe if she stays here with her sister rubbing her back, then none of this will be true – she won't be pregnant, she won't have these strange gripping pains in her stomach and it'll be a normal Saturday instead.

'It hurts,' Mary says. 'It already hurts. Is it supposed to?'

'Oh dear,' Pat says. 'What a fuss.'

Mary sobs properly then. She can't help it. She just can't hold everything in any more. She watches the tears drip onto her skirt and spread like flowers and she knows this is the end of every future she's ever imagined for herself.

1953 – a girl like her

Beautiful Robert Gibson, contracted for six months to work at the railway yard at Hexham. Mary had met him on the beach. She'd been daydreaming at the waves and he'd simply laid his coat on the sand and sat down beside her.

They'd talked for ages, sitting together watching the tide retreat when she should have been home hours ago. She knew Pat would be half-crazed with worry, but Mary couldn't seem to drag herself away.

They met every day after that. Why not? What harm? He collected her round the corner from the secretarial school and they'd go to the harbour and look at the boats or stroll along the beach. One evening, he borrowed a car and they went to Tiffany's and he was the best dancer there and it was Mary he wanted to be with. He told her he never imagined in a million years he'd meet a girl like her in a town like this. He said she *moved* him.

Another time, he invited Mary to his caravan and made her sardines on toast. It was all very proper. Nothing happened. Trouble was, Mary wished it had. Because surely, if she was with a man in that way, *properly* with him, wouldn't the world finally be enough?

He's sitting on the caravan steps drinking tea when she turns up. He has his shirt wrapped round his waist and when he grins at her, the whole morning seems to shine.

'I've brought a picnic,' she tells him, when he says he's expected at the yard, that it's Friday, that he won't get his wages if he doesn't go in. 'Look – bread, butter, even a tin of salmon. My sister's going to kill me about the salmon, but I don't care. I brought dandelion wine too, which sounds horrid, but is, in fact, rather delicious.'

He laughs. 'So now you're stealing your father's moonshine?'

'Can't help it.' She sets the bag down on the grass, holds out her arms to him. 'I'm a very bad girl.'

He looks her up and down appraisingly. 'Whatever are we going to do with you?'

'No idea.'

She buries herself in him, his bare chest and naked arms, the softness of his neck. She breathes in the scent of his skin, still sweet and warm from sleep.

'I can feel your heart,' she tells him. 'It's beating very fast.'

'Is it?'

She smiles. 'Does that mean you're afraid of me?'

'Should I be?'

'Perhaps.'

'And what about you, Mary Todd, what are you afraid of? Anything at all?'

She pretends not to hear, pulls him tighter instead. She doesn't want to tell him about how difficult things have been, how suspicious her family are. Pat's taken her purse and post office book away for safekeeping. Dad's taken to telephoning the secretarial school asking for details of Mary's attendance. Her world is closing in. She feels constantly observed, constantly disapproved of.

'I'm going to live in London,' she tells him, because if she's not going to talk about fear, then she'll talk about its opposite. 'I'm going to train to be an actress and then I'm going to get famous. My life's going to be startling. One day, you'll be telling your

116

friends you knew me and they won't believe you, just imagine!'

'Mary,' he says, 'I never met a girl like you before.' He pulls gently away so he can look at her. 'Tell me, since you're so good at predicting the future – what's going to happen today?'

She smiles up at him. 'I can think of plenty.'

He tells her he feels like he's cradle snatching as he leads her up the caravan steps.

Inside is a table and a bed. 'What else do we need?' he asks as he finds two cups and opens the wine.

Mary leans back on a pillow and quietly undoes the top two buttons of her blouse, so that when he turns round he'll see the way the sunlight falls on her hair and how the skin at her throat gleams.

He grins as he pours the wine. 'What are you trying to do to me?'

She smiles back. 'Nothing.'

'Do you know how a man feels when you look at him like that?'

She shakes her head, but she does know, has always understood it. Women are supposed to look demurely at their shoes, their laps, their folded arms, the floor. But it's thrilling to look men full in the eye, to meet their gaze.

'I'm going to have to kiss you if you don't stop.'

'Go on then.'

She doesn't take her eyes from his as he sits next to her on the bed. He looks like he's drowning as he reaches for her. It makes her want to laugh out loud. She feels wild and young and powerful. She is Mary Todd and she draws men to her. She can make their breathing change just by looking at them.

It's minutes before he gives a little moan and pulls away, sits apart on the bed, can't meet her eyes.

When he speaks, his voice is strangely quiet. 'Mary,' he says, 'I'm not sure about this.'

'Why not? I thought you liked me.'

'I do like you, that's the problem. I want you so much I can't think straight. But to do this now, well, it might not be the best idea we ever had.'

'It is,' she says, and she snuggles up next to him and rubs his thigh.

'Mary, don't. It's not that I don't want to. Christ, I want to so much. It's just, I don't want you to get hurt when I leave. I don't want you to get pregnant either.'

'You can't get pregnant the first time.'

'You can. I think you can.'

'My sister was in the Voluntary Nursing Service and that's what she told me.'

'Are you sure?'

She nods very slowly. Pat's told her no such thing and has never done a day's nursing in her life, but she doesn't want this to stop. She's certain it'll be all right.

Beautiful Robert Gibson, with his voice like melted butter. Both brothers went missing in action, his mother died of grief and he has eyes you can drown in. He used his demob money to start a printing press and now he's writing a novel. He's only on the railways to make a bit of cash.

'I want you to be my first,' she whispers as she leans in to kiss him again.

It's like a dance. He touches her breast through her blouse and she keeps kissing him to show how much she likes it. She runs her finger down the length of his spine and reaches for his belt. He undoes her buttons and they both smile at their fumbling fingers.

They lie on the bed. They press closer. He lifts the hem of her skirt. She touches the curve of his bare hip. It's a strange and wonderful dance. Better than any she's ever danced before.

I am alive, she keeps thinking. *Right now I'm alive, but if I was at home, nothing would be happening to me at all.*

Later, on the steps, he gets out his camera to take a photo. 'Look at you,' he tells her. 'You don't even know, do you?'

'Know what?'

'How bloody gorgeous you are. You really are. Everyone says so.'

'Everyone?'

'Down at the yard. Do you know what they call you?'

She shakes her head.

'Copper Box, that's what. And you are, with all that hair.'

'Is that a compliment?'

'You bet it is! It's after the fire box in the steam locomotive. Come on then, smile for the camera.'

She poses for him, one hand on her hip, the other gathering up her skirt to show him a bit of petticoat. 'Why is it a compliment?'

He winks. 'There's a high ratio of heat transmission in the fire box, you know.'

She laughs out loud. The shutter clicks.

The girl who suddenly appeared at her side said, 'Your favourite table's free if you fancy it.'

Mary tried to conjure Robert back by closing her eyes and imagining there were no sounds – no cars on the road, no bustle or chink from the café ahead, just her memories and her breathing. In and out.

'Mary?'

'Shush a minute!'

'I just wondered if you wanted a sit-down?'

119

'I'll sit when I'm ready, thank you. At the moment, I'm talking to Robert.'

'Ah, the beautiful Mister Gibson . . .'

'How do you know his name?' Mary gave the girl a stern look. 'Who have you been gossiping with?'

'You!' The girl smiled. 'He took you to Marine Parade. You'd always wanted to go and there was a big band and hundreds of people and you were the best dancers there and you stayed until the very end and then, when you got home, Pat was waiting up for you.'

This girl was astonishing. Mary gazed at her in awe. 'What happened next?'

'An inquisition.' The girl adopted a pose, looking every inch a school marm. *'Who was that chap in the car? You cheapen yourself kissing with a fervour I've only seen at the pictures!'* She wagged a finger, grinning now. *'Your behaviour is atrocious and I ban you from ever seeing Robert Gibson again.'*

'Ha! That'll never work!'

The girl laughed. 'It's one of my favourite stories, Mary. Along with the one about your waters breaking four weeks early and Pat making you squat over a saucepan on the kitchen floor.'

'You're a miracle knowing so many things!'

'Not really. You talk and I write stuff down, that's all. Walking helps you remember, doesn't it?'

Did it? Possibly. All she knew for sure as the girl chivvied her towards an empty table was that it had been worth it – to feel such voltage.

And to bear Robert's child. Ah . . . a daughter who would get all her love, all her grief, all her heart.

Fifteen

If only she'd let Mary keep walking. Or if only the café door had been shut so the smell of warm pastries hadn't been so enticing. Or if only Katie had managed to persuade Mum to let her take Mary on a bus and go to the seaside.

There were many ways it could have been. Many ways to have avoided Simona Williams from tutor group 13E (who everyone knew the rumours about) turning from the coffee machine behind the counter and frowning at Katie, gently puzzled. 'I know you, don't I?'

This was Mary's favourite café! Every day this week they'd come here and Simona Williams had never been waitressing before. Katie tried to scrabble up a menu so she didn't have to speak, could just go outside and convince Mary to leave right now!

But Simona said, 'Seriously, where do I know you from?'

Katie shook her head, wanted to say *never seen you before*, but all that came out was a whisper, accompanied by blazing cheeks and a thudding heart.

She'd have traded most things – a month of her life (she'd be on a summer scheme instead of under this girl's gaze), a week as her brother (how bad could Woodhaven School be?), or even a few hours as Mary, aimlessly shuffling salt and pepper sachets at a table beyond the café window – anything to avoid the dawning recognition on Simona's face.

But the reality was she was Katie Baxter and two minutes ago, the coffee smell coming from this café had been amazing and there were plenty of empty tables outside and she knew Mary would want her morning cigarette soon, so she'd encouraged her to find a seat and walked through the door and marched up to the counter and opened her big mouth and said, 'What cakes have you got today?'

And Simona Williams had turned round. And now . . . yes, now a cold light had crept into her eyes. 'You hang out with those morons, don't you?'

Swallow, try to stop looking mortified, try to return the gaze. 'I go to the same school as you.'

'Yeah, but you also hang out with those morons.' She thrust a menu at Katie and turned back to the coffee machine.

There were many ways it could have been. Many ways to have avoided the racing pulse at her neck, the hot shame on her face as she made her way back outside.

'The cakes look rubbish today,' she told Mary. 'Let's go somewhere else.'

Mary shook her head, took the menu. 'I like it here.'

'I've gone off it. Let's go home.'

'You go. I'm hungry.'

Katie sighed, took Mary's cardigan from the floor and hung it on the back of the chair and propped Mary's handbag where they could see it, trying to look busy and calm until her heart normalized. Finally, she sat down (chair facing the window . . . oh God!) and crossed her fingers that Mary would not start singing or stuff her pockets with sugar cubes or ask the couple on the next table if she might finish the pizza slice they'd clearly abandoned. She'd been guilty of all these offences over the last week. Why would today be any different?

'I wonder,' Mary said, 'what jerk chicken is? They never used to sell such things.'

She showed Katie the menu. Pictures of pasta and burgers and plates piled high with rice and curry swam in front of her eyes. She felt sick. She didn't want anything. She should never have offered to be Mary's carer. All these days of care for one party! It wasn't even a fair deal.

Mary turned impatiently to the window. 'Where are the people who work here?'

Behind the counter, ignoring them, that's where. If Katie leaned her chair back, she could see Simona chatting with the other waitress, the older woman, Angie, who usually served them. They were both laughing like there weren't any customers, or if there were, like they couldn't be bothered to serve them. Simona was wearing a T-shirt, shorts and a black work apron, and although Katie couldn't see her face properly, she could see the curve of her neck and the bare top of one shoulder.

'Hurry up, ladies!' Mary rapped on the window with her knuckles.

Both waitresses turned and looked right at Katie, as if it was her who'd knocked, as if she was arrogant enough to think they were servants you could summon. Simona frowned, wiped her hands down her apron and stalked towards the door. Katie saw the dark curl of hair under her armpit as she yanked it open. 'What?'

Katie shrank in her seat. 'Could we order?'

'I'm busy.'

She slammed back into the café and it was minutes before Angie sidled out. She gave Mary a beaming smile, but she picked up Katie's menu from the table as if it was contagious and shoved it under her arm. 'So, what are you having today?' Her voice was cold.

Katie ordered in the quietest voice possible, then checked out the street, the bus stop opposite, anything so as not to seem like someone who would usually hang out with 'morons'.

Mary minutely scrolled down her menu with a finger. 'Where are the ice creams?'

'You asked me that yesterday, darling. We've got lollies in the freezer for kiddies, but that's it. It's mostly cakes if you want something sweet.' Angie wiped the table with a blue-checkered cloth as she waited. She brushed up against Katie so close she could smell her perfume along with the disinfectant smell of the cloth.

Katie edged a fraction away, concentrated on the birds over by the dustbins. She liked the way they ruminated with their heads on one side as if they were thinking about going to other places, and what the best route might be and if was time to go yet. She wished she could swap – a whole day of her life for ten minutes as a bird. She'd get all the way home if she flew fast.

Mary took ages, but eventually ordered chocolate fudge cake and Angie left.

Katie got the book out, hoping she'd look like she was writing a novel. At least then Simona might think she had *some* sensitivity.

'Ah,' Mary said, stroking the cover. 'What's this?'

'Our book.'

'Ours?'

'Things you say.'

She laughed. 'Do I say interesting things?'

'You really do. And I write them down so you can remember.'

'A diary?' Mary waved a dismissive hand. 'My sister wrote pages in a diary every day – things people said, lists of complaints against the world. She was so busy writing she had no time left to do any living. No point in that kind of book now, is there?'

'This isn't that kind of book. This is to help with your memory.'

'Let me have a look.'

Katie handed it over. She risked a glance through the window while Mary fumbled at the pages, wondered how wrong it would be to leave before the food arrived.

'Here's a whole string of names,' Mary laughed. 'Are these your boyfriends?'

'Yours, not mine.'

Mary wagged a finger. 'Don't be so moral.'

'We made a list of everyone important to you. Look, there's Jean, the woman next door, and here's her son, Norman.'

'Ahh,' Mary sighed, tapping the page affectionately. 'I shared a lot of smooches with him. And who's this – *a winking man on a bus*?'

'He asked you out dancing. You couldn't remember his name.'

'John Farthing. Of course I remember. Worked on the boats.' Mary handed the book back. 'I got into terrible trouble when he dropped me home. Dad was waiting up for me and he couldn't abide shenanigans. Locked me straight in the coal hole.'

'That really happened?'

'Worth every second.' Mary smiled fondly. 'John Farthing was a wonderful kisser.'

Katie picked up the pen and wrote *John* in the margin.

'Pat let me out in the end. She always did. Oh, I felt so sorry for her. All she wanted was an easy life – Dad not to get cross, me to stop gadding about. Now, what are you doing scribbling away in that book?'

'Writing down what you're saying. Do you mind?'

'I'm honoured you find me so noteworthy. You carry on.'

Katie felt weird then, because was this an invasion of privacy? Was Mary technically able to give permission?

'Write this down.' Mary leaned across the table to whisper.

'Pleasure is spread through the earth in stray gifts to be claimed by whoever shall find. You know who said that?'

'No idea.'

'Me neither!' Mary laughed. 'We'll ask Jack when he gets back, shall we?'

'Back from where?'

'The gents. He just walked straight past us. Didn't you see him?'

Katie wanted to say, *Yes, Mary, I saw him and you're not crazy.* Would it help?

Mum thought reality was important, which is why she insisted on reminding Mary that she had memory loss and Jack was dead. But Katie was beginning to think it was easier to run with Mary's narratives. Jack was in the loo – why not? Mary was climbing down drainpipes or dancing the night away – absolutely. Time travel made the world a nicer place.

If Katie knew how to do it, she'd go back a fortnight to when she'd come out of that maths exam, and instead of walking over to Esme and that lot, she'd climb over the wall by the teachers' car park and scurry away unseen. At least then she wouldn't have laughed at Simona and she wouldn't feel so wretched sitting here now.

She dared another look through the window and tried to imagine walking in and apologizing. Simona was at a table chatting to some couple who were beaming up at her. She wrote their order on a pad, took their menus and walked back to the counter and out of sight.

Katie sighed and flicked through the pages of her notebook. The stories were building up. Here was the day Mary's father brought home all that beautiful silk. Here was Mary daydreaming on the beach, about to meet Robert. And here was the most terrifying story of all – Mary giving birth in her bedroom and Pat acting as midwife. Anything could've gone wrong.

Mary tapped a finger on the tablecloth. 'I'm going to order a knickerbocker glory.'

'You just ordered chocolate fudge cake.'

'It's for Caroline. She loves them.'

'Mum does? I doubt it.'

'I tell you what, I'll ask the nice waitress.'

'No, Mary, don't bang on the window again, please. They don't do ice creams anyway, she just told you that. I'll find the recipe on my phone if you like and then we'll know how to make it ourselves. I'll do it right now. Look, I'm doing it. Here we are, see – here's a picture. Is this it? Ice cream, fruit, whipped cream, sauce and a cherry?'

Mary clapped her hands with delight. 'Isn't that amazing? Look at that. Doesn't it look delicious?'

Katie saved the page to favourites, although if she ever brought the ingredients into the flat, she'd get bollocked. Mum might accept a smoothie, a handful of berries, some low fat yogurt, but not this calorific monstrosity. Mum and Mary were such opposing forces it was mad. Mary would probably pick the fruit out of the sundae and leave it on the side because it was too healthy. She might eat the cherry at a push, because she used to spit the stones across the garden when she was a kid. Katie liked cherries too. She used to loop pairs of them over her ears and pretend they were jewels.

It was good having cherries in common with Mary. Katie drew one at the top of the page and gave it two leaves and a stalk.

Inside the café, Simona was placing some kind of cake onto a plate using silver tongs. She put the plate on a tray and turned to the coffee machine. Katie found her gaze drifting to Simona's back, her hair, the tilt of her neck . . .

Christ, what was wrong with her? This was ridiculous! She got out her red pen and coloured in the cherry.

Mary looked up in anticipation as the door opened. 'Ah, here's the food.'

No, no! Katie couldn't look, couldn't speak – her face was one hot burning blush as Simona came over and rested a tray on the edge of the table. She motioned to the book. 'You want to lift that up?'

Katie slapped it shut, fumbled with the elastic, the pens, her bag, trying to clear a space as Simona carefully unloaded Mary's coffee and cake.

Mary practically pounced on it. 'May I say this looks delicious?'

'You may say that, thanks.' Simona put out napkins and cutlery.

Katie's heart was banging so loud she was sure this girl could hear it. She *had* to say something! Anything . . .

'Do you own this place?' Mary asked as she broke the cake into chocolatey lumps with her fingers.

'Sadly not. If I did, I'd give myself a pay rise.'

Mary laughed at the joke and Simona laughed with her, but it faded as she slapped Katie's teacake down. 'Here – don't choke.'

It was now or never. Katie dared to look up. 'Can I say something?'

'You're kidding, right?' Simona shot a suspicious glance around as if she imagined Esme or the others might be hiding under one of the tables.

'They're not my friends. I barely know them.' It sounded wrong, like she was making excuses, but she didn't know how else to explain. 'I was coming out of maths and there they were. I didn't know Amy was going to say that stuff to you.'

Simona narrowed her eyes. 'You laughed right along with them.'

'I'm sorry. I didn't mean to.'

'Oh, you didn't *mean* to? Not your fault, then? Your mates are total prats and you just got swept along.' She picked up the tray. 'Glad we cleared that up.'

'I'm sorry.'

'Yeah, I heard you the first time. Let's hope you feel better about yourself now.'

Tears stabbed Katie's eyes. She felt stupid, dumb and childish as Simona walked back into the café and she was left sitting outside with her teacake and latte. She didn't want them. She wanted to go home and go to bed and hide. She turned her back to the window, wishing she could peel her face off and swap it for someone else's.

Mary ate quickly, as if she hadn't eaten for days, sighing with pleasure at each new mouthful. She got chocolate everywhere – her chin, her cardigan, all over the table. When she stirred sugar into her coffee (three lumps!) she got froth all over the back of her hand and simply wiped it down her skirt.

People didn't do brave things. Not people Katie knew anyway. Dad was a coward who lied about having a girlfriend. Mary was a coward who gave up her baby. Mum worried about almost everything and Katie – well, it was clear she'd also inherited the cowardly gene because she should have apologized differently – louder, or for longer or more eloquently.

Chris was the only brave one – he had to be. No choice.

'Lovely,' Mary declared, pushing the plate away and turning her face contentedly to the sun. 'I could eat that all over again.'

'Why did you abandon your baby?' Katie asked her.

Mary opened one eye and frowned, as if the question stirred something deep inside. 'Did I?'

'Yeah, you left her with your sister and then you disappeared.'

'They told me to, didn't they?'

'Not your fault, then?'

Katie knew she was being mean, chucking Simona's words at Mary to stop the pain in her own chest. But she was on a roll.

'Mum was nine when you showed up again. Why did you do that to her?'

'Was it really that long?'

'She thought Pat was her mum. Imagine the shock when you turned up out of the blue and announced yourself.'

'I'm sure that's not what happened.'

Mary looked so confused that Katie felt instantly sorry and offered her the teacake to make up for it. Mary's delight in sweet things was spectacularly distracting as usual, but Katie felt wretched.

She got the book out again, turned it upside down and started a new page at the back. Under the header *Katie's stories*, she wrote:

Never come to this café again!

Make sure all future trips are OUT OF TOWN!!

Stop being weird.

Stop being a coward.

Stop being neurotic.

She wrote in small explosions of violence across the page:

Get Esme back.

Get some new clothes.

Get a boyfriend.

Knock ALL the boys dead at the party tomorrow.

Risk your heart and make things HAPPEN!!

Sixteen

Long-Lash mascara, Vamp lipstick, Pure Sheen foundation and Secret Shimmer eyes. It was just Katie inside, but outside you'd never know it. She looked utterly different as she smiled at herself in the mirror. She'd left her hair loose and it shone red-gold at her, complementing the colours in the dress perfectly – forest green, vivid emerald, charcoal black and every shade between – all shifting when the light caught them.

'For your party,' Mary had said when she pulled it from its carrier bag and handed it over. 'Go capture some hearts.'

When Mary had insisted on bringing her 'kissing dress' from the house, Katie had thought it'd be some old moth-eaten thing. She'd never imagined it to be vintage silk. Or that Mary would let her wear it. Or that it would fit like a glove.

Maybe it had transforming qualities. Maybe it would give Katie the confidence to chat and flirt and drink and dance like a normal person? She might become extrovert by proxy. It should definitely be possible to bewitch boys in a dress like this.

A rap at the door. 'Taxi's here!'

There was nothing Mum could do to stop it happening now. Katie gave herself one last smile in the mirror.

'That dress suits you,' Mum said. 'I haven't seen it before.'

Katie wanted to say, *It was Mary's*, but if she said that, Mum would think it didn't suit her any more, so she just nodded. And then she remembered Mum had been witness to Mary's hunt for it at the house and so this was probably a test.

'Mary brought it back with her. I think it's the one Pat made from all that silk.'

'And she doesn't mind you wearing it out tonight? It must be quite precious to her.'

'It's precious to me too.'

Mum flicked her a glance. 'Funny how you two get along.'

Katie shuffled her feet. She felt guilty and it was crazy, because shouldn't Mum be glad they got along? You'd think she'd be grateful. Relieved, even.

Mum rummaged for taxi money in her handbag. 'Can you give me the address where you'll be?'

'I'll text when I get there.'

'What if you forget?'

'I won't.'

'Well, make sure you ask to see the driver's ID.' She handed over twenty pounds, then stood in the lounge doorway watching Katie put on her jacket. 'You are just going to a party, aren't you?'

'Where else would I be going?'

Mum looked shifty and sad all at the same time. 'I don't know.'

Katie went into the lounge to say goodbye to Chris and Mary. They were watching the Nature channel. A monkey was breaking the windows of a house with a stick. He was wearing trousers and a T-shirt.

'He doesn't like living there,' Chris said without looking up. 'He wants to go back where he came from.'

Mary cheered as the monkey chased a woman across a car park. 'Run, girl, run!'

Katie leaned down to kiss her goodbye. 'I'm off to a party.'

'That's nice.'

'I'm wearing your dress.'

Mary waved her out of the way of the TV. 'Good luck with that!'

At the door Mum looked doubtful. In her opinion the world was teaming with muggers and rapists and drunkards and plain old-fashioned psychos with cleavers and scissors and knives. 'Please be careful, Katie.'

'I'll dodge all the bullets – promise.'

'Don't laugh. It's a dangerous world.'

'It's a party, Mum. It's supposed to be fun.'

Fear definitely travelled down generations. But tonight Katie was going to shrug it off. She took the lift (even though Mum would worry in case the cable broke, or the doors got stuck, or someone got in with a blade and a wicked grin) and at the bottom, she waved up the stairwell. Something unfolded in her stomach, like a fist unclenching as she eased the main door open . . .

It's 1952 and your father thinks you're asleep. You've feigned a cold and gone to bed early, made up some story about feeling unwell, even gone without tea to consolidate the plan. Downstairs, your sister writes her diary and imagines the man you will marry, the children you will have, the house you will keep and all the lovely things your husband will buy for you. You don't have time for this. You're climbing out of your bedroom window and tiptoeing across the grass with your shoes in your hand. You're wild. You don't want any of those things, thank you very much. Pat can dream them into existence for herself, not for you.

There's a big band, fifteen musicians and hundreds of people dancing. You jitterbug. You jive. You know all the steps to all the dances and you move beautifully with the music. You don't even know the names of your dance partners, but that doesn't

133

matter because it's exciting and hot and you swirl about and get breathless and then the music stops and you go back to your friends and wait for the next tune.

The world belongs to you. You can absolutely get away with anything . . .

Katie smiled. Here she was, over sixty years later, with the very same silk brushing her legs as she walked. No strappy dance shoes, but the heels on her boots made a satisfying clatter, like she was announcing herself as she walked the last few metres to the house.

The party had spilled outside and kids on the front lawn stood about in groups, smoking. Girls had their arms wrapped about themselves to keep warm. They shivered and stamped their feet like horses. A couple of girls looked up as Katie walked past. She didn't know them but she waved anyway.

Through the door and into a hallway. She peered into a lounge. Some boys were in there watching a football match on TV with the sound off. Music pumped out of a speaker in the corner. One of the boys was leaning with his back against the window. He looked Katie up and down.

Down some stairs and into a kitchen. It was big with wooden floors and had a marble island in the centre where bottles of beer were lined up in rows. Beyond the island, a door led out to a garden. Through the glass, Katie could see a crowd of lads standing out there looking awkward, gripping beer to their chests like they were waiting for something to begin.

It crossed Katie's mind that she was at the wrong party – no Esme, no girls from school, just a bunch of strangers and a pile of booze. She hadn't seen a single person she knew.

Go! said a voice in her head. *Run. No one will know you were here and no one will miss you. You can buy chocolate on the way home.*

134

She gripped the edge of the counter and breathed, trying to push away the rush of fear.

Over sixty years ago Mary held the shortest edge of silk under her chin, letting the length of it tumble to her ankles. 'There's magic in it, look. I reckon it'll make two dresses!'

Mary's father clinked his knife against the jam pot. He didn't want his youngest going to parties. She had too much fire and he could see trouble ahead. But if Mary was scared of him, you'd never know it.

Katie could feel a boy looking at her. He was leaning against the microwave, just staring. His gaze was like a light on the side of her face.

'You go to my school,' he said.

She didn't deny it.

'You do A level physics.'

That was true, although she didn't recall ever seeing this boy before. She tilted her chin and smiled at him.

'I'm in the opposite tutor group from you,' he said, smiling back. 'It's like I'm from another universe, but honestly, I do know you.'

'I believe you.' She walked over and stood in front of him. 'So, who else do you know?'

He looked about, slowly taking in the room. 'Surprisingly few people.'

'Well, that's OK,' she said, leaning in, 'because now you know me.'

He laughed. 'I guess.'

This was flirting. She'd stirred something in him and she'd done it on purpose. Ha! It would look cool if Esme came down those stairs behind her and found her chatting confidently to this boy.

135

'You want a beer?' she said. Because that would give her something to do – to go and get that for him.

'They're not actually free,' he said. 'You're supposed to put money in the box. Mel went to the cash and carry and bought them.'

Katie didn't know who Mel was.

'She's not trying to make a profit,' the boy said, 'but I guess she'd like her investment back.'

Katie shrugged and went to the counter and took one. She didn't put any money in the box.

'We can share it,' she told him. 'And maybe that means we don't have to pay.' She popped the beer open on the edge of the microwave door.

He was impressed, she could tell. 'So, who do *you* know?' he said.

'I'm a gate-crasher. I saw the lights, smelled the drugs, thought *why not?*'

It was easy. Nothing could be easier. It was like a game and you made the rules up as you went along. The dress rippled like water and the boy laughed at all her jokes. The boy thought she was amazing. It was as if she gave him secret signals with everything she said. She ran her fingers through her hair and smiled a lot and asked him loads of questions and looked really interested in all his answers. He totally fell for it. He was like a puppy and she was holding out her hand and feeding him.

But then Amy walked down the stairs and straight through the back door into the garden and that meant Esme was probably out there already. Why hadn't Katie thought of that? She should've checked. It should've been the first thing she'd done.

'Sorry,' she told the boy. 'I have to go.'

He looked a bit surprised.

'I'll come back,' she told him, although she didn't know if that was true.

There was a bench outside the kitchen door and Esme and Amy were sitting on it. Maybe flirting with the boy had made her brave because Katie walked straight up to them. 'Hello, you two.'

Amy said, 'What the hell are you doing here?'

'I was invited.'

Amy shook her head in disbelief, then whispered something in Esme's ear before standing up and stalking off down the garden path.

Esme looked awkward. And did she move a fraction away as Katie sat down next to her?

'So, how have you been?' Katie said.

'Fine. You saw me the other day.'

'Not for long though.'

Esme frowned, but didn't say anything. She had her hair tied up high above her head. She'd stuck her trademark Chinese paint-brushes in to keep it there. Katie knew she kept them in an oval-shaped dish on the dressing table next to her bed. The dish was cream and pink with a cracked glaze and she kept hair slides and bands in it too.

Katie was trembling. She hoped Esme didn't notice. 'I'm sorry about what happened at your house, Es. I'm sorry if it freaked you out.'

'Can we not talk about it, please?'

'It freaked me out too.'

'I really really don't want to have this conversation.'

'I miss you,' Katie said. 'I hate how you blank me. I hate how I text you loads and you never reply. I thought we were friends.'

'My friends don't jump me.'

'I didn't. You know I didn't. Why are you telling everyone that?'

137

They stared at each other. Esme's eyes glittered with something and it wasn't good. 'Just drop it, Katie, OK? We're at a party. Talk about something else.'

'All right,' Katie said. 'What shall we talk about?'

In the kitchen a big group had just arrived. They were pressing into the room, forcing the people already in there to squash nearer the back door. A couple of girls came out onto the step looking relieved. They smiled at Katie and Esme.

'They've brought stuff for cocktails,' one of the girls said.

'But they want to charge a pound,' said the other one.

'Happy hour,' Katie said, and both the girls laughed before walking off towards some chairs further down the garden.

People were shouting out cocktail ingredients — exotic names wafted through the kitchen door. Everyone sounded like an expert.

'I quite fancy getting drunk,' Katie said.

'Do you?' Esme didn't sound at all interested.

'I've got ten pounds,' Katie said. 'Let's get plastered.'

Esme didn't say anything.

'Don't you want to?' Katie said.

'Not really.'

It had been easy to talk together once. They hadn't even had to think about words. Now everything felt stilted and uncomfortable. Katie tried to dredge up something interesting or funny, some anecdote that would remind Esme why they used to be friends. Could she make herself sound heroic by telling Esme about looking after Mary? Could she make the claustrophobia of sleeping on the Z-bed amusing? Should she explain that Mary had the keys to the past, some kind of strange wonderland Katie wanted to explore? Or that she was trying to keep Mary's stories safe for her in a memory book? Or perhaps she should change tack and tell Esme how Mary cried in the night, keening like an animal, a sound so primitive and lonely that there were no words for it. How in the morning no one mentioned it, so Katie didn't know if Mum had heard or not.

'I miss us,' Katie said. 'There's so much you don't know.'

Esme was sitting on her hands and she suddenly leaned forwards like she was about to get up. 'This is really awkward.'

A moth fluttered past and they both watched it crash into the outside lamp a few times before flying off.

'Awkward sitting here with you, I mean,' Esme said. 'When you came up to me at school, I thought . . .' She looked confused. It felt like minutes as Katie watched her find the words. 'Look, I don't want to give you hope, or anything.'

'Hope?'

Katie leaned back on the bench and breathed. It was the subject they'd just agreed to drop and Esme was bringing it up again.

A flurry of people came out of the kitchen to smoke or take in the night air or whatever. They surged past, laughing and talking loudly and Esme turned her face brightly to them and smiled as if their presence was a relief.

More people swilled in the opposite direction, back into the house. It was as if the garden had to maintain some kind of equilibrium. Esme shivered as she watched them go.

'Are you cold?' Katie said.

'I was hot earlier,' Esme said. 'But it's colder outside than you think.'

Katie thought about offering her jacket, but knew it would be misinterpreted, so she didn't. An image of Simona flashed into Katie's head – she'd once seen her take her coat off and spread it on the grass for another girl to sit on.

139

'I should just get on with it,' Esme said, chattering her teeth together in an exaggerated way.

'Get on with what?'

'There's something I need to say. I wasn't going to, but Amy said I should.'

Some things get listened to more than other things. Every vein in Katie's body felt suddenly capable of hearing sound.

'People have seen you hanging out at the café where Simona Williams works. Beth saw you one time and Amy saw you again yesterday.'

Katie sat straighter on the bench. 'Mary likes going there.'

'Who's Mary?'

'My grandmother.'

'You haven't got a grandmother.'

'I have. She just turned up.'

Esme looked suspicious. 'And you take her to the same place all the time?'

How could Katie explain that she didn't really have a choice because Mary gravitated there? This morning had been really awkward – avoiding eye contact with Simona, praying another waitress would serve them. Katie knew how it looked from the outside.

'She refuses to go to anywhere else. It's her favourite café.'

'See, this just sounds like lies.' Esme turned round to face her, 'So, I'm guessing you've decided that's what you are now. Someone like Simona Williams, I mean.'

'What? No!'

'So, you really need to stop following me about and texting me all the time. I'm not the same as you. I have a boyfriend.'

'You do?'

'He's nineteen,' Esme said, like she was announcing he was from another planet. 'We drove here tonight in his car.'

140

Katie tried to smile, but couldn't quite pull it off. Her whole body felt heavy, as if she needed to lie down.

'I didn't tell you about him before because you've kind of been out of the loop.'

Katie picked at the dress. The fabric looked cheap suddenly, not sexy or retro or cool, just an old dress that smelled musty and had no transforming powers at all.

'He's in a band,' Esme said, studying her nails one by one as if they were entirely fascinating. 'He's the guitarist. He sings as well.'

'Multi-talented,' Katie said.

Esme frowned. 'Don't be a bitch.'

'I'm not.'

'I knew you'd be like this. It's why I didn't want to tell you.'

'I thought you didn't tell me because I was out of the loop?' Katie put 'out of the loop' into air commas to piss Esme off. It was one of her pet hates.

Esme looked at the ground and shook her head, 'You need to stop relying on me for everything, OK?'

'Relying on you?' Katie felt her throat tighten. 'What's that supposed to mean?'

'You don't have any other friends.' Esme sounded very certain. 'For months you've followed me around, and when I talk to other people you just sit there watching, like you're waiting for me to get bored and come back to you. Why do you do that?'

'I don't think I do. I think that's you making stuff up.'

'Are you calling me a liar?'

'You wanted to be my friend when I first arrived at school. You sought me out.'

'Sought you out? Is that what you think? Wow, that's just embarrassing. Look, I don't want you to be weirdly in love with me. I don't want you to be upset that I have a boyfriend.'

141

'I'm not in love with you! Are you nuts? I'm *happy* for you, Esme. I *love* it that you have a boyfriend. Where is he? What's his name?'

Esme shrugged. 'He's called Lukas and he's in the kitchen. There, see – by the door, with the black T-shirt?'

Like he knew Esme was talking about him, he turned to look. Esme waved him over and, like a boy in a trance, he came.

'Hey, gorgeous,' he said.

'Hey,' Esme said.

He looked down at her, right down at her pretty face as she turned it up to him. He wanted to kiss her. He wanted to lean right down and kiss her and take her in his arms and feel her swoon against him. Just looking at him you knew that about him. It was probably making him hard – the knowledge of how soft Esme might be. He knew you could sink into girl's bodies. Boys were all angles.

'Did you miss me?' Esme asked him, her voice soft and low.

'Course I did.'

'Fancy proving it?'

He smirked. 'Try and stop me.'

Maybe Esme was paying him. Maybe she'd actually hired a boy from an agency and he had certain lines that he was supposed to deliver at certain times?

When a girl with red hair sits next to me, come over and flirt, because I want to scare her away for ever.

Was kissing part of that plan?

Because this boy, this Lukas person who drove a car and was in a band, was leaning down, both hands resting on the back of the bench like he was going to do push-ups and he kissed Esme full on the mouth. And Esme let him. They kissed for a long time. Katie was right there next to them and she saw the flicker of their tongues and she heard the low moan caught in a throat that passed from one to the other, like something they shared.

Piña Coladas are white and sticky and look like medicine. They taste of coconut and pineapple and reminded Katie so much of summer that she had two. She didn't like Pimm's so much and could certainly have done without the fruit salad floating about in it. She scooped out the pieces of orange, apple, lime and cucumber from her glass and lined them up on the counter.

Someone had put crisps and slices of pizza out on plates since she was last in the kitchen. Whoever owned this house was probably a sweet parent, was maybe upstairs watching TV in their bedroom, hoping their home wouldn't be trashed. They'd probably rung around all the neighbours to warn them or maybe put notes through the doors. There was probably a time this party would formally end and the parents would come downstairs and start to make themselves obvious. Everyone was high or drunk or out of it in some way. The lovely parents would probably be very disappointed.

Sex on the Beach was so sweet and so red with cranberry juice it made Katie feel crazy just looking at it. She dumped it in the sink and poured herself a glass of some bright blue concoction from a jug. She had no idea if it had a name. Maybe someone had just invented it.

'What's this one?' she asked, waggling the drink at a boy who'd come up behind her.

'Blue Shark.'

She laughed. 'Did you just make that up?'

'No, it's made with Curaçao.'

She recognized him from earlier. It was microwave boy – the kid from a parallel universe. She smiled at him for a bit because she had

143

no idea what else to do. 'You're very clever,' she told him, 'but I have to go now.'

She had an impulse to go up and find the parents. They might let her snuggle down between them. She took a bowl of crisps from the counter to share with them. She knew this was weird and she knew she was drunk, but she didn't care.

She wandered up the stairs with the crisps and discovered an empty room. It was a kid's room with a bunk bed and aeroplanes flying across the wallpaper. In the corner a fish tank bubbled away. She went over to look. There was a bridge and a 'no fishing' sign and a castle and an Easter Island head and a single black fish swimming about looking lonely. She tapped on the glass and it came up to look at her, its fins billowing.

'Hello,' she said.

It opened and shut its mouth.

Microwave boy appeared next to her. The fish looked back at them curiously.

'Do you speak fish?' Katie asked.

'Let me out?' he suggested. 'Help, I'm drowning?'

Whatever it was trying to tell them, it gave up and disappeared under the bridge in a flurry of gravel.

'I saw you come in here,' the boy said.

Katie sat on the bed to see what would happen next and he sat down next to her. 'You're Katie, aren't you?'

She wondered about denying it, but he seemed like a nice boy and she was sick of lies. 'That's me.'

'Jamie,' he said and he held out his hand.

Katie looked at it and laughed. 'You want to shake hands?'

'Why not?'

She had a sudden desire to hug him. This boy had followed her. Esme had a boyfriend. And here was one for her.

144

'I'm not actually a gate-crasher,' she said, sliding closer. 'I was invited by some boys in my maths class, although they don't seem to be here. I only know one person and I've lost her.' She looked around vaguely. 'She's probably gone to one of the other bedrooms to have sex.'

'I hope not,' he said. 'My dad'll kill me.'

'This is *your* house?'

He nodded.

'It's *your* party?'

She couldn't believe he was the host! Here she was with the most important person at the party, just hanging out in a room. There were shelves and books and ornaments. There was a statue of three people holding hands in a circle. One of the people was a child. Was it supposed to be him?

'Does your mum live here too?'

'My dad and Mel. She's my stepmum.'

Well, that shattered the perfect parent myth.

She felt oddly dreamy suddenly. Maybe it was the booze. Or perhaps she was tired. She'd got up ridiculously early when she heard Mary crying on the landing. Christ! Home felt a million years away.

She hadn't checked her phone for hours and it crossed her mind to do it now. Jamie was craning his neck to look at books on the shelf. Had she even remembered to send Mum the address? Yes, look, here was the text. And what was the time? Only ten o'clock. Time passed slowly in the land of parties. She could be very drunk indeed by midnight.

'These books all used to be mine,' he said. 'I've read all of them and now they're my stepbrother's.'

She nodded politely. What was the right thing to say? 'You're prolific,' she told him.

'I see you sometimes,' he said, 'wandering about with a book in your hand. You're in the fiction section of the library a lot.'

She was so surprised she turned and looked at him properly. He had soft fuzz on his face, not quite stubble. He had broad shoulders. He looked suddenly handsome and mysterious in his jeans and T-shirt, knowing things about her.

'I do English lit as well as the science stuff,' she said. 'But if I drop one next year, it's going to have to be that.'

He shuffled nearer. He had a rip in his jeans at the knee and she could see dark hair through it. His knee was bony and so much more angular than hers. 'It's a good idea to drop one,' he said. 'They discourage you from taking four A levels into upper sixth.'

'I want to drop maths.' She sounded sulky, but didn't care. 'My mum says maths is the poetry of logical ideas, but she's quoting Einstein and actually doesn't know what she's talking about.' Why was she telling him this? Was it even true? When had she decided to drop maths? 'Grasping pi takes a certain leap of imagination, but apart from that, I'd rather have words than numbers any day.'

'Do you mind if I kiss you?' he said.

Was he asking permission? Is that what boys did?

'Maybe we should get a room,' she said. Because it felt like something to say and it was funny and also she was stalling.

But it seemed to mean something more to him, because he laughed in an embarrassed way and he leaned forward to kiss her and she let him. His lips were soft and tasted of coconut, although maybe that was her lips mixing with his. He may not have been drinking at all. She barely knew anything about him apart from his name. She'd never noticed him before tonight.

She shivered as he pulled away. He smiled and looked a bit pleased and a bit self-conscious. He had a cute smile – friendly and shy. In fact, he was so much more friendly than Esme out in the

146

garden with her hair and her chattering teeth and her cold eyes and her tongue in some boy's mouth – so much more friendly that Katie let him kiss her again. It didn't amount to anything much the second time either, but it seemed to make him happy because he held her hand and looked at her wonderingly.

'I was thinking . . .' he said.

But she couldn't let him do that. She hauled him up. 'There's someone I want you to meet, come on.'

He looked reluctant, but she dragged him out anyway, back onto the landing and down the stairs to the hallway and past the lounge. The football match on TV had finished and people were sitting about smoking. One kid was using the carpet as an ashtray. Katie wondered if Jamie was going to say anything to stop it, but he didn't.

Back in the garden, she could feel him behind her as she looked about for Esme. It was like having a loyal pet, one who would always be on your team. It was very inspiring. Right at the end of the path, under a tree that was hovering there, Esme was still wrapped up with Lukas. They were sharing a cigarette and looking about. Katie took Jamie's hand and pulled him closer, then turned around and kissed him. He was a bit surprised, but didn't object. She tried to make it long and slow and mesmerising. She tried to make the ground move for him.

Esme pretended not to notice. She yawned instead and stretched her pretty little arms above her head. Maybe the boyfriend kept her up all night.

'What's happening now?' Jamie asked as Katie pulled away. He didn't want to be let go of, that was clear.

She said the first thing that came into her head, which turned out to be that she wanted him to make her a cup of tea. He nodded and went off to do that.

'So,' she called over to Esme, 'that's Jamie.'

Esme frowned, like she was thinking, *why are you telling me this?* and Katie gave the thumbs up just to make it clear. 'This is his party and he's my boyfriend. I didn't tell you because you've been out of the loop.'

Esme had the grace to smile. The boy, Lukas, smiled too.

'He's funny,' Katie told them. 'I really like him.'

They both looked at her expectantly, but she didn't know what else to say. He's empathetic? He likes reading? He's interested in fish?

A girl yelled from somewhere down the dark garden. 'I am not drunk!' she yelled. She came running across the lawn, looked about wildly and sank herself into Esme's arms, where she promptly burst into tears.

Esme looked at Lukas with amused eyes. 'I better talk to her,' she said and stroked this new girl's hair and let her sob in her arms as she led her away.

How come that was OK? How come no one even blinked? If Katie had done that, the whole world would have collapsed.

'So, you like boys now?' Lukas said, and he pulled another cigarette from the packet and looked at Katie as if they were really going to have this conversation.

It was late. She should go. She could call the taxi to come early, keep in Mum's good books.

Katie could feel Lukas staring at her keenly from the bench. 'So what you did to Es then, what was that?'

'It was nothing,' Katie said. 'It was completely and utterly not important. Tell her goodbye for me, would you? I have to go now.'

She made it through the kitchen, down the hallway and out the front door before Jamie caught up with her. 'Why are you going?' He sounded disappointed.

'Something came up.'

'Don't you want this tea?'

She'd forgotten about that. He held it out to her like a gift. What a sweet boy. What a kind and lovely human being.

She imagined kissing him again. *Save me from this, Jamie. Save me from myself.* She could tell him to get rid of the tea, then leap into his arms and circle her legs round his waist and kiss him until everything stopped hurting.

His eyes were on her and she allowed hers to drift to his. They were brown. He had nice eyes.

'I was wondering,' he said, and even in the dark she felt him blush, 'if you wanted to go out sometime?'

It cost him to say that. It was a risk.

'We could get a coffee or something.' He had a soft voice – lilting.

'I'll see you at school,' Katie said. 'In the library.'

He smiled. 'Because you've got to get your poetry fix when your mum makes you drop English for ever?'

That was nice of him – to remember that. It was also funny. She'd been right about him.

'My parents met in a library,' she said.

'Did they?' That seemed to give him hope because he took a step nearer.

Her mum had very deliberately chosen her dad. He'd been studying for his accountancy exams and she'd seen him in the library several times with his books spread out on the desk. She'd sat opposite him with a magazine called *Accountancy News*. A studious and quiet accountant would give her studious and quiet children, financial stability and a life of harmonious monogamy. How wrong she'd been.

Katie stroked the material of the dress. It was smooth under her fingers and had a living warmth to it.

'A coffee sounds good,' she said. 'You want my number?'

'Great,' he said, grinning. 'I thought you were going to say no.'

They swapped numbers. *Jamie*, she wrote in her contacts.

How easy to make someone happy. He even wanted to walk her home. She told him she had a lift, that her dad was waiting round the corner. A father felt more certain than a taxi. This nice boy would want to walk her to a cab and check she was safe, whisper goodnight, keep the meter ticking.

'My dad's a bit possessive. It'd be easier if he didn't see you.'

She didn't know why she said this. She appeared to be turning into a compulsive liar.

She waved at him at the corner and he waved back. He looked very keen. It made her heart ache to look at him.

Seventeen

Something vitally important had happened and it was evading Mary's memory like a slippery fish. No, not a fish, more like a piece of fruit in syrup at the bottom of a bowl that you would chase around with a spoon.

She was standing in sunshine and she had no idea why. That was a church over there, wasn't it? Look – an arched doorway, a stained-glass window above. Was she at a wedding? There'd been singing earlier. A thin reedy sound. Blackbirds and gardens and broken mornings. She'd understand why soon, but all she had at the moment was the blank of it.

She looked around for the girl. She often knew the answer to things. There she was, standing with her brother and mother and several rather dour-looking gentlemen, all wearing black coats and shoes. One of the men wore a cape and seemed to be in charge. He held out a dish and said, 'Anyone who wishes to now come forward, please do so.'

And then a memory came. It dazzled briefly, like sunlight flickering through leaves and went away just as quick. *I had it then*, she thought, but then she got distracted by an angel standing guard on a plinth beside her.

'Hello,' she said. 'Aren't you beautiful?'

He had his wings wrapped around himself like a shroud and a

calm smile on his lips. His expression was curious, as if he'd never seen anyone like Mary before.

'Look at you,' she told him. 'All muscle and feather.'

She thought how wonderful if he unfurled his wings and shifted upwards in a cone of light. Wouldn't that be something to behold? What a clever, complicated thing he was.

The girl came up and took her arm. 'Who are you talking to, Mary?'

An angel, of course, but she wasn't sure why. She supposed they lived near churches. That would make sense.

The girl was staring, clinging onto her. 'You want to throw in some earth?'

Earth? What was the child on about? 'No thank you.'

'I'll do it for you then.'

The girl walked over to the man with the cloak. He offered her a scoop, but she shook her head, dipped her hand in the dish and pulled out a fistful of earth. Only now did Mary notice the gaping hole at their feet. There were chilling shadows down there. It was deep too. Mary leaned forward and caught a whiff of damp.

'Bye, Jack,' the girl said, letting the earth fall through her fingers and into the hole. 'I wish I could have known you.'

Jack was down there?

The boy was offered a turn with the dish, but declined. The woman took up the scoop and had a go. The man with the cloak said, 'We therefore commit this body to the ground. Earth to earth, ashes to ashes and dust to dust,' and all the other men with their black suits and white gloves bowed their heads and looked very serious.

And then it came crashing back. Jack was dead. Of course he was. Hadn't she heard him call her name? Hadn't she found him on the landing, his legs at odd angles? He made her pull that cord he

152

was always telling her not to touch and it flashed red, red, red on his face. He tried to speak, to tell her something, but the pain seemed to sweep at him, like some kind of terrible tide that sank him into the carpet.

And she'd begged him (she was ashamed to recall) not to leave her – *stay with me, I can't do it without you. Please, I beg you, Jack*.

It was only one man who had gone, but it felt like for ever, something so permanent and unstoppable that it blasted her. If she were a tree, she would drop all her leaves.

That's how it felt, Mary thought. That's what she wanted to say out loud to the grim little crowd standing around poor Jack's grave. And to all the angels with their calm sad faces. But what she actually said, half smiling so as not to scare anyone, was, 'Better to have loved and lost than never to have loved at all.' Which really was just a cliché and didn't come anywhere close to describing love. And its loss.

That was the point when she heard Jack whistling. That was the point he walked through the cemetery gate and waved at her. It was astonishing. Shocking. Had she summoned him somehow?

'I recognized you by your hair,' he said as she raced across the grass to him. 'My eyesight's pretty bad these days, so I have to look for the shape of things.'

Of course, she'd forgotten that about him – how he could only see the outside of the world and not the things in the middle. He used to tell her that he would always be able to see nature, but soon not books, not reading. Although, Mary thought, since he was actually dead, perhaps it didn't bother him so much now, perhaps he had no use for books any more.

She followed him to a bench by the church door. They sat together there.

He said, 'So, how have you been?'

'I've been missing you,' she whispered.

He smiled at her curiously, glanced about the churchyard for a few moments, and then leaned back. 'Not much of a crowd.'

'I'm sorry,' she said. 'I'm not sure anyone was told.'

'It's all right. I won't take it personally.'

'I should tell them, should I? That more people should be here. I could talk to the vicar?'

'I'm not sure they let you do it twice, sweetheart.'

And anyway, their voices were fading away. In fact, Mary wondered if they'd gone altogether – if perhaps the whole church-yard had disappeared. But she didn't want to check. If she took her eyes from Jack, he might vanish too.

'Don't worry, darling.' He shuffled closer. 'Why don't you tell me what you've been up to since I left?'

Mary laid her hands flat upon her lap. What could she say? How could she explain it? *I'm not sure what I'm supposed to be doing? Every morning I wake up with such certainty, and every afternoon it slips away?*

'I don't like questions much,' she said. 'Why don't you tell me about you instead? Are you allowed to talk about how things are for you?'

He didn't answer. She didn't know what that meant, but thought it probably meant no.

'I keep seeing you,' she told him. 'One day I saw you locking up your bicycle. One day I heard your voice in the bathroom. You often walk past me in the café and yet this is the first time you've stopped to say hello.'

'I didn't see you those other times,' he said. 'My eyes . . .'

'Should I let you know I'm there in future? Are there rules about things like that? If I see you again in passing, am I allowed to stop you? What if I call and you don't answer? I couldn't bear that.'

'I'll always answer,' he said. 'But if you see me and don't fancy talking one day, then just ignore me. Ask yourself, what will I regret when I get home? And don't forget, I can't see things very well, so I won't be offended.'

They sat in silence. Sunlight glimmered above his shoulder. At one point he looked at his watch.

'Do you need to go?'

'Not yet.'

But it agitated her, that he might be late for some appointment. It stopped her thinking of all the things she wanted to ask.

'I find things more confusing without you,' she said. 'People get cross with me. Sometimes it feels as if all the things I want to think are hidden under layers of cotton wool, like everything's dusty.'

'I'm sorry,' he said, 'that I'm not around to help.'

'Although,' she said, leaning towards him, '*you* seem very clear to me.'

His face glowed pink in the light, his grey hair seemed thicker.

He really looked very well, considering. He smiled fondly at her, then turned to look out at the graves. He started to hum. It was an old tune, Mary recognized it, sang along. It was about a man who'd lost his heart to a woman. A man who wanted to bring spring to her, who longed for the day he could cling to her – a man bewildered by love. She sang confidently. It was wonderful to be sure of the order of things.

'Sinatra?' she said.

He nodded. 'Lyrics by?'

'Rodgers and Hart?'

'Correct!' He turned back to her. She wondered if he knew he was crying. 'Mary, my love. I lost my heart to you a hundred times over.'

155

'That song's about me?'

'Not the bit about being cold. You were never that. But the rest of it.'

Mary rubbed her eyes with her sleeve, blinked at him. 'I'm sorry. I seem to let people down a lot.'

'No, you bewitch us all.' He glanced at his watch again. 'Tell me quickly – how's it going with that daughter of yours? Did my little trick work?'

'Trick?'

'With the medical bracelet. I had her phone number inscribed, hoping she'd feel obliged. Have you patched things up?'

'I'm not sure. I seem to upset her a lot.'

'Oh dear.' Jack's voice was impossibly gentle.

'She's very strict.'

'Poor you.' He went to put his hand on hers, but stopped himself. Would she have felt him? Would there be weight and substance to him? 'You were determined to find her, remember? It was important to you. There were things you wanted to sort out. Don't let that go. It'll make you feel better.'

She shook her head, wondered if he was teasing her. 'Perhaps you could write it down for me?' she suggested. 'So that I remember?'

'I can't, love. Not any more.' He patted the bench soundlessly. 'Don't worry, you'll get there in the end.'

'Sometimes,' Mary whispered, 'I think something terrible happened.'

'It did, darling. It's your blue blank.'

'Is that what it's called?'

'It's what I took to calling it on the days you cried. I so wanted to comfort you.'

'And you couldn't?'

156

'You wouldn't talk about it.'

'I'm sorry. Perhaps I was tired? I do get tired a lot. Sometimes I feel as if I'm a hundred years old.'

'That's the illness, Mary.'

'Or maybe it's because I'm not a good person. Maybe I don't deserve good things.'

'Now don't start believing your own bad press. Not after all this time. You deserve wonderful things. You certainly deserve your daughter back in your life. Your grandchildren too. They're growing up beautifully, by the look of it.'

Mary followed his gaze. There was the girl, standing with her arm around her brother – the pair of them washed in sunshine and surrounded by churchyard angels. 'She stirs me,' Mary said. 'Like she's got the edges of a jigsaw puzzle and all I have are a few pieces from the middle.'

'I'm sorry I can't stay to meet her.'

Mary knew he would leave now and that disappointed her. What had she hoped for? Her man back in flesh and bone? To have him sweep her up and hold her? To watch him unbutton his shirt and bare his chest and invite her to rest upon it?

Ah, she missed the heat of him.

She watched him stand and she knew she wasn't ready, that this hadn't been enough. She caught hold of his sleeve, but her fingers met air.

'What is it, love?'

She was shocked by the steady blue gaze that met her own. 'I know it sounds stupid,' she said, 'and I'm sorry if I seem different, but I can't let you go until I know what to do. All those things you said about Caroline – I'm going to forget them, I know I am. My head isn't right. Most days I feel as if I'm sliding off a mountain into the dark. How am I ever going to manage?'

157

'You want my advice?'

Mary nodded weakly. 'Something like that.'

He smiled. 'Well, that's a first!'

Mary fumbled in her handbag, found a pen amongst the mints and hankies and held it out to him. 'Help me.'

'You do the writing,' he said.

He told her what to write, and in big blue letters on the wrinkled skin on the back of her hand she wrote: *I am Mary Todd*.

'There you go,' he said. 'That's all you need.'

Mary looked up, confused. 'That's it?'

He nodded. She saw the hint of a smile. 'Didn't you always tell me it took courage for people to be themselves?'

'I don't know. Did I?'

'You used to say, "It's a life choice, Jack, and we only get one life." You were an inspiration, Mary.'

Again he went to go, and again she stopped him. 'What if I can't remember who I am any more, Jack?'

'That's why you've written it down.' He smiled sadly at her for a moment. 'Give Caroline the suitcase if you need to. Pat's been dead long enough. It can't do any harm now.'

'Suitcase?'

He nodded at the children. 'Ask for help if you need it.'

She wanted to ask him to sit back down and kiss her. She wanted to breathe him in. But she didn't dare suggest it.

'Bye, sweetheart,' he said. 'Take care of yourself.'

At the gate, he blew her a kiss. Mary followed his journey to the end of the street. He didn't wave and he didn't look back. At the corner he simply melted into the horizon.

She looked down at her hand. So what if she was Mary Todd? What difference did that make to anyone? Most days she could barely remember those eight letters herself. The only thing she ever knew for sure was the ache she felt inside, which she wished would go away. Was that important? She took up the pen and wrote her name on the bench. Perhaps repetition would help her understand what Jack meant. She wrote the word *courage* next to her name. Then she wrote: *Pluck. Valour. Guts. Audacity.* Ah, all those crosswords he'd encouraged her to do for years were paying off. Jack seemed to have reminded her brain about synonyms. Next, she wrote a string of words that came into her head. Things that required the aforementioned courage, perhaps? *Pat. Suitcase. Caroline. Blue blank.* It felt like a child's game suddenly and made her smile.

The girl, who appeared from nowhere, wasn't smiling. 'Mary,' she hissed, 'what're you doing? You're a total vandal!'

'I was reminding myself of things,' Mary said, offended.

The girl sat on the writing and tucked her legs under the bench and nodded at the boy and his mother, at the vicar, and at the men with the gloves who all came over to offer condolences before going off and standing in a little group outside the gate. She shuffled along the bench, demanded Mary's pen and scratched the words out. 'What's a blue blank?'

Mary shrugged. 'Search me.'

'What suitcase?'

'No idea.'

'Then why have you written this stuff down?'

'I don't know. Didn't Jack mention a suitcase? Don't I need to fetch it?'

The girl gave her a quizzical look. 'You mean the one at the flat?'

'A different one.'

'Fetch it from where?'

'Home, I suppose.'

The girl asked Mary questions she didn't know the answer to, like, 'Why didn't you get it the first time?' And, 'What's in it anyway?'

The girl said, 'So, let me get this right. You want to go back to your old house again?'

Mary nodded. That was exactly it. A day trip, that's what she wanted! 'Yes please.'

The girl thought about it. She made it look difficult. She made it look as if she would say no. She bit her bottom lip and looked over to the gate. 'Mum won't want us going that far.'

'Let's not tell her.'

'We might have to bring Chris. He's got PE tomorrow, so he'll try and pull a sickie and Mum's bound to let him.'

'The more the merrier.'

'He might blab. He hates breaking rules.'

'We'll bribe him. Boys are easily bribed.'

The girl smiled. She was extraordinary when she smiled – something knowing and a little bit dangerous flickered in her eyes. 'I think you might be a bad influence on me, Mary.'

'We're the same, you and me,' Mary told her, stroking the girl's arm. 'Somewhat foolish and somewhat brave.'

'Brave? I don't think so.'

'What did you say your name was again?'

'Katie.'

'Well, Katie, you definitely remind me of me. I was younger than you when I fell in love for the first time. Night after night, when my sister was asleep, I climbed out of my bedroom window to meet him – out into the dark, running down the street holding my shoes.' She smiled at the memory, so vivid she could see the swirl of her skirt as she ran, could almost smell the Arpege she'd sprayed at her throat. 'Robert borrowed a car and we drove to all sorts of places – supper at a hotel, or a dance hall. Sometimes we just went to his caravan. I thought I could get away with anything.'

'And could you?'

Memories flickered. Her father looking right through her as if she were a ghost, as if he'd decided she no longer existed. Pat being forced to translate every damn thing he had to say. The baby crying on and on.

'No, actually. It turned out that I couldn't.'

The girl eyed her for a moment too long. Perhaps Mary shouldn't have said anything – she didn't want to scare the child.

'OK,' the girl said eventually. 'Let's do it.'

Eighteen

'Mum's going to kill us.'

Katie turned from the departures board to scowl at her brother. 'Not if you don't tell her.'

Chris bit his lip, like he might not be able to stop words tumbling out of him. 'It's a crime scene. It's probably illegal.'

'How can it be a crime scene if there wasn't a crime?'

'It's a death scene then.'

Katie flicked a glance at Mary, sitting on the bench halfway up the platform – her eyes shut, her face turned to the sun like a flower. She didn't appear to have heard. Katie lowered her voice. 'Is it Jack you're worried about?'

Chris shrugged, scuffing his shoe in the dust.

'Because there's no such thing as zombies.'

He looked unconvinced. 'How come she sees him everywhere?'

'Because she misses him.' Katie cupped his cheek with the palm of her hand so he'd be forced to look at her. 'Don't you sometimes see Dad about the place?'

'He's not one of the undead!'

'He's not in your school canteen either.'

Chris yanked his face away from her. 'You don't know that!'

'What I *do* know is that mooning about Dad all the time is going to piss Mum off a lot more than us going on a little day trip, so how about we agree to keep some secrets?'

He knew it was blackmail by the scowl he gave her. 'Mum told me to text if I felt better.'

'You weren't sick in the first place!' Christ! It was hard enough to do daring stuff without Chris undermining her. 'Send her a text saying you're out of bed and doing your homework, then turn your phone off. It's going to be fine. We'll be back before you know it.'

'And what if we meet any weirdos?'

'Then you'll fit right in.' He rolled his eyes at her and she laughed. 'Nothing bad's going to happen, Chris. What else can go wrong? Dad's buggered off, Mum's a dictator, Mary's forgetting everything she ever knew and you and me are freaks. It can't get any worse!'

She had to stay strong. This new confidence of hers was tidal – coming in waves of strength this morning, but bound to retreat later, leaving her breathless with anxiety all over again. She didn't want to be afraid any more. She grabbed her brother's arm and linked her own through it.

'This suitcase is really important to her. Imagine what might be in it – maybe thousands of pounds!' She cast a last glance at the departures board as she steered him to Mary. Two minutes to go. 'Finding it might change all our lives. Mum could leave her crappy job and buy a massive house somewhere and we'd go to new schools and have exotic holidays and get new wardrobes and new friends and amazing new lives.'

Chris looked doubtful. 'What about Dad?'

'He'd leave his girlfriend and come and live in our mansion, of course. Everything would be fantastic.' Chris began to look convinced and she squeezed his arm. 'How can it be wrong to take Mary to her *own* home to look for her *own* suitcase? I would've told Mum we were going if she wasn't so stressed.'

'If the suitcase has got good stuff in it, can we tell her? She won't be mad at us then, will she?'

'She'll be ecstatic. We'll be heroes.'

Maybe it was the simple fact of moving at speed, but once they were settled on the train, Mary was the most content Katie had seen her. She gazed out at the retreating fields and sighed with happiness as they were replaced by row upon row of terraced houses, their back gardens sloping down to the railway track. Squat industrial buildings replaced the houses, followed by a series of bridges straddling a dual carriageway.

'Would you just look at all those cars!' Mary said. 'All off somewhere or other.'

Katie smiled. 'It's good to keep moving, isn't it?'

'Sit in a chair too long, my girl, and you might never get up again.'

'I was actually thinking of becoming a nomad. I might never go home.'

Mary whooped with laughter. 'That's the spirit!'

Chris pressed his leg more firmly against Katie's, which meant he disagreed with the entire conversation, but at least he was keeping quiet about it.

Katie tried to imagine staying on the train to the end of the line. The sky would stretch itself out and the horizon would expand and they'd end up somewhere totally new. They could reinvent themselves, have adventure after adventure . . .

Perhaps it was being on a train, but Mary thought the memory game might be getting harder. Today's category was babies and Mary wanted to think of the sleepy weight of her daughter, of that place at the top of her skull that smelled of newness, of her wise little face and her arms like sea anemones and her toes and fingers like tiny prawns.

But Pat and Dad kept getting in the way.

Here is her father growing colder, whittling Mary down with his silence and his little notes:

When are you leaving?

You can't stay here.

I don't want you under my roof.

Here is Pat, with her lists and plans, determined to find a solution. Poor Pat. She'd even gone to the yard to see if she could procure Robert's address, but all she discovered was what Mary already knew – that he'd broken his contract with the railway and gone back to his wife.

'So, there we are,' Pat says. 'He's got off scot-free, hasn't he?'

1954 – how to be a good mother

Two days after Caroline was born, Mary still hasn't stopped shaking. Even when she's wrapped up in bed with the electric heater on she shivers.

'It's the shock,' Pat says.

She brings Mary soup and sweet tea, rubs her back with menthol, gives her a hot pad for her feet and a smelling bottle to clear her head and takes the baby away for hours on end so Mary can rest.

'Maybe I'll feel better when my milk comes in,' Mary says.

But the milk doesn't come in. Not really. Not enough so the baby will ever stop rooting for more. It's as if Mary's cold in her bones, as if the very centre of her has become open to the elements.

'It'll have to be a bottle,' Pat says.

But Mary doesn't want that. She's made a promise to love this child. She hauls herself out of bed and puts a dressing gown over her nightie, a hat on her head and socks and slippers on her feet. She builds a nest of pillows in the armchair next to the heater and sits in it, wraps a blanket round her shoulders and tries once again to feed her daughter.

Outside the window, the sky is skittish with cloud and the cherry tree is bursting with blossom. Every time the wind picks up, petals flutter to the grass and Mary thinks of weddings. It doesn't help.

Her milk, what there is of it, is thin and pale and it's only minutes before Caroline whimpers in frustration. Mary scoops her up and holds her close.

'I'm sorry,' she says. 'I'm so sorry.'

The baby snuffles at her neck, but there's no satisfaction there and soon the child is wailing. Pat comes in to see what the fuss is about.

'Move the pillow,' she says, 'and change the position of your arm. You can't expect her to feed lying on a slope.'

'She sounds so lonely,' Mary says. 'Look how her jaw shudders.'

'She's hungry, that's all.'

Pat shuts the curtains so the sun won't get in the baby's eyes and turns off the heater in case it's sucking oxygen from the child's system. She gets a glass of hot cordial for Mary and sits on the edge of the bed and sighs as the baby desperately roots about.

'I can't bear it that she's starving,' Mary says. 'Tell me what to do.'

'Let me give her a bottle, that's what. I've done this before, remember? Hush now, hush, little one,' Pat croons. 'Don't cry, there's nothing to be sad about.'

But there is. This baby's mother is useless. Mary knows it. And now the child knows it too.

At night, Pat insists Caroline sleeps in the box room next to an open window. 'She doesn't want to be breathing in your stale air now, does she? And that back room's further from Dad, so he'll be less disturbed.'

But how do you check your baby's still breathing if she's all the way across the landing? And if she wakes in the night, shouldn't you go to her, rather than let her cry herself back to sleep?

'If you stop lifting her up and fussing her,' Pat says, 'she'll soon be feeding and sleeping at entirely predictable times.'

'How do you know all this?' Mary asks.

Pat merely scowls. 'Better to put a fence at the top of a cliff than station an ambulance at the bottom.'

'What does that mean?'

'It means that regularity of feeding, sleeping and bowel movements is best for a child.'

Now that Pat gives Caroline bottles, Mary resolves to help with other things instead. She watches her sister, eager to be as competent: the towel across the lap, the water at elbow temperature in a bowl, the cotton wool and baby powder. Pat demonstrates folding the nappy, how to tuck your fingers inside when using the safety pin so the baby doesn't get jabbed, how to tie the crossover vest with its ribbons, how to ease a nightie over the baby's head.

'I love you very much,' Mary tells Caroline as she struggles with socks and bootees. Because if she keeps saying it out loud, she might become a good enough mother to deserve such a lovely daughter.

But every day brings an increasing fear. Because what if Pat's right and Mary will never manage? And what if Dad really isn't going to ever speak to her again? Every time she walks into a room, he walks straight out. Every time she says anything, he pretends not to hear. What sort of atmosphere is that for a child? 'You,' she tells her baby daughter, 'you deserve better than this.'

Every time she cradles Caroline, Mary can't help thinking, *if I'm left alone with you for long enough, I'll do something wrong. I might accidentally drop you on your head or tangle you in cot sheets and suffocate you. And as you get bigger there are more ways to hurt you. I might give you the wrong medicine or let you run out into the road. And I have no idea what babies eat, so you'll probably starve and I can't knit or sew, so you're bound to get chills. Left to my own devices, you'll be lucky to make it to your first birthday.*

Then Mary feels terrible for thinking such horror, and holds her daughter tight and plants kisses all over her soft sad face.

She tries to tell herself that it isn't her fault. She goes over and over it. 'Listen,' she says to herself. 'It's simple. Not every woman is motherly. Some of us just don't have it.'

She tries to make up stories with happy endings, ones where she and Caroline live in London together and Mary is an actress and Caroline has all the children's roles, like Perdita in *A Winter's Tale* or Wendy in *Peter Pan*. But then Mary remembers that Perdita is brought up by a shepherd and Wendy flies away through a window and both end up motherless. Not even her fantasies come good.

Every morning, Pat makes up a bottle, feeds the baby in the kitchen, then puts her down for a nap. Pat makes Dad his breakfast, hands him his packed lunch and waves him off to work. Pat's started knitting again. She's bought pink wool and is making a matinee jacket, whatever that is. Mary can hear the needles from all the way upstairs. Clickety-click, clickety-click. Pat says there's nothing for Mary to do, except stay in bed and try to decide what the rest of her life might be like. But Mary can't get past the idea of taking her child and moving to London. Whenever she mentions this to Pat, she looks appalled, comes back at Mary with tales of mothers thrown out of boarding houses, of landlords taking advantage when they discover there's no husband, of women living in the streets, of babies getting tuberculosis or being bitten by rats.

Every possibility is taken away. Mary has no money, no prospect of work and nowhere to live. As Pat keeps telling her, 'You've really gone and done it now.'

One morning, Pat orders Mary to come downstairs and sit at the kitchen table. A paper and pen is produced. Pat's going to sort things out once and for all. This situation can't go on. She writes down Mary's options. These include getting the baby adopted (immediately crossed out, because hasn't there been enough loss in this family?), feigning the death of Mary's made-up husband in a car accident (crossed out because no one will believe it), Mary wearing a ring and pretending her husband works abroad (ditto), the entire family moving away and starting all over again (Daddy's too old and would never agree), Mary and the child staying locked in the house for ever (cruel to the child and at some point the neighbours will notice).

'Well,' Pat says, pushing the paper away, 'that leaves us with finding this baby a father.'

Mary sinks her head into her hands, fighting back the nausea that overwhelms her. 'Robert's got a wife.'

'I'm aware of that.'

'So what are you suggesting?'

Pat taps the pen against the table. 'How long since you last saw him?'

Mary's throat hurts. She wipes her eyes and looks at her sister. 'Four months.'

'And did you go with anyone else? I mean, you are sure he's the father? There couldn't have been a mistake?'

Pat says *mistake* as if she's swearing. It makes Mary smile, despite the threatening tears. 'I'm sure.'

'Well, we need to find a new man, then. One who won't mind taking on a child.'

Mary's heart sinks. What ridiculousness is this?

'Men have urges,' Pat says. 'Women have longings. It's a dangerous combination. Much better to put all that aside and sort this out in a practical way.' She taps the table three times and Mary thinks of a magician conjuring a rabbit. 'What about Lionel Dudley?' Pat writes his name on the paper. 'His mother's just died, so he owns that nice little house now. Daddy always speaks very highly of him. He dresses well. He's clean and quiet and must earn at least ten pounds a week. I imagine he even has prospects for promotion, despite his age.'

'What are you talking about?'

'Daddy's colleague from work.'

'What's he got to do with anything?'

'He might like a ready-made family. He needs a woman to keep that house for him now his mother's gone.'

Mary blinks at her sister. Doesn't she understand men at all? 'I don't think it's a wife that man's after. Don't worry, I'll bring my daughter up on my own.'

Pat glares at her. 'And where exactly will you do that?'

'I'll think of somewhere.'

'I will not stand by and see this family's reputation in tatters while you brazen it out with a baby and no ring on your finger!'

'Oh, don't worry about your precious reputation, Pat. I'll go to London.'

'You think anyone will rent you a room? And how will you pay for it? You'll be on the streets before you know it.'

Mary finds it hard to breathe suddenly. The room begins to slowly spin. 'I can't marry a man I don't love and that's the end of it. I refuse to spend my life in misery.'

'*Your* life!' Pat's voice is shrill. 'Never mind *your* life. You're giving no attention to the child. You of all people should know what it's like to grow up with a parent missing. But at least yours was decently buried and not married to somebody else!'

'Don't bring Mum into this.'

'Then don't talk to me about misery!' Pat stands up and jabs a furious finger at Mary. 'I gave up everything for you – grammar school, college, all of it. The reason I don't have a husband or family of my own is because of you!'

'Well, if you want a husband so much, why don't *you* marry Lionel and keep his little house nice? I'm sure you'll suit each other perfectly. Very convenient for both of you.'

There's silence. Mary's words echo. The kitchen reverberates with them.

Nineteen

'You all right, Mary?'

'Yes, thank you.'

'You know where we are?'

'Absolutely.'

It was tempting to check that she actually did, to ask her the name of the street or to see if she remembered why they'd got the train in the first place, why they'd walked up the hill from the station, what they were here for. But direct questions with only one correct answer were Mum's speciality and were beginning to seem cruel.

The keys worked, and there was no alarm. They went into the hallway and shut the door behind them, standing in a little bundle as their eyes adjusted.

'Are you sure it's not haunted?' Chris asked, peering into the gloom.

Katie gave him a warning nudge.

He frowned at her. 'Why's it so dark then?'

'It faces north,' Mary said sadly. 'However, if you go through to the back, you'll find a different story.' They followed her down the hallway and into the lounge. Mary went straight to the curtains and whipped them open, 'That's better.'

The room came into focus. The fireplace, the mantlepiece with all the trinkets, the armchair with its blanket, the wing-back chair with its tapestry cushion.

Chris sank onto the sofa in front of the TV. 'Does it work?'

'I don't see why not,' Mary said. 'You just help yourself.' She beckoned Katie over to the window. 'Look at this.'

Katie went to stand beside her and looked along the stretch of her arm. Outside, a set of traffic lights moved from red, through amber to green. It was shockingly bright out there – Mary had been right about that. Light bounced off the houses opposite and off the slow-moving cars. It looked like water on the road, a strange oasis shimmering on tarmac.

'There's a whole row of shops,' Mary said. 'You can get anything you want – newspapers, sausages, you name it, they sell it.' She laughed loudly, pressing her cheek against the window and steaming up the glass. 'And there's the garden, just the edge of it. You have to go through the kitchen door for that one.' She beamed at Katie. 'You want to go out there?'

'What about the suitcase? Shouldn't we look for that first?'

'If you like.'

But Mary didn't move. Chris gave Katie an I-told-you-so shake of his head as he flicked through channels with the remote.

Katie had imagined Mary like a hungry animal roving through rooms, foraging for the case. She'd find it in a wardrobe or under the bed and recognize it immediately. She'd produce a key from the depths of her handbag and open the padlock. It would be full of cash or maps or the deeds to a castle. But Mary was different from their last visit. Then, she'd been interested in the house and all it contained. Today, it was as if the outside world bewitched her – the street, the shops, the garden.

There was treasure to be found, Katie was sure of it. But how would she recognize it without Mary's help? Katie tried to recall the names, softly spoken by Mary last time they were here, each one an incantation, like words from another language. That was a Welsh dresser over in the corner, she remembered that – made of pine and very trendy in the seventies. And the armchair favoured by Jack was G Plan. The long low sideboard was teak and made in Scandinavia. That was a cocktail-cherry coat rack on the back of the door, very popular following the Festival of Britain and inspired by molecular models used in chemistry.

A strange excitement thrilled Katie as she recalled the details. These things were so alien, yet they were also part of her somehow, some long line of history that she'd now inherited. She grazed a finger across the top of the music box and lifted the lid. The plastic ballerina rose from her spring and wobbled drunkenly. Katie smiled as she wound the key. Mary, this house, even the tinny music coming from this box – for a brief time, maybe just for a few more days until Mum got a care home sorted, Katie had a stake in them.

'Shall I look for the case, Mary, if you'd rather not? Do you think it might be upstairs?'

'"Greensleeves",' Mary said. 'I can name that tune in one!'

Well, that sounded like permission.

The stairs creaked. Katie crept up holding the handrail tight and tried not to think about Jack lying on the landing and all the stuff that might've leaked out of him. She hoped there wasn't a stain. That would be too much to bear.

There were three doors, all closed. She was beginning to feel like Goldilocks. A suitcase was big. It would be easy to find. *Just keep breathing, Katie, you can do it.* The first handle she tried led to a bathroom – a bath, a loo, that was it. The second opened up into a small box room, and after a furtive glance under the bed (dust and a roll of carpet) and inside the fitted cupboard (rows

175

of shoes, shelves of jumpers), it was obvious there was nothing.

A splash of sunshine appeared on the landing and disappeared just as quick, like a torch flashing from the sky as Katie stood outside the last door. It startled her. What if someone was in the final room? What if Jack really was a zombie and that's why Mary kept seeing him? Or what if he'd been killed by a psychopath and they'd come back to finish off everyone else?

Don't be ridiculous, Katie. You can do this!

Yes – this was the master bedroom – a messy double bed (the last place Jack ever slept, but don't think about that now), a dressing table covered in trinkets, a wardrobe and an armchair. She whisked the curtains open to let light completely flood the room and took a big breath before kneeling to look under the bed (slippers, more shoes, more dust). The wardrobe doors slid open easily, to reveal nothing but rows of men's suits. She stroked the plastic covers, relieved and disappointed all at once. She considered the possibility of letting Chris know there might be some serious vintage up here, but dismissed it as soon as she thought it. Chris in a suit? When would that ever happen? And anyway, it would just make him think of all the men who were missing from his life.

She sat on the bed and closed her eyes to consider the options. Clearly, this was a stupid idea. They'd come all this way and were bound to get bollocked and Mary had probably made up the suitcase, and even if she hadn't then Mum had already gone through these rooms, so anything interesting or valuable would've been noticed. If the suitcase even existed, it most likely had boring stuff in it.

Mum had a fireproof steel box to keep all her important documents safe. She called it her life box, because it had her birth certificate in it, also her medical card, bank account details and marriage certificate. *Everything important in one place.* Katie knew that in the event of an accident or Mum being incapacitated in some way, in the box there was an envelope with a hundred pounds in cash, the local bank manager's phone number and Mum's life insurance documents. Katie wondered if this was also the place where Mum stored all the divorce paperwork she was refusing to sign, but that conversation was off limits. So was the box actually. The key hung on a green thread on a hook in Mum's bedroom and she was deadly serious when she said it was not to be touched unless there was a dire emergency.

So, Mum's life boiled down to some paperwork in a box and Mary's to a mystery suitcase.

What would Katie choose to keep? Family photos were on her phone, she didn't care about any of her clothes except Mary's silk dress (was that even hers to keep?) and her boots (and she'd probably be wearing those). Books, she'd be sad about, but that's why libraries existed. It shocked her to realize that there wasn't a single thing she owned that she cared about very much.

It was that thought that made her slide the wardrobe doors in the opposite direction. Because if there were men's clothes in there, perhaps there were women's in the other half and she might find something else worth saving.

It was the range of colour that was so surprising. None of Katie's clothes at home were turquoise or spicy orange or dark gold. And it was uncanny how things suited her complexion when she held them up to herself, as if Mary understood some secret about pale skin and red hair that Katie just didn't.

Several dresses were hand-made, they had to be. The bodice of this one was constructed of separate pieces of material woven together so it twisted into the waistband. A button was missing on the sleeve of this tea dress, but that would be easy to fix with a piece of the same fabric from the hem and a new button covered to match. The side zipper of this skirt worked well. Katie unzipped it, zipped it up again.

There was also labelled stuff – not just Marks and Spencer, but Biba, Mary Quant, and here was an actual little black dress by Givenchy. Some of these things were probably worth a fortune.

Would it hurt to try something on? Was it wrong?

Katie Baxter always wore jeans and jumpers and dreaded hot weather because it was more exposing. Katie Baxter wished her hair was a little less red and a little less wild. But this girl in the mirror looked confident! This olive shift dress totally complemented her hair. It felt exciting, the colour auspicious. Surely no harm could ever befall her if she wore clothes like these?

'Shoes,' Mary said, appearing suddenly at the door.

'Shit!' Katie's face rushed to blood. 'I didn't hear you come up.'

'Spare room, in the cupboard, down at the bottom.'

'I'm sorry, Mary, I should've asked.'

'What size are you?' She crossed the room and peered at Katie's feet. 'I think mine will be too small. I've got Alice shoes, patent court shoes, all kinds. Just help yourself.'

'I'll wear my boots, they go with anything. Are you saying I can borrow some of these clothes?'

'Keep them. What's mine is yours.' Mary leaned over and smoothed Katie's hair. It was perhaps the most intimate thing she'd ever done and it made Katie stand perfectly still. 'No need to look afraid.' Mary twisted a strand of Katie's hair between her fingers. 'You're always biting that lip of yours. It's Pat's fault, poor sod – always expecting the worst. She got numb. Like when you sit on your own leg. There's no purpose or meaning to that kind of life now, is there?' She rootled through her handbag and pulled out a lipstick. 'It's an old stub of a thing, but you're welcome to it. It's all you need to brighten that smile.'

It was ancient, all mashed at the end. Mary prodded at it with her finger and dabbed Katie's mouth. Katie tried not to think about where Mary's hands might have been and when she may have last washed them. She liked the taste though. It was waxy like candles, but tasted hot, like the burning red colour it was.

'You look like a Copper Top with that halo of hair.' Mary smiled at her. 'Now, let's get some sun on our faces.'

Katie got the key from under the sugar bowl and opened the door to the garden. It smelled fresh and earthy despite the heat. A bird with a bright yellow beak looked at her from a branch with its head on one side like it was saying, *Who are you?*

'Good question,' Katie said.

Mary brought out a chair and found a patch of sun right in the middle of the grass and sat in it. She named the flowers, although Katie wasn't sure they were the right names. 'Jack grew the lot,' Mary said. 'Like little poems, all of them.'

Katie sat on the doorstep. She pulled up a clump of grass and sprinkled it on her lap. She found a twig, snapped it in two and planted both halves in the dry earth.

'Maybe they'll grow,' she said when she caught Mary looking.

'Best hope for rain then.' Mary held her palms to the sky as if it would surely never rain again.

'Are you worried about the garden, Mary? There's a bucket there. You want me to water Jack's flowers?'

Mary nodded benevolently. 'If you like.'

So she did. It was the least she could do in return for the clothes. Back and forth into the little kitchen, watering the flowers pail by pail, Katie felt like a kid. She had a sudden memory of filling a paddling pool like this once, under the summer sun with Dad sitting in a deckchair watching. There'd been a table with glasses of lemonade and a jug. It seemed a long time ago.

179

Mary sang as she watered. 'K-K-K-Katie, beautiful Katie, you're the only g-g-g-girl that I adore. When the moon shines over the cowshed, I'll be waiting at the k-k-k-kitchen door.'

And it was fine. So fine. Better than anything. Katie felt like she lived there. They'd stay for ever, watch the flowers grow, sit on the grass, talk. Later, they'd go into town and check out the nightlife. Mary would be up for that. It'd just be a case of persuading Chris to leave the TV behind.

Mary lit a cigarette as Katie watered. She blew smoke up into the sky. 'Nancy, Nora, Norman, Nelson,' she said. 'Now your turn.'

'Norway,' Katie said. 'Netherlands, Namibia, Nicaragua.'

'Ha!' Mary cackled. 'Very good. I can name millions. Towns, villages, flowers. You ask for it, you can have it.' She smiled contentedly. 'I could give those people on TV a run for their money.'

'I think it's easier to remember stuff when you're here, isn't it, Mary?'

'Easy? I call it blooming marvellous. I call it summer arriving!' She waved her cigarette. 'You can stick that in your pipe and smoke it.'

It was wonderful. Like a veil had lifted.

'What about the suitcase, Mary? You wanted it and I looked for it and I can't find it. You remember it now?'

'Absolutely. Come with me.'

She went down the path to the shed and pulled on the handle, but the hinge was broken and the bottom of the door scraped the ground. Katie helped her – with both hands she lifted it and hauled it open. She was half expecting wild animals inside – cats, foxes or even something ridiculous like a tiger. She wouldn't put anything past Mary.

'Jack's den,' Mary said as they stepped in. 'He comes here to smoke and look at ladies.'

'Ladies?'

Mary raised an eyebrow coquettishly and pointed to a picture tacked to the wall. It was a woman – a curvy, fifties, black-and-white woman smiling at the camera.

Katie leaned in closer. 'Wow, is that you?'

She was stunning. Her hair in dark waves, her skin glowing, her eyes huge and full of 'come-hither' fire as she posed, one hand on her hip as if saying, *I will stand here for this photo, but only because I choose to.*

Katie peeled it from the wall and turned the photo over, but there was nothing on the back – no name, no date, no clue.

'Robert took it,' Mary told her. 'Jack was sad it wasn't him I was posing for, but you can't know one person for ever, can you? Now then, remind me what we're doing in here again.'

'Suitcase?'

'Ah, yes.' Mary pulled open a drawer and rummaged through. It appeared to be full of gardening things – packets of seeds, a ball of twine, a bundle of wooden sticks, several brown paper bags neatly folded, a single leather glove. 'Not in here.' She shut the drawer and opened the cupboard above and peered in. 'Is this what we're looking for?'

It was a battered overnight case in red leather. Katie pulled it out of the cupboard and laid it on the bench.

'It has a silk lining,' Mary said. 'A pocket for an alarm clock and elasticated loops for a bottle of perfume or travel shampoo. There's plenty of room for a change of clothes, a facecloth and makeup.'

She sounded as if she was reeling off the original advert. 'What's inside now, Mary? Anything?'

'I wanted glamour,' Mary said, ignoring Katie and lovingly wiping dust off the case. 'I wanted a place in London with big bright rooms and gilded mirrors that reflected the light. I wanted plush white

181

sofas and a chandelier. I wanted a different life from my sister. Pat had a housecoat in quilted nylon. She used to make rags from old sheets and tie them to her feet to polish the lino. She used to darn socks and alter clothes with pin tucks and pleats and gathers.' Mary leaned over the case as if the memories weighed too much. 'I took this case when I left. It was a present from my father years before. He was always buying me gifts, though he stopped all that when the baby came.' She tapped it with a finger. 'I wrote letters to Pat every day, and – do you know? – she never replied. I thought perhaps she was throwing them away, but she saved every single one.'

'Is that what's in the suitcase, Mary? Your letters to Pat?'

She nodded very slowly. 'And other special things.'

'Shall we open it?'

'If you like.' She looked up at Katie, her eyes full of hope. 'I expect you'll know what to do with it all.'

1954 – how to be a good mother, part two

Mary sits at a table in the corner of the staff canteen and waits for the new girl (Joan, is it?) to register what she's just said.

'A baby?'

Mary nods, tries to smile. 'Yes, nine weeks ago.'

'And you did *what* with her?'

'I relinquished care and responsibility to my sister Patricia and her husband Lionel and have no further claim.'

Second time round, the words hold the same foreboding. Mary feels as if she's placed a funeral brochure on the table amongst the tea cups.

'Blimey.' Joan gives Mary's hand a small and sorry stroke. 'I'd never have guessed.'

'I send letters,' Mary says. 'And each Friday I send money.'

'You must miss her though?'

Every minute of every hour, Mary wants to say. *And nothing fills the gap. It's as if my life has stopped, as if there's an invisible tie that binds me to a child I fear I may never see again.* What she actually says, however, is, 'Well, it helps to know she's in such good hands. Lionel's a friend of our father, a little older than my sister. He's a good man, and marriage suited them both. Pat will make a wonderful mother. She's very sensible.'

Pat always turns out lights and locks the door at night. She

183

understands how to get the washing line to stay up with the clothes prop and what halibut oil is for and how to administer it. Both of these arts escape Mary. In fact, if she really thinks about it, the list of things Pat's capable of is endless. The child will flourish, Mary must keep telling herself this.

'There was always cake for tea,' Mary says, 'all the way through the war.'

Joan grins. 'Nothing like cake in a crisis.'

'And it's comforting to know that if the baby gets a fever, Pat'll be able to tell if it's the kind that requires a doctor, or the kind that needs putting to bed with wintergreen and eucalyptus. I'd probably just put the poor thing in a cot with a hot water-bottle and hope for the best.' Mary tries to laugh, but it comes out like a strangled cough.

'And can you visit whenever you like?'

'I'm letting them settle. My sister only just got married and so this is all very new for her. I'll go up at spring bank holiday, I expect.'

Mary swirls the dregs of tea round her cup and gulps the last of it down, tries to swallow the doubt along with it. Despite all the careful negotiations, all the wording gone over and over, the signatures, the promises – not a word! Pat, who was always so fastidious about keeping in touch, about thank-you cards and gracious little notes to shopkeepers, has not replied to a single letter.

'And tell me,' Joan says darkly. 'Most girls would have taken something. I know at least two who have. They get a bottle from the chemist and nothing's said.' She leans in closer. 'Didn't you think you might do that?'

'Only at the very beginning. Not really.'

A pang of fear for the child strikes Mary again – like a wound in her chest, something primal that makes her want to run screaming from the table and go and find her daughter and snatch her back.

'Well, I think you're very brave.' Joan pushes her plate of chips closer and gestures that Mary help herself. 'Let's cheer ourselves up before we get back to the grind, shall we?'

The monotony of working in a factory canteen doesn't help – the scraping and chopping, the heat of the kitchen and the washing of pans, the mixing and stirring, the tedium of it all – it gives too much space for thinking. Mary tells herself she deserves it. What else had she expected? She has no qualifications, no talents, never passed the typing course, never did understand shorthand. Pat was right all along – she'll come to no good.

She tries to do her tasks without her mind being present, her real self buried somewhere deep down, like a hibernating thing. But every now and then she thinks of Caroline and wonders what she is doing *right now, this very minute* and it makes her stop in peculiar places and have to breathe very slowly and deeply. Sometimes she even hears a voice inside her head reaffirming what she suspects already, that her life is going to be exactly like this for ever. This is all there is, a kind of never-ending sadness, broken only by moments of sheer terror.

She tries to pull herself together, tries to blame it on lack of vitamins and boredom. She makes an effort to vary her routine, maybe a cup of tea with Joan at lunch time, or a bit of supper. Sometimes she attempts to surprise herself by going to see a film on the way home from work. But mostly, she just goes back to the bedsit and writes her daily letter to Pat, has some tea, then gets ready for bed. She sits there unable to sleep, her blanket at her chin, her knees hugged in to herself, gazing out at the night.

* * *

31st May, 1954

Dear Pat

I have been longing to hear from you and feel sure that you must be all settled down now. Could I have news? Anything you feel able to tell me. Of course I want to know about the wedding and how it all went, but more than anything, I want to hear of Caroline.

I know at the moment it's impossible to see her and I'm sure you are quite right (again) when you say she needs to settle in, and of course I know she's well loved and cared for. It's just that I miss her in ways I can't begin to put to paper. Didn't you always tell me that words were never enough? Well, how right you were about so many things.

Nothing seems to matter so much as it did - I haven't been dancing since I got to London and have no desire for it either. All the things I yearned for - the music and lights and laughter - well, they belong to another girl in another life.

Please excuse more now, Pat. I will say bye but will write again tomorrow. Give my love and a kiss to the babe.

Yours,

Mary

It's a shock not to be able to shrug off the grief. Something so animal in Mary that she wakes up with her pillow damp from dreams of loss. She longs for this baby who has gone, who she's chosen to give up. She's giddy with it and no one seems to notice. Joan keeps inviting her to things, as if a night at a dance hall or a few drinks at the works social club will cheer Mary up.

'You might surprise yourself,' Joan says.

'I doubt that.'

'Come on. It'll be fun. Quite a few of the chaps have been asking after you.'

But a chap isn't what Mary needs, much as it surprises her to admit it. That part of her life is over. She sees something in other women that seems to have faded in her – something hot and quick that used to draw life to her, that used to make her feel alive. What's the point of pretending to enjoy a dance?

Mary tries every argument, tells Joan she has no special clothes, even embarrasses herself by saying she can't afford it, is ashamed when Joan offers to lend her money.

By the height of summer, Joan's stopped asking. Mary feels almost invisible. Barely anyone speaks to her at work and she hardly lifts her eyes to meet those of anyone else. She knows people talk about her, knows she's perceived as strange, sees herself as they must see her – half withered inside like a crone. Sometimes when she's alone in the canteen, clearing tables after the rush of hungry workers, or mopping the floor, she has a sense of foreboding, as if a shadow has crossed her soul. She sees herself speeding towards death, feels herself being watched, feels the tick of death's heart close to her own.

She has to give herself a good talking to on more than one occasion. Such a drama queen! Wasn't that what Pat always told her?

She writes letters and postcards daily, begging for news. Four months old now and what can Caroline do? Can she sit up yet? Reach out for toys? Recognize faces? And at last, at last, she gets back from work one night to see Pat's meticulous handwriting on an envelope. Someone's placed it on the hall table and she sits on the stairs and holds it to her breast. Perhaps it will be an invitation – *come quick, she misses you* – or perhaps a photograph or some funny anecdote about her daughter. No. When she eventually dares open it, it's a rather dull note from Pat detailing the weather and the price of things. The only news of Caroline is that she's 'a good girl' and is 'doing well'. Much as it's a relief to hear anything at all, it's the *detail* that Mary craves.

2nd July, 1954

Dear Pat

Thank you for your letter. Will you let me telephone you? A chat would be so much better. There's so much to say and a letter doesn't seem enough. And you write so rarely, Pat - you, who used to keep that diary so religiously. I tell myself that you're busy keeping house for your new little family.

I'm sure you can imagine how I'm feeling. She was such a darling and I miss her so much. Can you assure me that you haven't changed her name? Also, I'd treasure a photo if you had one. Could we come to some agreement about me visiting soon? You don't need to be afraid of me, Pat. I'm not out to make trouble.

I know I did the right thing for the future happiness of my child. You know how grateful I am for your kindness.

Mary

She buys a book and studies the stages of development. She discovers that Caroline should quieten to the sound of a voice and turn towards it, that she ought to be able to follow a brightly coloured object with her eyes if it's held eight inches away from her.

She will have been smiling for weeks. And children have more bones than adults, does Pat know this? If Caroline falls badly, she'll be more likely to bend a bone than to break it because her periosteum is stronger and thicker.

What's a periosteum?

Mary borrows a medical encyclopaedia from the library, takes it home to bed and traces with her finger the diagram of a baby's skeletal structure, the spine like a string of pearls. She learns that the skull of a new-born consists of five main bones and there are soft spots on a baby's head allowing the plates of the skull to flex during birth.

She studies the blood system, the respiratory system. She learns the names of every bone. It's like a whole new language. Neurocranium. Cartilaginous. Olfactory. She can even make up sentences that make sense with words such as these.

'Did you know,' she asks Joan, 'that the neurocranium has cartilaginous supports and olfactory receptors?'

Joan frowns, 'Are you swearing at me now?'

'No,' Mary says. 'It's simple – it means in your head there's a nose. That's all.'

She continues to write daily letters, spending a fortune on stamps. She asks if Caroline can sit up yet. Has she started to crawl? Is she babbling any recognizable sounds? How long is her hair and has Pat bought ribbons or bands? Should Mary send some, would that be welcome? She also tells Pat that the most common fractures to look out for in children are the incomplete ones such as greenstick or buckle. The former involve a bend on one side of the bone and a partial fracture on the other. Is Pat aware of this?

The letter that comes back is curt. Pat would find it a great relief if Mary could stop sending letters. Pat is a busy woman and doesn't Mary have better things to do than give unsolicited lectures on child welfare? In fact, it would probably be better if all correspondence was limited to birthdays and Christmas from now on.

7th Sept, 1954

Dear Lionel

I write to you, not to go behind Pat's back, but to ask you to speak to her on my behalf. I would very much like to have news of Caroline more regularly than twice a year. I cannot believe that Pat really means this.

I think of the babe often and I hope you know I am being truthful when I say I will not do anything that will jeopardize her happiness. I'm sure her new mummy and daddy love her very much and that she is happy.

Will you please also ask Pat to let me visit? Our original agreement allowed for regular news and contact and neither of these have been forthcoming. You can never know how much it would mean to be able to have one small peek at Caroline. It would give everything meaning.

With very warm regards

Your sister-in-law Mary

10th September, 1954

Dear Mary

I was greatly surprised at your cheek in writing to my husband. Lionel and I are in complete accord about things and have no secrets, so please don't assume that you are able to persuade him of anything.

It seems I have to remind you of our formal agreement. These are the actual words you signed to:

"I hereby covenant that I will not nor will any other person or persons on my behalf at any time molest, disturb or in any way interfere with Patricia

or Lionel Dudley in the upbringing, maintenance, education or otherwise of Caroline."'

Remember? I know you are upset, but it was what we agreed.

You had every chance to keep the child yourself, although I imagine if you had gone down that road, you would be sleeping rough by now and forced to wash at the railway station out of a fire bucket.

I promise I will send word twice a year at birthday and Christmas. You will have to trust me. I will also enclose photos at that time. This is more than you would have if you'd had her adopted through an agency and you know it.

I feel as if you are unwilling to move on and let us have our time with her.

Best wishes, Pat

13th Sept, 1954

Dear Pat

You have broken your word. This is not what we agreed. You said I could visit and now you have changed your mind.

You are acting as if I have no feelings at all, as if I am dead to you. I am not dead! If I were, I would come and haunt you. I would throw your furniture around and never leave. I would scare the living daylights out of you!

If you don't formally agree a time for me to come and see Caroline, I will get a train and come and knock on your door. What's to stop me sitting on your gatepost and telling your lovely new neighbours that you are refusing to let me see my own daughter when we agreed that I could?

I beg you to reconsider.

Mary

Less than a week later, she gets a letter from Dad. She sits in the hallway staring at his handwriting on the envelope. It stuns her. This man, who has pledged never to talk to her again, has written. It's a good sign, surely? Perhaps he's intervened and spoken to Pat. But no. It's a formal little note. He hopes she's well. He's finding the weather very hot. He finds it hard to breathe sometimes and the doctor thinks he might have a touch of asthma. But aside from that, he wants her to know that Pat, Lionel and the baby have moved. Lionel applied for a promotion and has been successful and his new job has taken them many miles away. Jean from next door is kindly doing his suppers now, so he's managing all right. For now, he's unable to forward Pat's new address.

Unable? *Unable!*

Mary lies on her bed and wishes an answer to come hurtling from the ceiling. The pain in her chest is overwhelming. She wants her own mother back to advise her, to rock her and hold her and tell her what to do – the right thing to do. Should she get the train up and make Dad tell her where the baby is now? Should she hire a lawyer?

She goes over the details. She kissed her daughter goodbye. It was six in the morning and daylight was just beginning. Pat had already fed and changed her and Caroline should've been asleep, but when Mary bent over the cot, her daughter was awake and smiling.

'Not old enough to smile yet,' Pat said when Mary told her.

But Mary knew what she'd seen.

She also knew that she wouldn't see another smile from her daughter for a while. And yes, she'd signed an agreement, she didn't deny it. As Pat had so clearly explained – if you love someone, you must do what's best for them and put yourself second. And what was best for Caroline was two parents and a mother who knew what to do.

But Mary had never imagined she would be barred for so long.

20th Sept, 1954

Dear Dad

Every part of me hurts. I don't know what she looks like. I have no idea of her. It's as if she haunts me. I see her everywhere in every child. Since you won't tell me where she is, I'm going to hire a detective. And then I'm going to fight to get her back. I don't think the agreement we signed was legal, and since I was under a great deal of pressure from you all at the time, I think I have a very strong case. Please could you inform Pat of my intentions?'

Mary

PS I am sorry you are ill. I hope you feel better soon.

24th September, 1954

Mary

I am not going to respond to blackmail or threats. I am not going to respond to further letters, although I will (I am a creature of my word) send you an occasional package containing a photo and a report of progress.

I will remind you that it will hurt Caroline very much to be told the truth of her origins when she firmly believes herself to be mine and Lionel's child. I would also like to warn you that we would fight back harder and with more financial clout than you could ever muster should you choose to go down a legal path.

You are selfish and had your chance. You are young and can have more children (although I suggest you find a husband first). Stop trying to take away what I have.

Growing up, you had the best of everything. I gave up all hope of a bright future when I became your surrogate mother at twelve years old. You got to swan about looking pretty and being Dad's special girl while I cooked and washed and tidied and asked for nothing. I was a home body, remember? And you had all the fire.

Well, now I have something I want – a husband and a child – and I thank you for them both. But they are not yours to have any more.

Please leave us alone.

Yours sincerely,

Pat

The detective's office is seedy and Mary isn't sure he's any good. How do you tell? What's to stop him only pretending to look for Caroline, but taking Mary's money anyway?

He asks her to explain the circumstances under which she's left her baby. He asks to look at her copy of the agreement along with Pat's letters. He asks why she wants the child back so badly.

'I'm her mother,' Mary says. 'I should never have left her.'

'You can't just take her back. You'll get yourself arrested.'

'I'll think about the particulars when I know where she is.'

'It's hard to bring up a kid on your own,' the detective says. 'Let's say I find her, how will you manage?'

But Mary doesn't want to think about the practicalities. She wants her baby back. And she's offering to pay this man, isn't she? She doesn't want his questions, just his skill at finding missing children.

'I don't require a lecture on parenting, thank you,' she says. 'Now, do you want the job or do I need to go elsewhere?'

He smiles. 'I see what your sister means about fire.'

He takes a deposit. He explains that he'll require expenses plus his weekly fee in advance each Friday. He promises to keep his costs as low as possible. 'I'll stick lunch on someone else's budget,' he says. He requires a final payment when he hands over proof of the child's whereabouts. He imagines this won't take long since he assumes Pat still makes visits to their father.

194

Mary cuts down on spending. She moves into a smaller room and turns down the heating. She wears a hat to bed. Apart from the detective's fees, her major expense is stamps. She still writes letters to Pat every day, sending them via Dad. She has no idea if he ever forwards them. Or if he does, if Pat ever reads them. She tries to keep them chatty, newsy, friendly. She doesn't want Pat getting suspicious and moving house again.

Weeks pass, then one morning two envelopes come at once. The first contains notification that the detective has found Caroline. She's living in North Bisham, a small town not far from the coast. It's not a place Mary has ever been. *Bisham*, she mouths. She wonders if there's a railway station. The detective goes on to say that if Mary would like to come into the office he'll be glad to pass on the full address once he's received payment for the enclosed invoice.

The second envelope contains a brief note from Dad. *We had the christening last week and Pat asked me to forward the enclosed photograph of the baby surrounded by her pretty cards.*

Caroline's sitting on a lace coverlet with a cushion behind her. She isn't smiling, but is looking up at the camera with such intelligent curiosity that Mary clutches a hand to her heart. It's as if she has a window into her daughter's soul. She sees possibilities in that gaze – of a toddler, of a girl, even of a woman. Her hair looks golden (hadn't Mary's own hair been light until she was older?) and her arms are beautifully chubby. She wears a christening bracelet on her left wrist and behind her, on the mantelpiece, a row of cards is clearly visible. Mary counts them – seven! Dad will have sent one, of course, and maybe the neighbours. The rest must be from Lionel's family. Mary's never considered them before – his parents are dead, but perhaps there are aunts or cousins?

Mary sits on the edge of her bed and feels anger leak out of her.

Here is Pat's new lounge – the mantle with its clock and its cards, the hearth with Lionel's pipe and ashtray. There are some rather nice curtains at a sparkling window. Here is a coffee table with a neat stack of coasters. On the carpet by the fireside is a magazine rack, and isn't that the button jar sticking out of Pat's sewing basket? So much is familiar, and yet dotted about are items that suggest new routine – a basket of toys, a teddy slumped on a cushion, a cot blanket folded over the arm of a chair.

None of this is posed, none of it for effect. This is how they live, what they do – this is the detail, the ordinariness of their lives. It isn't something Mary can offer – cards, christenings, aunts, mantelpieces. It's very clear to her now.

That afternoon she goes to see the detective, tells him she no longer wants the address, but when he insists (she might change her mind and he's gone to a lot of trouble) she slips it into her purse. Her daughter looks just like her, he says. Had he actually seen her? Oh yes, he had to make sure she was the right kid.

She sits on a chair, weak at the knees. This man has seen her daughter with his own eyes. 'Tell me,' she breathes. 'How was she?'

'She seemed very well.'

'That's it?'

'Pretty much.'

'What was she doing?'

'Lying in a pram being pushed about the place.' He shrugs. 'What else do babies do?'

Mary asks what she'd been wearing and had there been toys in her pram? She asks if Caroline's hair is long enough for ribbons now, or had she been wearing a bonnet? Where had Pat been taking her, did he think? The shops? The park? To feed the ducks?

For a detective he isn't very observant. All he knows is what he's told her. The baby had been with Pat, he'd watched them leave the house together and followed them only a few yards before tracking back to speak to neighbours and then off to the town hall to check official records. He hadn't realized Mary wanted him to make notes on clothes or hairstyles.

'The neighbour said they seemed a nice family,' the detective says. 'Decent and quiet.'

'That's no surprise,' Mary says.

Why is nothing ever enough? Why does she crave the detail?

Perhaps he feels sorry for her, because he accepts only half his outstanding fee before shaking her hand and wishing her all the luck in the world. 'Should be an actress with your looks,' he says. 'I could fix up a meeting if you're interested.'

She tells him she'll think about it.

When she gets home, she sits down and writes Pat a letter.

Dear Pat

I am sorry for any distress I have caused. I appreciate the photo very much. It has made all the difference in the world to me - to see Caroline's beautiful face and to have a glimpse into your life together.

I am sorry if I scared you by being too forthright. I would like us to get back on track. I would like to accept your original offer of a package every now and then. If you could include photos or anecdotes, even a lock of hair, I would love that.

I enclose a separate note. Would you be so good as to read it out to Caroline? She won't understand, I know that, but I want her to know how dearly I love her.

I look forward to your next package, and please be

assured that if you ever felt it appropriate for me to visit (I could be Aunty Mary and very well-behaved!), I would get on the first available train.

Very best wishes
Your loving sister, Mary

Darling Caroline,

This is a message from your first mummy. Yes, you have two! Aren't you lucky! I will always be your first mummy. Always. Even when the world is a million years older. But I have to do what is best for you, sweet girl, and I can't offer you all the things children need to grow up and be happy.

I want you to know that those short weeks we spent together were the best of my life. I spent every day astonished at your loveliness. I leave you to your new mummy and daddy now. You will be very safe with them. I will think of you every single hour of every single day. Never doubt it.

Mummy

Twenty

It was as if the dark called to Katie, as if the very fact of the day fading caused some primal heat to rise. Like a fever. Or when she had that virus once and it got worse at night. Perhaps she should go to bed instead of going out. She wouldn't though. Nothing was stopping this now.

She wore sweatpants, a T-shirt, her boots and a hoodie. 'Just going for a walk,' she said from the doorway, keeping her voice light.

Mary and Chris didn't look up from the TV, but Mum frowned at her from the laptop, its shine reflected in her glasses. 'I don't want you going anywhere. You've caused enough trouble today.'

'I just need some air.'

'You don't feel well?'

'A bit woolly, that's all. I know it's late, but I just need a quick walk round the block.'

Mum considered this. She was probably thinking that if she actually grounded Katie she wouldn't be able to ask her to look after Mary tomorrow.

'Just a walk?' Mum said.

Katie nodded. When had she started to lie so much? It was recently. When Mary arrived, was it? Did it matter? It was only a small lie.

'Half an hour max,' Mum said, 'and take your phone.'

Half an hour? That wasn't going to be long enough. Katie shook her head in disbelief as she sidled out to the hallway. Why did Mum have to be so strict about everything? Why could she never just relax?

Katie had been convinced the suitcase would change things. She'd let Chris do the honours, proudly telling Mum where they'd been and what they'd done. Katie had genuinely thought Mum would be elated, because here was concrete proof that Mary had loved Mum after all. One of the letters had almost made Katie cry. '*I will think of you every single hour of every single day. Never doubt it.*'

But instead of being thrilled, Mum was furious – Chris was over-excited, Mary was exhausted and Katie was both a liar (for saying she'd stay local when she clearly had no intention) and a busybody (for stirring up the past). Nice. Thanks for that, Mum.

'But Mary hired a detective,' Chris kept saying. 'Don't you think that's cool? She found out where you lived and everything.'

'And then didn't bother showing up.' Mum put her hand up to mark the end of the discussion and marched off to the kitchen to open a bottle of wine, even though it wasn't six o'clock yet. She relegated the suitcase to the broom cupboard.

Never mind. Never mind any of that now . . .

Katie ran down the stairs two at a time, and at the bottom eased the door open, slipped through the gap and let it close gently behind her. Empty grass. Empty wall. No one by the dustbins or under the fire escape. She took a breath, filled her lungs with the dark.

It had rained earlier and the air had a fresh-washed smell about it. The sky was grey now, edged with darkest blue. It looked like a healing bruise. She stood there for a moment and breathed. She

200

liked the way the trees moved in the wind, as if they were dancing. She liked the scent of wet earth and growing things.

She shoved her hair into her hoodie and zipped it up.

One, two . . .

She walked quickly, skirting the grass. She didn't look back or up at the windows. She didn't want to falter if Mum's disapproving face was up there looking out.

The temperature changed as she jumped the low wall and jogged along the pavement. A coolness of space, of trees, of more air, of being away from enclosed buildings. She ran past the pub, past three lads sheltered in the doorway with pints clasped to their chests. She could feel them watching, but they didn't say a word, didn't tell her to slow down or speed up or come over or anything and so who knows what they were thinking, which meant maybe nothing, but which also meant she could give them anything to think. Like, *that running girl looks completely normal, wouldn't you say? Yep, she doesn't look like she's on a special mission at all . . .*

The main drag was quieter than daytime, barely any cars, never mind people. It was like she owned this town! Like being on holiday. No – like being older. Like maybe she'd left home and gone to university and tonight, after lectures, she'd come out for an adventure, with the trees dripping overhead and the beautiful empty street to run into.

It took almost ten minutes to get to the garage, which was longer than she'd imagined. But what the hell? She'd simply have to run home at top speed. Here was the library, and next to the library was a bus stop and over the road was the café

It looked shut. The outdoor lamps glowed red but the tables were bare and inside was dark, definitely empty or closing. This wasn't what Katie had imagined. She wanted crowds of people and a quick flustered moment with Simona to pass her the note before running home again.

As Katie stood catching her breath she had the feeling of being on the edge of something. She thought back to Mary on the train – the fire in her eyes as she'd sifted through the suitcase, plucking out photos, letters, even the adoption agreement from all those years ago. How courageous she'd been, how she'd fought for Mum despite everything.

Katie had read some letters out loud. She loved the crisp dryness of the paper, the antique look of the ink, the passion in the words, the knowledge that day after day Mary had spilled her heart before sealing the envelope, licking the stamp and walking to the post box.

No one made that much effort any more. Now, it was all texting and Snapchat and Facebook and instant messaging and so, when they got back to the flat (after the protracted bollocking from Mum) Katie had gone upstairs and written a letter – longhand on a sheet of paper from a stationery set she'd got for her birthday years ago. It was gilded with gold. It meant business.

The café door opened. Katie shielded her face and peered towards the oncoming traffic, trying very hard to look as if she was waiting for a bus. It was an older waitress – one Katie had never seen before. She looked up briefly, one hand on her hip as if she was exhausted. The neon sign behind her flashed *Latte, cappuccino, pasta, pizza* over and over into the dark. She stacked four chairs into a pile and dragged them beneath the window. She hauled a table across to join them and chained all the legs together, as if she was in a Western and was hobbling horses for the night. Katie imagined a camp fire, Simona strumming a guitar . . .

The waitress went back into the café. Maybe she was going to get Simona to help with the other tables. There were a lot of them.

Or maybe she was going to call the police. *'Yeah, there's this strange girl across the road staring at me and to be honest I think she's a psycho . . .'*

Oh, this was ridiculous! Where had Katie's courage gone? She just had to cross the road and deliver the letter. She didn't even have to speak!

Simona was standing behind the counter cleaning the coffee machine. She was wearing a T-shirt and jeans and her work apron. Katie didn't knock on the window or make any sound – she simply stared at the bare arc of Simona's shoulder, at the place at the nape of her neck where her hair was shaved. And maybe Simona had special powers, because only a few seconds passed before she turned from the machine and looked at Katie. Right at her and no one else was there. Now Katie was going to look like some kind of stalker and Simona would be revolted. She already looked annoyed, giving a kind of 'what-the-hell-are-you-doing-here?' frown as she wiped her hands on her apron and came to the door. She didn't smile when she opened it. She barely opened it in fact, just peered out. 'We're shut.'

Katie couldn't speak. She'd been mad to come. What had she been thinking?

Simona said, 'Did you hear me?'

'I wrote you a letter.' Katie's voice was a cracked whisper and yet she imagined everyone on the street hearing. She imagined the other waitress listening in, her shoulders stiffening with disapproval somewhere inside the dark of the café.

Simona opened the door, stepped through and pulled it shut behind her. She leaned on the glass, her eyes suspicious. 'What kind of letter?'

Katie fumbled at her pocket, pulled it out. It looked crumpled and ridiculous, not at all as she remembered it. 'Here.'

Simona shook her head, as if she couldn't believe this was happening. A flood of fear rushed Katie's heart as she watched Simona rip the envelope and pull out the single sheet of paper. The letter said:

Dear Simona,

I kissed my best friend and she told everyone. The day I laughed at you was the first time anyone had spoken to me for weeks. I felt included. This is absolutely not an excuse, more a way of explanation. I'm sorry. Truly I am.

I'm looking after my grandmother, Mary, at the moment and she loves your café, which is why we've been every day since I made my first terrible attempt at an apology. If our visits are awkward for you (because you think I'm a moron), please text me on the number below and I'll try and take her somewhere else instead.

Thanks,

Katie

A slow smile lifted the edges of Simona's mouth. 'I'd say less of a moron and more someone with truly terrible taste in friends.'

'Yeah. Except for Esme, they're idiots – sorry.'

'Esme's the one you kissed?'

'Yeah.'

'She doesn't sound much of a friend either, to be honest.'

'It's not her fault. It was a misunderstanding.'

Simona raised an eyebrow. 'Is that right?'

Was that a question? Did it require an answer? Simona kept looking at Katie. The way she kept looking made Katie look away.

The pavement outside the café was littered with things that Katie only noticed now that she was trying hard not to look at

Simona – a sweet wrapper, three chips, a plastic fork, a ball of tissue scrumpled up under the pile of tables.

'It's all right,' Simona said. 'You don't need to tell me. I should probably get back to work anyway.'

Katie felt suddenly hot in her layers of running stuff. She counted how many items of clothing she was wearing and it came to eight. She counted the number of tables in the stacked pile and it came to four. She was aware that Chris did this kind of counting – when he felt ashamed, uncomfortable.

'I wish everything could go back to how it was,' Katie said. Her voice sounded strange – high and uncertain. 'I wish Esme would talk to me and her mates would stop staring. Every time I walk past them, it's like being on stage in the worst possible way.'

She waited for Simona to say something, but she didn't. She waited for her to open the door and escape back inside the café, but she didn't do that either.

'My parents split up last year,' Katie said, 'which is why we moved here and why I changed schools. My brother still goes to his old school. He has special needs and they send a bus for him. It's funny, I never really envied him before, but I wake up most mornings wishing a bus would come for me.'

It was easy to talk to someone in the dark, someone who felt like they might know what you were talking about. Katie had a sudden desire to ask Simona if the rumours about her were true. And if they were, then how long had she known and what had been the signs, the very first signs? And did her parents know, and how did she tell them, and were they handling it or were they falling apart? She didn't ask though. Of course not.

'I'm sorry,' Katie said. 'You have to get back to work. I should go.'

'You say sorry a lot.' Simona's sandalled foot slid forward and tapped Katie's boot. 'Why's that?'

Katie's chest constricted. It was suddenly hard to breathe. 'I don't know.'

'Probably not a good habit to get into.'

A sandal and a boot. Bang, bang.

'I'm not saying *never* apologize,' Simona said, 'because the letter's kind of sweet and I appreciate you bothering to come here and explain, but you should be careful you don't end up saying sorry for who you are, if you know what I mean . . .'

Katie feigned fascination with the street, the trees beyond, the glitter of the tower blocks in the distance. Simona's sandal was rapping on her boot and it felt like a test. She was completely aware of it. What did it mean? Was she supposed to do something, say something? Simona would probably deny all knowledge. *My foot knocking yours? You think that means anything? Are you crazy? That's just a coincidence.*

There was silence again. Rounds of it, like a boxing match.

Simona said, 'Do you fancy a coffee?'

'I thought you were shut.'

'I don't mean here.'

Katie flicked her a look and Simona smiled that slow smile again. And it was like Katie's eyes got snagged and she couldn't look away.

'I can't.'

'Why not?'

'My mum's really strict. I told her I was just going for a walk.'

'So, tell her you're just going for a coffee.'

Something's going to happen, Katie thought, *if I say yes.*

It was like an energy building, the two of them looking and all the seconds ticking between them.

Katie looked away first. 'I have to get back. If I'm late home, it'll really stress my mum out.'

'I would've thought your mum was nicely distracted with your grandmother the way she is. I would've thought she wasn't actually taking much notice of you at all. Maybe you just think she is?' Tap, tap went Simona's foot again. 'Maybe you're just looking for an excuse?'

Blood washed up from Katie's chest to her neck to her face. She had to get out of there, had to get home. She'd been an idiot. Why had she written a letter asking if she could come to the café more often? She should have written one pledging never to return. 'She relies on me. I couldn't do it to her.'

'Do what? Be yourself?'

'Let her down.'

'Well, that's that then.' Simona folded the letter and put it in her pocket. 'I just thought you might like to talk.'

'I can't. Sorry.'

'Apologizing again?' Simona grinned as she opened the café door. 'You really want to stop doing that.' She went through the door and shut it behind her. She walked back to the counter, picked up a cloth and returned to cleaning the coffee machine.

Katie ran. She didn't look back, not even a glance. She ran across the road. The lovely road. Away from the café. She ran along the pavement. Cars swept past. A group of people walked into the pub. A late-night corner shop was still open and its lights winked at her. She ran faster, putting distance between her and Simona. She ran until her lungs were screaming with the rush of sharp air. All the way home.

Mum was sitting at the kitchen table with a cup of tea and the open suitcase. 'Well?' she said. 'Nice walk?'

She didn't seem mad that Katie was late. She was clearly making an effort. What could Katie tell her? Not the truth. *I went to deliver a letter to Simona Williams who, incidentally, is a lesbian and who asked me out for coffee.*

'So,' Mum said, 'I've been looking through some of this stuff.'

Katie stood in the doorway and stared at her mother and all she could think was – *coffee is a euphemism. In every movie and book, people never mean coffee.* And why did that knowledge make her pulse speed? She thought Mum might be able to tell just by looking, and she didn't want to walk into that warm kitchen and sit opposite her mum's sleepy face and destroy the rest of her life. So she made some excuse about how she was tired and maybe they could talk tomorrow.

Mum didn't say anything, but Katie could tell she was disappointed. It's not what she expected. Chris was supposed to be the moody one and Mary was supposed to be the one who was always leaving. Katie was the good one, the one who helped, the reliable one who could cope with anything.

Good old Katie, that was her.

Twenty-one

Fantasizing about members of the same sex does not necessarily mean you're gay. Straight people often have same-sex fantasies. But fantasizing mostly about members of the same sex is a pretty strong indication that you lean primarily in that direction.

Katie deleted her browsing history, slapped her laptop shut and looked out of Mary's bedroom window. Correction – *her* bedroom window. It looked pretty mundane out there – grass, litter, other people's windows. No drama. Nothing much to see.

Surely it was just that Katie didn't know any boys? She'd had two kisses in her whole life. The one with Esme had been far more meaningful and passionate than the one with Jamie, but that was probably because of their friendship. If Katie's best friend had been called Eric instead of Esme, then Katie would probably have kissed him just as ardently. Nothing to do with gender at all. Although, that didn't explain why she'd spent all morning thinking about Simona . . .

Katie knew from biology that to keep a memory you have to keep *having* the memory, using it, revisiting it, so that the neurons become imprinted. When Mary had her own stories told back to her, she eventually found them easier to access by herself. So neuron behaviour also explained why Katie was being haunted by

Simona. If she wanted to forget about her, she had to *stop* reliving last night's conversation over and over.

Katie moved away from the window and over to the wall. Maybe she could do some more work on it? That would be nicely distracting. It was building up – several photos of everyone now, each with a name card above them. The map of Bisham was new, allowing Katie to plot their morning walks to see if there was any logic to Mary's wandering. So far, the only constant was the café. Katie traced the most direct route with her finger. Approximately one and a half kilometres. She wondered if Simona was working today. She wondered if Simona would text or call now she had Katie's mobile number.

No, this kind of thinking was not helpful! She unlocked her mobile and texted Jamie: YES. It was the second time he'd asked to meet. A walk in the park would be lovely and it was the quickest way to kill the synaptic connections between her and Simona.

Now all she needed was something to wear on a date with a boy. Katie went to the wardrobe and rifled through some of the clothes Mary had given her. The tea dress was her current favourite – moss green with pink rosebuds – a perfect combination of sexy but sedate. She crept across the landing to borrow Mum's button jar and sewing box and spent the next hour mending a rip at the seam, a small tear on the hem and covering a button and stitching it on. She spent ages watching YouTube videos on fifties and sixties fashion and was just sorting through her very minimal eye shadow collection to see if she had a black eye liner (Audrey Hepburn's eyes were smoking hot) when Mum opened the bedroom door. She opened it warily, like she was expecting someone else. 'Katie?' She shut the door quietly behind her. 'You've been up here a long time.'

She sounded disappointed. Katie scooped the makeup into its bag and zipped it shut. 'Sorry.'

'Look what I found in the suitcase.' Mum sat next to Katie on the bed and tentatively held out a photo. 'It's my parents' wedding – Pat and Lionel.'

Katie had never seen such a miserable-looking couple. They were standing outside a church, arms stoically linked. There was scaffolding up and all you could see of the church was the door and the edge of a window and it had clearly been raining, since the ground was pot-holed and puddled. Behind the bride and groom, a small group of guests stood in a bundle smiling grimly at the camera.

'See him?' Mum said. 'That's my granddad, and these two are relatives of Lionel's, though I don't remember them very well.'

It was the saddest wedding in the world. Everyone looked dour and old. Except . . . Katie leaned closer . . . a baby, wrapped up in a blanket and held in one of the old women's arms was laughing! The only bit of life in the picture. She was reaching out a fat baby hand for something beyond the frame of the photo. Maybe the trees were waving in the wind and she was waving back.

'Is that baby you?'

Mum nodded. She looked pleased to be recognized.

'You don't look like you belong to them. Look at you – all joyful, while they're all frowning. You're laughing like Mary does. You look just like her.'

'Is that right?'

Mum's voice held a warning, but it was ridiculous being offended at having similarities pointed out. 'Weren't you even a little bit pleased to discover Mary was your real mother?'

'Pleased? What sort of question is that? A total stranger turns up and flips my world on its head. Why would I be happy about it?'

Because Mary was lovely? Because Pat was a liar? Because it must've been difficult living with such dour and cantankerous-looking people? But Katie knew if she said that, Mum would walk out the door, so she smiled an apology instead. 'Can I keep the photo? I haven't got Pat or Lionel on the wall yet. Or your granddad.'

Mum shrugged. 'If you like.'

Katie knew Mum was staring at her as she found Blu-Tack and put the picture up. It made her feel uncomfortable. The photo was probably meant as a peace offering. Perhaps Mum thought if she handed it over, Katie would open up about last night and where she'd gone and why she'd got back late and run up to bed so quickly. Katie gave a quick glance over to her laptop to make sure it was shut. Yes, and her phone was locked.

'Have you been mending something?' Mum said. 'I see my sewing things are out.'

'I had a button missing.'

Mum picked up the tea dress and examined it. 'This isn't yours.'

'Mary gave it to me.'

'You brought clothes from the house as well as the suitcase?'

'Just a few things. She said I could have them.'

Mum sighed. 'You know, it kind of annoys me that you see only the good in Mary. You think the past is some kind of romantic story and it isn't like that at all.'

'What's it like then?'

'Why are you so fascinated?'

'It's my history, my inheritance.'

'Your inheritance?' Mum shook her head. 'I'd say that's ten pounds and your brother. Although I might chuck in my iPad if you're lucky.'

Mum was trying to lighten the mood, but it wasn't funny. Katie hated it when Chris got handed over like that. It made the future lie flat, as if it was completely predictable. Much as Katie loved him, she didn't want Chris shadowing her life, making sure she had to be sensible and well-behaved for ever. She moved over to the desk and sat on the chair. She could hear kids playing football out in the ball court. Their shouts echoed off the walls of the flats. She swivelled the chair closer to her mother and plonked her feet on the bed, making it bounce. She knew Mum thought she'd done it on purpose, but she hadn't.

'Do you remember when I did that project at primary school, Mum? The one where I had to draw a family tree? Dad told me Pat drowned and then you walked into the room and got upset. You even wrote a letter of complaint to the school. I ended up imagining all sorts, probably worse than anything that really happened. All these years later, I still know nothing about my own family.'

They stared at each other. For one appalling moment, Katie thought her mum was about to cry. But she took her glasses off and rubbed them with her skirt instead. 'What exactly do you want to know?'

All of it. Every detail of every person from every year. But Katie knew that was pushing it. 'Why did Mary show up on your doorstep when you were nine? She'd had your address for years and never used it. Why then?'

'I don't know why. To this day I haven't a clue.'

'You never asked?'

'I was a child. I wasn't going to sit down and interview everyone.' Mum put her glasses back on and peered at Katie over the top of them. 'I've always assumed she was busy getting on with her career and just happened to be passing by that day.'

'Did she just knock on the door and announce herself?'

'No, she came up to me in the street.'

'Pat wasn't there?'

'She was indoors. Kids played in the street in those days.'

'So, Mary just walked up to you and said, "Hi, guess who I am?"'

'Of course not.' Mum smiled wearily. 'Listen, Katie, if I tell you what happened, that's the end of it, OK? No more meddling in the past after this.'

That was a terrible deal, but Katie nodded anyway. She didn't want to scare Mum off, didn't want her knowing it wouldn't be the end of it at all. Mum was like a bird on a lawn. Any sudden movement and she'd be frightened away.

Mum brushed at her skirt, picking off imaginary fluff. 'Well, I was living here in North Bisham, as you know. And I was happy, I really was. I had a mum and a dad and a house and garden and friends. I think that's why I wanted to live back here – to try and capture that happiness again. Stupid, really . . .

'Anyway, it was the summer holidays and I was out playing with the rest of the kids from the street when we heard the ice-cream van and we all ran indoors to beg our mothers for sixpence. But my mum was lying on the sofa with a flannel across her forehead and the curtains drawn and I knew I shouldn't wake her. So I went back outside and sat on the gatepost and watched my friends queue up at the van and wander off with their Zooms or Treble Hits or whatever and felt very sorry for myself.

'About five minutes later, a lady appeared. I didn't see where she came from, but she seemed to materialize as the van drove off and she stood right in front of me and smiled and said, "Hello, Caroline." And she was just so pretty – young and glamorous and so unlike anyone I'd ever met, that instead of asking how she knew my name, or being suspicious in any way, I said hello back.'

Katie shifted forwards on her chair. 'Why did you think she was glamorous? What was she wearing?'

'Oh, she looked so modern. All the kids were staring. We were used to our mothers, who wore aprons and slippers and had scarves over their curlers as they went about their housework, but this woman looked like she'd walked off a movie screen with her bobbed hair and slacks.

'She told me she'd come to take me for ice cream at the coffee bar at the end of the street. I asked her if my mother knew and she leaned in and whispered, "Does she have one of her headaches today?" I nodded, amazed that she knew both my name and this very private thing about my mother. "Well," she said, "then she won't miss us." So I hopped off the gatepost and took her hand. I remember feeling so special as we walked past all the other kids – chosen, I suppose. A boy asked who she was and I didn't know what to tell him, but Mary turned to him and smiled and guess what she said?'

Katie shook her head, her heart at her throat.

'She told him she was my fairy godmother. And do you know, I actually believed her.'

Katie could imagine that – both that Mary would say it (she'd love the drama) and that Mum would believe it. Poor little nine-year-old Mum. And it was odd, because although Katie knew this story was going to end badly, she also felt sorry for everyone in it. Pat was the villain (although neither Mum nor Mary seemed able to admit this out loud), but she wasn't evil – just a misguided woman who'd been desperate to keep a child she'd fallen in love with and have a different kind of life.

'The coffee bar had recently opened,' Mum went on, 'and it wasn't a place my mother would ever have taken me. It had a jukebox and little booths with Formica tables and it sold milkshakes and coffee and snacks. It also sold ice-cream sundaes and I'd admired the pictures in the window lots of times.

'I made that ice cream last for ages. Every single mouthful was delicious. Mary told me wonderful things about London – about plays she'd been in and parties she'd been to.'

'Plays?' Katie sat up straighter. 'She got to be an actress after all?'

'Only in rep. Small-town stuff. She never made it to the silver screen.'

'But it was her dream. It was the thing Pat and her dad banned her from doing and she got it anyway. That's amazing.'

Mum scowled. 'I knew you'd be like this – all delighted that Mary got what she wanted, and never mind the cost to anyone else . . .'

Katie gave Mum an apologetic smile. She didn't want her stomping off downstairs and not finishing the story. It *was* amazing though. And ironic that Mary won more freedom by being pregnant and disgraced than she'd ever gained by being well-behaved. 'So, when did Mary tell you she was your real mum?'

'She didn't. I only found that out when I got home.'

'Pat told you?'

'She was on the doorstep when we got back and saw us coming up the street. I got my legs slapped for going off with a stranger and Mary got the door slammed in her face. It was only because she started calling through the letterbox that my mum let her in. I was sent to my room, but I crept out and stood on the landing.' Mum ran her hands through her hair, pulling it into a ponytail, then letting it go. It wasn't a gesture Katie had ever seen her do before and it made her look young. 'There was a lot of shouting. My mum was afraid Mary had come to take me away. She said that just because Mary gave birth to me, it didn't mean she could have me back.'

216

'That's how you found out? You overheard?'

Mum nodded. 'I overheard a lot of things that day. They weren't very discreet. I didn't understand it all, but I certainly worked out that my mum was actually my auntie and had married my dad for convenience sake and was desperately unhappy. *Marriage isn't what I was expecting*, she said.

'Mary had a lot to say on that subject. She thought my mother's headaches were my dad's fault, that happiness was important, that divorce was no longer taboo, that my mother should get herself a job . . . oh, there was a whole list of things she thought my mum could do to improve her lot.

'My father turned up from work, but instead of calming things down, he joined in. He told Mary about my mother's funny turns, the amount of days she spent on the sofa and the amount of times he had to make his own tea. My mother started to cry and said she should never have married him. I remember thinking that Mary seemed able to make people say things they'd usually keep quiet about.

'Mary offered to take me away for a few days while they sorted themselves out, but my mother thought she'd never see me again if that happened, so Mary was told to leave. I watched her go from my bedroom window and it really was like she had magical powers, because even though I was hiding behind the curtain she waved up at me.'

Something melted inside Katie as she gazed at her mother. It was as if her eyes opened to something startling that had been right in front of her all along. 'Mary ruined everything by showing up, didn't she? No wonder you're mad at her.'

Mum smiled limply. 'It was certainly a difficult time.'

Even Mum and Dad breaking up hadn't been that dramatic. At least Katie had seen it coming and been old enough to cope, and she'd had Chris to share it with . . .

'How long until you saw her again?'

'Months. My parents separated and I went with my mother to live with my grandfather. I lost my friends and my father – and in many ways I lost my mother because her headaches got worse and she spent a lot of time in bed and my grandfather had to look after me. I got very close to him.'

'And did Pat realize you knew the truth? Did she know you overheard?'

Mum shook her head. 'I'll tell you something. I used to look for evidence. I wanted to find something conclusive, a photo or a letter or some kind of absolute fact in black and white which would prove I hadn't imagined it. I wanted to take it to Pat and say, *Tell me about Mary*, but despite rootling around in wardrobes and cupboards, I never found a single thing. All those letters you brought back yesterday would have been somewhere in that house, but I didn't see them. I guess when Pat died, Mary took them. Maybe she was trying to protect me from knowing I'd been stolen away.' Mum gave Katie a grim smile. 'It's just a pity she feels compelled to stir everything up now.'

'It was me who went looking for the suitcase, Mum. It's me that's been stirring things up.'

'She mentioned it to you though, didn't she? At the funeral. You went looking on purpose?'

'Only because she wants you to know how much she loves you, before she forgets.'

'Charming!'

Katie smiled. 'That didn't come out right.'

It was true though. Mary would forget everything one day. The pictures on the wall might help her remember names and faces, but they wouldn't help her remember who she loved.

'So what happened next?' Katie asked. 'Did Mary just show up again one day and take you to London?'

'What happened next was a girl at school told me my mother was a slut. I had no idea what that meant, but I knew it was bad, so I told Pat. She was mortified, and said something like, "I assure you she's not referring to me." I asked her if the girl meant Mary and Pat looked at me in such shock that I realized I'd finally let slip I'd overheard. I was glad though – at least I didn't have to pretend any more.'

'It was my granddad who sat me down and told me the story. Mary had been very naughty having a baby without a husband, he said. She hadn't been able to cope and Pat and Lionel had stepped in to save the day. When Mary ran off, they thought she was never coming back and so it was agreed I'd become Pat's little girl.'

That was a terrible version of the truth and Katie bit her lip so she didn't slag off Mum's granddad. OK, he had a dead wife and a broken heart, but he'd refused to talk to Mary when she had the baby. He'd called her a slut and told her to leave and he let his other daughter marry some prehistoric mate of his. In fact, Katie's great granddad could be the new villain. She flicked a look at his photo – grim, unsmiling, dressed in a million layers of tweed. Yeah, he looked the part.

'Mary was allowed to visit now I officially knew,' Mum went on, 'but her visits always upset the household for days. My granddad would sit in another room and refuse to talk or share a meal and Pat would go brittle like she disapproved of everything and Mary would be oblivious. She'd swan in with her fancy presents, looking gorgeous, stay a few hours and then disappear for weeks. If I wore a dress she'd bought me or read one of the books she gave me, I'd get frowned at by Pat and tutted at by Granddad, and so I started keeping them secret and I'd get them out and look at them when no one was there. I used to long for her visits and dread them at the same time.'

'How long did this go on for?'

'I was twelve when she finally took me away - so she'd been visiting for a couple of years.'

'Why did she take you away?'

'Pat was ill.'

'What was wrong with her?'

'No, Katie – you asked what happened when Mary showed up and I've told you. All you need to know is that my place should have been with Pat, and instead they let Mary take me away and it was awful. A total disaster. Honestly, I can't talk about it, Katie, I'm sorry. There's not much more to the story. I stayed nearly two years with Mary in London – it took that long for Pat to get better – and it was a nightmare. I was very glad to get away from the city and back home where I belonged.' She laughed without humour. 'Living with your fairy godmother isn't quite as glamorous as you might think.'

And that was all Katie was getting. It boiled down to Mary showing up out of the blue and a little girl's world being smashed apart. But why did she show up? She'd got the address from the detective years before and decided not to use it. She'd fervently believed her child was better off with two parents and then she'd changed her mind.

Katie shut her eyes and concentrated on the pink glow the sun made on her eyelids. If she could turn back time, would it be best not to have found the suitcase? Mum wouldn't have discovered Pat broke the contract, Katie wouldn't have written Simona an idiotic letter. They'd all go back to last week, when life was simpler – Mum happily thinking Mary hated her, Mary happily wandering about not remembering much, Katie not yet making a fool of herself running through the dark to the café. Ah! Even thinking about it made her want to hide her face.

She opened her eyes suddenly. 'What ice cream did you order?'

Mum looked puzzled. 'Why?'

'Mary asked me to find out the recipe for a knickerbocker glory the other day. She said you loved them.'

'Really? I'm surprised she remembers.'

'It *was* a knickerbocker glory?' Katie scrabbled off the chair in excitement. 'That's where she's trying to get to every day – the coffee bar she took you to.'

'She'll be lucky. It's been gone for years.'

'She doesn't know that though, does she?' Katie went over to the Bisham map. 'What was your road called?'

'Victory Avenue. But they changed all the names when they built the bypass. A lot of houses got knocked down.'

'She mentioned Victory Avenue the first morning she was here. Was it number twenty-three?'

'How do you know that?'

'She wrote it on the sofa. It took me ages to get the mark out.' Katie traced the route to the café with her finger again. 'Here it is – Park Avenue. There's a café we go to. Mary loves it. We always end up there. I bet you a million pounds it used to be the coffee bar. It's opposite the library – do you know the one I mean? Is that near where you used to live?'

Mum looked uncertain. 'Mary wouldn't remember. It was years ago. She only visited once.'

Katie thought back to all her morning wanderings with Mary. Something was nagging at her, something important. Mary claimed to recognize loads of places in Bisham – the railway station, the park, the cemetery. Katie had always thought she was just confused. But what about the day Mary left the flat before anyone was

221

awake and knocked on that woman's door? Was that random? It was the day they'd gone to the café for the first time. They'd walked for ages afterwards and ended up outside the primary school. Mum had to rescue them because Mary was utterly felled by being there. It was like when she sun downed at night – like she was taken over by ghosts.

Now it made sense!

Katie sat on the bed and scooped her mum's hand up in her own. 'Mary knocked on a woman's door once, claiming Pat lived there. I didn't tell you because I knew you'd freak. Mary said she watched the place from the café window. The woman thought Mary was nuts, but what if Mary was re-enacting something she used to do years ago? What if she used to get the train and go to the coffee bar and sit watching your house? What if she didn't just come to Bisham once, Mum, but loads of times? Think about it – it makes perfect sense. She even recognizes the school you would've gone to when you were a kid. The day she actually showed herself to you was because you were the only one without an ice cream and she couldn't bear it. How else did she know your mum used to lie on the sofa with headaches? She'd been peering through the windows, watching you for years! That detective gave her the address when you were a baby, and all that time she'd been checking you were safe, not interfering, allowing Pat to get on with it. She didn't mean you to find out who she was that day, but Pat saw you and the whole thing blew apart.'

Mum often looked as if she was out of reach. Even if you tied a rope to her and reeled her in, she'd probably stick her foot in the door and refuse to get close. But now she gazed at Katie with an open and vulnerable expression.

'So you think when she had a day off at the theatre or something, she used to come here?'

222

Katie laughed. 'Yes! I think you had your very own fairy god-mother watching you after all.'

'So when she runs off every morning, she's not actually trying to get away from me?'

'She's trying to *find* you, Mum. She wants to sit in that café and watch her little girl. It's like an ancient memory pattern or some-thing. It's totally awesome!'

Katie had a sudden desire to hug her mum, to nudge her nose into the space between Mum's chin and shoulder. It'd been years since she'd done it, but she remembered the warmth and comfort of it from when she was much younger, and she'd feel like a small creature, a baby bat or a mouse – totally taken care of and completely approved of.

But Mum stood up and brushed at her skirt. 'Right, well I better go and see what's going on downstairs.'

How could she shove her feelings away like that?

'And you should be getting on with your personal statement, shouldn't you, Katie, instead of faffing around with musty old clothes?'

Her beautiful softness had gone. It was like watching someone come out of their house to sunbathe for a second and then dash back inside and slam the door.

PART TWO

Twenty-two

The memory game was getting dangerous. Today's category was: blue blank, and it was going to hurt. Blue meant sad. Blank meant forgotten, Mary knew that much. She also knew there was no avoiding it. The day was approaching when memories would slip through her so quickly that she'd only be able to stare at the space where they'd been. She'd be in nappies by then. Drooling. Silent . . .

She knows it involved a garden.

She knows there was a fox calling in the dark, and somewhere at the top of some stairs a child cried and cried.

Hunting for a memory is like peering through fog. You know it's there, but you're not sure if it's friendly or terrifying or even of this world and it keeps moving about. You catch glimpses, tantalizing fragments. She remembers a baby, for instance – sleep warm, milk and powder, the smoothness of skin, the weight in her lap. Then it is gone, whisked away and replaced by a crowd of people staring down at her.

What's this picture now?

Come on, Mary, you can do it. Think, woman, think!

She's in a railway station, is that right? When you are old, people often look through you, but now their attention is upon her. She feels their hot, pitying gaze.

Someone says, 'Her breathing's very rapid. You think she needs an ambulance?'

I am sitting in a railway station and there are people looking at me.

'It could be a panic attack.'

And somewhere in a garden, a blackbird trills and somewhere a child weeps.

'Or a shock. Sometimes a shock causes this reaction. Is she with anyone? Does anyone know her?'

'Jack,' Mary says. 'Jack knows me.'

But no one seems to know Jack. They take her to hospital instead, just for one night. She is cold, so cold that they wrap her in silver foil and she's sick in a bucket. It takes her hours to warm up. Hypothermia on such a warm evening. How did she manage that?

She has no idea. She has to sit here in this memory and see what happens next.

What happens next is a woman appears in front of her holding a plate of biscuits. 'Did you take your tablets?'

'Are you a nurse?'

'No, I'm not.'

'Are you real?'

'Yes, extremely real. Now, did you take them or not?'

A blink and the hospital has gone. A blink and the terror abated.

A quiet breath in and out and Mary found herself on a sofa in a lounge.

The woman with the biscuits was still there. She said, 'Did you hide the tablets again? Is that what happened?'

The best policy in such situations was to keep quiet and pretend you hadn't heard. Mary took a sip of the tea that had appeared in front of her and avoided eye contact.

228

'Are they down here?' The woman held the plate out of reach and slipped her hand down the edge of the chair. First one side, then the other. 'Thought so.' She showed Mary two white blobs congealing on her palm. 'What are these?'

'No idea. They're not mine.'

'Then who do they belong to?'

'Not me, I assure you. Now, how many of those biscuits are for me?'

'All of them if you take these tablets.'

'I'm not touching those. You found them down the side of the chair.'

The woman tutted. 'They're perfectly fine. Just swallow them.'

'They'll hurt my head.'

'The doctor said they might do that for a bit, but then they'll stop.'

'I don't want them to do it at all.'

Mary reached for a biscuit, but the woman held the plate higher, as if Mary was a child and this woman was in charge – holding things out of reach because little fingers mustn't touch and little ears mustn't listen and little girls mustn't climb trees or kiss boys, but must sit in chairs and keep safe.

'Bugger off,' Mary said. She liked how it sounded. 'Bugger off, missus, why don't you? I want the other one. What have you done with her?'

'You mean Katie?'

'That's it. Sweet little girl with the red hair.' She stabbed a finger at this officious woman. 'No one's taking her away again, I tell you that for nothing.'

'Christ! I give up. This is ridiculous, this charade every day.'

The woman stalked off, slamming the lounge door behind her. She thought she was in charge, that was why. It was no good trying to make friends with her either. If you took her hand, she'd snatch it back. If you reached out to stroke her face, she'd shake you off. She was never relaxed, always rushing everywhere. If she kept bossing people around and never sitting down for even a minute, she'd have a heart attack. She should be careful.

Ah, who was this, coming now? What a beautiful face on her.

'You need to take your tablets, Mary.'

'Someone else just told me that.'

The girl laughed. 'We have to get to the café. It's sunny, really lovely. You, me and Chris are going together.'

'That sounds wonderful. Shall I get my bag?'

'I don't think Mum's going to let us go anywhere until you take your tablets. She's out in the kitchen crushing them up and then she's going to hide them in a chocolate biscuit. But, hey, maybe they'll taste better like that?'

Mary smiled at the girl. She looked particularly beautiful this morning, as if she was tipping towards something lovely. 'And then we'll go to the café?'

'That's right. And see if there's anything on the menu you haven't tried yet.'

'And talk to the waitress you like.'

The girl gave her a startled look. *Yes*, Mary thought, *I see you. I see your fire and heat, don't think that I don't.*

'Anyway,' the girl said, 'Chris is coming with us today, so things might be a bit different. But we'll sit at your favourite table and you can still wave at people who walk by and chat to everyone.'

'Perhaps Jack will be there,' Mary said. 'Perhaps we'll see Caroline.'

'All things are possible, Mary.'

'And you're coming with me, aren't you? You're special, anyone can see that. You have the face of an angel.'

'Do I?' The girl's eyes shone with laughter. 'I wish other people could see what you see, Mary.'

The woman came back with only a single biscuit on a plate and a sullen boy at her side.

'Why do I have to do what they want?' the boy said. 'Why can't I decide what I do?'

'Stop fussing,' the woman said. 'I'm sure you'll have a nice time when you get there.'

'Not in a stupid café I won't.'

'Please, Chris, don't do this to me now.' The woman handed the plate to the girl. 'You try.'

The girl stroked Mary's cheek. 'This is a special biscuit and you need to eat it. It's the only way for us to get out of here. Would you like to give it a go?'

Mary found her hand, curled their fingers together. 'You want to share it?'

'No, it's all for you.'

'Well, you're very generous, thank you very much. I asked that lady there for a biscuit just now, but she wouldn't give me one at all.'

Katie's heart lurched with pity. Every morning it was the same, like some kind of ghastly comedy sketch. She hated the whole ritual of it. She hated the way Mum stood over poor Mary, insisting and insisting.

Why was it so important to take the stupid tablets anyway? The consultant had said they 'might' slow down the progression of the disease, but he'd also said it was impossible to accurately diagnose Mary in the first place. She 'probably' had vascular dementia, she 'almost certainly' had Alzheimer's. He'd been pretty clueless.

He showed them the CT scan, pointed to some black smudges

231

with the tip of his pen and said Mary had plaques in her brain. It was about the only thing he was certain about. He used the analogy of a forest – one day a tree crashes to the ground and bang, the recipe for lasagne you've known for years falls out of your head. The next day a different tree silently collapses and bang, the memory of your first kiss disappears for ever. Eventually Mary would forget how to use the toilet, how to walk, how to eat. Until, one day, the forest became a wasteland and she forgot how to breathe.

'Silent, deadly and irreversible,' the consultant said.

It was the worst analogy in the world and he was the worst doctor. Would the tablets stop the trees falling down? No. Would new trees get planted? No. All the tablets 'might' do was slow down the process of deforestation. The tablets might have side effects as well – headaches, nausea, diarrhoea, insomnia, loss of appetite, lethargy. Like Mary needed anything else to put up with.

Mum seemed to think it was all totally worth it. She'd even mentioned Mary's irregular sleep patterns to the doctor and let him prescribe sleeping pills and anti-depressants, although he'd advised saving them for later, once the main tablets kicked in.

That still hadn't happened though. If anything, the tablets appeared to make Mary worse. She was often tired. She seemed slower, sadder. She said her head was 'all muddled' and sometimes she seemed to have no purpose beyond sitting in the chair. It took ages to get her up and ready and out of the flat these days.

Mum was late for work nearly every morning, which was probably why she was looking so anxious now, picking up her bag and groping about in it for her purse. 'Stay together, the three of you, won't you? And here you go – subsistence money.'

Thirty quid! Mum wasn't going to be able to keep that amount up every day of the summer holidays.

'Right,' Mum said, snapping her purse shut. 'Do as your sister tells you, Chris, OK?'

'How come she's in charge?'

'We discussed this. You know the deal.'

'But there's somewhere I want to go.'

Why was nothing easy? Katie wanted him in a good mood today, she needed a favour. 'Where do you want to go?' she asked.

He tapped his nose. 'It's a secret.'

Katie smiled, despite herself. 'Well, I like secrets. Maybe we can go together later, how about that?'

'Cool! I'll get my stuff.' He rushed off, slamming out of the lounge and up the stairs.

'Don't let him do anything stupid,' Mum said. 'And keep in touch with me at all times.'

'When will you be home?'

'I've already told you.'

'Tell me again.'

'Christ, don't you start forgetting everything I say as well! Six thirty. And remember to get stuff for supper. The list's in the kitchen along with the sun cream.'

'You don't expect me to cook as well, do you?'

'Well, if you get time, that'd be great, but if not, don't worry.' Mum laughed, as if she was being totally generous, when actually she'd probably be disappointed if there was nothing bubbling away in the oven when she got home.

When Mum had rung school and confirmed Katie was doing her work experience being a carer, she doubted the Head of Year realized it would turn into a long-term job. Katie didn't actually mind – she had no other plans for the summer holidays anyway, but now Chris was off school and part of the care package, was it fair that she was supposed to make supper as well?

Katie curled her fists into two neat balls as she followed her mother down the hallway and watched her grope with the mortise lock. She looked so desperate to get away that Katie thought she was going to leave without saying goodbye, but at the very last second, she turned in the doorway.

'I couldn't do this without you,' she said. 'I'm deeply grateful.' She leaned in and kissed the top of Katie's head. 'You're my good girl.'

Which showed how much she knew.

Twenty-three

Here's what happened, exactly how it went.

A week after Katie gave her the letter, Simona said, 'I wondered when you two were going to show up again. I was beginning to miss you.' She took their order and served it. Over the course of the morning, she threw an occasional smile in Katie's direction. When she brought their second tray of drinks, she leaned in and whispered in Katie's ear. 'You sure it's Mary who wants to sit here all day, and not you?'

Heat rose in Katie like mercury. And she knew Simona saw it because she smiled that slow smile of hers, and Katie's heart beat so fast she thought she might die at her feet.

The next day, Simona said, 'Can't keep away, can you?'

And Katie wanted her to understand that she was here for Mary, not for herself, so she told Simona about Victory Avenue – how Mary used to be an actress, and every time she had a day off she'd get on a train and sit in this café to watch over the daughter who lived across the road. And Simona really listened. She listened so hard, she pulled up a chair and sat down.

Mary couldn't recall the plays she'd been in when Simona asked her, but she was so charmed to have the waitress sit with them that she took hold of Simona's hand. 'Funny ones. Popular ones.'

'A different play each week?'

'That's it,' Mary said. 'All over the place.'

'Repertory theatre,' Simona said. 'I did my drama project on that.'

Katie watched their hands, all her attention focused on the way Simona smoothed her thumb across Mary's palm and she noticed (not for the first time) that Simona wore a thumb ring and that she had long slender fingers, unlike Katie's fat sausage ones, and could probably be a surgeon or a pianist if she wasn't interested in going off to do drama and English at university in four months' time.

'But only if I get an A and two Bs.'

'I'm sure you will,' Mary said (still holding her hand). 'You seem so lovely and clever.'

Simona laughed. 'I should get back to work. But we'll talk again later, yeah?'

It went on like that for days. Katie worried that someone would see her. Kids in her year were doing their work experience in shops and offices in town. She saw people she recognized everywhere, especially at lunch time as they walked back to the flat – the grass opposite the café, the benches outside Lidl, the steps of the library, hanging around the market stalls. She imagined the gossip if Amy or any of that lot noticed – *Katie Baxter's still going to that café every morning, even though she's got a boyfriend. Yeah, she's obviously two-timing him. It's so disgusting. Can you imagine what her and that dyke get up to?*

It would be easier to stay in bed, to draw the duvet up and tell her mum that she was sick, she had a fever and couldn't possibly look after Mary any more.

Jamie's texts didn't help. He thought the walk in the park had been 'LVLY'. He thought the coffee they'd had together was 'GRT'. But would she be free to go to the arts centre one afternoon next week? There was a film on he thought she might like. She told him yes because she couldn't bear to tell him no. She knew how being told no felt. She wasn't sure when, though. She'd let him know. Because if Mary wanted to go to the café all the time and Mum was paying Katie to take her, what spare time did she have?

Simona joined them for a few minutes each day. She said her boss didn't mind, that good customer relations were all part of the service. She started putting a reserved sign on one of the outside tables, so Mary could smoke. Then one day as they arrived at the café, Simona said, 'Got something for you.' Katie thought for one startling moment that she meant something for her, but no, she had a book for Mary about theatre in the fifties and sixties. She'd sent off for it and it was Mary's to keep. It was mostly pictures, Simona said, so why didn't she sit with them and they could look through it together?

Mary turned the pages and Simona talked about different theatres and different plays and how actors received four pounds a week, and digs cost two pounds with all the food and laundry thrown in and how most actors did a different show every week and only got Sundays and Mondays off.

Mary listened as if she was falling under a spell. Katie too sat completely tongue-tied. She couldn't stop looking at Simona's long brown legs, her gaze travelling down them to her sandals and the purple nail varnish and the ankle bracelet with little silver beads.

'I remember the audience always laughed,' Mary said. 'And they always clapped very loudly.'

She went on to tell them about the men who waited for her at the stage door each night, and how she was always being invited out to dinner, and how one young man kept buying her roses and how one of the others demanded he take his roses away and when the first man refused, the second man invited him to roll up his sleeves and sort things out and they both got bloody noses.

'Noses instead of roses,' she chuckled.

They all laughed at that and Mary beamed with delight because she loved being funny. Then she asked if she could cut out the pictures in the book and Simona said, 'Sure,' and got her some scissors.

'We have a wall,' Katie said, as Simona sat back down, 'in my bedroom, where we stick important stuff. If Mary sees the same thing over and over, it helps her remember. That's why we come here so much.'

'Is that right?' Simona's slow smile drew light and dark into Katie's belly at once. 'And there's me thinking I was the main attraction.'

Neither of them looked away. Katie felt as if she was plummeting downhill and nothing was stopping her. She found herself saying, 'Can I ask you something?'

And the whole café seemed to slow down and go suddenly silent. The people at other tables faded into the background like they do in movies when someone's stopped time. Even Mary blurred at the edges. Only Katie and Simona had definition or focus.

'Are the rumours about you true?'

Simona's eyes brightened with laughter. 'What rumours are we talking about?'

'What they say about you at school.'

'What do they say?'

Heat rose in Katie again. She was flushed with it. 'Never mind.'

Simona was nearly eighteen, soon to be out of here. Katie was only just seventeen, shipwrecked for another year with no way out. When Simona went off to university, which she was bound to do, Katie would be immersed in gossip – the only one left, the only one to be stared at and scorned.

Simona said, 'I think it might be time for that chat we never had, don't you?'

Katie wanted to say, *What chat?* But she knew it would sound like a lie, so she kept quiet.

Simona leaned closer. Katie could feel the warmth build along her right arm – through her cardigan and her dress, until it bloomed on her skin.

'I tell you what,' Simona said. 'I'll make it easy for you. You get to ask me three questions and I promise I'll answer truthfully.'

She stood up and started collecting the plates and Katie thought maybe the offer wasn't on now. Maybe you had to answer quickly or things got cancelled. The café spun back into life. Mary turned a page of her book, tea cups wobbled, somewhere a phone chirruped.

'What kind of questions?' Katie's voice sounded hoarse.

'Whatever you can think of.'

'When?'

'Whenever you're ready.'

Twenty-four

Now. She was ready now. It was all arranged.

Katie put ten pounds on the table in front of Chris. 'Wages for one hour, OK?'

'You're not supposed to leave me. Mum said not to.'

'You'll be fine. All you have to do is sit here and keep Mary company. If you want anything else from the menu, just order and I'll pay when I get back.'

'Where are you going?'

Mary snapped her scissors merrily. 'Off for an adventure with all that beautiful hair.' She'd finished her coffee and cake and was cutting out pictures from Simona's book again. 'I would if I were you. I'd run like the wind.'

Chris frowned. 'Why can't we come?'

'I won't be long. Don't do anything mad. I'll be back soon.'

He buried his face in his arms on the table and started doing his ragged breathing trick. A couple of people glanced over and Katie nearly changed her mind. The only reason she didn't was because if she didn't show up at the library garden in the next five minutes, Simona might come looking for her. She might insist on Katie asking the questions in the café. In front of an audience!

'Just do this for me, Chris, and I'll do whatever you want later, OK?'

'You won't.' He sat up and glared at her. 'I bet you a million pounds.'

'Why? What do you want to do?'

'See Dad.'

'You're right, I'm not letting you do that.'

Mary laughed. 'I'll take you. Who is it you want to see?'

Chris slumped back down again. 'I knew it. I knew today would be terrible.'

His voice was too loud for the café and Katie put her finger on her lips to let him know. 'I have to go. Drink your hot chocolate, Chris.'

'It's cold chocolate. It got cold really quickly.' He pushed the mug away, sloshing cream and milk across the table.

More people were looking – the old man at the corner table, a couple of women by the door. They were pretending not to, but they definitely were. Katie frowned at them before grabbing a napkin and mopping up the mess. 'You're just going to have to trust me on this one, Chris.'

'You sound like Mum.'

She leaned down and whispered, 'I never ask you to do anything. Please, just do this one thing for me?'

'You're not the boss.'

'No.'

'Stop telling me what to do.'

'OK, I'm going. Look after each other.'

As she walked away, Katie felt as if she was shrugging them off, as if she was turning into somebody else. She was wearing the Givenchy dress and she'd left her hair loose. She felt like a girl in a magazine.

Simona was sitting on a bench at the back of the library garden. She had her eyes closed and her face turned to the sun. The place

241

was empty, like a walled garden in a fairy tale. Light danced through leaves and dappled the grass.

Katie stood at the gate for minutes. She thought of all the things she knew about Simona now. The list was adding up. She worked in a café to save money for university. She wanted to be a theatre director. Katie had never seen her afraid. She was kind to Mary. She'd agreed to answer three questions truthfully. Katie wasn't sure what happened after three. Would she tell lies after that?

Katie opened the gate. Simona sat up blindly, briefly dazzled by the sun. She shaded her eyes as Katie walked over. It seemed a very long walk with Simona watching. Katie stood on the grass in front of her.

Simona said, 'Little black dress today, is it?'

'Mary wanted me to wear it.' Total lie, but Katie didn't want Simona to think she'd worn the most valuable dress in Mary's collection for her.

'I like your hair. It's better loose.'

Having Simona look at her outside the café was something else – too bold or too electric. Like an alarm.

'I haven't got long,' Katie said. 'My brother's sitting with Mary and he's a bit upset, so shall I just get on with it?'

Simona said nothing. She licked her lips and frowned.

'I wrote them down,' Katie said. She sat on the bench and opened her bag. She'd planned to say something about how long it had taken her last night to think of three really good questions and how she'd written a whole load at the back of Mary's memory book, how she'd divided them into two columns – safe and dangerous – and then ended up writing a stream of consciousness monologue which ended with the lines, *Why the pain? What's the deal? Is it wrong to feel this real?* But none of that felt appropriate now. The only way to manage this was to be efficient and business-like. Katie would only ask questions that Simona was expecting and she would definitely not ask any questions from the dangerous list. Actually, sitting here alone with Simona in the garden, even the safe questions seemed too much.

Katie said, 'OK, my first question is the one I asked you before. Are the rumours about you true?'

Simona sighed. 'That's your first question?'

Katie nodded very slowly.

'That's a total waste of a question. You already know the answer.'

'Rumours don't make something true.'

Simona shrugged. 'No smoke without fire.'

'That's rubbish. Some of the things people say about me are crap. Like the stuff about Esme, about me jumping her.'

'Oh? What wasn't true about that?'

'I didn't jump her. She was totally up for it.'

Simona laughed. 'I bet she was.'

What was that supposed to mean? Was she being ironic, like no one would want Katie to jump them because she was so ugly? Or was she being serious, like she could understand the attraction? And why was it so much harder to meet Simona's eyes now they were alone? At the café there was stuff to look at, other people around. Here, it was just the two of them and it made everything more exposed.

'All right, well, I'll scrap the first question.' Katie knew she sounded hostile. 'When did you first know?'

Simona didn't even hesitate. 'I was three years old. I fell in love with my nursery teacher. There were tell-tale signs every day after that.' She raised a jaunty eyebrow. 'Next question.'

'Do your parents know and, if they do, how did they find out?'

A tiny pause. Did she flinch? 'That's two questions.'

243

'They're related. They count as one.'

'OK. There was this girl, Anna, who I met when I was thirteen. We went to the same drama group and by fifteen we were going out. I never actually told my parents, but I didn't hide it either. I was sixteen when they finally sat me down and asked. I didn't deny it. There were tears – mostly because my mum was convinced she'd never have grandchildren, but I put her right on that and they were pretty cool once they got used to the idea. But Anna totally freaked out. She was terrified my parents would tell hers. She stopped speaking to me, left the group, wouldn't reply to mails or texts. Later, I heard she moved house, so I never saw her again. End of story. I found out the hard way that most people will go to ridiculous lengths to deny who they are.'

'What if Anna didn't know who she was?'

'Is that your last question?'

'No, it's just she might not have been certain.'

'What, you think maybe I jumped her?' Simona raised her eyebrow again and Katie smiled. She couldn't help it.

'You're very pretty when you smile,' Simona said.

Katie looked away, feigned interest in a spot at the end of the garden. She could hear her own heart hammering.

'Don't worry,' Simona said. 'It's just an observation.' She pulled up a clump of grass and sprinkled seeds on her lap, sifting through them as if she was looking for something.

'I've had a couple of dates with a boy,' Katie said. 'Just walking and coffee and stuff. I like him – he's funny and kind, but I don't . . . Oh, I don't know. It's hard to talk about.'

'You don't fancy him?'

'I think I say yes to the wrong stuff sometimes, you know what I mean? It's difficult to be certain about things. That's what I mean about your friend Anna – maybe she wasn't as sure

244

as you thought. Maybe, when her parents found out, she—'

'Believe me,' Simona said, cutting her off, 'she was very sure.' She pulled out another bunch of grass. Katie could hear the rustle of the stems, the dry earth resisting. She could hear the soft strim as Simona stripped the seeds. Why did everything sound so loud and so close? Katie's eyes travelled back across the garden to the gap between Simona's skirt and her T-shirt. Her skin was just visible.

Simona looked at her then. And the way her eyes fingered Katie's hair. She wasn't imagining that, was she?

Katie said, 'Teach me.'

Simona laughed, it fell out of her. 'Did you just say, *teach me*?'

'I want to be sure.' Katie's voice was a whisper, but she wasn't scared. Isn't this why she was here, why she'd come? All the dangerous questions were summed up in those two words. *Teach me*. Yes. It was exactly what she wanted. 'Teach me about love with a girl.'

Simona leaned against the back of the bench looking at Katie. 'You mean physically?'

Katie nodded, couldn't speak.

Seconds went by, minutes maybe, and then Simona narrowed her eyes like she'd decided something. 'Would it have to be a secret?'

'Yes.' Katie's voice was very quiet. How did Simona know what she was thinking?

'So, you want us to get together, but you wouldn't want anyone to know? No one at school, not Mary or your mum or anyone at the café. You want me to promise not to tell?'

'Yes please.'

Simona leaned in close, her breath hot on Katie's shoulder. 'The thing is,' she whispered, 'I'm not much good at secrets. I tend to let things slip. I might need to urgently hold your hand in the street, or smell your skin or suddenly sit right down on the pavement and lick your feet. How would that be?'

Fear saturated Katie's body. She knew Simona saw it, maybe even expected it, because her eyes hardened.

'This isn't something I pick up and put down.'

'I know that.'

'I'm not going to hide just so you can conduct your research.'

'You don't have to. I'll be the one who's hiding.'

Simona pointed to the road beyond the little gate. 'Look over there.'

'Look at what?'

'At the world over there. The shops, the people.'

'So?'

'So, they're just people. Most of them are idiots and none of them are worth cowering for.'

Katie didn't want her to do this. She'd felt so certain before and now Simona was spoiling it.

'Admit it,' Simona said. 'That was probably the worst idea you've ever had. Teach you! Ha! I mean, I can see you like hanging round with me and I can't say I blame you – I'm wildly attractive and in huge demand.' She raised an eyebrow self-mockingly. 'But I'm afraid I'm not able to make the necessary sacrifices.'

'OK, let's drop it.'

'No, let's not.' Simona held up a hand as if asking for silence. 'Lesson number one . . . you can't have the strawberries without the shit. There – you can have that bit of wisdom for free.'

Katie stood up, needed to get away. It was humiliating and embarrassing and she was an idiot. Had she really just asked Simona Williams to teach her? Her face was one hot flush of shame as she jogged towards the gate. Out there was the street. The café. Mary.

Chris. She'd take them home. She'd shut the doors and draw the curtains and never come outside again.

'Hey!' Simona came running up behind Katie, caught her arm and swung her round. 'Don't leave.'

'I have to get back to Mary.'

'She'll be all right for a minute.'

Katie didn't understand. Hadn't Simona just laughed at her? Hadn't she just suggested Katie was a total coward? So why was she pulling her towards the side of the library? It was shady, damp, hidden from the road.

'Let go of my arm, Simona.'

'I can't. My fingers are stuck.'

'Don't be ridiculous.'

'Serious. You're going to have to kick me or something.'

'Please let go. Where are you taking me?'

'I want to talk to you, come on.'

'There's nothing to say.'

'There's always something to say.'

But this didn't feel like talking as Katie found herself against the shadowed brick of the library wall. Simona let go of her arm and stood in front of her. 'Lesson number two – you're not as fragile as you feel.'

'What does that mean?'

'You might feel it, but that doesn't mean you *are* it.' Simona took a step forward. 'Believe me, I know what I'm talking about.'

Katie took a step back, but behind her was the wall of the library and there was nowhere else to go. 'Please, I need to leave.'

'Just listen for a minute. My mum cried loads when she found out about me. She'd come in my room and hold my hand and say nothing at all. She was adjusting, you know – giving up the daughter she thought she had and getting used to the new one. It was

247

really difficult for both of us and it wasn't that long ago. I do understand.'

'I'm not like you. If my mum did that, I'd crumble.'

'You might not.'

'I would. I'd completely deny everything. I'm rubbish at being brave.'

Simona smiled. 'You're very hard on yourself, aren't you?'

Katie looked away because Simona's smile was beautiful and it got her in the gut every time. She'd have to be strong and not look. She'd have to never go to the café again either. Maybe that nice woman whose door Mary knocked on would let them bring a thermos and sit on her lawn instead.

Simona said, 'I shouldn't've taken the piss, I'm sorry. It's just . . . well, it's tough being the only one with my hand up sometimes. It gets kind of lonely.'

Katie looked at her boots. She knew if their eyes met, she'd be trapped.

'I used to have this fantasy,' Simona said, 'that the head teacher would stand up in assembly and announce she's gay and all the kids and teachers who were sympathetic to how bloody hard it is to be different would stand up to support her. I wanted all the ones left sitting down to be in the minority. But I've left school now, so that's never going to happen, is it?'

Katie dared to look up. 'You think the head teacher's gay?'

'Definitely.' Simona took two more steps and stopped right in front of Katie. They were so close. Face to face, just standing there. Simona smiled that amazing smile of hers and Katie felt herself falling.

'What are you doing?' Katie whispered.

'Nothing. I thought it was you.'

'Don't do this.'

'What?' Simona said as she inched closer. 'What am I doing?'

Katie's back was against cool brick. Over Simona's shoulder, the little garden was bathed in sunshine. Beyond the wall was the road, the shops, the lunch-time traffic. But here they were out of sight, separate.

'I might have been a little hasty,' Simona said. 'I actually think I'd make a brilliant teacher.'

Every night Katie dreamed of her – her lips, the curve of her belly, the arc of her spine, her fingers, her smile.

Simona said, 'How about a taster session, see how we get on?'

Katie nodded. How could she resist? They were so close they were sharing air and it was so sheltered by the wall she felt as if she was asleep or had fallen through some kind of vortex to a world where things were hidden and private and no one would ever know.

'We can discuss the small print later,' Simona said. 'There's always a way around things.' She reached out and brushed Katie's cheek with the back of her hand, then she ran her fingers along the line of Katie's jaw to her neck and slowly across her bare shoulder.

Katie thought, *What is she doing? Where will this end up?*

It was like being sketched – down her arm to her hand, across the waistband of her dress to her other hand. She could feel Simona's breath on her face. She could smell the perfume she always wore – something warm and musky and familiar. Simona's eyes were brown, flecked with gold and she smiled as if she knew what Katie was thinking as her fingers travelled the path of Katie's shoulder and slowly climbed the back of her neck.

'Lesson number three,' Simona said as she closed her hand, tangling her fingers in Katie's hair. 'Dare to see yourself in your own future.' She pressed nearer, pushing Katie's shoulder blades against stone as their lips brushed. 'Dare to see all your possibilities laid out.'

There's no going back from this, Katie thought. Her shoulders rasped against the wall as their tongues met, as she wrapped her arms around Simona's waist and pulled her closer.

But then, in the middle of something so miraculous, came something terrifying – the creak of the gate, muffled footsteps.

'Someone's coming!'

'Don't worry,' Simona whispered. 'They'll go away again.'

Over Simona's shoulder a boy walked across the grass towards the bench.

'I know him!'

'Shh, keep still.'

But how could she? It was Lukas, and walking just behind him was Esme. He waited for her, took her hand. They continued towards the bench. They were going to sit down. And as soon as they did, they'd see Katie spread-eagled against the library wall with Simona pressed against her. There was nowhere to hide, nowhere else to go. Any second they'd look over, and how could this ever be made to look like anything other than what it was?

'I don't want them to see us. Please don't let them see us.'

'It's all right,' Simona said gently. 'They're only people. What can they do?'

Katie heard a noise in the back of her throat that didn't belong to her as she pushed Simona away. She didn't fall. It wasn't hard enough for that. It was a discreet, quiet shove that said, *Get off, go away, I don't want to be seen with you.*

Simona didn't even stumble. Lukas and Esme didn't even turn round. All that happened was that a strange darkness spilled from Simona's eyes.

'Get down,' Simona said. 'Stay close to the wall. I'll distract them.'

'No!'

'Just do it. I'll meet you at the café.'

Katie did as she said. She didn't even hesitate. She crouched down, staying low and in shadow as Simona stepped brazenly into the middle of the sunlit grass and jogged up behind Esme and Lukas. She tagged their shoulders and ran to the bench. She sat down on it and grinned up at them. 'Morning, lovebirds,' she said. 'How's it going?'

They stood open-mouthed, staring at her.

'We were just going to sit there,' Lukas said.

'Plenty of room.' Simona patted the bench either side of her. 'Snuggle down next to me.'

Katie edged along the wall in terror. Simona was capable of anything. But perhaps she was simply making herself a target so Katie could get clear of the garden. And if someone was prepared to make that kind of sacrifice, then you had to do as they said, didn't you?

'That's completely unreasonable,' Lukas said.

'She's always like this,' Esme told him.

'You know her?' He sounded surprised.

'She's the year above me at school. She's a nutter.'

Simona feigned offence and demanded Esme apologize. Esme said it should be Simona who apologized for stealing their seat. Simona said that actually, since she was offering to share it, she'd done nothing wrong. Esme said if she didn't get off, she was going to make her. Simona said she'd like to see her try.

On and on it went as Katie sidled along the wall to the gate, keeping in shadow.

She thought how slowly time moves, each second ticking by one after the other.

She thought – *count up to twelve and it will be over. You will be at the gate and you'll be free. You can run to the café, collect Mary and Chris and pretend none of this happened.*

She thought how cowardly she was, how shameful to be creeping along like this, and really she should go and be with Simona. She should walk over and proudly take her hand. Then she thought how Simona had university to go to, whereas she had to go back to school, and there was no point bringing the world crashing down.

As she crept closer to the gate, she told herself, *One day this will be a distant memory. I will tell this story at a dinner party and everyone will laugh.*

Esme was trying to force Simona off the bench now. She had her by the arm and was yanking on it. Simona was clinging onto the back of the seat and laughing and Lukas was telling Esme to leave it because Simona wasn't worth bothering with.

'She can't leave it,' Simona laughed. 'She loves touching girls. She can't get enough.'

No, no, Katie thought, *don't go there. Why would you do that?* She felt anger surge through her – panic, heat of all kinds.

At the gate, she didn't even feel relieved. Look at Esme's face – she was freaking out and Simona made that happen. Why? Was she stupid?

Katie stood in the street, shielded by the hedge and watched. *Leave it now*, she willed Simona. *Stop causing chaos. Walk away.*

Simona leaped off the bench. 'All yours.'

Lukas stepped forward and blocked her path. 'You want to explain what you meant by that last comment?'

Simona looked at him calmly. 'Not really.'

'What that girl, Katie, did to Esme wasn't something she wanted. You do know that?'

252

Simona put her hands in the air, Italian style, as if all things were possible.

'I don't care what she thinks,' Esme said. 'Just drop it, Lukas.'

'I'm not going to drop it,' Lukas said. 'It's not fair on you.'

But Simona was walking away now, spinning and weaving her way to the gate, laughing at his confusion. Esme sat on the bench, and maybe Lukas felt stupid chasing Simona on his own because he sat down too and Esme picked up his hand and held it.

Simona waved goodbye, shut the gate behind her and walked over to Katie. 'You got a mention, did you hear?'

Katie could barely meet her eyes. She was feeling a million things. Shame and fear, but mostly a feeling that people might see them together. She was aware her legs were shaking.

Simona said, 'So, what happens now?'

Katie didn't know what she meant. Did she mean specifically or generally? Would Katie always be such a coward, or where was she eating lunch?

'I'll get Mary, take her home.'

'I thought you might say that.'

'Well, she'll be tired.'

Simona looked along the street to the café as if she'd be able to check Mary's status from across the road. 'Fine. Go home. It's probably best.'

It was only a short walk. Katie walked slightly behind, not quite with Simona. Not quite.

Mary was thrilled to see them and asked if they'd be ordering something from the menu now because she quite fancied a curry and Chris said, 'Are we seeing Dad next?' And all Katie could think was, *Let's get out of here. Let's go home. Please, please let's go home.*

She didn't say goodbye to Simona, didn't say anything to anyone as she ushered Mary and Chris from their seats. But Simona insisted they wait while she scooped up the pictures Mary had cut from the theatre book, and as she handed them over to Katie she leaned in and said, 'To thine own self be true.'

Which was a quote from Shakespeare and meant Simona was showing off and had no clue about anything. Katie felt something angry pulse up from her gut and she was glad. She wanted it to take over from everything inside her that was swooning.

1966 – Red Gloss

They've decided to picnic in the car because of the weather. They're in the Humber – the green Humber belonging to Stanley Wiltshire, the producer fellow Mary met at the 100 Club. It's a lovely car, with seats made of grey leather and polished wood trim on all the interior doors and around the glove box. They've parked on the South Bank, hoping for a good view of the Thames, but rain lashes the windows and the river is almost invisible.

Very disappointing the weather, really, but they're making the best of it. Mary sips her coffee. Stan smokes a cigarette. The wind rocks the car.

And from the back seat, a voice. 'What if the handbrake slips?'

Caroline. Beneath every sentence lurks a terror that Mary has no idea how to manage. The girl is afraid of *everything*.

Stan laughs. 'Nothing wrong with my handbrake!'

'But if there was, we'd go flying in the river and smash on the rocks.'

Mary twists in her seat. 'The car's parked in reverse. Even if the handbrake slipped, we wouldn't go anywhere. And I'm pretty certain there aren't rocks in the Thames.'

The girl nods but doesn't look reassured in the least. She stares grimly out at the river as if only she understands what trouble lies ahead. It must be very tiring, Mary thinks, to be so vigilant.

Stan pats Mary's hand. 'Your daughter has a wonderful imagination.'

They smile at each other and Mary feels a small rush of love. *Daughter.* The word thrills. It's worth it. The pain is worth it. Caroline will settle soon.

'Want an olive?' Mary asks her. 'Or some onion dip?'

'I'm allergic.'

'You can't be allergic to everything new,' Mary laughs. 'You've been used to Pat's food, that's why – tapioca, porridge, boiled eggs. You need to spread your wings.'

Caroline sits forward in her seat. 'When can I see her again? You said we'd go on the train. You promised and we haven't.'

'She isn't well enough for visitors.'

'If someone's sick, isn't that the exact time people should visit?'

Stan eyes her in the mirror. 'Why don't you talk about this with your mum later, love? We're on an outing now. We're supposed to be having fun.'

'Fun?' Caroline shakes her head bemused, as if she's never heard the word.

Mary's throat tightens. She'd do anything to protect this child from pain – dive in front of buses, fight off lions – but perhaps she's already failed her by not predicting how Pat would whittle away at her.

Of course, living with Lionel hadn't helped. Pat had known his proclivities when she married him, but still thought it the perfect solution – she'd keep herself to herself, get independence from Dad at last and bring Caroline up with a decent father. But not to be loved? Not in that way, not even once . . . What did that do to a woman?

Mary's heart melts for her sister every time she thinks about it, because Lionel was the man suggested for *her*, and perhaps if she'd married him instead, things would have turned out better. He wouldn't have minded her having lovers. He'd probably have taken some for himself. They could have been friends.

What a fool she'd been all those years ago thinking her life had to be so perfect, that she couldn't marry a man she hadn't loved, yet allowed Pat to do it on her behalf. What had Pat said to her then? 'This isn't about you.' And she'd been right. It should only ever have been about the child.

'We'll have a party tonight,' she announces. 'How about it?' She twists round to look at Caroline. 'We'll buy you something lovely to wear and invite a few people over.'

'I won't know anyone.'

'You'll know me.'

'I'd rather stay in my room.'

'What about if we make it a supper party? You could just join us for dessert, if you can't bear the whole thing. Just a quick hello and let people have a look at you.'

'Can't we go and visit the hospital instead?'

'She'll be wonderful in Chekhov,' Stan says. 'All that longing to be elsewhere.' He turns to grin at Caroline. 'You're hired. You start Monday.'

It's supposed to be a joke, but Caroline looks aghast and her eyes fill with sudden tears. Mary sends Stan away to fetch more cigarettes and gets into the back of the car. It's wonderful to put an arm round her daughter, to stroke her hair and wipe her tears away.

To prove to Caroline that she isn't alone with fear, Mary tells her about the night during the war when she hid in the wardrobe instead of going to the shelter – how her father and Pat had looked for her and then left the house without her. How Mary had sat with a saucepan on her head surrounded by her mother's coats.

'I went through the pockets,' she says, 'and guess what I found?'

'Money?'

'Lipstick. I dabbed some on my lips and cheeks and I knew for sure I'd be safe. It was a sign from my mother, I thought. And you know what? Every raid after that, I kept it with me and our house never got damaged, not even a window out.'

'That's just a coincidence.' Caroline has stopped crying now and shrugs off Mary's arm. 'There's no such thing as magic.'

'What about magic squares?' Mary says. 'You can't deny they exist. Not if you like maths.'

Caroline frowns and Mary reaches for Stan's newspaper and tears off a corner, rummages in her bag for a pen and shows Caroline the trick a man in a bar had shown her once – a grid where all the numbers in every row, column and diagonal add up to fifteen. The girl's impressed and Mary feels more glad about that silly trick than about the curtains and sheets she's chosen with such care, the new clothes in the wardrobe, the cookery books and pans she's purchased, the rule she's made with herself to never let a man stay the night now her daughter's in the house.

She hands Caroline her brand-new stick of Red Gloss. 'In case you ever need to feel brave.'

The girl gives a small smile. That's more like it.

Twenty-five

Mary slapped her empty tea cup on the table and gave the girl a glare. She'd been scribbling away in that book for hours.

'You fancy a shopping trip?' Mary said. 'How about Carnaby Street? We could go right now if you like.'

'No adventures for me, Mary. I'm going to live a nice safe life from now on. The world's got too many difficult things in it.'

'Let's go out, come on. Why not wear the lipstick I gave you? That'll keep you brave.'

'The one you gave me at the house?'

'In the car. When you first arrived. It's a shame to be frightened and London's not as big as you might think. It's divided into smaller places, like villages or towns. They all have different names. There's Hackney, of course, and Enfield where I used to live and Covent Garden where I work and Soho where I go out to dinner or meet friends. And there are buses and tube trains and trams to get between the places. It's like a puzzle that joins up into a wonderful whole.'

The girl eyed her with interest, but said nothing.

'I'm an actress, did you know? I've just done a season at Cromer, on the end of the pier. That was nice. I'm not working at the moment because I want to concentrate on you. I just turned down a job in Venice. That's in Italy.'

'Yes,' the girl said. 'I know.'

'Ah,' Mary laughed. 'Good at geography as well as maths, eh?'

'I think you may be talking about Mum?'

'My mother's dead. I'm not talking about her at all.'

'I mean *my* mum – Caroline.'

'Yes, that's it.'

'I'm Katie.'

'Of course you are. I knew that.'

Mary leaned back in the chair to work it out. She sat there for minutes as the girl carried on with her writing. Katie was Caroline's daughter. Caroline was Mary's daughter. Mary had a mother, who had a mother of her own. Back and back it went, like Russian dolls.

But you could get lost like that. You could end up in darkness, sitting in a cave with Neanderthals . . .

Mary swallowed, tried to focus, yanked her thoughts back to Caroline.

She'd come to stay, Mary knew that much. She was unhappy, Mary knew that too. The child wanted to return to Pat, didn't understand why she couldn't. Things needed explaining. Despite her father swearing Mary to secrecy, the truth was surely best.

'Excuse me,' she whispered to the writing girl. 'Do you happen to know where Caroline is?'

'She's upstairs. I'll get her.' The girl pushed her chair back from the table and jogged out of the room.

Darling, I need to explain about Pat . . .

Sweetheart, there are some things you don't know about Pat . . .

Beautiful girl, I know you miss Pat, but there are very good reasons we can't visit her . . .

None of it was right. Words didn't quite cut the mustard. But what else could she do? Write Caroline a letter? That was still made of words. Mary had written hundreds of letters in her life, and had any of them done any good? Perhaps the only hope was to keep trying? After all, if you give a monkey a typewriter and enough time, one day it will write a sonnet.

A woman said, 'You wanted me?'

Mary turned to her. 'I wanted Caroline actually.'

'For goodness sake. I *am* Caroline!' The woman swilled liquid around the bottom of a glass, tipped her head back, gulped it down.

'I was talking,' Mary said, raising all the dignity she could muster, 'about my daughter.'

'That's me,' the woman said. 'I *am* your daughter.'

Mary considered this. 'She's got different hair.'

'Copper and gold. Yes, I know.' The woman slapped a bottle and the empty glass on the table and sat next to them. 'I got old.'

She *was* old, it was true. She had long greying hair that dragged her face down. And those glasses certainly didn't help.

'Have you ever thought of contact lenses?' Mary asked.

The woman laughed, a scoffing kind of laugh that was really rather unpleasant, considering Mary was only making a polite enquiry. The woman turned to the bottle and sloshed some more out. It lapped up the glass like a little red tide. 'Tell me,' she said, 'since you seem to be wanting to talk. What do you want to do about a bath tonight? It's pretty late, so do you want to wait until the morning instead?'

'I don't need a bath. I want to talk about Pat, about all of that.'

'You do need a bath actually. We've got an important visit tomorrow. You remember where we're going?'

Mary felt an urgency – she had to get together the right amount of words and they had to mean the right thing. But inside her head was a softening, a sliding away.

She looked about the room for clues. This was a lounge clearly – a table and chairs and in the corner a television. On the sofa, knees curled up, a girl with flame-red hair was looking rather sheepish.

'Should I be here?' Mary asked her.

The girl gave her a weak smile. 'Probably not, but I'm glad you are.'

Mary gazed at the window, how dark the day was. Perhaps it was winter . . . She drummed her fingers on the arm of the chair. 'I got a telegram from my father. *Come quick*, it said.'

'Can we get back to discussing the bath, please?'

Who was this woman who kept interrupting? A telegram definitely rang a bell. Had there been a cat? A clock? Something melting in an oven? Birds?

An image of Pat scattering spent matches in the garden landed squarely in Mary's head. Yes, that was right – Pat thought that if the matches received sufficient moisture they'd germinate. She'd raked a thin dressing of sand on top as she explained, 'They'll turn into something warm, I hope – red-hot pokers, or toadflax.'

'Pat was ill,' Mary said. It was a sudden revelation. She was pleased with the memory. It felt very solid.

Pat had been pegging tins onto the washing line to keep the birds away. They shone and chinked. Bottle tops too, rasping in the breeze. To make light of it, Mary reminded her that magpies might be attracted to the silver. Pat was afraid. She thought they might come swooping and scurried up the path to safety dragging Mary by the hand. They stood together at the kitchen door. Pat kept shushing Mary, kept telling her to listen. Could she hear the whirring of wings?

'My father begged me to help,' she said. 'My sister was unwell and needed a break. She had no joy in anything and neither did Caroline as far as I could tell. She needed some life breathing into her.'

'Some life?' The woman with grey hair sounded furious, took another swig of her drink. 'You took your daughter away from everything she knew because you wanted her to have some *life*?'

'I took her to London,' Mary said quietly. She remembered this bit very clearly. Such high hopes she'd had. Her daughter and her together at last! It had been a slow blossoming. 'She was a funny little thing,' Mary said. 'Nothing like me at all. Very quiet, very good at maths.'

'I wasn't what you wanted, was I? I was a complete and utter disappointment.'

'Were you?'

'You really want to discuss this? OK, then.' She sat forward on her chair. 'You remember taking me to Oxford Street? It was right at the beginning, almost as soon as I'd arrived. "It'll be such fun," you said, but you never asked me what I wanted and I ended up with a silver minidress and some leather boots. You said I'd be the height of fashion, but I hated wearing them. I hated the way everyone stared. You kept inviting people round – all your friends, people I didn't know. They only came because they wanted to be nosy. And there was ridiculous food, nothing I ever wanted to eat . . .'

'*You* were at my house? Are you sure?'

'Absolutely. Your friends sat about drinking and smoking and playing music. I kept in my bedroom, knowing if I came downstairs they'd all look at me and tell me to come and join in, sit down, have a glass of something. Sensual parenting, you called it. You remember what that is?'

'No idea.'

'It's having no boundaries and accepting no responsibility for anything.' She stuck her hand out to count off on her fingers. 'No regular meals. In fact, rarely any food in the house at all. No bedtimes. No homework. No settled adults in your life.' She wiped her hand on her skirt as if rubbing the list away. 'You were always showing me off like some kind of prize. *My daughter*, you used to announce and it really annoyed me. It felt so unfair to Pat, who was in hospital having a terrible time. I wanted to see her, wanted to phone her or at least write her a letter, but I kept being told no, not yet, maybe later. For nearly *two years*.'

Mary blinked. That wasn't true, was it? They'd sent plenty of letters. But when Pat was in that hospital she couldn't have visitors.

'I was like a little alien among all your friends, being petted and shown about and taken for dinner at fancy restaurants and meeting different men every five minutes and having to call them Uncle this or that and being taken to parties after the show when I really should have been in bed. You used to make me a nest in a corner and encourage me to sleep while you lot moved the chairs to one side for dancing. How was a kid supposed to sleep through that?'

Mary leaned forward. This story was stirring something. 'Excuse me? Are you a police officer?'

'Why? Are you feeling guilty? You should be. Here's a thing – one night everyone had to go round and do an act. You had a beautiful voice and you sang something lovely and they all looked at me – what could I do? But instead of protecting me, saying I was shy or tired or too young, you were the worst. You kept saying, *You must know something, surely there's something you can do, some kind of turn?* But there was nothing. I couldn't even remember any jokes. My head was entirely empty and I looked at you and saw your disappointment and knew I wasn't the plucky, extrovert daughter you wanted me to be. I wasn't pretty enough or bold enough. You should've left me with Pat, you should never have taken me away.'

The woman leaned back in her chair and looked sternly at Mary. It made her feel rather uncomfortable. Was she obliged to listen to this?

'Sometimes you went out to the theatre and didn't come back at night.'

'Are you sure?'

'When I woke up in the morning, you were still out. So I got dressed, had some breakfast and went to school. What else could I do?'

Mary nodded. 'You sound sensible.'

'Oh, I was. I didn't mention my mother's absence to any teachers. I knew they'd be upset, knew it would get you into trouble. When I got home, I was very relieved to find you sleeping in your bed.'

'Oh,' Mary said with a sigh, 'that's all right then.' She was glad the story had a happy ending.

'Not really, because it happened once a month at least, no warning at all, which meant I was never sure if there'd be anyone there or not when I woke up in the morning. So because I could never be sure and because it was so terrible to creep along the hallway to see if you were missing, I made a decision. Do you know what that decision was?'

Mary shook her head. Best to keep quiet.

'I decided never to check. I decided I *wanted* to be alone, that it was preferable. So now when I woke up, I didn't bother looking in your room, I merely went downstairs, made my own breakfast, made my own packed lunch and went off to school. I was careful to shut the door properly, careful to take a key. After weeks of this, it was as if I lived alone. It became commonplace for me not to seek you out if I needed anything, commonplace not to talk to you, or to require anything from you. And do you know how old I was at the time?'

'Fifteen?' Mary suggested.

'Twelve. I was twelve years old.'

That did seem young to be doing so much. Still, Mary had been younger than that during the war and everyone had been expected to muck in. Perhaps she should mention this?

'I used to think,' the grey-haired woman said, 'that it was my fault, that if only I was more interesting, you'd want to spend time with me. But as I grew older, I came to realize you were extremely selfish. You needed constant admiration. Whatever kind of child I'd been, you'd still have dumped me as soon as any man gave you the wink. I was so glad to get back to Pat as soon as she was better. Nearly two years with you was *more* than enough!'

The flame-haired girl stood up. 'Mum, I'm not sure this discussion is doing anyone any good.'

The grey woman scoffed at her. 'It's doing *me* a lot of good, I can tell you.'

'Please, Mum. Why don't I make us all a coffee? Let's talk about this tomorrow.'

The woman shook her head. 'You wanted to hear about London, didn't you? Well, here it is, in all its glory. Not so romantic now, is it, Katie? I'm here all the time for you and your brother. All the time! I gave up any notion of a career to look after you both when you were younger, and now I actually have a job I say no to extra hours and put myself out of the running for promotion. You know why? Because you still need looking after! I help you revise, help you with homework, I know your teachers, come to every damn parents' evening, every concert and play. I look after you when you're sick. Have you ever had to spend a night alone in this flat? No. Have you ever come home to empty cupboards or had to get the nits out of your own hair, or had to plan how to make food last until there was more money available? Never.' She was furious. Shouting with it. The girl had a hand over her mouth, listening to her. 'But Mary – well, I'd put very good money on betting she got pregnant on purpose. Ha! That never crossed your mind, did it, Katie? She knew her dad would throw her out, knew Pat would offer to look after me, knew she'd finally get the freedom she wanted. How about that, eh? Is she so wonderful now? She sacrificed me so she could have the life she dreamed of.'

Mary leaned back in her chair. She'd heard this speech before somewhere. It hurt to hear it now. Like pinpricks of sharp light biting the back of her eyes. 'I'd like to go home now,' she said softly. She hoped someone would show her the way.

Twenty-six

A woman met them in the lobby. 'Ah,' she said, 'I've been expecting you.' She was wearing a badge with her name on – 'Eileen' it said and underneath, *Manager*.

'Sorry we're late,' Mum told her. 'We had a little attack of nerves.'

'We' meant Katie. She'd spent the last ten minutes refusing to get out of the car in a final attempt to get Mum to change her mind.

'Nerves are entirely to be expected,' Eileen said, 'but I assure you we're a friendly lot.' She winked at Katie. 'How about a guided tour and then you can see what you think?'

Katie let Mum go ahead with Eileen, then took Mary's arm and followed behind.

'We'll start with The Willows,' Eileen said as she punched a key code into the door, 'our high dependency unit.'

As they followed her through to a corridor there was an immediate whiff of institutionalised food and a stronger, chemical smell above that.

'Willows?' Katie leaned into Mary. 'I bet there won't be a tree in sight.'

Mary chuckled, although Katie hadn't meant it as a joke.

During the forty-minute car journey, Katie had tried to imagine

St Catherine's care home (specializing in caring for people with dementia). Mum had said it had a person-centred approach and was in a wonderful setting, but Katie couldn't get beyond the idea of the hospital in that Jack Nicholson movie. Of course, that wasn't actually a care home, but it was still an institution that took away all your freedom.

Mary had been busy admiring the scenery, excited as a schoolgirl on an outing, not realizing she was about to be betrayed. So Katie told her the bit in the movie where Jack's character breaks everyone out and they all go fishing. Mary didn't seem that interested, so Katie told her the bit where he gets put in a straitjacket and has his brain fried. It was such a relief when Mary looked horrified and demanded Mum turn the car round.

Mum refused to do that (of course) and told Katie to stop stirring things up, to keep 'blinking quiet' and accept this was 'the best solution for all of us'. She went on the hard sell after that, talking about entertainers and outings and living in small units like a family.

But Mary already had a family. She didn't need a new one made up of a bunch of abandoned old people. 'The only criteria,' Katie told Mum, 'should be if you wouldn't mind living there yourself.'

'I wouldn't,' Mum snapped. 'It'd be a blessed relief.'

And that was the difference. Mum liked safety and closed doors and windows and regulated meal times and people being the same every day and no surprises at all. But to Mary, a life like that was a nightmare.

'This corridor is actually a loop,' Eileen said as she encouraged them along. 'It circles the entire building and all the rooms lead off from it, so everyone gets a view – the courtyard, or outside across the fields, or for some lucky residents, towards the sea.'

'The sea?' Mary said.

'We passed it,' Mum said. 'Remember?'

Mary frowned. 'I don't think I was there.'

'You said the stones on the beach looked like pearls.'

'It's just across the road,' Eileen said. 'We're in a wonderful location.'

Mum smiled, but Katie wasn't going to be seduced by the sea and Mary wouldn't be either. She *had* seemed excited to see it, sniffing the air as if it stirred some ancient memory and she'd definitely made the pearls comment, but she wouldn't like watching it from a window. She'd want to get up close and splash about. And Katie would bet any money that no one in St Catherine's was going to let her do that.

A woman appeared at the curve of the corridor, gripping the handrail as if she'd fall if she let go.

'Ah, here comes Doris,' Eileen said. 'A lot of our residents like to walk, so a looped corridor provides that opportunity in a safe environment.'

They walked in circles all day? Indoors? That was terrible. That was worse than hamsters on a wheel. They all stared as the woman got closer. She didn't acknowledge them as she shuffled past, despite Eileen's cheery, 'You off for a walk, Doris?'

Katie flicked a look at Mary, but she was gazing with great interest out of the window and across the car park.

'Sometimes we stick a duster in her hand and get her to polish the rail,' Eileen said, smiling at Doris's retreating back.

'You could get my mother to generate your electricity,' Mum said. 'She can walk for England.'

Eileen laughed. 'You're not the first person to suggest that about someone, believe me.'

Were they mad? That wasn't even funny.

'Mary walks into town every morning,' Katie said. She was

looking at Eileen, but speaking to Mum. 'I let her go wherever she wants, so she has some control over her life.'

'Well, that's lovely,' Eileen said. 'We operate a key worker system here, so your gran can walk into the village any time she fancies.'

'The sea!' Mary said, stabbing at the window with a finger. 'There it is.'

'Yes,' Eileen said, 'you get a very good view from there.'

Never mind the sea. A random village wasn't the same thing at all. Mary wouldn't be able to go back to her past in any old place. She needed Bisham, she needed Victory Avenue (the café would have to be avoided until Simona had gone to university), she needed Katie to read out stories from the memory book until they settled back into solid shapes. There was no way some unknown key worker would have the patience or inclination to give Mary her memories back on a daily basis.

They weren't allowed in any of the bedrooms because residents' private spaces had to be respected, but one of the rooms had its door open and no one was there, so they stood in a huddle and peered in, which was pretty disrespectful in Katie's opinion. She tried not to look out of principle, but her eyes were drawn to the cluster of photos on the wall. Someone else's family spread across the years. She felt the hairs on the back of her neck prickle.

'There's an unoccupied room in Beeches Unit,' Eileen said, 'so we'll have a proper look when we get there.'

'Unoccupied?' Mum said. 'I thought there was a waiting list.'

'It's one of our respite beds, so it has a separate list handled by social services.'

'So it might be available?' Mum was positively beaming. 'Should I speak to the council?'

Eileen looked doubtful. 'I imagine they've got someone in mind,

271

but you could certainly let your mother's social worker know you're interested and they'll be able to handle any referral.'

Ha! Well, that sounded fantastically complicated and Mary didn't even have a social worker, so none of that was happening. Mum looked pretty gloomy again, but it served her right.

Eileen whisked a door open. 'Shall we have a peek in the lounge?'

There were about a dozen people sitting inside. At least half of them were asleep, their heads lolling against the wings of their chairs. Some of them were probably younger than Mary, but they looked older. Even the ones who were awake looked as if they'd been unplugged. The TV was on, but no one was watching it. No one was even talking to anyone else. Maybe it was something to do with their eyes – as if no light was reflected there, or maybe it was because Katie didn't actually know them, but they seemed like shapeless bags rather than people.

'Morning, everyone,' Eileen said cheerily. One woman looked up at her as if she was miraculous – the most interesting thing to happen for hours. Eileen gave her a wave, 'All right, Nancy?'

Nancy lifted a withered hand. She was so thin, so frail, she looked like a waving skeleton. Katie imagined she might have hollow bones.

'She's our longest-serving resident,' Eileen said. 'Twelve years you've been here, haven't you, Nance?' Nancy gave a gummy smile and waved some more.

Twelve! How was it possible to survive so long in a place like this?

'Shall we go and sit in the car?' Katie whispered to Mary.

But Mary nudged her away, was chuckling at some crappy TV advert where a cat was running down a hill with a stick in its mouth, pretending to be a dog.

Katie turned to Mum, hoping to give her a look that said they

272

should get away from St Catherine's as soon as possible. But Mum was asking Eileen about activities and Eileen was getting all animated telling her about their amazing coordinator who ran 'singing for the brain' sessions.

Singing? Where was the philosophy club, the ballet company, the troupes of actors? Where were the movie nights? Eileen was going on about visiting hairdressers and chiropodists now, school-kids who came for tea, a trolley that came round every day with toiletries and chocolate.

Mary had found a seat and was looking longingly at the biscuit tin. Katie wanted her not to be doing that. Katie wanted her to be resistant and full of rage. Mum had clearly arranged to visit in the afternoon on purpose. Mary was always more pliable when her morning energy ran out.

Katie squatted down next to her. 'Let's get out of here.'

Mary shook her head. 'I'm busy.'

Katie deliberately bumped Mum's arm as she stomped past her and out of the lounge to the corridor. Someone had to show her this was wrong. She leaned against the wall and stared out the window at the view. Not the sea from here, but green fields, trees, a few scattered sheep. Dull, dull, dull. Katie checked her phone to see if this place even had a signal. Two bars. Not brilliant, but enough to have got a text from Jamie.

STILL OK 4 MOVIE?

She texted back, YES.

She wrote a text to Esme after that, THRD DATE WTH JAMIE. EXCITED! She wanted Esme to know she wasn't 'weirdly in love' with her or relying on her 'for everything'. She pressed send and it swooped away.

Only a few seconds later she got a reply: WE NEED TO SPK. CALL ME.

Not Esme, but an unknown number. Katie felt the heat of a blush sweep her face. Simona.

'Ah, there you are,' Mum said, coming out of the lounge with Eileen and Mary in tow.

Katie turned her phone off and rammed it in her pocket and zipped the pocket shut.

'We're off to look at Sycamores' dining room,' Mum said. 'Then a quick cup of tea in the office. That all right with you?'

It sounded like torture. And what was Eileen doing with her arm linked through Mary's? And why did Mary have two cookies in her hand? Eileen must've given them to her as a bribe. Katie gave Mary a fierce look, but she just twinkled a smile as she walked past.

'We try to keep the menu varied,' Eileen said, pointing out a whiteboard on the wall as they passed the dining room. 'And we source most ingredients locally.'

'Shepherd's pie today,' Mum said with a nod at Mary. 'And plenty of cakes, look. Lemon drizzle, Victoria sponge . . . see them written up there?'

'All home-made,' Eileen said.

'Well, I do like a cake,' Mary agreed. She turned to Eileen and patted her arm affectionately. 'I don't know how you find the time.'

Mum and Eileen smiled at that, like Mary was just so cute for thinking Eileen did all the cooking. And Mary grinned back at them, because she liked people thinking she was funny.

'She hates fish pie,' Katie said. 'And salad.'

'Never could abide salad,' Mary agreed. 'I'm not a rabbit.'

'I'm sure there are alternatives,' Mum said. Her voice held a warning, but Katie chose to ignore it.

'Last time we went to the café, you had jerk chicken, didn't you, Mary?'

Mary looked enchanted. 'Did I?'

'I think,' Katie said, 'you might actually throw up if you ate liver and bacon.'

'That's enough,' Mum said. She said it quietly, like she meant it.

'Now,' Eileen said, 'this is a typical bathroom.' She swung open a door and encouraged Mary to peer in.

Mum lagged back. 'Why are you being like this?' she hissed at Katie.

'Like what?'

'Rude and disrespectful.'

Katie shrugged. She could say the same about Mum last night – all that hurtful stuff she'd said to Mary. If she wanted to start making accusations, she should be careful.

'Oh, for goodness sake!' Mum said. 'It's the silent treatment now, is it? I really don't need this.' And she huffed off to look at the bathroom.

It was enormous, completely covered in white tiles. The hoist was pointed out, the walk-in bath, the raised toilet seat, the hand-rails and emergency cord. Mary stared at that for a long time – it had a little red winking light where it joined the ceiling.

'If someone's not a fan of water,' Mum asked, 'how do you manage?'

This was code for *Mary hates washing*. Eileen clearly understood because she launched into a complex explanation about the balance between a client's autonomy and their best interests. As she moved off down the corridor with Mum to the next set of swing doors, Katie waited with Mary. The winking light had hypnotized her and Katie knew why.

She took Mary's hand. She knew what she was about to do was wrong, but Mary had been seduced by sugar and the buzz of new things. She couldn't see the danger and Katie was her advocate.

'When Jack had his heart attack, you pulled the alarm cord, didn't you, Mary?'

Mary looked astonished. 'Jack had a heart attack?'

'I'm so sorry, Mary. He fell over on the landing and he called your name and you went to help him. He always told you not to touch the cord, but that day he asked you to pull it. You were a hero, Mary. You got the ambulance to come.'

It was obvious from the pain in Mary's eyes that she remembered. Katie felt terrible hurting her like this. 'And now you live with us in Bisham and you often see Jack about the place.' Katie gently squeezed Mary's hand, noticed for the hundredth time how thin her skin was. 'I'm sorry, I don't want to upset you, but if you live here, Jack won't know where to find you any more. So I think you should tell Mum you want to stay with me. Tell Caroline you want to stay with Katie, OK?'

Right on cue, Mum appeared through the swing doors. 'You two got stuck?'

Katie shook her head. 'Mary's had enough.'

'Come and look at the garden,' Mum said. 'It's really lovely.'

'Yes, come and see,' Eileen said, coming up behind Mum. 'We even grow our own runner beans.

But Mary wasn't interested in runner beans. Mary's eyes were locked into Katie's. Katie had never seen her look so terrified – not even when she first came to stay and didn't know any of them. This fear looked like it came from somewhere deep inside, somewhere primitive that she'd just been given access to. And Katie had done this to her.

'I'm sorry, Mary,' she whispered. 'I'm so sorry. It's just that no one else knows you're amazing. Only I know. And I don't want to lose you. Good things happen when you're around.'

Mum came scurrying closer. 'What's going on?'

Mary scrabbled at her. 'How can I leave without saying goodbye? Why would you make me?'

Katie watched something dark flicker across her mother's face. 'I'm not making you do anything,' she said. 'We're just having a look around the care home to see if you like it.'

'But I'm helping. Steve wrote to me and I'm helping. I don't want to go.'

Mum shot Katie the weirdest look in the world – furtive and searching – as if she was checking: *You're not getting this, are you?*

Katie kept her face utterly deadpan, pretending she wasn't even listening. But Mary knew Dad's name. Mary said Dad had written to her. Was that just a mad coincidence?

Tears filled Mary's eyes. Katie took her hand again and stroked it with her thumb, over and over. She felt as if she would rasp down to the bone. But she wanted to make up for what she had done, wanted Mary to know she was loved, that Katie would take care of her, that no one was going to rip this family apart again.

Mum took off her glasses and rubbed at her eyes as if she had grit in them. 'We should go.' She turned to Eileen. 'Do you have any literature? An application form we can take away? Perhaps a price list?'

Eileen nodded. 'Reception has those. We'll get them on the way out.' She leaned across and patted Mary's shoulder. 'I'm sorry you didn't get to see our lovely garden. Maybe another time, eh?'

Twenty-seven

Jamie appeared from the side street and surprised her. He was breathless as if he'd been running. Katie found it difficult to meet his eyes.

'I was trying to get here first,' he said.

'Sorry, I was early.'

'I didn't want you buying the tickets.'

'I haven't.'

He grinned. 'Is that because you thought I wouldn't turn up?'

That hadn't even crossed her mind, but the idea seemed to make him happy, so she nodded. He'd texted her three times that day already, so she'd known he was going to show. She hadn't bought the tickets because she was worried about leaving Chris in charge of Mary. He hadn't seemed to mind and he swore on his life he wouldn't tell Mum, but she'd have to turn her phone off inside the cinema, and even if she left it on vibrate she wouldn't be able to answer if he rang.

'Listen,' she said. 'Are you sure about the movie? It doesn't sound much like a boy's film to me.'

'I don't mind.'

'No car chases, no guns . . . ?'

'It's fine.' He opened the door for her. 'Also, it's buy one, get one free, which makes you an incredibly cheap date.'

She laughed, even though she didn't mean to. 'You know it's in French and it's got subtitles?'

'*Absolument!*' His gaze was clear and kind as he smiled down at her. 'You will let me know if I'm trying too hard here, won't you?'

She'd forgotten he was funny. Why did she keep forgetting that? 'Let's go halves at least.'

He shook his head. 'You pay next time.'

Next time? There was going to be a next time? Well, that was good, because today she was going to let him kiss her again. They hadn't even held hands on the walk round the park or the time they went for a coffee, but if Katie was going to move forward and stop thinking about Simona and stop being freaked out every time she texted: U HVNT CALLED (five times now), then kissing Jamie happened next. At the party she'd been drunk, but today she was totally sober and there was going to be proper, full-throated snogging.

Jamie went over to the ticket machine in the corner and pulled up the menu. He looked very confident doing it. Perhaps he'd done it before for other girls on other dates. She was surprised to feel a stab of envy.

She stood by the wall and pretended to be interested in the movie posters. She picked up a leaflet and skimmed through it, but couldn't concentrate, so folded it and put it in her pocket. She went to the window and looked at the world out there. The pavement was busy with people. Grey cloud hung low in the sky. It wouldn't rain though – it hadn't rained properly for ages. Every day it looked as if it would, and it never did. Tomorrow would be hot and muggy again. And the next day.

As Jamie walked back with the tickets, Katie almost believed in God because Jamie was carrying a big tub of popcorn and two

279

Cokes and it made her want to cry with just how lovely it was to have this level of kindness thrust upon her.

If they carried on dating, she'd be able to say the words *my boyfriend* in sentences. *I went with my boyfriend to the cinema and he paid for everything. My boyfriend is very generous.* Esme would stop thinking she was weird and invite her to hang out. She'd be included when the girls did each other's makeup or braided each other's hair, and when they walked round school together with their arms linked or did work in the library with their heads touching. Katie would at last be able to take a shower after PE without feeling shame.

They sat in the middle of an almost empty cinema. Katie switched her phone off and shoved it in her pocket. Sod it. What was the worst thing that could happen? Chris was fourteen and definitely sensible enough to manage Mary for a while. Jamie switched his phone off too. It was like they were agreeing to be on a desert island together, even if it was only for an hour and a half. He pulled out a glasses case and made an apologetic face as he showed her the frames.

'They're only for screens and driving,' he whispered.

She didn't know he could drive. She barely knew anything about him, in fact. 'They suit you.'

How easy he was to please. If you said nice things, he grinned as if he'd won a prize. She smiled back at him and tried to think of other compliments to make him happy, but the lights went up briefly and then dimmed.

'Here we go,' he said.

There were trailers for forthcoming movies, for snacks and local businesses and other things coming on at the arts centre. In the dark, Jamie's knee pressed against her leg. She wondered if he knew this.

'Aren't you hot?' Katie whispered, because she couldn't think of anything else to say and she wanted to let him know about his knee.

'Hot?' Jamie said and he shone his teasing smile at her. 'Do I look hot?'

He meant something else by it. He was more confident today than he'd been the other times, which meant he was doing the leg thing on purpose.

'It's boiling in here,' she said, 'and you've still got your hoodie on.'

'Better take it off then.' He shrugged it off and laid it on the chair next to him. She wondered if he'd do anything she suggested.

Mary said that in any relationship one person does the chasing and the other does the running away. 'With Jack,' she said, 'I let him chase me until I caught him.' It had made them all laugh, even Mum, but then Mary had gone on to say that she thought she must have a secret powerful magnet hidden inside her because even when she was with Jack, men were drawn towards her.

'Because you led them on,' Mum snapped. 'Take some responsibility for once.'

Maybe she was thinking about Dad and the night she'd discovered he had a girlfriend. 'You're ten years older than her!' she'd yelled. 'You're making a fool of yourself.' He'd raised both hands as well as his eyebrows, as if to say, 'What can I do?' as his girlfriend's secret magnet dragged him out the door.

Katie had a grandmother who was a man-eater and a father who was a lothario. What chance did she have of being decent and honest and kind? She'd kissed two girls and one boy in the space of a few weeks, so these things were clearly genetic. And that must be why she was leading Jamie on right now. Because he was

281

pressing his knee against her leg again and she wasn't stopping him.

On the screen, a man set up a camera. He was going to interview everyone who knew his wife. She'd died several weeks previously and he was convinced she'd been having an affair. His friends simply thought he was missing her as they sat one by one in a chair and spoke at great length while he filmed them. After a while, Katie stopped reading the subtitles and let the foreign words wash over her because the whole length of Jamie's leg was pressing against the whole length of hers.

Surely the fact that Jamie seemed to like her so much was a start? There were girls all over the world in much worse positions. There was that girl at her old school, Adina, who didn't come back after the summer holidays and everyone said she'd been sent abroad to marry her uncle. And there were young women Katie had heard about on the radio who came over to this country with their boyfriends and were then totally betrayed and sold as house slaves while their 'boyfriends' pocketed a fee.

Jamie was kind and funny and intelligent and not bad-looking and surely she'd grow to like him? His hand slid from his lap to the side of her thigh and his little finger began to stroke the seam of her jeans.

The film cut to footage the man had taken when his wife was alive. Here she was looking out of a window. Here she was reading a newspaper. Here she was sleeping.

Jamie leaned in. 'Did you say there was a car chase?'

'Yeah,' Katie whispered back. 'Right after the gun fight.'

He laughed. His breath was warm against her neck.

The woman on the screen was dancing now. She had a cigarette in her hand and she blew a kiss to the camera with such confidence that for an instant she looked like Mary. Katie smiled, and maybe

Jamie saw and thought it was encouragement because he picked up her hand and threaded his fingers with hers and laid both their hands back on her thigh.

A boy's hand in hers! A boy's hand in the dark. His hand was warm and the lacing of their fingers together was so intimate it shocked her.

The film droned on, but none of it mattered. She could feel Jamie's pulse in her palm and it felt much more meaningful than kissing him at the party.

'I really like you,' he said.

She didn't say anything. She sat there like an idiot with her heart going nuts and she'd bet any money he was looking all serious and vulnerable and if she did turn towards him or say anything, he was going to kiss her and she wanted to please him, but . . .

Should she tell him? *Before I met you, I kissed a girl. Since I met you I've kissed another one. I may not be the person you think I am.*

The trouble was, there was something so lovely about his attention that she didn't feel quite ready to give it up yet.

'You have such amazing hair,' Jamie said, his voice gentle. He leaned closer and kissed her lightly on the side of her head. 'Your eyes are amazing too.'

He was interested in her in ways that no boy had ever been before, and Katie felt moved by him and sorry for him. She ached with it. It reminded her of seeing really old people scrabble for money in their purses.

'I really like you,' Jamie said. He laughed softly. 'Did I already say that?'

'I like you too,' she said, because she did, and also because it would make him happy and what else are you supposed to do with so much feeling?

It was nice kissing him again. His skin was soft and his lips were soft too and he was gentle, his kisses like small enquiries. He ran his tongue along the edge of her top lip and when she did it back, he did it again. He ran his tongue along her bottom lip. She dared to touch the tip of his tongue with hers. It was like a conversation – each gesture a new sentence. It was complicated, but interesting.

It was nice stopping kissing him too. She particularly liked his arm round her. She felt gathered, like wool being wound in, as he pulled her close and she leaned her head on his shoulder and they went back to watching the movie.

It was weird coming out of the arts centre into bright daylight. The sky had cleared of cloud and the street was busy. There were tons of little kids being dragged about now there was no school to go to.

'We could go for a drink if you like,' Jamie suggested. 'What time do you have to be back?'

She turned her phone on but there were no messages. 'OK, let's get a coffee somewhere.'

'You fancy a pub instead?'

'Will we get served?'

'I've got ID. And you're so sophisticated, no one will ask you.'

Sophisticated? No one had ever called her that before. 'Do you know a nice one?'

He looked about as if a pub would suddenly appear before their eyes. 'The one on Sidmore Street has a beer garden. You fancy that?'

He didn't try to take her hand again as they walked, but he softly bumped against her twice and she knew he was doing it on purpose. He dared to link arms as they crossed the road. It was old-fashioned and she didn't mind it. When they got to the pub they found a table easily and he asked what she wanted and she told him a rum and Coke because she wanted to keep being sophisticated.

'Crisps?' Jamie said.

'No, I'm fine. But let me pay.'

She handed over ten pounds, and although he hesitated he took it.

What was astonishing was that when he went off to the bar, she missed him. She actually felt shy sitting amongst the other people in the beer garden – friendless again, alone. She looked at her phone to give her something to do, but there were still no messages. Strange to be this free suddenly.

She texted Chris: OK? She considered texting Esme: ON THRD DATE, but that would look strange and desperate, so she didn't.

She got out the cinema leaflet and flicked through it. She'd choose a movie and invite Jamie out again. It would be her treat. Jamie had done all the work for this date – all the texting and arranging, all the hand holding and daring to touch. On the walk round the park he'd also asked most of the questions, done most of the listening and said most of the lovely things. She'd soaked it all up like some kind of parasitic sponge and spent most of the time wondering if she even fancied him, so it was only fair that she treated him.

But there, right in the middle of the brochure was an advert for next week's French film. In the photo, two girls stood in such proximity that the only outcome was a kiss. The girl on the left had her eyes wide, her mouth slightly open in anticipation as she leaned down. The girl on the right had her eyes almost shut, but her lips were also parted as she craned her neck up. She had blue hair. It was a three-hour film based on a graphic novel, following a blossoming love affair between two young women. *Warning: contains explicit sexual content.*

And that's when Jamie came back with a drink in each hand and a packet of crisps swinging from his mouth. And that's when she slapped the brochure shut like it was porn.

And maybe the universe punishes people for doing one thing and thinking another, because that's also when her phone rang. It was Mum. She was furious. She'd come back to the flat and found the door unlocked and nobody in.

'What's going on, Katie? Where the hell is everyone?'

Twenty-eight

The bus was full of people and Mary was struck by how young they all were. Every single one of them younger than her. She wasn't sure when this happened, but she knows that it had, like the balance of the world had shifted when she wasn't looking.

The boy sitting next to her was plugged into things, the light from some gadget shining on his face, his fingers tapping at it. 'Mum keeps ringing,' he said. 'But I'm not answering. I'm just texting that we're fine and we'll be back later.'

He looked upset. Mary touched his arm to comfort him, but he shrank away. Sometimes she wondered if she drained energy from the world. Sometimes she felt like a hole in a plane, sucking lap trays and coats and babies at great speed out to an empty sky.

She nudged the boy again. She wanted to say, *I was your age once. Every morning when I wake up, don't you think I'm shocked to look in the bathroom mirror and see this battered peach?*

But when the boy looked up, all Mary could think of saying was, 'How quickly it goes.'

When every damn thought was so much richer, so much more than that. Like a rock pool, she thought, with your hand plunged deep in cold water and bright fish threading your fingers and you want to catch one in your hand. You want to hold it up, trapped and shimmering and shout, *Look! Look!*

The boy said, 'Now Katie's calling. I'm gonna turn it to silent. That'll shut them up.'

Who was he? Mary stared at him, willed a name to pop into her head. Nothing. She nudged him again. 'Do I know you?'

He sighed. 'I'm Chris.'

'How old are you?'

'You're always asking that. Fourteen.'

'That's a good age.'

'That's what you always say.'

Perhaps she should label things – butter, fridge, tables and chairs. That might help. Perhaps this child wouldn't mind wearing a badge?

He tapped away at his gadget again. 'Katie says if I lose you, she'll never forgive me, so I'm telling her to sod off.'

Who is keeping who company? Who is looking after who?

'Would you do me a favour,' Mary said, 'and tell me to go home if I look lost?'

The boy frowned. 'Are you OK? You're not feeling sick again, are you?'

Sick? Perhaps. Because every damn thought kept slipping away. And her head was full of memories that weren't in any order at all. Why, for instance, did Pat pop into her mind now? Pat bending down to her saying, 'People drown in that water. I don't know how many times I have to tell you that only paddling's allowed.'

And now Mary as a child, in a red swimming costume and sun hat.

And now the day on the beach when Pat looked away for a moment. A beach well known for its terrible tides and its secret shifting sand.

It was so peaceful. Mary lay on her back in the water and watched the clouds spin. She was there for ages floating about.

288

She was a mermaid, a dolphin, a drowning princess. She only began to be afraid when a flock of seagulls settled on the cliff to watch and she realized her face was under the water.

Later, Pat wrapped her in a blanket and held her on her lap. Mary was so surprised to be alive that she couldn't think of a single thing to say. Instead, she found a small space in the crook of her sister's elbow and buried herself there.

'You were so nearly lost,' her sister whispered. 'I will never be so careless again.'

But she was. She was very careless.

1968 – the point of you

They say if you spend five days in water you start to melt. If someone grabs your dead hand to haul you out, your hand comes off in theirs. Your eyes are fish blown, your hair has turned to seaweed. You are salty and swollen, more water than earth or air. You are soaked, full as a sponge. You come out dripping and bloated and heavier than you've ever been. Your bones have absorbed it, your head is full of brine like a pickled boar. Every orifice leaks as they drag you up the beach and lay you out.

Mary sits with a small crowd in the parlour and Pat lies in her box and Jean from next door says, 'He'll be lost without her.' And they all look at Dad, who has still not spoken a word to Mary. Who has curled Caroline's hand in his own as if it will save him.

Pat knew how to make mock cream from cornflour and margarine, a sauce from Creamola when there was no custard to be had. Pat knew how to bank a fire, how to manage a larder, how to take a pint of sour milk and turn it into a scone.

How would any of them cope without her?

That night, Mary lies in bed and listens to Caroline breathe. Then she sits up and looks at her. *You are my child*, she thinks. *You have a sweet, sad face and I am your mother. We will go back to London again together soon and all will be well.*

Outside the church after the funeral, Jean mops her eyes. 'She was a wonderful neighbour,' she says. 'Always so neat and houseproud.'

'She was indeed remarkable,' the vicar agrees. 'A woman who lived a life in sacrifice and put others' needs above her own. This young lady in particular owes her a great debt.'

Mary owes her? Does she?

Oh yes. It was the younger sister's fault. It had been too much for Pat to take responsibility for a child when their mother died. Was she never to have a life of her own? It was her nerves – anyone could see. Selfish Mary. Contrary Mary. That Pat loved too much, and too hard.

And in later years, it was Mary's fault for visiting so rarely, for living so far away, for never using the telephone, even though that was why Pat had one installed (at great expense, mind you!).

'That wasn't how it was,' Mary wants to scream. 'Pat lied to me. She stole my baby and never let me see her. I let them be together over and over.'

Maybe that's why she finds it so hard to wrench the girl from her grandfather. They just keep holding each other, their hands across the kitchen table as she passes him tissues, her arm round his shoulder as she watches his favourite programmes with him.

In the days leading up to Christmas his tired old eyes light up only if the child is near. Caroline reads to him, something Mary's never considered doing in her life. Caroline knows how to bank the fire and stack his pipe and when he says he wants no festivities, no gifts or tree or special dinner, the girl agrees and they spend Christmas Day huddled together, looking at photos of Pat and talking about how valiant and exceptional she was. When all Mary can think is, *How dare she? How dare she steal my daughter and break her heart? How dare she die?*

Mary shares Caroline's room at first, like camping, like maybe

291

after New Year they'll wake up and it's just been a holiday and Caroline will want to leave now.

But no, Caroline just gets on with things – goes back to school when term starts, does her homework, has her tea, watches TV, does more homework, drinks a mug of Horlicks, kisses her grandpa, who was off for a walk (again). The amount of walking that man does, he should buy a bloody dog. Or walk the circumference of England.

'You're staying then?' Caroline says to Mary one night.

'I am,' Mary answers. 'If you want privacy, I'll move into the spare room, but that's the extent of my leaving. I'm your mother, aren't I?'

But claims of motherhood incense Caroline. And Mary's attempts at domesticity infuriate her more. She stalks about the house, tutting when Mary uses the wrong cups or fails to ram the lid back on the tea caddy or puts a wet spoon in the sugar or slops water on the carpet and wipes it in with her foot instead of bothering with newspaper and cloths. The day Mary witnesses Caroline mopping the kitchen lino with rags tied round her slippers, she knows it's too late. The girl belongs to Pat. And guilt will keep her there.

And Mary is giddy with missing London. She thinks of her suitcase under the bed. Her manuscript. The lines she's supposed to be learning. The panto would be over by now, and the company would have a short break then start rehearsals for *Uncle Vania*. She'd been promised the role of Yeliena. Would they have recast yet?

One day towards the end of January, Caroline politely knocks on Mary's bedroom door. 'You may as well go back,' she says. 'I mean, they want you in London, don't they? And really, you're no use here. I don't see the point of you. So why not just leave? Come and visit if you like, send money when you can, but you're only under my feet here.'

Was she remembering this right? Had a fourteen-year-old child said this to her?

'Come with me,' Mary says. 'Don't stay looking after him. The only reward will be people telling you what a good girl you are and, believe me, you can live perfectly well without any of that.'

'He needs me. And anyway, it's what Mum would've wanted.'

She was right about that.

And Mary's failing, her very great and terrible failing, had been to listen to the words of a broken girl. She should've hoisted Caroline onto her shoulders and carried her off. Instead, she abandoned her to an old man, to his teeth in a jar, to his back bent with age, to the gip in his knee and the tremors in his hands and eventually to his incontinence and night terrors. And because she felt so guilty, poor little Caroline bent her head in acquiescence and got on with the task in hand, which turned out to be caring for her grandfather for fifteen long years.

Twenty-nine

It was like running back in time – back to the wide pavements and long sloping front gardens and detached houses of her old life. The lawns were vivid green, like in picture books, and there was the familiar tang of earth, wet and dark from so many sprinkler systems. How could Katie have forgotten that smell?

She dismissed it with a wave of her hand. No, she didn't need it. She wouldn't look. It could all piss off. She'd come here to do one thing – get Chris and Mary and haul them away.

She ran faster. The breeze lifted her hair and her legs began to burn and she could feel her own sweat, could taste salt on her lips, but she was going to keep running until she got there and when she got there, Chris was going to be in such trouble. She was going to yell at him. She was going to do more than yell at him, in fact, because how come he couldn't do one thing right? And how come whatever happened for the rest of her life, Chris would be her responsibility? Had she asked for it? No. But Mum went on about it all the time – *Look out for your brother, Katie. He's not as clever as you. He doesn't have your opportunities.*

Well, that could all piss off too. Because this was the last time, the very *last*, that Katie would look out for anyone other than herself. She'd been on a date! She'd been trying to be normal! Well, tonight, when she got home, she'd tell Mum that yes, she would in fact like to go to the Oxbridge Summer School, and after that she wanted to spend the rest of the holiday studying. Mum would be a total hypocrite if she refused. She'd have to look after Chris and Mary herself and Katie could get away from them all, pretend she was going to the library and then sneak off and have a regular teenage life.

She had the beginnings of a stitch. It was so hot it looked like water was beaming at her from the horizon. She slowed to a walk and laid a hand over the pain, trying to breathe deep. A long hedge packed with pink flowers lined the fence. Peonies. She'd forgotten about them too. How they'd be in bloom at this time of year. Blowsy, Mum used to call them. Two white butterflies chased each other through the leaves.

There was the gate ahead of her. The gate that always clicked or squeaked, that her dad could never silence no matter how much oil he put on its hinges. It used to sing in the night if it wasn't secure on its latch.

Katie could feel her blood pounding, her breath coming quick and shallow. She was utterly aware of the house and its windows and the front door and the shadows stretching across the lawn. It was so familiar and yet it felt like the one place in the world she shouldn't be.

There was Mary! On the bench under the holly tree, gazing up at the house. She was alone, which meant what? Chris was inside? No, there was Chris lying on the grass on the other side of the front garden. He was doing his pattern thing, waving his hands in front of his face and watching the light through his fingers. Katie checked all the windows – they were blank, the front door was shut, the garage was closed, no sign of life. Maybe they'd get away with this after all.

She lifted the latch and pushed the gate. Chris looked up

expectantly as it squeaked and then collapsed back on the lawn.

'Get up!' she hissed.

'Get lost.'

She marched over and rammed his leg with her boot. 'Before anyone comes!'

He slapped her away. 'I'm not leaving.'

'You bloody are.'

'I'm waiting for Dad.'

'Do you know how much trouble you'll be in?'

Chris looked at his watch. 'He gets back from work at six, so I'm waiting for that.'

'Are you insane? Have you had some kind of breakdown? You can't just camp out in Dad's front garden.'

'I want to see.'

'See what? His girlfriend? The baby?' She kicked him again. 'Come on, get up.'

'No!' He slammed his arms over his face. God, he was infuriating.

'He won't want to see *you*, Chris, that's the point. It'll be really embarrassing and he'll call Mum and yell at her for not keeping you under control and you'll get taken to that counsellor again.' She knew she was being a cow, but she didn't care. He'd ruined her date! One thing she'd asked him to do, just one – look after Mary for three measly hours – and he hadn't even been able to manage that. 'Please, Chris, come on! They're probably on holiday anyway. It all looks very quiet. They've probably gone somewhere lovely where we've never been – the Caribbean or somewhere.'

She looked down at his too big body sprawled on the grass and the way he just lay there hiding under his arms, like it was perfectly routine to get on a bus and come and see Dad and if he hid his face, he'd just be allowed to get on with it, and he suddenly seemed to have it easy. No responsibility for anything! How great that must be. No exams, no revision, no school. You couldn't call Woodhaven a proper school when all they did was cookery, tech and art. If Chris concentrated for one whole day, spoke up in class and was friendly to the other kids, he got treated like some kind of superstar and came home clutching a certificate of merit. He probably wouldn't even be told off about coming here if Mum found out – Katie would! *I left you in charge! I thought I could trust you!* Well, maybe instead of apologizing, Katie should start screaming and bang her head on the floor like Chris used to before he could talk. What would Mum do then?

Chris said, 'I was all right until I rang the bell and then I felt sad.'

'What did you expect? Cosying up to Dad and his new family is hardly a recipe for happiness.'

'I'm not cosying, because he's not in!' His voice was muffled from talking under his arm. 'And it's my fault.'

'That he's not in?'

'That he left.'

'Your fault? Where the hell did you get that idea from?'

'Josh told me.'

'And who's Josh?'

'A boy at school.'

'Well, since I've never heard of him and since he's clearly never met Mum or Dad, I don't see how he'd know anything about it.'

Chris rolled away from her as if the subject was closed, but she wasn't having that. She stepped over him and sat on the grass by his head. 'It's not your fault, Chris.'

'You would say that.'

'Because it's true. Dad left because he found a younger woman. It's a total cliché and nothing to do with you.'

'She can give him good babies.'

'What's that supposed to mean?'

Chris looked at her briefly, then closed his eyes again. 'Nothing.'

'Is that what Josh said? That you're not good enough? He sounds a total prick. Next time I come to your school, you point him out and I'll break his neck.'

'I can fight my own battles,' Chris said stoically.

It crossed her mind this might be why he was so often reluctant to go to school. Then it crossed her mind she should probably hug him, but she was still angry and didn't want to. She leaned over instead and tried to get him to open his eyes by blowing on them, but he rolled away again.

'Well,' she said, 'if you ever change your mind and want me to kill Josh, you just let me know . . .'

'You can go now actually.'

'I'm not leaving without you.'

'And I'm not leaving until I see Dad.'

'Well, you're not getting the bus on your own again.'

'I wasn't on my own.'

Katie wasn't sure that being with Mary counted as adult supervision. She cast a quick glance at her over on the bench. She was still staring at the house as if it was totally fascinating. 'I can't believe you brought her here.'

'You take her to places all the time.'

'I'm supposed to. Mum's paying me. God, why are you so annoying?'

'I dunno. Why are you so mean?'

Katie slumped on the lawn next to him, burying her face in the warm grass. It made her feel heavy thinking of Dad walking in and catching them here. The girlfriend would probably be with him, and she'd be all glam and look at them with pity in her eyes, and the baby would be gorgeous and Mary would come bounding over to coo at it and Chris would start asking awkward questions and Dad would phone Mum and there'd definitely be shouting.

She rolled onto her back and stared at the sky. A tiny silver aeroplane was making its way across the blue, its wings glinting.

Katie sat up to look at the house. It blushed with warmth on such a sunny day, even with its shut curtains and the ivy gathering up the brickwork. Later, the sun would sink behind the garage roof and the tops of the trees in the back garden would be washed with light. She'd thought she'd never see it again. She'd thought it would be sold and Dad would move, probably abroad, and that'd be the end of it.

The garden seemed smaller and shabbier. The paint on the swing was peeling off and the seat was lopsided. Had it always been like that? She supposed Dad would get a new one when he eventually moved house. Probably a slide as well. Maybe a climbing frame.

'You know, Chris, I dreamed about the baby one night.' He didn't answer, but she thought he might be listening. 'I was at a railway station with Dad and his girlfriend and they asked me to look after the baby while they went to buy tickets. She was older than in real life and toddled off and I just let her. I remember thinking I didn't want to fuss about everything like Mum does. I wanted to be cool and impress Dad. So they came back from getting tickets and asked me where the baby was and I pointed to the platform and the girlfriend clapped her hand on her mouth and said, "You let my baby near the trains?" And it was suddenly really obvious from the crowd and the silence that the baby was dead and it was all my fault.'

Chris turned to look at her. 'Shit!'

'I couldn't get it out of my head all day.'

'Did Dad get mad at you?'

'I don't know. I woke up.' She turned to smile at him. 'I miss him too, Chris. It's horrible that he lives here and we don't. It feels like some terrible joke.'

Chris sat up. 'If you think about the word "forever" a lot of times, it does your head in.'

'I don't want to think about it.'

'I do it all the time. I can't help it.'

Katie sighed. 'We can't stay here, Chris. I really don't want Dad to come back and find us, it'll be horrible. And I really don't want to leave you on your own. How about we get the bus home and I promise I'll help you come up with a plan?'

'To get them back together?' He sounded excited, as if she were capable of miracles.

'No, of course not. A plan to see Dad. Properly see him. How about it?'

She turned to look at him and found him smiling right at her.

He held out his hand. 'Deal.'

The corner of the garden where Mary sat on the bench was so dark it looked damp. Walking into shade from the sunshine made the skin on Katie's neck tingle. 'We're going now, Mary.'

'I keep hearing noises.'

'What kind of noises?'

'Crying.'

'Well, I can't hear anything. Let's get you off this bench and into the sun, shall we?'

Katie put out her hand to pull Mary up, but she shook her head like an old horse troubled by a fly. 'I'm not going without saying goodbye.'

'Goodbye to who? There's no one in.'

'Up there.' She pointed to Katie's old bedroom window. 'See the curtains shivering?'

'I think it's you that's shivering, Mary.'

Chris came over. 'I just looked through the letterbox and there's loads of post on the mat.' He looked up at the window. 'Is someone in?'

'No,' Katie said. 'It's just shadows.'

'Maybe it's a burglar. Or maybe Dad's girlfriend's holding him hostage.'

'Or maybe it's Mary's imagination.' Katie was beginning to get a headache. Why wasn't anything easy? 'Right, let's get to the bus stop. I think the newsagent's will still be open, so if you're lucky, I'll buy you both a choc ice.'

But Mary was making a soft noise, like the whimper of an animal. It was horrible. And her eyes were bright and strange.

'She's been here before,' Chris said. He nibbled a fingernail as he gazed up at the house. 'She said it when we arrived.'

'That's impossible. We moved here when you were tiny and she never came to visit.'

He shrugged. 'I'm only telling you what she said.'

Mary talked nonsense. Mary thought she'd been everywhere. She probably thought she'd been to the moon if you got her on the subject of space travel. But still, it stirred something in Katie, because imagine if it was true? Imagine Mary visiting for lunch on a Sunday or picking her up from school or coming to a birthday party. Jack could have come too. It would've been great. Maybe everything would have turned out differently.

Katie plonked on the bench next to Mary and stroked her arm. Chris sat on the other side and stroked her other arm.

If Dad walked in now, they'd look insane. Three stooges. Three monkeys. Three sad idiots.

It was very quiet suddenly.

A memory of Simona flashed into Katie's mind. Why now? A vision of her laughing, the gleam of skin at her throat. Last week, was it? It felt like a clip from a film. Yes, they'd been at the café and Simona had brought Mary a samosa and Katie a can of cold lemonade. Mary had asked Simona to join them. 'Don't worry about the boss,' she'd said. 'I'll tell her you're my sister.'

It was wonderful, the three of them laughing. Simple and lovely.

OK, this was definitely a sign of sunstroke. Katie pushed the memory away and gave Mary one last rub on the arm. 'Time's up. Let's get out of here.'

Mary turned to Katie in absolute amazement. 'I know what this place is. I can place this place – what house this is, what town. I know where the railway station is, the post office. I've had such a busy time. It's been very overcrowded.'

'We need to get the bus.'

Mary shook her head. 'I don't want to be inside anywhere at all, but I don't want to leave. I feel it everywhere – even in my hands.'

Katie took a deep breath. This was awful. It was like Mary had gone away and been replaced by someone else. Not a word of that made sense.

Chris looked at Katie, wide-eyed. 'She wasn't like this before.'

Katie held out a hand and Mary took it. She gently stroked Mary's fingers with her thumb. The skin was so thin she could see the blood pulsing underneath, the purple knot of veins near Mary's knuckles, the brown age spots, like gravy splashes, over the back of her hand. 'I don't know what to say about any of that, Mary. I'm wondering if you're feeling ill? Do you think you might need a glass of water or something?'

Tears welled in Mary's eyes. 'I was there,' she whispered. 'Just now I was there.'

Chris stood up and peered down at them both. 'What's going on?'

'No idea.'

The two of them watched Mary cry. Katie felt useless. Chris rocked backwards and forwards on his heels. Heel, toe, heel, toe. He was humming too, which was a bad sign.

Katie was going to have to call Mum to come and get them. Mum would definitely go mad. She'd feel betrayed by Chris and stressed by Mary's bizarre new behaviour and furious that Katie had abandoned them again and she'd ask questions about where Katie had been and why she lied and maybe she'd insist on immediately dumping Mary in that stupid care home.

Mum picked up on the first ring. 'You found them? Is everyone OK?'

'Mary's a bit upset. Could you come and get us please?'

'Where are you?'

'Um, sorry, Mum, but . . . we're at the old house.'

'What do you mean, the old house?' The chill in her voice was instant. 'You mean *our* old house?'

'Dad's not here though, it's OK. The whole place is locked up.'

'I want you to get out of there right now.'

'There's loads of post on the mat, Mum. I think he's probably on holiday.'

'You're not listening. I want you to leave.'

'We can't. We're in the garden and Mary won't move.'

'Then make her.'

And it landed slap in Katie's head that Mum wasn't worried about Dad turning up. If the house was empty and he was clearly away, then why couldn't they just sit in the garden and wait? No, she was worried about something else.

'Has Mary been here before, Mum?'

'Katie, I'm not going to have a conversation with you. Now, just get her out of there. Bribe her – I don't care what with – and start walking. I'll call you when I'm close and see where you are.'

'She's more upset than I've ever seen her. She said she recognizes the house.'

'She says a lot of things. Please, Katie, just do as I say and I'll be there as soon as I can. I'm going to put the phone down now.'

Guilty. Guilty. Katie could hear it in her voice. Mum was definitely hiding something.

Thirty

Mum got the doctor round. She was kind and sat on the sofa next to Mary and asked her questions. Mary was slow in her responses, she struggled to find words and once lost the thread of conversation completely, at which point she patted the doctor's hand and told her she was lovely and the doctor said, 'Well, you're lovely too,' and they both laughed.

The doctor thought Mary might have had a vascular incident, where her brain had temporarily been deprived of blood. She stood in the hallway with Mum and Katie and told them there wasn't much anyone could do. The disease was progressing.

All Katie could think of was the forest analogy and how a whole copse had been destroyed in Mary's head in one afternoon.

'She'll probably plateau out for a while,' the doctor said. 'You might get a good few weeks or months before the next incident.' She looked sadly at Mum. 'It's hard for you. Home-based care is tough on everyone.'

Mum went and ruined it by saying Mary wasn't supposed to be living with them, how everyone was passing the buck and no one seemed to care. 'Sixty nights she's been here,' Mum said. She made it sound terrible. She made it sound like she had a calendar where she crossed each night off with a permanent marker.

Mum asked the doctor if she'd write to mental health services and try and get Mary up the list for a care home and the doctor said, of course, she'd do anything to help.

'She's wet the bed a couple of times recently,' Mum said. 'All the sheets had to be changed and the mattress wiped and aired and turned over. I had to persuade her into the bath and put her night clothes in the wash and make sure they were dry again by bedtime, because she'll only wear one particular nightie. Once, it was more than just a wee, if you know what I mean. There was a terrible mess.'

Katie swallowed hard. Why hadn't Mum told her any of this? Was it even true, or was she trying to make things sound desperate for the doctor's benefit?

'I can't understand why dementia is treated so differently from other illnesses,' Mum said. 'If she had cancer she'd be whisked into hospital with board and lodging thrown in. But with dementia, we're all fighting each other over care home places and we're supposed to see it like a hotel and pretend it's marvellous, and only fair that we top up the fees ourselves. All my mother's money, every bit she's earned over her lifetime, will be eaten up. It's not her fault she's sick, is it? Why don't we ask cancer sufferers to pay for their care?'

The GP had no answer, but she patted Mum's arm sympathetically and said she'd write the letter that evening, and Mum could pick it up at the surgery in the morning.

'It was Dad's house that freaked her out,' Katie said as Mum closed the door. 'Mary recognized it. I'm telling you, we just need to find out why and she'll feel much better.'

'And I'm telling you,' Mum snapped, 'that I'll feel much better when you stop playing the amateur detective.

'She's got a blue blank.'

'A what? What are you talking about?'

'Blue for sad and blank for forgetting. Jack made it up. She's mentioned it a few times. It describes how she feels when she gets upset and doesn't know why. Do you think that's what's going on when she cries at night?'

'Did you hear what I just said?' Mum looked old and bitter as the words twisted out of her. 'What she needs more than anything is reliable care. I thought I could trust you, Katie, and you left her. You lied to me, then rushed off on a date with some random boy and abandoned your responsibilities completely.'

'I was gone a couple of hours. I didn't know Chris would take her there, did I?'

'Just imagine if Dad had been in! How mortifying that would have been.'

'Has Mary been there before though? Did she ever visit or anything?'

'Would you just stop with this, Katie! What's got into you? I can't be doing with this now.'

She knew something. She definitely did and there were only three ways to find out what. The first was to ask Mary, and given she was so unwell, that was a no-no. The second was to ask Dad. After all, Mary had mentioned his name at the care home.

'Email him,' Katie told Chris. They were in his room, away from Mum's prying eyes. 'Tell him to meet us.'

Chris was elated. He thought Katie was keeping her promise. It hurt to watch him write: *Do you want to meet up? I'd really like it.* He added a whole row of kisses and grinned like Christmas was coming when he pressed send.

It only took Dad fifteen minutes to send a reply saying how lovely it was to finally hear from Chris and how it had really made his day. He asked after Katie. He even asked after Mum. Then he asked if Mum knew that Chris had emailed? Because if she didn't, Chris should probably tell her.

307

'No way!' Chris said.

Dad ended the email by saying that things had been tricky between him and Mum, but if Chris were to tell her that he was keen to meet up, perhaps she'd agree at last. *I'd love it*, he said. But then he went and ruined it by saying he was *on holiday in France until August* (which explained the empty house) *so let's do it after that*.

'That's another fortnight,' Katie said. 'Who goes on holiday that long?'

'People with babies,' Chris said gloomily.

When had Katie or Chris ever been on a holiday that lasted that long? Never, that's when. But Dad didn't mind gallivanting off with his new family for weeks on end. It made Katie want to cry, and that surprised her, because it was usually Chris who had all the feelings about Dad. It also made her want to go running to the café and tell Simona how shitty everything had turned out, but if she did that, Simona was hardly going to dish up sympathy, was she? She'd have a go at Katie for never replying to texts (seven, now), for pushing her, for acting like a coward, for asking for things she didn't really want (Katie groaned inwardly whenever she thought of the words, *teach me*) and for generally wanting the strawberries and not the shit.

There was only one place left to look for the secrets of the past and it was the most illicit. If anyone ever betrayed Katie the way she planned to betray Mum, she'd never forgive them. But what choice did she have? She wanted Mary back. She wanted her well. She didn't want her having vascular incidents every five minutes because she couldn't remember something she wanted to remember. Katie had given her back her memory of the café and Victory Avenue and it had helped. Mary had been content. Well, going to Dad's house had ruined that contentment and Mary clearly needed to understand why.

The next day, when Mum went off to collect the GP's letter and take it the council offices, Katie made Chris a milkshake and set him up with snacks and her laptop so he could watch YouTube videos in the kitchen. She switched the TV on for Mary and then locked the front door and put the key safely in her pocket. She went upstairs to the room she shared with Mum and shut the door.

Katie told herself she could stop at any moment as she opened Mum's wardrobe. She took a photo of how everything was in case Mum had set a trap – the gaps between clothes on the hangers, the particular angles of the shoes, the boots on their sides, the zipped plastic bags of jumpers, protected from moths in a neat row.

Katie put her winter gloves on. She knew it was ridiculous, as if not touching anything with her bare hands would make a moral difference, but she did it anyway.

She pushed the hangers to one side and picked up Mum's grey box by its handle. It wasn't heavy. She put it on the bed, then worried it would leave a mark on the duvet, so put it on the floor.

'Only in an emergency,' Mum always said. Well, given that an emergency is an urgent and unexpected occasion that requires immediate attention, this definitely counted. Although Katie imagined Mum wouldn't agree with her if she ever found out.

The key on the hook was hanging at an angle and the green thread was twisted. Katie took another photo. It was useful growing up with a watchful mother. Katie had clearly learned some of her skills. They'd both make excellent detectives.

Her hands were trembling as she fitted the key into the lock and turned it. She could still stop, but she didn't. She watched herself keep going. She lifted the lid.

There were four suspension files, all buff brown, each marked

309

with a sticker in Mum's neat writing – *Finance, Insurance, Documents, Arrangements*. The writing made it worse, like she was about to look into Mum's soul. If Katie went ahead with this, it would be, without doubt, the most terrible thing she'd ever done. This was Mum's special box that she'd set up in the event of her death so that Katie would know what to do, how to handle things and manage her affairs. She was a cautious and careful mother who loved her children and Katie was about to betray her.

But Mary was downstairs with all her memories running out of her head like sand and Katie had to help. She had to keep guilt out of this. She nudged the file marked *Finance* tentatively open with a finger. She didn't want to look at Mum's bank statements, or take any money from the envelope marked 'cash', but she did need to check there was nothing relevant to Mary in each file. Knowing Mum, she'd hide the real secrets in the most unlikely place. But apart from her Post Office card and the savings book for the account Dad had set up (and Mum refused to use), there was nothing.

Insurance was the thickest file, but only because Mum clearly never threw any policy records away, keeping old booklets alongside the current ones for both home and car insurance. Katie flicked through them all in case Mum had hidden anything between pages. Nothing. At the back were her life insurance documents. Sum assured: £500,000. Term of cover: life. There followed a list of things Mum wasn't insured to do, which began with mountaineering and potholing and went through loads of activities she'd never dream of doing anyway and ended with skydiving, base jumping and motorcycle racing. Right at the bottom it stated they also wouldn't pay out if Mum died during a war or if she took an accidental drug overdose or committed suicide.

Katie wondered if Pat's life had been insured and, if so, if her insurance company had refused to pay out. She'd never learned to swim, after all. Pretty silly to go in the sea . . .

The next file was marked *Arrangements*, which sounded odd – arrangements for what? Inside was a single typed sheet of paper, headed *Funeral*. The top half was a list of people Mum wanted contacted if she died. There were email addresses and phone numbers for Dad, people at work and organizations, such as the mortgage company and the bank. Christ, imagine phoning total strangers up and telling them Mum was dead. Imagine phoning Dad up! Would he come back from holiday? Would they have to go and live with him? The second half of the page was headed *Plot* and had the address and phone number of a funeral director, along with the fact – the gruesome and terrifying fact – that Mum had already paid for her funeral and gravestone and the plot was number seventy-eight in the cemetery in North Bisham – *'the plot can accommodate three, so depending on the circumstances of my death, there could be room for all of us.'*

Katie sat back on her heels and laid her hand in a patch of sunlight that splashed the carpet. She tried not to think of how deep graves were – how dark, how terrible to have all that mud pressing down on you. She tried not to think of the circumstances that would require her to be buried with Mum and Chris – a car crash, a psychopath, a gas explosion. She tried not to think of the girls at school who would come to the funeral and witness that even in death Katie wasn't allowed to separate from her mother. But the thoughts came crashing in anyway, along with a feeling of utter claustrophobia, like she couldn't breathe, like the walls were pressing in and the windows had shrunk.

If they all died today, Katie would be buried in North Bisham for eternity. Her bones entwined with Mum's, the same soil plugging their mouths, the same earth weighing them down. How dare

Mum make arrangements for Katie's funeral when she wasn't even dead! What if she wanted to be cremated? What if she wanted to be buried in a wood, somewhere beautiful? Why, even in death, did Mum get to make all the decisions?

Katie raced through the last file, but *Documents* held nothing other than child benefit letters, medical cards, birth certificates and the divorce papers Dad sent months ago that Mum wouldn't sign (let him take me to court). Dad had cited Mum's unreasonable behaviour as cause for divorce, stating that she was emotionally absent from the marriage and frequently displayed a patronising and condescending attitude to him. Great! Another thing Katie didn't need to know.

She felt furious as she spaced the files back along their runners. Her dad was prepared to say anything to get shot of them and her mum was planning everyone's funeral. She felt sick. You can't unknow things. You can't shove information to the back of your mind and not have it hurt you. You can lie to yourself (she jumped me, honest!), you can refuse to think about it (just drop it, Katie, OK?). You can even get dementia and have memories fall away. But the really important ones are like blue blanks in your head – they have an emotional charge that never leaves. They spill and hurt and damage.

The files didn't look right. Too neat? Too far apart from each other? She should've taken a photo of the interior of the box. She ran the files to the top end and squashed them together to see if that looked more familiar and that's when she saw the book lying along the bottom of the box. It was grey, easy to miss, camouflaged. The story of Bluebeard flickered in her head – the last key, the last room, the secret that awaited his innocent wife behind a closed door.

Sod it. She swung the files to the other end and lifted it up, turned it over. It was marked *Diary 1968* in gold letters. On the first page, *Property of Patricia Dudley (née, Todd), Strictly Private.*

Thirty-one

If Katie opened Pat's diary, it would be a direct link to the time when Mum was back living with Pat after nearly two years of being in London with Mary. The year Mum turned fourteen. The year Pat drowned. It would be like sitting inside Pat's head and swilling about in her thoughts. It'd be like eavesdropping on private conversations. Katie shivered, glad for once that she wasn't in Mary's room with all the ancestors looking down at her. They'd definitely disapprove, especially the old ladies in the wedding picture. *Betrayal! Betrayal of the dead!* they'd be yelling if they still had voices.

Well, they could sod off. The only dead person whose opinion mattered in relation to this diary was Pat, and given that she was the one who'd ruined everything between Mary and Mum in the first place, she'd just have to understand that Katie needed to betray her in the hope of restoring peace.

But, in a nod of respect to her great-aunt, Katie would set some rules. First, she'd only look at the diary for ten minutes. Second, she'd never look at it again after today – this was a once-in-a-life-time opportunity. Lastly, she'd never use anything she discovered for her own gain, only to help settle the feud between Mum and Mary.

Rules set, she put her phone on timer and opened the diary.

January 1968 was, Pat noted, a time when the 'character of England seemed to be changing'. No one seemed to have any morals and everything scared her. This resulted in her having some 'very dark moods'. The war in Vietnam frightened her, as did the marches against it. She was fearful of decimalization ('why do they have to change the money?') and definitely against the abortion act ('it encourages promiscuity'). 'If things can't innocently stay the same,' she wrote, 'then I want to be beyond it. That seems a peaceful option to me.'

It struck Katie that Pat had lived all her life (apart from the few years in Bisham with her 'marriage-of-convenience husband') in the same house with her father. She'd slept in the same bed, shopped in the same streets and undertaken the same daily domestic tasks for years. No changes at all. Even the little sister she'd brought up had been swapped for a very similar little girl. But the world outside the windows was changing and there was nothing Pat could do about it.

As Katie read the next pages, she was made aware of a woman who was clearly not enjoying life at all. There were floods, there was a power cut, the butcher only had 'scrag ends' and the grocer was selling bad apples. To top it all, a woman at the post office assumed Pat and Lionel were still together. 'The horror of divorce never leaves,' she wrote. 'Years on and I still get nosy parkers stirring up the past.'

There was no reference to Mum at all. Perhaps Pat was too sad and self-absorbed to notice her? The only mention she got in the whole of January was, 'Caroline watching too much rubbish on television,' which resulted in *Top of the Pops* being switched off because the men were wearing makeup and the women were wearing 'hardly a stitch'.

'I thought I'd learned to live with "black moods",' Pat wrote a few days later, 'but they are getting more frequent. They get in the way of seeing the good things. They hide the light. On a good day, it's as if the curtains are fluttering and I can see it's sunny outside and maybe I'll go out later. I have a certain optimism. But on a bad day, it's dark, dark, dark.'

This was followed by a series of scribbles, in black ink, like smudges of sadness. Then two weeks of blank pages. Then, 'How do I go on? So many days in a row that I don't get out of bed.'

Katie's heart slammed. This woman clearly had depression! Was this the illness Mum mentioned? The illness that had put Pat in hospital? Is this what Mary meant when she said, Pat had 'no joy in anything'?

Even the so-called 'good days' were boring. Pat might dare to go outside in the garden or even wander into town with her shopping trolley. But mostly she seemed to fritter away her time with pottering about and small domestic tasks. 'Sewed a button.' 'Darned two pairs of Dad's socks.' 'Wrong delivery from milkman, so left note of complaint.' The surprise of reading the diary, Katie thought, was just how little Pat actually did.

'Was I happy in the war?' she wrote towards the end of February. 'I don't remember thinking it at the time, but there seemed such purpose to everything and now there isn't.'

She made a list of books she'd like to pick up from the library, but never seemed to get them.

Pat went the whole of March without leaving the house, relying on Mum to get the shopping and make meals. Katie skimmed, looking for news of doctors or hospital check-ups or visits, but there were none.

It wasn't until the beginning of April that anything changed. Pat's father contacted Mary, requesting she visit. 'He tells me I'm unwell again,' Pat wrote, 'but I tell him it's just that Caroline looks at me with different eyes and I can hardly bear it.'

Different eyes? No, Pat – you're ill again. Go to a doctor and get some medicine – stop holding your daughter responsible.

Here, on 15 April was the visit from Mary in full detail – she was half an hour late and 'flaunted herself to the neighbours before even crossing the step'. Norman (still living next door apparently) had a 'crush', despite the fact that Mary was dropped off by 'her latest fancy man' who managed to 'look very married' before zooming off in his Mercedes. Her outfit ('a low-cut thing') was 'inappropriate' and the gift she brought Caroline (tickets to a festival in August) was going to 'cause a row'. Katie felt Pat's envy of Mary in the pages – this sister who seemed to have everything and got away with so much.

'Dad's eyes lit up when she walked in. So much for her being "ruined". It took him a full fifteen minutes to recall he's "unable to forgive" her and leave the room. Caroline could barely stop grinning either. It won't be long before they're all best pals, mark my words. And where will that leave me?'

Mary's suggestion that Caroline go back to London after her exams was dismissed outright by Pat. Later, on the same day she wrote, 'Caroline assures me she has no desire to live in London again, but I don't see her fitting in here. She has Mary's ways about her now.'

Mary's ways? Mum did? Only last week, she'd told Katie that living in London had been a nightmare, that she'd felt like a fish out of water with all the socializing and new people. But moving anywhere different changes you, makes you aware of other choices. Here was Mum, back in her birth town with a depressed mother and a dull routine, with antimacassars and ticking clocks. Mum was too dreary for Mary and too wild for Pat, and perhaps didn't fit in anywhere any more?

Mary's visit had clearly tripped some kind of switch, because

Pat's attention turned to Mum. 'Asked Caroline to post a letter and she was gone forty minutes.' 'Secret laughter on the telephone.' 'Car stopped outside at tea time and I thought it was Mary. My heart plummeted to the ground.'

On 28 May she wrote, 'Spent an afternoon raking through knitting patterns, but gave up. What's the point of bothering when Caroline refuses to wear anything but the angora sweaters Mary brought from London?'

Mum had said she'd avoided wearing the gifts Mary bought her. And here was Pat writing that she brazened it out, even suggesting Mum wore them to annoy her. The truth, Katie thought, is a slippery thing.

Everything Mum did seemed to stir Pat to fury:

'Caroline came in from school and I try to be kind, but she's very frustrating. Suddenly allergic to everything she used to like. Cook your own meals from now on, I told her!'

'A boy walked Caroline home and when I ask who he was, she ran up the stairs and slammed her door. None of my business, she thinks. Well, I put her right on that.'

'I can see that Caroline is embarrassed by the level of conversation I'm able to provide, so I decide to keep silent.'

'Caroline watched the demonstrations in Paris on the television. Off she trots upstairs when I switch it off. Even though I kept my mouth zipped, she said I have no tolerance. Who does that sound like?'

'Caroline comes in with a pair of purple trousers from the market. I break my silence to tell her she looks ridiculous.'

On 22 June, Pat heard 'from a spy' that Mum had been kissing a boy in a shop doorway. She hauled Mum straight to the bathroom and ordered her to wash her makeup off. She then did a recce of her room and discovered (listed) hair curlers, Tampax ('expressly for married ladies'), a pack of cigarettes and a lighter, a passport photo taken in a booth with 'some boy pressing his face against hers'. Mum had secret makeup, secret earrings, secret money hidden in her underwear drawer. And as for the underwear, well, where had she acquired a scarlet knicker and bra set? And why did she need it?

Several items were confiscated, and when Mum refused to relinquish a lipstick, Pat grabbed it and mashed it to pulp beneath her heel. Later, she made Caroline clean the carpet ('vinegar did the trick'). Katie's heart ached with pity. Not only was it cruel beyond measure, but what if the lipstick had been the one Mary had given Mum to encourage bravery?

Later that night, Pat regretted what had happened but: 'Caroline not interested in truce and spent the evening with Dad. Thick as thieves. "Come back," I told her at bedtime. "I want my little girl back."'

She'd be lucky. She must've totally alienated Mum by trashing her room, and even if depression was the cause – well, some things were unforgiveable.

Katie skim-read the next few pages, she only had forty seconds left on the timer and she had to get to the end.

'Dad sent for Mary. Wants me back in that damned hospital. "You think Mary's a better mother?" I ask him. He couldn't answer, because he knows she's not. Did Mary mop Caroline's brow when she had tonsillitis, or nurse her through measles and mumps? No – she turns up for the easy bits. Mary Todd the hero, trampling over everyone to grab what she wants.'

More blank pages, more dark scrawls, words written and scribbled out that Katie can't access now. 'Everything is monotonous and dull,' Pat wrote in October. 'I am drawn to the beach. Such a beautiful expanse of nothingness. I have a desire to walk into it and never come back.'

Drawn to the beach? So, Pat didn't drown because she couldn't swim, she drowned because she walked into the sea on purpose! She killed herself!

Katie rested the diary on her knee briefly. The timer was about to go off, but she couldn't read when her eyes were filling with tears. Why hadn't Mum told her? How could she keep something this massive a secret? Why hadn't she said, *My mother suffered from years of depression and was actually pretty abusive and then she committed suicide, so, I'm sorry I come down hard on you sometimes, Katie, do you forgive me?* Mum could write a misery memoir and make a fortune. Katie wiped her eyes, turned back to the book.

Pat had only weeks to live and was clearly plotting. Katie had sworn to dead Pat that she wouldn't go beyond ten minutes, but as the timer went off, she knew she was going to keep reading. These last pages were vital. *Sorry, Pat*, she breathed. *Just one more minute.*

'I cannot bear it, how different my life is, how dreary it all seems, how pointless. Soon, Caroline will leave me and Dad will die and what will I do then?'

'Letter from Mary. "Send her," she begs. "Reconsider, why don't you?"'

Now came more blank pages. Here, in what was now November, a list of essentials. Sheets and towels were required apparently, 'to dampen and stuff under doorways'.

Definitely planning on harming herself. Didn't Sylvia Plath stick her head in a gas oven when her kids were upstairs sleeping? Didn't Virginia Woolf walk into a river with stones in her coat pocket? Maybe Pat had heard of them? Maybe, in her depression, she thought such things romantic and hadn't considered the irreparable damage she might do to Mum.

319

Mary is coming to 'give her a rest' and Pat 'can't bear it'. Mum gets blamed, accused of making secret phone calls, of conspiring and scheming, despite her protestations that she doesn't want Mary to come. 'Caroline swears she didn't invite her,' Pat writes, 'but I see the lying look in her eyes.'

'I've made up my mind what to do,' she writes on 5 November. Katie imagined fireworks exploding outside and perhaps Mum out with her friends (stay out, Mum – never go home!). Because here was Pat, mired in depression, writing, 'I refuse to watch Mary steal all that I love. I must take action before she gets here. Not pills. Not gas oven. Not Dad's car. The sea. I want all that water to wash me clean away . . .

'Spent the afternoon washing and sorting shells. The ones Mary gathered from the beach all those years ago. Listened to the water's roar by placing the largest of them next to my ear and yes, I have decided . . . All that is left is to say goodbye.'

And now, the saddest thing of all, the saddest saddest thing, was a series of one-liners. Scrawled sentences crossed out, as if Pat was determined to get the wording right.

'It won't hurt they say, it's painless.'

'Don't cry for me.'

'Look after your grandfather. That's all I ask of you.'

'I know what you see in her – all that wild energy and light. Well, fine – do what you must. But I can't any longer.'

On and on. Page after page through that week in November. Blank pages, torn pages, little dark blots, stains and smears as if the ink was running away from her.

Thirty-two

'What the hell are you doing?'

'Shit!'

Mum stood in the doorway, her face ashen. 'Why is my box out of the wardrobe?'

'I was . . . I was just looking for something.'

'Is that my mother's diary?'

They both looked at it in Katie's hands. There was no denying it.

'That's private.' Mum marched over and snatched it back. 'Were you reading this?'

Katie hunched lower on the carpet. She had no words.

Mum glared furiously down at her. 'I asked you a question.'

Katie nodded, tried to make herself smaller. 'I'm sorry.'

'How much of it?'

'All of it.'

Mum lunged at her. She grabbed a handful of jumper and pulled Katie up from the floor. 'Why would you do that? What gives you the right?'

'Mum, you're hurting me.'

'They're my private things.' She gripped Katie tighter, her fingers feeling like stubby claws. 'How dare you go through them.'

'I'm sorry. I didn't mean to.'

'You don't accidentally read someone's diary!' She pushed Katie roughly towards the bed. 'Sit down. Go on. Sit there and explain yourself.'

Katie felt her chest heave, her brain swirl. No! She didn't want her mother looming over the bed with that awful, disappointed look on her face.

'You said you were looking for something. Was it the diary you were looking for?'

'I didn't even know it existed.'

'What then?'

Katie's throat hurt. She swallowed hard. 'Something to help Mary.'

'Help her with what?'

'She was upset at Dad's house.' Katie found herself fiddling with a corner of the duvet, twisting it round and round her fingers. 'I wanted to know why, but when I asked, you wouldn't tell me.'

'So you trawled through my things?'

'She keeps crying at night. You know she does.'

'You break my trust and completely disrespect my privacy because she *cries*?' Mum sounded wounded as well as furious now. Like the fact that Katie wanted to help Mary was the most shocking and unbelievable part.

'I thought you were hiding something.'

'I can't believe this. I can't believe what I'm hearing.'

'And you *were* hiding something,' Katie whispered. 'Pat drowned on purpose. She committed suicide. Why didn't you tell me?'

'Because it's none of your business.' Mum's eyes were gleaming and Katie didn't know if it was with rage or tears. 'I've had enough of this. I'm not putting up with it any more.'

Katie stared in horror as Mum turned to the wardrobe and

322

hauled a suitcase from the top shelf. It had jumpers and winter clothing in it and she tipped them on the floor.

'What are you doing?'

'Packing Mary's things. She's got to go.'

'This isn't her fault!'

'That woman's wrecking our lives.' Mum turned in the doorway. 'You've changed, you know that? I don't even know who you are any more.' She marched across the landing with the suitcase and slammed into Mary's room. Katie raced after her.

'You can't just send her away.'

'Watch me.'

'Where will she go?'

'Back to the hospital.' Mum yanked open one of the bedside drawers. 'I'll leave her in reception and I won't give a damn.'

'You can't dump her!'

'Oh, yes I can.' Mum pulled knickers and socks and tights from Mary's drawer and threw them in the case. 'Why not? You do whatever you like with no regard for anyone else, so why shouldn't I?' She glared at Katie triumphantly. 'You lie about where you are and who you're with. You get drunk at parties. You go on dates with boys I've never heard of and now this – you go through my private things as if rules don't apply to you.'

'I'm sorry. I said I'm sorry.'

'That doesn't make it better. Nothing does. You've changed because *she* changed you. You're not mine any more.'

'I wasn't yours in the first place. What does that even mean? I don't *belong* to you.'

Mum opened the next drawer down and dragged out Mary's cardigans. She ripped her nightie from under the pillow. There was no going back from this. If Mary walked upstairs now, she'd be traumatized. Katie stood with her back against the door.

323

'Mum, this is so unfair.'

'Don't talk to me about what's fair. You were the one reading my mother's diary when I walked in the room.'

'I'm sorry. I'm sorry I found out about Pat. But please don't punish Mary.'

'You invaded my privacy!'

'I know, but don't invade hers. She had nothing to do with it.'

Mum didn't answer, didn't seem to hear. She opened the wardrobe and pulled dresses and skirts from their hangers and chucked them in the case. 'My mother died of a broken heart, you know that? Mary broke it. And then she broke mine.'

'Please, Mum, just stop.'

Mum ignored her, kicked Wolf Mountain out of the way, grabbed the framed photo of Jack from the bedside table and threw it on top of the clothes. She swept Mary's makeup bag and cleansers from the shelf. 'All her life she's only cared about herself. You think she's so brave having an illegitimate child and leaving home? It'd be more radical to bring the baby up herself or go off to university and get an education. But no, she buggers off to London to follow her dreams.'

She looked so ugly saying such mean things. Her mouth was a thin line and her eyes were all narrow.

'And so what if she pops back to gawp at her child through some damn café window every now and then? What good does that do anyone, eh? She should have left us alone. We'd have been fine without her.'

Katie stared at her mother, at the way her mouth moved. She curled her hands into fists and her mother's mouth kept moving.

'For weeks I've watched you trot after her like some kind of disciple. And yes, I asked you to look after her, and yes, I needed to go back to work and yes, I was grateful. But I didn't expect it

324

to drive us apart. I didn't expect you to get all secretive or start raking through the past like it belongs to you.'

It was all flooding out of her. All the resentment, all the unsaid things. Mum tugged Mary's clothes from the washing basket and rammed them in the case with the clean stuff and she just kept talking.

'All I ask of you is that you work hard at school and you stay out of trouble. You think I ask that for my own benefit? For my health? Or maybe you think I'm just trying to limit or annoy you? I ask you to do that stuff because I care about you – and see how you repay me? See what you do?'

Katie felt a churning in her stomach like that time she'd got food poisoning – a cramping, a hot ache, where the only way to feel better was to throw up. She took a step forward. And maybe Mum sensed a shift, because she turned round.

'Get out, Katie.'

The heat climbed. Katie could feel it pulsing. 'It's my room. I lent it to Mary, but it's actually mine – remember?'

'I don't care. Just get out of my sight. This is nothing to do with you.'

And hearing those words, Katie felt the heat turn to fury. 'It *is* to do with me. Pat was my ancestor. Why keep what happened to her a secret? What's so shameful about it? You never talk to me about anything that matters. Why not? You're not an island. Look at you getting rid of Mary. This is just like when you chucked Dad's stuff out.'

'I'm serious – you need to leave.'

'Are you going to hire a skip for Mary? Are you going to ban us from seeing her?'

'Don't be ridiculous. Get out, go on. You're giving me a headache.'

'You always do this. You always make out you're the victim when you don't want to listen. Don't I have a right to talk?'

'You don't get any rights.'

'So I can't even know about my own family? I can't ask any questions about it?'

'The person invading the other person's privacy gets no rights at all.' Mum turned to the wall and started pulling photos off. All the tender effort Katie had put in and Mum was just yanking at them. She looked like she was enjoying it. She looked like she could just keep doing this – going through room after room and destroying everything.

Katie took another step forward. 'Do I get any rights about where I'm buried?'

Mum stalled for a moment and Katie was glad. *Got you*, she thought.

'What are you talking about?'

'I'm talking about the fact you bought a hole in the ground with all our names on it.'

Mum turned round and stared at her in disbelief. 'You read that paperwork as well? You actually went through everything?'

Katie nodded.

'You shouldn't have done that.'

'And you shouldn't arrange a plot in the cemetery without asking.'

'It's not for you, it's for me.'

'It's for three people!' They'd both raised their voices now and Katie didn't care. 'Don't you see how creepy that is?'

'You have to state the size of the plot when you buy it. You can't add to it later.'

'Why buy it at all?'

'Because when you're the only adult running a household you

have to think about things like that. You have to think about wills and funeral arrangements and what happens to your children in the event of your death. You also have to consider terrible possibilities, such as your children dying with you. Who would organize a funeral then, eh?'

'Dad would.'

'Would he? He'd probably just dig a hole in his garden and chuck us all in.'

'So what? So what if he did?'

Chris and Mary might be listening downstairs. The window was open and maybe people outside could hear too. Mum would usually care about things like that, but she didn't and Katie didn't either. They faced up to each other and it was exhilarating. It was like all the cosmic plates had shifted and in this room right now was the exact place to spill your soul.

'Me and Chris want to see him.'

'Go ahead. You're not banned from seeing your father.'

'We pretty much are. Whenever we try to talk about him, you clam up.'

'That's not true. You can talk about him whenever you want.'

'What, like we can talk about Pat? Or Dad's girlfriend? Or our new half-sister? No, you'd like to think we're all best mates, but we're not. You make us rotas and timetables and charts and you tell yourself you're the best parent on earth, but other kids' parents don't do any of that.'

'I'm not interested in what other parents do. My only concern is you two.'

'And that's the point! This family's so small and so lonely. It's like we're breaking off person by person and you just don't care. All this secrecy about Pat. All this fury at Mary. I could've known her for *years* and you made sure that didn't happen. She's my *grandmother*.'

327

For a second Katie saw something in her mother's eyes she'd never seen before. Was it fear? It made Katie feel bigger than herself, bigger and more powerful and more right than her mother.

'You don't know how lucky you are, Mum. I never do anything wrong. I'm not a junkie or pregnant. I'm doing well at school. I help out all the time – I cook and shop when you ask, I've looked after Mary for weeks and you're pretty much planning I look after Chris for the rest of my life, and still nothing's right for you, is it?'

Katie could see her own face in the wardrobe mirror and it was strange, like when she'd been a kid and watched herself cry. It made her self-aware, so she banged the door shut with her foot. Mum flinched.

'If we talk about Dad, you change the subject. If we say we want to see him, you go all cold. We're so scared of hurting you, we never tell you anything. Can you see that? We creep about trying to avoid anything real because it's like you might melt or explode. And you make all these plans and expect us just to fall in with them. How do you think Chris feels having his weight chart slapped on the fridge for everyone to see? How do you think I feel when you tell me which university to apply for or want to write my personal statement for me? All the things I want to say about myself are just swept to one side.'

Mum stood very still. Katie could hear her own breathing, like she'd been running. She couldn't hear Mum breathing though. Maybe this was killing her. But she didn't care if it was. She didn't care that the fire had gone out of Mum's eyes either.

'I can't wait for school to be over,' Katie said. Her voice was very quiet. She felt almost calm. 'I can't wait to get out of here. I'm going to apply to go to university in Edinburgh or New York, so I can do whatever I want without you breathing down my neck.'

328

The sun shafted through the window. Dust spun in the air. Mum's face seemed bleached out.

'Can you go now,' Mum said. 'I want to be by myself.'

'Tough.'

'Please, Katie. I just need some space.'

'No, this is my room. Mine and Mary's.'

Mum stood staring at her, not saying anything. She looked small and defeated. She shook her head a couple of times, like she wanted to shake away all the things Katie had said. And then, without warning, she walked out the room and shut the door.

Katie was glad. There was nothing else to say. She'd said it all. She felt wonderfully empty.

Thirty-three

It was over an hour later when Katie went downstairs. She'd put all Mary's things back except for the photos. She figured she and Mary could do that together after supper. It'd be fun to rearrange them. She'd decided to feel good about things.

She'd also decided that if Mum had another go at her, she'd demand a truce. They'd both done – and said – awful stuff, but Katie wasn't going to cower. There was no point going backwards.

But Mum wasn't there. Mary was drinking tea and watching TV and Chris was huddled by the balcony doors staring out at a darkening sky.

'What's going on, Chris?'

'She's gone.'

'Mum has?'

He nodded. 'She's never coming back.'

'Is that what she said?'

'It's what she meant.'

'What did she actually say?'

'She's gone to a hotel and if there's an emergency we have to call nine-nine-nine.'

Jesus. So now they were alone. Katie had never known her mother walk out. She'd been angry before. She'd slammed doors and shouted, but she'd never just disappeared.

'She won't go,' Mary said. 'She won't go out in all this rain.'

'She already has,' Chris said, and he looked mournfully down at the courtyard. 'She got in the car and drove off.'

'She'll be back,' Katie said, but she wasn't sure.

Mary banged her cup down, rattling the saucer and making the table shake. 'She's always leaving. Good riddance, I say.'

In the kitchen, Katie sat at the table and put her head onto her arms. She'd been so sure earlier. She'd felt as if she had right on her side but now she didn't know. Should she call Mum and apologize? Or was Mum being manipulative and it was best to sit it out? How was it possible to be so clear about a situation one minute and so confused the next?

'Shall we phone Dad?' Chris said, sidling into the kitchen.

'He's in France. What's he going to do?'

He walked over to the sink and looked out of the window. 'I keep thinking she's going to come back.'

'She will.'

'It's raining loads though. What if she has a car crash? What if she goes for a walk somewhere lonely and breaks a leg?'

'She's got her phone.'

'It's switched off.'

So, he'd tried calling her. Katie propped herself on one elbow and looked at the shape of him against the window. He looked like a cut-out with all that cloud and silver rain behind him.

'She'll be fine, Chris. She's probably raiding the mini bar and ordering room service right this second.'

He turned to look at her. 'What were you arguing about? Was it me?'

'Not everything's about you.'

'What then?'

Shame hit her in a great wave. Going through Mum's stuff was

331

so obviously wrong all over again. She couldn't tell him. She didn't want him to hate her as well. 'How about a takeaway, Chris? We can put it on my credit card.'

He shrugged and he looked so young, just a kid whose Mum and Dad had left him.

Food, when it came, didn't cheer him up. It didn't cheer Mary up either. She didn't want supper, she wasn't hungry and anyway, she hated pizza. Katie had never heard her dismiss any food out of hand before. She gave Mary's share to Chris, but as soon as he'd finished it, Mary asked why no one was giving her any pizza, and was she invisible or what? Chris said it wasn't his fault there was none left and Mary said, 'Whose fault was it then?' Chris buried his face in the sofa, so Katie switched the TV to some fast-moving game show and tipped a load of chocolate biscuits on a plate for them to share. She was clearly terrible at looking after people. They'd both be hyper with screens and sugar by bedtime.

She sat in the kitchen and tried to figure out what to do if Mum didn't come back tomorrow. She couldn't decide if she should keep taking care of things herself, or if she should let Dad know. She washed up the plates and dried them and put them away. She tried to watch TV, but couldn't concentrate. Chris kept flicking channels, and when he wasn't doing that he was sighing or looking out of windows. Mary seemed restless too. She said everything ached, but when Katie tried to hug her, Mary pushed her away.

Katie veered between ashamed and furious. She preferred furious. It was like grabbing an oar when you'd fallen from a boat. It felt safe and sure and Katie enjoyed feeling things shift back in her favour. Parents shouldn't just walk out if you yelled at them. They had to be able to withstand more than that. Wasn't that the point of them? It was completely irresponsible of Mum to bugger off.

Fury was hard to hold onto though. It kept slipping away. Maybe it was the rain. It was hitting the windows and bouncing off the balcony furniture and didn't look as if it'd ever stop. Katie kept thinking of that scene in *King Lear* when the mad old king goes out in a storm after his daughters betray him. Didn't he die in the end?

She decided to follow Mum's usual routines. It wasn't like she didn't know what they were. She made a pot of chamomile tea and encouraged Mary to drink because she needed to 'keep up her fluids' and because it'd help her get 'quality sleep'. She even sounded like Mum. She ran a bath and cajoled Mary upstairs and into the bathroom. She wasn't sure how far Mum went in forcing Mary to undress and actually get in the water. What had Katie been doing every evening at this time? How come she'd never been part of the bath ritual?

'I don't need a bath,' Mary said. 'I'll wash when I get home, thank you.'

'How does Mum make you do this, Mary?'

Mary folded her arms. 'No one makes me do anything.'

Mary smelled Elizabethan when she was stripped down to her underwear and standing right in front of you. Why hadn't Katie ever known this about her? Was it only true today? Katie felt weary. When the anger fell away, she was left with only sadness and a kind of hollow panic.

She gave up on the bath and let Mary put her nightie on and go downstairs again. Chris was back in the kitchen, perched on the sink and staring gloomily down at Mum's empty parking space. Katie retrieved his 'Call of Duty' game from where Mum had hidden it with the cookery books and handed it back to him.

'I'm not supposed to have it,' he said. 'It's an eighteen. She might not come back if I do stuff she doesn't like.'

'That's ridiculous. She's never going to know.'

'I'm still not doing it.'

Fear was contagious and Katie despised it in him, even though it was ratcheting up in her. She wanted him to be brave. She wanted him to cock a snook like Mary had once advised them and not try to pacify Mum in her absence and not give a damn that he was an overnight orphan.

She texted Jamie, THNKNG OF U. He texted straight back and invited her out for a drink and she replied that she couldn't and hoped she sounded mysterious rather than trapped. It was comforting to know he was in the world. At least someone liked her.

Texting him must've opened the airwaves because her phone immediately rang. Chris jumped down from his perch by the sink. 'Is it Mum?'

Katie shook her head and they both stared at the screen.

'Who's Simona?' he said. 'Aren't you going to answer it?'

What would she say if she did? 'Sorry' over and over? There were no other words for what had happened at the library, no possible explanation for ignoring texts for days. Clearly, Simona was getting angry now. She'd moved from texts to calls. She wasn't letting this go.

She didn't leave a message though. That was a relief.

Guilt and fear were terrible things. *Come back, fury*, Katie thought. *I prefer you.*

The evening went from bad to worse. Mary tore up a packet of tissues and confettied the carpet. She claimed she knew nothing about it when Katie confronted her. She seemed both embarrassed and puzzled. Later, she said a woman in the toilet asked her to leave and Chris freaked out until Katie turned the mirror to the wall and Mary decided the woman had gone.

At ten o'clock, Katie suggested it might be bedtime, but Chris put his coat on and said he was going to find Mum. Mary said she'd join him because she fancied a walk. Katie locked the door and hid the key in her pocket and Mary banged on the door with her slipper and urged Chris to call the fire brigade.

'No one's calling anyone,' Katie said. She could hear the anger in her voice. She sounded more like Mum with every breath. 'You're both going to bed.'

'I'm not sleeping until Mum gets back,' Chris said.

Mary folded her arms. 'Neither am I.'

Katie slammed the kitchen door on them both and stood against it. She wanted to run away. She wanted to be outside with the wind-whipped trees and the lashing rain. She wanted space – to run into it and always have it in front of her – endless space. If she ran fast enough and for long enough, maybe she could disappear from the world.

Instead, she made three cups of hot chocolate. She put the Nature channel on and encouraged them both to sit back down and watch a programme about orphaned sloths. She hoped it wouldn't upset Chris, but he didn't seem to get the connection.

Mary sipped her drink really slowly, like she wouldn't have to go to bed until it was finished. Katie kept peeking at her, trying to understand why the balance of their relationship had changed. Was it simply because Mum had gone and Katie had become parent and jailer? Or was it to do with Mary being sicker? Whatever it was, their old warmth had disappeared.

A new programme began and Chris said he wanted to watch it and Katie said no and turned it off and hid the remote and Chris said she wasn't in charge and she asked who was then and he said, 'Mum.' And Katie said, 'She's not here though, is she?' And Chris said, 'Because of you!' and glowered furiously at her before stomping upstairs. So maybe he'd heard the whole thing after all. Maybe he knew about the diary and maybe he hated her.

Mary still refused to go to bed. She said the stairs weren't real, they wouldn't work, were not to be trusted. Katie ran up them to prove they were fine. She jumped up and down on the treads until Mary was persuaded.

They went up arm in arm. That was nice.

'Where is your mother?' Mary asked politely as Katie helped her into bed.

'A hotel.'

'All right for some.'

'Not really. I did a terrible thing and now she hates me.'

'Mothers never hate their children.' Mary sounded extremely sure about this. It was very consoling. 'They love them with all their hearts.'

Katie leaned down and kissed her cheek. 'I miss you. Where have you been all night?'

'Right here,' Mary said as she snuggled down. 'And don't you ever forget it.'

Katie sat on the edge of the bed. She wanted this Mary to stay, but she was already fading, her eyes losing focus, heavy with sleep. Katie felt the loss so completely. One day soon, there'd be no moments of clarity or connection at all. It was inevitable, and just around the corner. She leaned down to give Mary another kiss. 'Who will I be when you forget me?' she whispered.

Mary drowsily tapped her hand. 'You will be you.'

Within seconds she was asleep. Katie got under a duvet on the floor next to her and lay there watching shadows on the ceiling. There was a strange light shining in through the curtains. She thought it might be the moon, but couldn't be bothered to check. If she moved her head slightly, it shone right across her face.

She thought of the forest in Mary's head, how it was probably moonless. She wondered if more trees were crashing down right this minute. She imagined an elephant banging about in there, a mad lumbering elephant with a chain round its belly yanking all the trees down. It was brutish and it had heavy animal breath, and in the morning Mary would wake to more devastation. She would be emptier and the spaces inside her head would be deeper. She would be less.

Katie thought of Mum in the hotel and wondered if she was asleep. Then she wondered if she'd secretly crept back in the flat when they were watching TV and was hiding in her bedroom. Katie was suddenly so certain of this that she had to go and check, but there was no one there.

She went downstairs to get a glass of water. She unplugged the TV and checked the door was locked. When she came back, Mary was out of bed and staring at the wall like some kind of ghost.

'What are you doing?'

Mary frowned. 'It's my room, isn't it?'

Actually not, Katie thought, and it shocked her to realize how immediately irritated she was. 'You slept for precisely twenty minutes, Mary, that's ridiculous.'

'I'll have you know I've been asleep for hours.' She narrowed her eyes. 'Some of my things are missing.'

'Your photos? They're on the cabinet. You want to put them back up?'

Mary didn't answer, so Katie decided to just get on with it, hoping Mary would either join in or get bored and go back to sleep. She peeled a few pictures from the bundle and pulled globs of Blu-Tack from the corners and stuck them on again neatly. As she pressed them to the wall she whispered the names. Here were the film stars – Lauren, Grace, Ingrid, Audrey. Here was Mary, more stunning than any of them with her nineteen-fifties curves and come-hither eyes. Mary came and stood next to her, holding out more photos, and Katie felt ridiculously pleased. Here, at last, was something they shared.

'This one next,' Mary said. 'This little girl and me.'

Katie took it from her. She assumed it would be Mary and Mum, but it wasn't. She couldn't believe what she was seeing. She sank onto the bed holding the photo and stared and stared at it. She felt like she'd been pulled down a rabbit hole to a topsy-turvy world where nothing made sense. 'This is you and me, Mary.'

'If you say so.'

'But I'm a little kid. How can it be us if we never met?'

'Of course we met.' Mary shook her head, as if Katie was being ridiculous. 'We're here right now, aren't we?'

'When I was young, I mean. I look about four in this picture.' She was wearing a green T-shirt she had no memory of. She had a fringe, which she didn't remember ever having either. And she was on Mary's back, her arms wrapped round Mary's neck and they were both laughing. This was Mary as Katie had never seen her before – a woman with short, razor-cut hair who wore lipstick and eye shadow and had diamond studs in her ears. But it was definitely her and it was definitely Katie, and that was definitely the back garden of the old house – the edge of the shed, the paddling pool out on the grass. 'Mum said you never got in touch, never visited us once. She said you weren't interested.'

'I was very interested. I'll have you know I was sent for.'

'Mum asked you to come?'

'No,' Mary said. 'It was a man. He wrote me a letter.'

It was Dad who'd written! Of course. That's what Mary said at the care home. 'Steve wrote you a letter?'

'That's right,' Mary said proudly. 'It said, *come quick, we need you.*'

Dad *needed* her? What the hell for? At the care home Mary had said she was helping. But helping with what? Katie peered at the photo looking for clues. She and Mary looked happy enough, so it wasn't that some shocking tragedy had occurred. In fact, they looked *very* happy. Mary looked like the kind of grandmother you'd see in movies – someone who'd take you to a fancy restaurant or a night at the theatre, who had energy for things and was always up for a laugh. She wasn't the young beauty from the photos, or the old woman in front of her now. She was someone entirely new. And Katie – well, she was grinning like the baby in the wedding photo, like Mary sometimes did – head tipped back, eyes shut, total joy. Tears pricked Katie's eyes. She never laughed like that any more.

'To tell you the truth,' Mary said, sitting next to Katie on the bed, 'I have a very bad feeling about this.' She tapped the photo with a finger. 'I keep meaning to ask what happened in the end, because I have to say, it feels as if someone made a terrible mistake.'

It was upsetting her and there was nothing Katie could do about it. She passed Mary a tissue, then wiped her own eyes too. They sat there looking at the photograph together and neither one of them had a clue.

Is this what dementia felt like? It was horrible. It felt like going mad – being presented with evidence that something had happened when you had no memory of it at all.

And this picture must've been in Mary's possession all this time. Where had it been? Not on the wall certainly, or Katie would have seen it. Had Mum trashing the room brought it to the surface somehow?

'Sorry,' Mary said, dabbing at her eyes. 'It's a terrible lost thing that happened, that's why.'

'It's a blue blank, Mary. For both of us.'

'Is that why I can't remember?'

It hurt. It felt raw and terrifying. Katie held the photo out so they could both see it clearly. She wanted to know what it meant with such urgency. It felt like the answer to everything. But getting stories out of Mary was like trapping a wild animal. You had to be patient. You had to not let her see you were coming. You had to go cautiously down pathways, and if they were blocked you had to turn round and go back on yourself. 'It's a lovely garden,' Katie said. 'I like the paddling pool.'

'Beautiful,' Mary agreed. 'We could water the flowers.'

'Did you ever go in the house?'

'I was in charge if you want to know the truth.'

'In charge of the little girl?'

'Although I have to tell you, it didn't end well.' Mary wiped a fresh tear away. 'Sometimes I think the wolves took her, because I never saw her again.'

Katie nodded, best to agree, best to open all the doors and let this story out, whatever form it came in. She wished she knew how to hypnotize people. She held the photo higher and let it glimmer in the light shining through the curtain. She hoped it was mesmerizing. 'A long time ago,' she began, 'you went to see Katie and Chris and Caroline and Steve.'

'No,' Mary said, 'Caroline wasn't there.'

Katie's heart leaped. Mum wasn't there? She took a breath, started again, 'One day, Mary Todd got a letter from Steve and the letter said, *Come quick*.'

'No, the letter said, *Where's my wife, do you know? My wife has completely disappeared*.' Mary snapped her fingers. 'Just like that.'

She made it sound like a terrible magic trick. She made it sound as if mothers were liable to vanish at the drop of the hat. 'Where was she?' Katie asked. 'Do you know?'

'Having an adventure.' Mary leaned in as if they might be over-heard. 'I was relieved, if you want to know. I didn't think she had it in her.'

Katie didn't either. Mum as adventurer wasn't someone she recognized. 'So, Steve sent for you and you arrived at the house . . .'

'That's right. I walked round the side of the house and there they were in the garden – three of them in a little row.'

'Steve and Katie and Chris . . .'

'That's it.' Mary's eyes were bright as she studied the photo. The air felt full of memories. Katie could almost hear long-ago voices stirring to life.

'I walked up the path,' Mary said and she sounded very sure, 'and there was Steve, standing at the back door with the baby in his arms and Katie at his side, her hair bright as flame.' She smiled, losing herself in the memory. 'I had never met her, but every inch was familiar.'

Here it comes, Katie thought. *Bring it on . . .*

2000 – what sort of mother?

Mary shakes Steve's hand, agrees that yes, she does travel light as she puts her suitcase on the grass. She coos at the baby, then crouches down to get a proper look at her granddaughter. 'Hello, Katie.'

'Hello.' The girl's eyes are merry with the strangeness of it all. 'Are you really my granny?'

'I really am.'

'I never had one.'

'Well, now you do.'

They gaze at each other.

'I made lemonade.' Katie points to a rickety garden table and a jug full of melting ice. 'It's got real lemons.'

'Took her hours,' Steve says.

'Is that right?' Mary says. 'Well, I'd love some. Lemonade is just about my favourite thing.'

'Mine too,' the girl says approvingly. 'You should've come to my party cause we had lots. I was four and I had a caterpillar cake.'

Mary smiles. Caroline has slipped through her fingers for years, but here is a new opportunity. A beautiful granddaughter!

'Does my mummy know you're here?' Katie asks.

'Well . . .' Mary begins.

Steve ruffles the child's hair. 'Talking of cakes, how about you

342

fetch the one we bought, Mrs Chatterbox? You think you can manage that?'

The girl nods, suddenly solemn with responsibility. 'Shall I get plates?'

'Napkins. And I'll pour the lemonade.'

Mary is given the baby to hold. He reaches out to pluck at her nose. He fills up her mouth with sweet baby fingers.

Steve says, 'You wouldn't think to look at him now, but that little fella was up half the night.'

He'd said on the phone the baby cried a lot, was a fussy eater, slept badly. But he isn't crying now. And Mary enjoys the weight of him, the warmth, the way he nuzzles into her neck as she sits down on a bench by the back door. She nestles him closer and leans in to smell the top of his head, because she knows there's a place there, a soft place, right at the top of the skull, which smells of life. She breathes him up. She thinks of the sons her mother lost – Herbert, Stanley and William. Like prayers, those names.

And this boy, this little Christopher, is alive and in her arms. He gives a yawn. She sees right inside the soft oval of his mouth. What a miracle he is. And despite what Steve said on the phone, you can't tell, just by looking, that there's anything wrong with him at all.

Steve hands her a glass of lemonade. The ice cubes creak like tiny glaciers. 'I'm really grateful,' he says. 'I feel like the walls are closing in. I can't believe she ran off and left me to manage the kids.'

Ah, Mary thinks, *I see*. And the picture slides into focus. 'Tell me more about this little one,' she says.

'He has an undiagnosed disorder.' Steve takes a swig of his drink. 'Whatever the hell that means. On one hand, the sky's the limit, isn't it? No one can ever say, "Oh, he'll never be able to do x or y."

But with no prognosis, it's like you're stuck in the dark. Will he walk? Will he run or jump? Will he talk? Will he be dependent on us for ever?' Steve gives Mary the smallest of smiles. 'Every time we take him to a specialist, I think, *don't tell me they've found anything, some terrible genetic thing*. But another part of me thinks, *please give us some information*. All they've said so far is that he has some kind of global developmental delay.'

Mary takes a sip. It's sweet and sour at the same time. Pat used to make lemonade like this. She swallows. 'Have you heard from Caroline since we spoke?'

'A postcard, that's all. She misses us, and she's sorry. Nothing to say if or when she's coming home.' He gives a hurried look into the house, perhaps making sure Katie isn't listening. 'You think you know someone, don't you? But it turns out I married a stranger.'

'She'll come back,' Mary says. 'You'll work things out.'

He sits down heavily on the bench next to Mary and stares at his son. 'Or she won't. And we won't.'

The baby's eyes are heavy with sleep. Mary wills him to give in to it. She wonders if this situation has ever occurred before in the history of the world – a man begging his mother-in-law to help with his children when she's never met them before and is entirely estranged from their mother. 'She doesn't know I'm here, does she?'

He shrugs. 'How can I tell her if she doesn't phone?'

'She'll call eventually. Will you tell her then?'

From somewhere inside the house, there's the sound of cupboard doors opening and shutting. 'The one under the kettle,' Steve calls, 'by the biscuit tin.' The baby's eyes flicker open and immediately close again. Steve gives Mary a weary smile. 'I'll say I asked you to stay, that I needed to get back to work.'

'And what do you think she'll do?'

'Be grateful? Shouldn't a grandmother be the perfect solution?'

'I doubt she'll see it that way.'

'Well, I don't know what else I was supposed to do. We don't have any other relatives.'

From the kitchen now, the sound of drawers opening and closing. Mary shifts the baby's weight on her arm.

When Steve had written it had crossed her mind to write back and tell him no, he should sort this out himself, it risked too much – the last thing in the world she wanted to do was hurt Caroline by interfering where she wasn't wanted. But a chance to meet her grandchildren? Just to spend a day or two, a week or so, in their company . . . And if Caroline needed time away and her husband couldn't manage, then perhaps this was a way of supporting her? Steve had put his phone number at the top of the letter. How could she resist?

She'd talked it through with Jack. 'What if she comes back and finds me there?'

'You'll talk, that's what. You'll mend this falling out at last.'

'She might not want to talk. My being there might make every-thing worse. It's a big risk to take, Jack.'

'When did a big risk ever stop you doing anything, Mary Todd?'

They laughed at that.

'Seriously,' Jack said, 'you should go. I haven't known you long, but I know this is breaking your heart.'

Ah, she was going to miss him.

'She told me she was going swimming,' Steve says. He sounds sullen. 'She took nothing except her passport and purse and she got on a plane and went to Malaga. I didn't see her note until the afternoon, by which time I was frantic.' He turns to Mary, his eyes

345

glistening. 'Why would she do that? What sort of mother just leaves her children and walks out the door?'

All sorts of mothers, Steve.

'So I wrote to you,' he says. 'So what? I'm sick of this rift between you two. On and on it goes. I mean, it's not as if you actually killed Pat with your bare hands, is it?'

A blackbird sweeps across the garden and settles on a branch by the shed. Mary watches its throat quiver before it spills liquid notes into the sunshine. She puts her lemonade down and moves the baby back to her shoulder. Her arm's gone numb with the weight of him.

'You want me to take him?' Steve says.

She shakes her head. 'Caroline came to visit me when she was pregnant with Katie. Did you know?'

His frown tells her he didn't. This man is discovering new things about his wife all the time.

'She just turned up on the doorstep. She said becoming a mother made her realize how furious she was with me and she needed to get it off her chest. She didn't want to come into the house, didn't want a cup of tea, so we stood in the front garden and she let rip.' Mary laughs, a soft sound. She's surprised to be laughing. 'I decided the best policy was not to interrupt, but by the time she'd finished, everything I wanted to say just sounded like an excuse.' She turned to Steve. 'I caused her immeasurable pain and I had no words for her.'

'You wrote. She was always getting letters.'

'Oh, letters. What good are they? I should've taken her away from Pat sooner. Either that, or left her alone completely. She belonged nowhere, that's what she told me.'

'She kept the letters. That's how I got your address. That's got to be a good sign, right? I mean, how long can someone hold a grudge?'

Mary has a feeling he's about to find out. Most men can't let their woman run off and not want some kind of revenge. She wonders what Steve is capable of. It depends exactly what Caroline's up to, of course. And who with. And how long it takes her to come home.

'Anyway,' she says, 'I'm here for her now. If she needs time for herself, then so be it. If this little one is hard work, then I'll do what I can. I want nothing more than to be part of this family.'

Katie comes wobbling down the step with a plate of Battenberg cut into very large slices. She holds it out proudly. 'I cut it by my own. With a knife.'

'Jesus,' Steve shakes his head. 'I look away for five minutes!'

'Not the sharp one, Daddy.' She holds the plate with one hand and wiggles some fingers at him. 'See?'

He takes the plate. 'Don't tell your mother. I'll never hear the end of it.'

'She's not here.' She wiggles the other hand. 'So I can't.'

'I mean when she gets back.'

'Will it be soon, Daddy?'

He distracts her with cake. She takes a piece and twirls off across the lawn.

'She asks me every day,' Steve says quietly.

Lemonade is drunk and cake is eaten. Afternoon sunshine spreads across the lawn. Mary shows Katie how to make a daisy chain. The baby wakes up howling and is taken inside for a drink and a nappy change. Katie shows Mary where the paddling pool is kept, and together they heave it out from the shed and fill it with warm water from the kitchen tap. Pail by pail they fill it, splashing their toes. By the time it's full and Katie throws herself in, the water's already cold and she whoops with laughter.

'I know what we'll do if you don't want to sit in it,' Mary says. 'Let's give Mummy's flowers a drink.'

347

She wants to care for Caroline in her absence. She wants to care for the things she loves, and that includes not only her children but also her flowers. Jack has taught her the names and she recites them for Katie as they make their way round. 'Poppy, buddleia, campion, aster, pennywort, hawksbeard, forget me nots.'

Hours go by. Mary wonders how many afternoons like this there will be. How long it will take Caroline to do what she needs to do out in the world and come home again. It'll be enough time to fall in love with one little girl and one little boy. She's certain of that.

She's already falling.

After supper is made and eaten and baths are supervised, Steve puts the baby to bed and Mary takes Katie out into the garden in her pyjamas to watch the sun sink beyond the fence. There are midges dancing above the paddling pool, so she pulls the child onto her lap and wraps her shawl round them both.

Katie tells Mary they are one fat lady. 'We're called Rosie,' she says, 'because of our hair.'

I have never been happier, Mary thinks. *This is exactly where I should be and exactly what I should be doing.*

She takes a strand of Katie's hair and lets it fall through her fingers. 'Mummy has our colour hair. Do you think she'll fit in our shawl? We could be an enormous Rosie if there were three of us.'

Katie looks delighted. 'We can have three breakfasts.'

'Like Goldilocks?'

'And three chairs and a giant bed.'

They giggle together. It's wonderful to imagine the three of them together in a fairy tale.

Katie nudges closer. It's getting cold and Mary rubs her legs through her pyjamas to keep her warm. 'If your teeth start to chatter, we have to go in.'

The blackbird makes a last visit. A moth bumps into the kitchen window. Mary watches Katie notice these things. *You*, she thinks, *ah, the brilliance of you*.

It's like being given another chance, a chance to get it right, to do it better.

Mary pops a kiss on the top of Katie's head. 'We're going to have fun, you and me.'

The girl twists to look at her. 'What are we going to do?'

'All sorts. We'll make a list.'

Katie nods. 'OK.'

Mary wonders if she should ask Steve before making promises, but she'll check with him later – what the rules are, what she's allowed to do or not, what's expected.

'I choose the zoo,' Katie says. 'And swimming.'

'And I choose a place where you can buy the biggest ice cream in the world. It's so big not even an enormous Rosie could finish it. It's made of all sorts of amazing things and it's called a knicker-bocker glory.'

Katie laughs. It falls out of her. 'That's a silly name.'

Mary whispers it in Katie's ear to make her laugh again. She can feel the girl's laughter in her own bones.

PART THREE

Thirty-four

Katie wasn't surprised when her mother's car pulled into the court-yard just after dawn. She'd sent Mum a text over an hour ago: PLSE CME HME. Since then, Katie had been sitting on the balcony, drinking coffee and preparing for what lay ahead. She knew what she had to do, and everything was set up, but still, she was afraid.

She watched her mother climb out of the car and lock the door. She looked so familiar down there, yet everything was different between them after last night and would never be the same again. Katie tried to hold onto the fact that change could be positive and that what she was about to do might distress her mother, but hope-fully wouldn't kill her.

Fairy tales always have a heroine who is set difficult tasks, like spinning gold from straw or carrying water up a mountain in a jug full of holes. By completing the challenges, the heroine gets some reward – she marries a prince or she gets to live in splendour for the rest of her days. But sometimes, all she gets is a spell broken – the one that silenced her or bound her to the wrong life. Her reward, better than princes or castles, is to be free to be herself.

If Katie had only one wish for today, it would be that by the end of it, after all the tasks she'd set herself were complete, she'd have that kind of freedom.

She shut the balcony doors, went into the kitchen and had one last look at the photo while the kettle boiled. Her mind still buckled when she looked at her four-year-old self laughing on Mary's back. She could almost feel the sun on her face, the warmth of Mary's neck, the scent of flowers in the garden and the birds singing. Mary had told the story in such a visceral way that Katie's whole body had roared with knowledge. She and Mary had met before! Not just met, in fact, but known and loved one another. The deep familiarity Katie felt in Mary's company finally made sense and it was such a relief.

Katie tucked the photo in her pocket as she heard Mum's key in the lock. She felt calm, more certain than she had for weeks.

'Katie,' Mum said as she walked into the kitchen. Just that. Nothing else. Like an acknowledgement of being in the right place at the right time. Her eyes skimmed the room as she took off her coat and sat down. Perhaps she was surprised it was tidy, or that Chris and Mary were still asleep or that Katie had made coffee and arranged biscuits on a plate.

Katie pulled out a chair and sat opposite her. 'Thanks for coming back.'

'Of course I came back.' Mum frowned gently at her. 'I was always going to come back.'

'I wasn't sure. I thought you might enjoy being in a hotel room on your own.' Katie kept her voice light to show she didn't mean it badly, that she understood the stress of being constantly in charge. 'I wish you'd texted to let us know you were safe. We were worried.'

Mum nodded, like she knew she should've done that. 'I wasn't thinking straight. I'm sorry.'

'Chris found it difficult.'

'I'll talk to him when he wakes up.' Mum took a sip of coffee. She had dark circles under her eyes and her hair was all greasy and flattened against her head.

Katie clenched her jaw tight against the softness she felt creep up from her heart and pulled the photo from her pocket. She slid it to the middle of the table.

Mum didn't pick it up, but stared down at it. 'Where did this come from?'

'It's Mary's. She showed it to me last night.'

'Your dad must've taken it.' She shook her head as if she couldn't believe what she was seeing. 'I had no idea.'

'You knew Mary came to stay with us though? You knew I'd met her before?'

Mum took off her glasses and rubbed at her eyes. She looked exhausted. 'Do we have to do this now?'

Katie was aching to say, *Yes we do! I want to know why you left us. I want to know how long you were gone and what happened when you got back. I want to know why you lied for years and said I'd never met my own grandmother.* But she knew she had to tread softly if she was going to get what she needed.

'Mary's got a blue blank.'

Mum frowned. 'A what?'

'It's the phrase Jack invented, remember? I told you before. It's like she's got the pain of a memory and none of the details. Anyway, it's to do with this photo and the old house and I was thinking maybe you could tell her anything you might know about it so she wouldn't feel scared.'

'Scared?' Mum looked startled. 'What's she been saying?'

'Just that you went away and Dad wrote and asked her to come and help look after us. She couldn't remember anything else.'

There was a horrible stillness, a moment when Mum's whole face tightened. She could say anything, deny everything, make up any old story.

'She cried herself to sleep last night, Mum. She couldn't get beyond the lovely garden and the sweet little kids and all her plans for the summer. Whatever she's forgotten – she really needs it back. It's what made her freak out at Dad's house, I'm convinced of it. She thinks something terrible happened.'

For what felt like hours, but might only have been seconds, Katie waited for Mum to say something, and when she didn't Katie stood up. She felt a stab of fear as she pushed her chair under the table. 'I'm going out now, Mum.'

'What? Where are you going? It's barely light.'

'I'm meeting someone for breakfast.'

Mum opened her mouth, but quickly shut it again. Perhaps she thought she wasn't in a strong enough position to protest. Katie pulled on her jacket. She picked up her bag and put it on the table.

In some fairy tales, the heroine has to give away her most precious possession in order to save those she loves, but knowing that fact didn't make unzipping her bag any easier. Katie knew she was trembling as she pulled out the book and placed it gently in the middle of the table. 'I'd like you to read this.'

'What is it?'

'It's a memory book.'

Mum shook her head. 'I don't want it.'

Katie wanted Mum to look at her, but she wouldn't. She wanted them to look at each other and understand they'd reached the end of something and had to start some new way of being. But perhaps it was easier not to be looked at as you handed over the story of your life. 'It started off as a family tree, then I began to write Mary's stories in it so I could tell them to her when she forgot. Then I turned it upside down and started my stuff at the back.'

'Your stuff?'

It wasn't too late. Even now, Katie could snatch the book up and

356

run out the door. She could buy matches and burn it. She could go to the library and shred it. She could hurl it from a cliff. 'Some secrets are bad for your health, Mum.'

Mum looked up, aghast. There was a sudden vulnerability about her that made Katie ashamed. 'What's that supposed to mean?'

'There are things you don't know about me.'

They kept looking at each other. Mum didn't look away, although perhaps she wanted to. 'What kind of things?'

'Things I've been struggling with.'

'Struggling?' Mum whispered.

Katie buttoned her jacket and shrugged her bag onto her shoulder. 'I better go now, or I'll be late.'

Mum put her head in her hands. 'Oh Christ, what am I going to find out?'

Katie thought of the dead ancestors upstairs – Pat's critical gaze, Great-granddad's stern frown, all the old ladies in the wedding photo with their tight lips. *Young people should be seen and not heard! Respect your elders! Don't hurt your mother!* Then she thought of Mary up there asleep, and how she navigated by stories. They represented a place to rest, something she was sure of.

Watching Mary face up to emptiness made Katie want to walk beside her. Giving her own story away was her first brave act. It was like shouting, 'This is me!'

'Read it, Mum. But start at the back.'

Mum moved the book tentatively towards her as if it was hot. She turned it, so the back cover was facing her.

Katie knew exactly what was written on the opening page – *Stop being weird. Stop being a coward. Stop being neurotic*. Words she'd written weeks ago, nothing too incriminating. But then would come the list of difficult questions for Simona, the ones Katie had never dared ask: *How do I tell my family? Will life always be this*

357

tough? What do I do about bullies? How do I meet other people like me? What should I do next? And then came the monologues, the poetry . . .

'Don't hate me,' Katie whispered as Mum opened the book.

Mum's shoulders sagged as she began to read. She got smaller on the chair.

Katie had done this to her.

She felt transparent, exposed, as she walked out of the kitchen and very quietly left the flat.

Thirty-five

Katie knew she looked like an idiot sipping her latte in silence, saying nothing about why she'd asked Jamie to meet her so urgently. He'd think she was unstable. She was actually shaking as the silence grew bigger. All sorts of ridiculous words came into her head. Words everywhere pressing to get out.

Jamie said nothing. He took a bite of his breakfast muffin. He licked his lips and frowned. He chewed thoughtfully. He swallowed and took another bite.

Katie said, 'For so long I've felt terrible. Closed in or closed off or something.'

'Sorry,' Jamie said, pointing at his plate. 'Do you want some of this? Should I cut you a piece off?'

Katie said, 'There's this girl, you might know her actually because she's the year above us at school. She's called Simona and she works in a café. You know who I mean?'

And still Jamie didn't answer. And then Katie realized what the problem was. She was speaking so softly that her lips didn't move and no sound came out at all.

She said, 'I'm really sorry, but I kissed her and also I keep thinking about her and most nights I actually dream of her. The other thing you should know is that I also kissed my ex-best friend, who incidentally is a girl too, and lots of kids at school know this, so you're bound to find out soon and that might be tricky for you. So, that's why I can't go out with you again. It's not you, it's me. You're lovely. I wish I fancied you.'

Jamie said, 'So, there's this gig on Friday. Do you think you might like to go?'

Speak, Katie, speak! You are pathetic! Open your mouth and say these words out loud!

Around her, people were talking and laughing and sipping their drinks and all the sounds they were making seemed bizarrely amplified. Also, Jamie looked so sweet and vulnerable sitting there opposite her asking her if she wanted to go out with him again, risking his heart like that.

'Shall I tell you something?' he said. 'About why I'm really glad you said yes when I first asked you out.'

'No!' she yelled. 'Don't tell me anything! Absolutely don't say anything nice to me ever!' But that wasn't out loud either.

He told her how he'd noticed her around school and had always thought her hair was lovely, like polished conkers. And he told her how he used to have a girlfriend called Martha, but he realized whenever he was with her that he was actually thinking about Katie instead. 'I wanted to ask you to my party so badly. I think I even decided to have the party just so I could invite you, but then I didn't dare and no one seemed to know your mobile number and I tried to pluck up courage so many times and I even spoke to some lads in your maths class and told them to tell you about it.' He smiled. 'I know I'm sounding incredibly uncool here, but I guess I'm trying to tell you why I was so stupidly keen at the cinema.'

She missed the next bit. Something about how he couldn't believe his luck when she turned up at the party, how it made his night, how he'd even told his parents, who incidentally had invited her for supper next week, though of course he didn't expect her to

360

come. In fact, he was going to slow right down and maybe they should just have one date a week and she could set the pace and how would that be?

And then he stopped talking and the only words she could hear were in her own head. They didn't seem to belong to her, like her head was a cave and the words were an echo from someone else. 'I want to tell you something true,' reverberated off the walls. 'Can I trust you?' dribbled down the stalactites. 'Because if you're sickened at what I'm about to say I'm not sure I'll cope . . .' She really needed to say this out loud, because this was really what she wanted to say and Jamie deserved more than her silence. And how are you supposed to find out exactly how you fit into your seventeen-year-old skin and how everything works and what it all means if you aren't prepared to take risks?

'I've got something to tell you.' The words tumbled out and Jamie definitely heard them because he stared at her.

'OK,' he said carefully.

'It's a pretty big deal.'

'You're not dying, are you?'

'No! Of course not!'

'Sorry.' He looked immediately shamefaced. 'Really sorry. I'm a tosser.'

'You're not. It's just what I'm going to tell you is really hard to say and I haven't told a single person in the whole world. Well, not out loud anyway. I wrote it down for my mum. She's reading it right now, in fact.'

'Christ! It sounds pretty massive. Maybe you shouldn't tell me.'

'I should. You're absolutely the person I should be telling. It's just, well, the thing is . . . I'm not sure I like boys.'

He half smiled, not sure if this was a joke perhaps, or if he should feel insulted. 'Specifically or generally.'

'Generally. All boys.'

'You don't like them?'

'I have this friend, Esme, well, she's an ex-friend actually . . .'

'I know who you mean.'

'Well, a few weeks ago, I was round her house and we kind of got together.'

'Yeah, I heard something about that.'

'You did? What did you hear?'

'It doesn't matter. I'm fine with it. People do all sorts of crazy stuff.'

'It does matter. It wasn't crazy. She went round telling everyone I jumped her, which was complete crap because it wasn't like that at all.'

'What was it like?'

'It was reciprocal.'

Jamie looked confused. 'So, what exactly are you saying? You're going out with her now?'

'No! She hates me. Looking back, I think she knew I liked her and maybe she was curious, or maybe it made her feel powerful or special or something, but we're not friends any more.'

Jamie sat looking at her, not saying anything. It went on for ages.

'Aren't you going to say anything?' she asked eventually.

'I don't know what to say. You said you'd never told anyone, but you're also saying loads of people know. You and Esme kissed. Now she hates you. What exactly are you telling me?'

That she wasn't curious about boys. That she had no desire to undo a button or to explore the particular texture of skin on their hands or neck or inner thighs or anywhere else. She felt about Jamie's body the way she felt when she saw Chris come out of the bathroom and wander about in a towel. *Oh, your leg hair is darker than mine. Oh, you have muscles. Oh, you have chest hair.* Objective about it. When she thought of Simona, she thought of the scent of her – coffee and hot skin and something underneath that even, something familiar and alive and pulsing. And how kissing her at the library wasn't like kissing Jamie. There was heat and urgency. It was like she could climb inside Simona and still not be near, never be close enough.

She couldn't tell him that though because it would hurt him, so she told him about the weeks of being blanked by girls at school, about going to his party and hoping to sort things out with Esme. She told him about seeing Simona at the café every day and realizing she wasn't just going there for Mary's sake. 'I wanted to *be* Simona,' she said, 'but I wanted to be the customers she was flirting with too. It was the maddest thing. I couldn't work it out. Then a couple of weeks ago, we kissed and I'm sorry, because that wasn't fair on you. What I'm telling you, Jamie, is that I don't really fancy boys. I like you loads, but I don't think we should see each other any more.'

Jamie was in pain. It was palpable. It was like watching someone fall from a building and as they fell, they bumped against sharp edges and all you did was watch, you didn't even bother putting a mattress at the bottom.

He said, 'So, I was some kind of experiment?'

'No, you're lovely and I wanted it to work out.'

He didn't look convinced.

'Jamie, if I didn't have these feelings for girls, I would totally snap you up. I'd marry you in fact. You're gorgeous and funny and kind and I wanted so badly to fancy you.'

'But you didn't?'

'No, I'm sorry.'

'Great. That's just great.' His eyes shone with tears and she wanted to hold him or something, but he shook his head when she leaned across to stroke his arm. 'I'm going to leave now,' he said. 'I don't want my coffee if that's OK with you?'

He pushed back his chair and stood up. It was horrible watching him walk away. People stared and she wanted to tell them to piss off, because this wasn't a lovers' tiff and they shouldn't be looking. This was about humiliation and not feeling worthy, about believing you weren't enough. She knew how it felt, and now so did Jamie and she wanted to run after him and tell him she was wrong and they'd work something out because vulnerability was excruciating.

She found him outside the café, just leaning against the wall looking sad. 'I forgot to pay,' he said. 'I shouldn't just walk out and expect you to cover it.'

What a lovely boy. Of all the boys in the world, this one would pass all her mother's tests.

'It's all right. I left money on the table. This one's on me.'

He nodded. 'Well, I'll see you after the holidays or on results day, or whatever.'

'We could meet before then if you like. As . . . friends?'

'I don't think so.'

And again, she wanted to tell him she was wrong, because he was so nice and the alternative was so difficult. But she had to let him go, so she said nothing and he simply shrugged and walked away. She counted seventeen steps until he turned the corner and was gone. And in the space he left behind, in the loss of him, she felt an actual physical pain in her belly.

She'd lost a friend and she didn't have many of those.

Thirty-six

There was a woman in the kitchen and she was crying.

'You all right?' Mary asked her.

The woman nodded, wiped her eyes with her fingers. 'Sorry. I didn't know you were awake.'

'What's made you upset?'

'Nothing. I'm fine. You go in the lounge and I'll bring you some tea.'

Such pale skin she had. And just like Caroline used to get when she was upset, a purple bruise of shadow bloomed beneath her eyes. 'Was it me?' Mary asked. 'Did I do something wrong?'

'No, of course not.'

'Maybe I did something I've forgotten about? That happens sometimes.'

The woman shook her head. 'No, you didn't do anything. I've been reading a book, that's all.'

Well, that was a relief. Mary had imagined something much worse. A much more complicated problem. 'Is it a sad book? Does somebody die?'

'Nobody dies, no.' The woman pushed her chair back and stood up. 'It's painful, that's my best description. It's very difficult and it hurts a lot.'

'Oh dear, I'm sorry to hear that. Why don't I put the kettle on?'

'Don't worry, I'll do it. You go and join Chris in the lounge and I'll bring you some tea and biscuits.'

The television was on. A boy was lying on his tummy in front of it, his bare soles pointing at the ceiling.

'You've lost your socks,' Mary told him.

The boy turned and smiled. 'My feet were hot.'

Mary nodded. Her own feet were cold, but there was nothing she could do about it. She settled herself in a chair and the boy turned back to the television. 'There's a woman in the kitchen,' Mary told him. 'Did you know?'

'That's Mum.'

'I don't think so.'

'*My* mum, not yours.'

'Oh, well, there's something wrong with her, whoever she is.'

The boy turned to look at her again. 'What kind of wrong?'

'She's upset.'

'That's Katie's fault.' He sat up, glanced furtively at the door. 'They had a big row. You do know who Katie is, don't you? My sister.'

Of course Mary knew her – all that hair, like a waterfall tumbling. She'd met her plenty of times. She was the one who'd sung her to sleep, who'd held her hand in the dark. Or was it the other way round? Had Mary done those things for her?

'Well,' the boy said, 'she's gone.'

Gone? Mary felt her body clench.

A woman came in with a tea tray and set it down. Mary clutched at her. 'Where's the girl?'

'Katie? Out for breakfast apparently.'

'Is she coming back?'

'I certainly hope so.'

The boy drummed his heels on the floor. 'It's pretty unfair that

366

she gets to go out and have breakfast when she's the one who yelled at you and made you go to a hotel.'

The woman gave him a watery smile. 'Is that right?'

'She should be in trouble, shouldn't she? She's the bad one.' He flopped back down on the carpet. 'If it was me, I'd be grounded for *years*.'

The woman sighed as she sat in the chair next to Mary. She had the sad book with her and she put it on her lap. 'Tell me,' she said. 'Do you know someone called Simona? She works at the café Katie takes you to.'

'Café? Does she?'

'Every morning until very recently Katie's taken you there.'

Mary closed her eyes to imagine it. She followed the banister all the way down the stairs and out the main door. It was desolate outside. It was raining and bits of rubbish whipped across the courtyard. There was no girl. Mary opened her eyes and reached for a comforting biscuit. 'I don't know anything about anything,' she said, taking a bite.

The woman poured the tea. The boy was asked to turn the television off. It got very awkward and quiet. Mary could hear herself swallow. Every crunch of her biscuit sounded like shoes on gravel.

The woman said, 'What about you, Chris? You've been to that café, haven't you?'

'Only once and it was horrible.'

'Did you meet Simona? She's a waitress.'

He shrugged. 'There were lots of waitresses. They didn't tell us their names.'

The woman thought about that. She reached down for her handbag and rummaged around in it. She pulled out her purse. She said, 'Why don't you go to the shop and buy yourself something?'

The boy looked surprised and also a little afraid. 'You don't like me going to the shop on my own.'

'You'll be fine. You're fourteen.'

He narrowed his eyes suspiciously. 'Are you trying to get rid of me?'

'I'm trying not to cross-examine you.'

'What does that mean?'

'I'll tell you later.' She pulled a note from the purse and handed it to him. 'Get yourself sweets or crisps. Share them with the kids outside. It's sunny out there now.'

'Why would I do that? I don't even know them.' He looked at the money in his hand as if that would explain the situation.

Mary laughed at his puzzled face. 'I'll introduce you if you like,' she said, wanting to help. 'I know plenty of people. You want me to come?'

He shook his head. 'How long should I be?'

'As long as you like,' the woman said. 'Take your phone and answer if I call you. Make sure it's turned on.'

After he'd gone the woman picked up the book again. She hadn't been reading for long when she began to dab her face with her sleeve. Mary wanted to comfort her, put an arm around her, stroke her hair, wipe her tears away, but she felt very far from the action. It was like watching television. She felt curious to know what the matter was, but she didn't seem able to move.

She closed her eyes and let the sun warm her face as it filtered through the curtains. Her thoughts dismantled one by one.

Thirty-seven

Katie stood over the road from the café and stared at Simona. She appeared to be sleeping, just sitting at one of the outside tables with her eyes shut. Usually if she was on a break, she'd read a book or go for a walk, or chat to the other staff, so it was weird she was sitting there on her own. She didn't look anything like herself.

Katie crossed the street. Her heart was hammering, but she was determined to do this. Task number three. She pulled out a chair and sat opposite Simona. 'I sent you a text.'

Simona opened her eyes and for a moment it was as if she forgot to be furious. It was like watching something lovely skim the surface of a river.

Keep looking at me like that, Katie wanted to say. *I can keep being brave if you just keep looking at me like that.*

But Simona's face closed down as quickly as it had opened. 'I deleted it.'

'I was hoping we could talk.'

'I'm busy.'

'You don't look busy.'

Simona narrowed her eyes. 'Can you go away? You want me to get sacked?'

'I thought your boss liked you talking to customers.'

'That depends on the customer.'

Angie opened the door and stepped out. She folded her arms and glared at Katie. 'You causing trouble?'

'No, of course not!'

'Because if Simona doesn't want to talk to you I'm going to have to ask you to leave.'

She sounded like a bouncer. She sounded like she'd be more than happy to escort Katie off the premises. Simona must've told her about the library, about all the ignored texts. Katie could barely meet the older woman's eyes. 'I only just got here. I don't know if she wants to talk to me.'

Angie turned to Simona. 'Do you?'

Simona gave her a smile. 'No, but I can handle it.'

'You sure?' Angie looked Katie up and down as if checking for weapons. 'Where's Mary?'

'At home. She's not well.'

Angie looked sceptical. 'What's wrong with her?'

'She had a vascular incident.' Katie tried not to let the words affect her voice, but they did anyway.

Angie's face softened, 'Ah, poor lamb. Is she going to be all right?'

Katie shook her head, aware Simona was staring at her from across the table.

'What's a vascular incident?' Simona said.

Katie knew the concern in Simona's eyes was for Mary, but still – it was as if they were on the same side for a moment. 'It's like a mini stroke. She's a lot more confused now.'

'And she won't recover?'

'She'll plateau out, but it'll happen again.' Strange how using the same words as the doctor made it sound so certain.

'That's horrible.'

'Anyway,' Angie said, 'I'm going inside now, so give her my

regards, won't you. And you two be nice to each other, you hear me?' She gave Katie a final glare. 'Especially you.'

Katie felt more exposed once she'd gone because at least her anger had warmth in it. Anything was better than watching Simona's face freeze over.

'Five minutes to talk,' Katie said. 'That's all I need. There aren't even any customers.' She waved a hand at all the empty tables to prove it.

Simona scowled. 'What's so urgent? If it's anything to do with libraries, gardens or your stupid mates, you can forget it.'

'They're not my mates and I came to apologize.'

'Apologize?' Simona's eyes glittered. 'Do you ever do anything else?'

'That's not fair.'

'Life's not fair.' Simona picked up her phone. 'I'm setting a timer. You've got exactly two minutes and then you're leaving.'

Katie leaned forward, put both hands on the table, palms down. 'I'm sorry. I really am. I was a complete coward at the library. I totally messed up.'

'You pushed me.'

'Yes.'

'You didn't reply to a single text or call.'

'I know. I was scared. It won't ever happen again.'

'Damn right, cause I'm never texting you again.'

They looked at each other. Katie hated how cold Simona looked.

Katie said, 'Something massive happened last night. Me and my mum had this row and she stayed out all night and left me in charge.'

'You're always in charge, so if you want sympathy – forget it.'

'I'm not after sympathy.'

Simona shrugged. 'Your mum relies on you too much, that's all I'm saying.'

Katie stalled. Kind words affected her strangely this morning. She wanted to take notice of each one, like rare flowers, but Simona was looking at the timer.

'Last night was different because Mary's different,' Katie said. 'She's much harder work, and I guess I saw things from my mum's side a bit – you know, the stress of being responsible and having to make difficult decisions. I actually began to see why Mary might need to be in a nursing home.'

Simona sighed, like that was obvious, and if it meant they never came to the café and she never saw Katie again it wouldn't bother her in the slightest.

'Anyway, when Mary went to bed, she showed me a photo . . .' Katie leaned closer, hoped Simona would lean in too, but she didn't, she looked at her phone instead. 'Simona, please, stop checking the time.'

'Fifty-five seconds.'

'I know you're pissed off, but I'm trying to explain something.'

'You said you wanted to apologize. This is all about you.'

'It's back story.'

Simona tapped her fingers on the table. 'Go on then, but you better be quick.'

'So, basically the photo shows me and Mary from years ago, which means I've met her before, even though my mum said I hadn't. And I realized, for the first time ever, that truth doesn't exist.'

Simona laughed, a bitter sound. 'Truth doesn't exist?'

'I don't mean because my mum lied, I mean because everyone's got their own side of a story. So, there's this photo and I'm too young to remember anything about it and Mary starts talking and I

372

think, yeah, actually I do remember – she stayed with us for a while and every night she wrapped me in her shawl and we sat in the garden. But was I really remembering or just adopting the bits I liked? And I absolutely guarantee my mum'll have a completely different take on it. If there's no real truth, then all we can do is offer up our own stories and listen to other people's and try and make sense of it all.'

Simona said, 'I know a really good story about a waitress who met a coward at a library. You want to hear that?'

Katie looked at her hands, still flat upon the table. She hated her hands. A coward? Yes, she deserved that. There was another account, where a girl bravely asked a waitress some questions and they kissed and then the world crashed in and the girl got scared. But the end result was the same – Katie let Simona down.

Simona made a great show of checking the time again. 'Eleven seconds. Nearly done. Hurrah!'

Katie took a breath. 'So, what I came to tell you is that I gave my mum a book I've been writing in for weeks. I finally gave her *my* version of *my* story.'

Simona slightly, ever so slightly, frowned. 'What story?'

'The one where I like girls.'

The alarm went. Simona snatched it and turned it off. 'What happened? What did she do?'

'Nothing yet. I only just gave it to her. But whatever she does, I don't care.'

'You should care. You just unleashed a storm.'

Katie shrugged, feigned indifference. If she really thought about the fact that Mum might be reading the book right now, she'd probably cry. There must be a word for being certain you'd done the right thing, but simultaneously terrified. But if there was, Katie didn't know it.

'Your mum's going to go mental, isn't she?' Simona said. 'What if she kicks you out?'

'Then I'll come and live at yours.'

Simona shook her head as if Katie was a complete fool. 'I've had enough of this. I'm going back to work.'

'No, set the timer again.'

'There's nothing to say.'

'There's always something to say.'

Simona smiled. A tiny shadow of a smile, creeping along her lips from the edge of her mouth. 'You've got a good memory for crappy one-liners.'

'When do you finish? We could go for a walk later.'

'No we couldn't.' Simona swept a hand across her face, rubbing the smile out. She looked past Katie to the street.

'Or we could get a bus somewhere. See where we end up?'

Simona shook her head again, wouldn't look.

'You don't have to accept my apology, Simona. I just wanted to let you know I'm an idiot and you're not. You said no one puts their hand up, that you feel alone. Well, I came here to tell you that I'm putting my hand up.'

'Bollocks.'

'Seriously, I promise. I'm not going to hide any more, however hard it is.'

Simona sighed. The window of the café was glazed with fragile sunlight. She leaned back on her chair and was bathed in it. 'Careful what you promise.'

'I mean it. Why should I be careful?'

'Because something happened.'

'What happened?'

'It was the day of the library. After that.'

'What was? What are you talking about?'

374

She looked steadily at Katie. 'It's why I kept texting you. When I finished work, that girl, Amy, and a couple of her mates were hanging around outside the café. I guess they must've heard I took the piss out of your friend in front of her bloke, because they decided to have a go. Usually I can handle things like that, no problem, but they started following me and saying stuff, and maybe I was tired but for some reason I just took it. I kept walking, kept my mouth shut and let them talk shit. They were saying there was something wrong with me, that I should stay away from people, go to a doctor, whatever. Then Amy said I'd infected you and that you'd tried to infect Esme.'

'Amy's such a bitch.'

'Yeah, and you know what? I actually let them get to me. I went home and sat in my room for hours thinking about what they'd said. Then my mum got in from work and we talked it over. She insisted on reporting them, which hadn't even crossed my mind. I'd convinced myself they had the right to say that stuff – it was their opinion, you know, and maybe it was true, I had infected you.'

'That's ridiculous. I asked you to teach me, didn't I? I want this.'

'What – this life?' Simona leaned forward into shadow again. 'I don't think you do. I think you're a tourist. I think you're someone who imagines they can come on to me whenever they like and then back off when things get tough. I think you're someone who turns up with their, "I'm sorry, it'll never happen again" crap and thinks I'm going to take it. But I'm not. I'm sick of it. It was bad enough with Anna. I'm not doing it again.' She looked at Katie and it was strange, because even though she was angry she looked more weary than Katie had ever seen her. 'If you ever get followed by Amy, if you ever have to listen to that shit, you'll definitely backtrack again. So, don't make promises you can't keep, OK? You want my advice? Go back to your boyfriend.'

'I don't have one.'

'You ended it?'

'About an hour ago. Told him why too.'

Simona shook her head. 'Text him. Tell him you were joking.'

'I can't do that.'

'Well, you should.' Simona stood up. 'Beg him to take you back, then go home and tell your mum you never meant anything you wrote in that book.'

'Where are you going?'

'Back to work.' She yanked open the café door and shut it behind her, like it was all decided and Katie would just go away and do as she suggested.

Tears tightened Katie's throat. She swallowed hard, looked down the length of the street and blinked a few times. There was the newsagent's, the butcher's, the card shop. Outside the DIY shop, a man stopped to adjust his shoe. A woman came out of the news-agent's and stood counting her change. She put the money in her purse and clicked it shut. Normal things. Ordinary people. So why did Katie have a physical pain in her chest? It surged through her and hurt when she breathed.

She tried to distract herself by staring at a seagull pecking at a takeaway box by the bus stop. Another gull swooped down to join it, then a third, and they flapped and shoved, stabbing at the paper with their curved yellow beaks.

Behind the bus stop was the block of flats where Mary had knocked on the door, where Mum's old house used to stand. On one of the balconies, a man was hanging out washing and a little girl hung her arms over the wall and looked at the birds.

Katie stood up and slowly pushed her chair back under the table.

Through the window she could see Simona behind the counter. She was at the chalkboard, rubbing out one of the items from the menu with a duster. Katie wanted to bang on the window. She wanted Simona to come rushing out and say that everything was going to be all right.

As she crossed the road and walked away, Katie thought of all those fairy-tale heroines storming up hills and hacking through forests and putting their lives in danger, and she wondered how they got to be so courageous. They didn't expect anyone else to save them. They just got on with it. All Katie had done was hand over a book, dump a boy and say sorry. Of course that was never going to be enough.

She had to do something new. Some brave and wonderful task that would prove she was worthy of being the heroine of her own story.

The trouble was, she had no idea what it should be.

Thirty-eight

Mum was crying. Katie stood in the doorway between the lounge and the kitchen and stared at her. Mary was sitting on the sofa and she was staring too. Mum hadn't cried for years – not when Dad cheated on her or when his girlfriend got pregnant, not when Mary arrived, not even when Katie yelled at her yesterday. But she was crying now – sitting on the sofa next to Mary with the memory book on her lap, looking as if her whole world had ended.

Mary got a hankie from up her sleeve and dabbed Mum with it. 'There,' she said, 'there, there. Let it all out.' Katie felt fear rise up her throat. Mary said, 'You could stick the kettle on if you want to be useful. Make this poor woman a cup of tea.'

Katie watched them from the kitchen as she waited for the kettle to boil. Mary stroked Mum's arm, squeezed her hand, whispered soft words in her ear. It made no difference. Mum was broken and Mary couldn't fix her.

Katie brought in the tea and still the tears were falling. Should they call emergency services? Could you get an ambulance for someone who wouldn't stop crying?

Katie gave the cup to Mary who tried to get Mum to take a sip. But she wouldn't. Mary put the cup on the table. 'I think you need a hug.' She put her bony arms round Mum and pulled her close. 'Is this any better?'

Mum folded into Mary like a child and shut her eyes.

'Hush,' Mary told her. 'There's my girl.' And she stroked Mum's hair with a wrinkled hand. Over and over, like spinning a cocoon.

Katie couldn't bear it. She crept upstairs to talk to Chris, to see how long this had been going on, but he wasn't in his room. She phoned him, but he didn't pick up. Well, either he'd run away or he'd been farmed out somewhere. She missed him with sudden urgency. She went into Mary's room, closed the door, sat on the bed and tried him again.

He picked up this time. 'What?'

'Where are you?'

'Outside.'

'I didn't see you.'

'I'm in the ball court playing football.'

'Does Mum know?'

'She told me to come out.'

So, whatever was wrong with Mum was so momentous that she was prepared to risk Chris's life by sending him to play with the rough football boys, the kids she'd always thought would force drugs or alcohol on her precious son within minutes.

Katie wanted to say, *It's my fault Mum's crying, Chris. I told her who I really am.* She wanted to say, *Promise not to hate me when you find out.* But those words were bottled tight inside. She sat not saying anything, just listening to her brother breathe until he said, 'I have to go,' and she said, 'Sure,' and he hung up.

She went to the window and looked out. There were kids swarming the courtyard on bikes and a couple of women sitting on the steps with mugs of tea. Katie looked left, towards the fenced-off ball area, and there was Chris. He was in goal, which she knew was the worst position, but maybe there was a hierarchy and you had to work your way up. He looked happy enough. One of the regular football boys – Luke, or Lewis or something, from the block opposite – ran up to shoot. Chris didn't save it, but another boy came running over and slapped Chris's back in a friendly way as if he was sorry, as if he was saying, *better luck next time*.

Weird how watching Chris negotiate the world made Katie feel sad, like he was growing up and would need her less. She felt as if she'd lost something. She wondered if this was how Mum felt most of the time. But she didn't wonder it for long because the door opened and Mum peered warily in. 'Can we talk?'

She came in and shut the door quietly behind her. She walked over and stood next to Katie at the window. She smelled of smoke. Maybe she'd had a few drags on one of Mary's fags, or maybe all that proximity meant Mary's scent had rubbed off on her.

'Sorry about the tears,' Mum said.

Down in the courtyard a couple of older kids were navigating planks of wood on skateboards. The ones on bikes continued weaving about the place.

'Is it OK if I say a few things?' Mum said. 'Would that be all right with you?'

Katie wished she was one of the really little kids – that one there with the dungarees, sitting next to her mum on the step – innocent, young, everything ahead, plenty of time to do it all differently. That girl wouldn't have given a book to her mother because she probably couldn't write yet. That girl's mother wouldn't be walking away from her, sitting on the bed, waiting for permission to speak.

God! Holding your hand up was lonely. Simona was right.

'Say whatever you want, Mum.'

'I'd like to know that I've understood correctly.' Mum's voice cracked. She coughed and started again. 'There's a lot of confusion in that book, Katie, but my understanding is that you like this Simona girl. She means more to you than just a friend?'

She waited for Katie to answer, but all she could do was nod. A seagull had appeared in the sky. It wheeled in lonely circles above the flats. She wondered if it was one of the ones she'd seen earlier by the café.

'Do you think some of what you're feeling might be because of Mary? You've been stuck with her for weeks, you haven't seen your normal friends, you've been dragged to that café every day. I make you look after Chris and he gets so much of my attention. Then there's your dad leaving. Is it because of that?'

'It's nothing to do with that stuff.'

'I'm just trying to understand. I thought it might have affected you – Mary being here for so long, I mean.' Her voice trailed off. 'To be honest, I thought you had a boyfriend – that boy you went to the cinema with.'

'Jamie. He's a friend.'

'Have you never wanted a proper boyfriend?'

Katie shrugged. Her throat hurt. What did Mum mean by 'normal friends' or a 'proper boyfriend' anyway?

'Has this Simona ever dated boys?'

Katie couldn't stand this. Did Mum think Katie knew the answers?

'Can I ask you,' Mum said, 'when you dream – do you dream about girls?'

That was surprising. Katie hadn't expected that. What did Mum do – go online and download twenty questions to ask a sexually deviant daughter?

'Have you ever felt like this before?' Mum said.

'Please stop asking all these questions.'

'Do you feel different from the other girls at school?'

'I don't know. I can't answer any of this.'

Mum sighed, lay back on the bed with her hands under her

381

head and stared at the ceiling. Katie thought Mum might cry again and she didn't know what she'd do if that happened.

'Young people often experiment with their sexuality,' Mum said to the ceiling. 'Do you think you might just be experimenting?'

Hadn't Katie just asked her to stop? It felt like being under a microscope. She turned from the window and Mum leaned up – all jutting chin and hopefulness. She wanted reasons. She wanted Katie to describe the day something happened to send her off on this strange tangent. Maybe she'd caught a bug and it sent her mad, maybe she'd seen a DVD that was too old for her, maybe she'd been talking to people she shouldn't. She'd surely been influenced in some way.

'I'm not experimenting, Mum. Not in the way you mean. I've felt it for ages. It was just difficult to admit. Then I met Simona.'

'At the café?'

Katie nodded.

'And how does she feel about you?'

Katie shrugged, because how could she ever describe the complexities of what she imagined Simona may or may not feel? Anyway, it was none of Mum's business.

'So, you're sure about this, are you?'

Katie nodded very slowly.

'Do your friends know?'

'I guess.'

'And what do they think about it?'

'Not much.'

Mum sighed. 'You see, that frightens me. That makes me think you won't live an ordinary life. Oh, I know there's less stigma these days, but I can't help but feel you'll be marked out in some way and people might hurt you.'

The words hung between them. They felt so heavy and terrible, like they'd last for ever and always be true. If you put them in land-fill and buried them, they'd still be there, exactly the same in a hundred years.

'You hate me for this, don't you, Mum?'

'No! Of course not.' Mum scrambled up to sitting. 'Oh, Katie, I'm sorry – I love you. That should've been the first thing I said – I love you, of course I do. I'm surprised, that's all. I had no clue about any of this and you seem so sure.'

'Some people know when they're three.' Katie looked back at the seagull, still circling overhead. 'I knew a long time ago. I just never said anything.'

'Why not? Why didn't you come and talk to me?'

'Because we're completely rubbish at communicating.' The gull looked like a sailing boat gliding across some blue ocean with its white wings outstretched. It made Katie think of what Simona said about daring to see yourself in your own future with all your possibilities laid out.

'Am I really so hard to talk to?' Mum said. 'You make me sound like a monster.'

'It's just you get disappointed so easily. There's no room to fail.' Katie walked over and sat next to her on the bed. She noticed for the first time how the grey in Mum's hair was outweighing the gold. She was getting older day by day. 'I shouldn't've read Pat's diary and I'm sorry I did.'

'It's all right. I don't mind so much today.'

'This is going to sound weird, but when I was reading it, I kept wishing I'd known you at that age. If we'd been at school together, we might've been friends and we could've shared our problems.'

'Is that why you gave me the memory book? You wanted that teenage girl to read it?'

'Maybe, yeah. Then neither of us would be so alone.'

383

Mum smiled and the corners of her eyes crinkled. Her eyes were mostly pale blue, but today, in this room, they were the colour of rain. 'It's ironic, because that teenage girl was going to be a brilliant parent. She was determined her kids would be able to talk to her about anything. She wanted to repair all the stuff that had gone wrong with her.'

'You're not a monster, Mum.'

'I'm too involved. You were very eloquent on that subject.'

'At least you care about us. You're always there, you're interested in our lives, you said it yourself – you know about friends and home-work and come to every school event.'

'But all that stuff you wrote in the book, all these big things you're telling me – I'm not sure I know what to do about any of it.' She looked very serious. 'Katie, if you don't do what's right for you because you think I'll be disappointed, that would be terrible. If you go to some overseas university just to get away from me that would be terrible too. Don't get me wrong, I'm certainly not glad about this, but I don't want to lose you either. Do you understand? Pat lived her whole life trying to please her father and look how it worked out for her. I wasn't much better, spending my best years looking after the miserable sod because I felt so guilty I'd pushed Pat over the edge. Mary didn't get it right either – all that running about doing whatever she wanted might look very glamorous from the outside, but she had to pay a hefty price, didn't she?'

Sunlight escaped briefly from behind a cloud, sliced across the carpet and up onto the bed before being chased away by shadow again.

'I'm a bit worried,' Mum said, 'that I'm not going to handle this very well. I don't have any gay friends. I don't know anything about it. I'm not sure I know how to be a good mother to a seventeen-year-old daughter who's telling me such enormous things.'

384

Katie thought of what the perfect mother might be like – one who approved of you and loved you and was interested in all that you did, but who had a fascinating life of her own so you didn't feel guilty about leaving her. A mother who was at home when you needed her, but absent when you wanted space, who would sew on your buttons and help with revision, but was also scintillating company and completely cool in the eyes of your friends. Katie thought this mother was possibly a combination of Pat, Mary and Mum and that made her smile, like it was feasible to take the best bits from three women and make a perfect parent.

'OK, Mum, here's something you can do. One day, sometime in the future, maybe I'll bring a girl home to meet you.'

'Simona?'

'Or someone else. And maybe we're holding hands, me and this girl, because we're nervous and this is a big deal for us. But when we come in the flat and I introduce her, you're completely unfazed. You just say hello and ask if we want a cup of tea or something to eat and we sit down in the kitchen and you make us sandwiches and drinks and then you join us for a while and chat.' Katie shrugged. 'That's it. That would make you a brilliant mother.'

'That's it?'

'It's as mundane as that.'

Mum smiled gently. 'What kind of sandwiches would you like?'

Katie felt her throat clench. That was the trouble with sympathy and kindness – they pulled your defences open and exposed you.

Thirty-nine

It would be nice, Mary thought, to understand why she was gripping so tight to the handles of her handbag. Her fingers had become mottled with the strain. She looked down at her hands. They were like chicken flesh. Damp and white and her thumb the drumstick.

This made her chuckle. She quite fancied a bit of chicken, could just imagine the satisfying crunch of bone between her teeth. She was still smiling when she heard a click and the door opened.

Ah, here was Jack. Mary wanted to share the joke – how her hands had turned to poultry in front of her eyes – but seeing him standing there, the words slipped away. Had she always been able to see right through him?

'Morning,' she said. 'You all right?'

'Yes, love. Just let me catch my breath.' He stood there wheezing, one palm flat against his chest. 'I've got some news.'

'Not bad, I hope?'

He shook his head, breathing hard. 'Caroline's coming to talk to you.'

'Who?'

'Caroline. She wants to tell you about the photo. You and the little girl, remember? You and Katie? This is the moment we've been waiting for.'

His words swilled around inside her head. Mary tried to grab them, but they eluded her, made no sense. All she was aware of was the immense pain they brought. She hid behind her fingers. 'I don't want to.'

'You do,' Jack laughed. 'Come on, don't hide that pretty face. You've been desperate to talk about what happened for years.'

'I don't believe you.'

'Well, it's true anyway. It's been hurting you ever since we met. It's not fair that you're always painted as the bad one.'

'I *am* the bad one, everyone says so.'

'That's a job you can give up now. Time to share it out.'

Mary risked looking at him. 'Will it hurt?'

'Let's hope not. The girl's set it all up for you, so I think it's going to be all right.'

There were footsteps in the hallway. A click at the door. Jack was beaming with excitement. He looked very sure of things. 'Time to face the music,' he said, and he hobbled off and stood by the curtains.

Mary blinked at him. Surely he hadn't always shimmered at the edges? 'Jack?'

But he waved her attention towards the woman coming through the door. 'Here's your daughter. Recognize her?'

'Caroline?'

'That's it.' Jack clapped, his hands no louder than a whisper.

The woman came in, shut the door behind her and leaned on it. She said, 'I think that's the first time you've ever used my name.'

She was older than Mary remembered, her hair streaked with grey. 'It is you, isn't it? You are Caroline, all grown up?'

'Yes, Mum.'

'Where have you been?'

'Upstairs, talking to Katie.'

'She's back, is she? Well, that's good. Is she going to come and see me?'

'Yes, of course. She just needs a couple of minutes to herself.'

'And what are you up to? Are you going to sit down and have a little rest? You look like you're about to walk straight out that door.'

'No, I'm not leaving. In fact, I'd like to talk to you, if that's all right?'

Mary waited, but Caroline didn't speak. In fact, she looked as if she couldn't. She looked as if she'd turned to stone.

'You're not saying anything,' Mary told her. She turned to Jack for guidance. He was still by the window, nodding and smiling like this was the most amazing thing that had ever happened.

'She'll speak in a minute,' he said. 'Give her time. She wants the girl to be here.'

The way the curtains rippled behind him reminded Mary of a walk they'd made once through a ploughed field. She'd been wearing high heels and carrying a picnic basket and Jack had given her a ride on his back so she didn't ruin her shoes. She remembered the heat of him as she wrapped herself tight around him. How safe she'd felt. She couldn't remember when it was, exactly. Only that it was a lifetime ago.

Jack smiled gently at her, as if he too recalled that picnic. 'You need to concentrate on the matter in hand, darling,' he said. 'Ask to see the photo. She's got it with her somewhere.'

'Photo?' Mary whispered.

'You remember it?' Caroline said from the doorway. 'You remember showing it to Katie last night?

'I don't know.'

'Well, you did and then Katie asked me to talk to you about it. Did she tell you?'

388

It was Jack who knew what to do. 'Ask her to sit down. Ask her to sit right next to you.'

Mary patted the space beside her on the sofa and Caroline walked over. It was a strange, reluctant walk. She sat down, looked at her feet for a bit and then looked right up at Mary. 'I haven't treated you well.' She spoke very slowly as if she'd been practising. 'I haven't been as kind as I should. When we picked you up from the hospital that first night, I found it very painful that you didn't recognize me.'

What was she talking about? Of course Mary recognized her. It was just that she had so many faces. This one was lovely though, this one right now. It was soft and vulnerable and looked like it was telling the truth.

Caroline shuffled her feet. 'Anyway, you kept leaving the flat every morning and running off. I don't know if you remember any of this?'

Mary remembered putting slippers over her socks and holding the banister all the way down the stairs and finding a coat on a hook by the door. Sometimes, there'd be a hat that had no head to wear it, or a listless scarf with nothing to do, so she'd stick those in her pocket. And every morning, like a miracle, the girl would come dashing to meet her.

'You were looking for Victory Avenue,' Caroline said, 'but I didn't know that. I just thought you were trying to get away, that you couldn't bear to be with me.' She bit her lip, a terrible habit that made her look afraid. 'If I'm being honest, which I'm trying very hard to be, I was jealous of how much time you spent with Katie. She seemed to have a way to reach you. Maybe she just listened to your stories, maybe that was it.' She stroked the book lying on her lap. 'I've learned a lot about you both from here.'

'Ah,' Mary said, 'she's always scribbling away in that thing.'

'Yes,' Caroline said, 'my daughter certainly has a way with words.'

'I like words,' Mary said. 'Although I don't know as many as I used to.'

'Oh, Mum.'

'I think I might have a hole in my head.'

'Is that how it feels?'

Jack coughed over by the curtain. 'Stick to the point,' he said. 'It's your blue blank you want to know about.'

'Blue blank?' Mary echoed. 'What about it?'

Caroline opened the book, slid something out and handed it to Mary. 'Here – this is a photo of you and Katie. It was taken a long time ago.'

Mary felt her throat tighten. This was the photo she kept with the wolves in the mountain. They were the guardians of this. How had it got out into daylight?

Caroline said, 'You came to look after Katie and Chris because I'd gone away. My husband, Steve, wrote to you. You stayed for nearly eight weeks and I need to tell you what happened when I got back, because Katie says you can't remember and it's causing you pain.'

Here was a garden, a sunny day. Here was Mary laughing. Here was the child with hair like burnished copper, her arms wrapped round Mary's neck. Here was the scent of warm, sweet skin. Here was the sound of a blackbird singing.

Mary's throat hurt, a dry panic. She didn't want to cry. Swallow. Swallow it down.

'Focus, sweetheart,' Jack whispered. 'You can do this.'

Here was the paddling pool, the watering can, the heady perfume of wet soil, the grass like silk beneath naked toes.

'Ask a question,' Jack said.

Mary blinked at him. What kind of question? Nothing she could say would be right. All she could do was nod and smile like a buffoon as she tried to push the grief back down.

'Go on, beautiful,' Jack urged. 'Anything you can think of will be fine.'

Mary took a breath and tapped a finger at the photo. 'Is this true?'

'All true, Mum. And I'm sorry if this is going to make you sad and I'm not sure how much you're going to remember, but it feels very important that we try and go back there. I think Katie's right that keeping everything hidden isn't good for anyone's health.' She sighed and stroked the book again. 'I'll call her, shall I? I'd like a witness to this story.'

Mary didn't like the sound of that. She pointed at Jack, needed Caroline to know he was listening to every word. He nodded and waved, but Caroline ignored him.

'Photo!' Jack hissed. 'Wave it under her nose. Flap it about.'

Mary did as she was told. 'You going to tell me about this?'

'Yes, Mum.'

'Are you going to tell me now?'

'Just as soon as I pluck up the courage.'

Courage? But this daughter was so certain of things, so full of words. How right she always seemed when she said those words out loud. Although looking at her now, it was true she was different. The word for it evaded Mary's mind. Unwrapped, was it? Unlocked? Like that door earlier. Ajar?

'We'll just wait for Katie,' Caroline said. 'She'll be here in a minute.' She took off her glasses and rubbed at her eyes.

Mary flapped the photo. Jack had told her to and she was going to keep doing it until things began to make sense.

'Sorry,' Caroline said, putting her glasses back on. 'She really is on her way. Let me check Chris is OK outside and then I'll give her a call.' She got up and went out onto the balcony. She brushed right past Jack, didn't notice him at all. He beamed at her, didn't seem at all offended.

'That Katie's a right old dawdler,' he said.

Dawdler. That was a good word. Mary liked the sound of it. It made her think of girls in summer dresses dragging their feet on the way home from school.

She could see the bones at the top of Caroline's neck as she craned to look over the balcony wall. Imagine tracing each vertebra with your finger? Imagine the spine like a rope of pearls. A baby has over three hundred bones, and as she grows cartilage is replaced, smaller bones join together and she ends up with only two hundred and six.

So many things get lost as daughters grow.

She smiled at Jack across the carpet. He was lost too, she knew this. There was no coming back from where he was.

'Don't worry about that now, darling,' he said, winking at her. 'You just focus on one thing at a time.'

'He seems quite happy out there,' Caroline said, coming back in. 'I'll just leave these doors open, then at least we can hear him scream if the other kids turn on him.' She raked a hand through her hair. 'Why did I say that? That's not even funny.'

She opened the lounge door and called for the girl. While they waited for her to come, Caroline sat down next to Mary and they looked silently at each other and it was the strangest thing, as if years tumbled away and within this woman, Mary saw all the layers, like the rings of a tree exposed, all the people this daughter had been.

'You are my heart,' Mary said. 'I miss every single one of you.'

Caroline ran a hand across her face. 'Don't say that, you'll make me cry again.'

'I'll keep quiet then.' Mary found her daughter's hand and curled their fingers together. 'I'll just do this.'

Mary could feel Caroline's pulse trembling. The skin at her wrist was thin and pale. There it was again – a fluttering, like something trapped. How fragile we all are. It never stops.

The girl arrived and waved at Mary. She settled herself on the chair opposite. She looked very serious.

'She's going to write everything down,' Caroline said, handing the girl the book. 'I want her to do that.'

The girl nodded. 'I'll give it back to you when you need it, Mary.'

'Katie tells me to think of you as a time traveller,' Caroline said. 'So, I guess this is the bit where we get in the time machine.'

Mary felt a churning in her belly. She both longed for and never wanted this. She touched the photo with their joined hands. It was all she was sure of.

Caroline smiled at her rather sadly. 'Hopefully it will give us a new start. I don't want to lose you. You're my mum and I should never have let you go in the first place.'

'You let me go?'

'Well, yes – although strictly speaking, you did it to me first.'

Over by the curtains, Jack chuckled, a soft sound. 'Like getting blood from a stone.'

Mary frowned at him. Caroline was scared, that was all. But she was also soft, as if her edges were smudged. Tender, that was the word. Like a bruise.

'Guilty,' Jack said. 'That's a word too.'

Mary shushed him and he laughed again. 'All right, you win,' he said. 'Just tell her to get on with it.'

'Come on then,' Mary said. 'Before we forget where we're going.'

'We have to go back thirteen years,' Caroline said. 'It was a Thursday evening and I'd just got off a plane. I was expecting to come home to my husband, but instead you were there – fast asleep on the sofa.'

There was a noise, like the blades of a windmill turning far away. Something to do with light and shade. A breath of air stirred the room and Mary felt a chill at her neck. She looked over at the girl, her legs curled up on the chair, all that hair tumbling round her shoulders. 'Were you there?'

'I don't know, Mary. I've never heard this story before.'

Mary turned to Caroline. 'Where was she?'

'Asleep upstairs.'

'And the boy?'

'Oh God,' Caroline said. 'This is so hard. I can't believe we're doing this.'

'Was he upstairs too?'

'They both were. You'd put them to bed and then fallen asleep yourself. Steve was away on some conference, but I didn't know that. I thought he'd be there to greet me. When I saw you on the sofa, it was such a shock.'

Somewhere, deep inside Mary's skull, a memory stirred. 'You woke me up. You were very brown.'

'I'd been to Spain.'

'That's right. You had an armful of bangles.'

How strange, Mary thought, that this was the moment. She'd dreamed of this moment for so many years, played it over in her mind, all its possibilities, and here it was. She was living it right now, it was really happening.

'You woke me up,' Mary said, squeezing her daughter's hand. 'And what happened after that? Please do carry on.'

2000 – Blue Blank

'What the hell are you doing here?'

Mary opens her eyes and there's Caroline, standing at the end of the sofa glaring down at her. Is this a dream?

'Where's Steve?'

'You're back.' Mary struggles to sit. 'I can't believe it. Did you just get off the plane? Goodness, you're brown.'

'I asked where Steve is.'

'Um, let me think . . . He's on a trip, just some overnight thing. I can't remember where now. Colchester, is it? Chichester? Back tomorrow. Does he know you're here?'

'Where are my children?'

'Upstairs. I put them to bed. Sorry, I must've fallen asleep.' She runs a hand through her hair. It takes a while to wake up to reality these days. Sometimes if feels as if she's waking up through mist. But this is definitely her daughter. She's becoming more vivid by the second.

Caroline says, 'Are you drunk?'

'Of course not. I was just having a little rest.' Words too take a while to grapple with. She wants to say something profound, but all she can think of is the kettle. 'Shall I make some tea?'

'No, you need to leave.'

'Now?' Mary feels vulnerable sitting there in just her T-shirt and shorts, half asleep, like she's done something wrong, like she's been caught in flagrante. She shakes that thought away. Ridiculous. She's got nothing to feel guilty about. 'It's the middle of the night.'

'It's half past nine. Trains will be running for hours.'

'Please, Caroline, don't do this. Steve wrote to me. I was happy to help.'

'I bet you were.'

'He didn't want to leave the children with strangers.'

'You *are* a stranger.'

'No, no . . . I was, but I'm not any more.'

Caroline gives Mary a long look. Mary returns her gaze, but it makes her feel uncomfortable. She should say something, but she doesn't know what.

'I'm going upstairs to see my children,' Caroline says. 'Please pack your bags.'

Mary puts the kettle on. She thinks about phoning Steve, but decides against it. He'll be home tomorrow, and perhaps if she and Caroline have space to talk tonight, they might resolve things. How wonderful that would be. Katie would love it. For a brief minute, Mary allows a narrative to unfold in her head – one where Caroline is grateful, where Mary lives close by and comes round every day to look after the children while Caroline's at work.

Mary closes her eyes, aware of a dark space in her head that seems to be expanding. It's fear, panic, something of that nature. She rubs the back of her neck to ease the pounding. Caroline is here and she isn't ready yet.

She can't bear to lose the girl.

Mary gives up on the tea and opens a bottle of wine instead. She gets two glasses and a bowl of olives and spreads some cheese and crackers on a plate and arranges everything on the kitchen table. She opens the back door. She feels as if a wild creature has come into the house – a she-wolf looking for her cubs and she needs to give her an escape route, to show she's on her side and means no harm.

She drinks a glass of wine and feels more like herself. She eats three olives and half a cracker. She worries Caroline has fallen asleep, thinks perhaps she should go and check, but stops herself. If she goes upstairs, Caroline might remind her to pack her bags. She's on her second glass of wine when Caroline finally comes down. She stands in the kitchen doorway looking at all the things Mary has put on the table. She shifts from one foot to the other.

'Chris has grown,' she whispers. 'I hardly recognize him.'

Mary pours her a glass of wine and slides it towards her.

Caroline doesn't move. 'Can you believe I left them? I walked out the door and I went to the airport and I got on a plane and left my children behind.'

'You had your reasons.'

Caroline flicks her a look. 'Where does Katie think I was?'

'Steve told her you were on holiday.'

'Without her? Is that the best he could come up with?'

'She didn't need a grand explanation. Children are very forgiving.'

'Is that right?' The way Caroline clenches her jaw reminds Mary of the times she'd watched her sleeping all those years ago. That little Caroline used to have a recurring nightmare about falling planes.

'Are you hungry?' Mary asks. 'Why don't you come and sit down. There's cheese and crackers if you fancy it.'

Caroline shakes her head. 'Why are you even here? What are you doing in my house offering me food? You know nothing about domesticity. You can't even boil an egg. What was Steve thinking of, getting in touch with you?'

'He thought I might know where you were.'

'As if I'd tell *you* anything!'

'He thought your leaving had something to do with the past, so he wrote to me.'

'And then what? You inveigled your way into my home?'

'I phoned him, we got talking. He was struggling on his own and asked if I could lend a hand. I said yes because I wanted to help you.'

'Don't pretend you did this for me,' Caroline hisses. 'Not on my account. I didn't ask you to come and I had no idea Steve would be so stupid.'

'I don't expect you to be grateful,' Mary whispers, 'but there's no need to be cruel.'

'Cruel?' Caroline leans on the doorframe and narrows her eyes. 'Exactly how close have you and my husband become?'

'Don't be silly.'

'I wouldn't put anything past you.'

'Well, put that past me, because that's you being angry and has no basis in reality. You think Steve would look at an old woman like me? You think either of us would do that to you?'

Maybe it's raising her voice. Maybe it's the certainty with which she says it, but Caroline seems to lose her fire. She sort of crumples. Her shoulders sag first, and then she looks suddenly pale. She walks over to the table, kicks off her sandals and pulls out the chair. 'I'm sorry, that last remark was out of order. I'm tired. I don't know what I'm saying.' She picks up the glass and takes several long gulps.

Somewhere outside, not far away, a fox barks. It sounds eerie, painful.

Caroline says, 'I rang Steve yesterday. It was the first time we'd spoken since I left. Did he tell you?'

Mary shakes her head. Quiet, quiet.

'I had this fantasy he'd have taken time off work, that over these last weeks he'd been caring for the kids himself. I thought he'd finally understand something about my life.' She chews on her lip, another gesture from childhood. 'But he got you to come and look after them instead.'

'I'm sorry.'

'When he told me you were here, I went nuts and slammed the phone down. I thought he'd know I'd come straight back. I thought he'd ask you to leave.' Caroline pours herself more wine, then curls her hands tightly round the glass. 'I have no idea what to do now.' Her hands are shaking. She can't stop, not even when Mary puts her own hand on top of them.

'You don't have to do anything. Just sit here. Eat if you're hungry, talk if you want to. I'll leave tomorrow if that's what you want.' Mary butters some crackers so that things will seem ordinary, so that Caroline won't feel watched. She cuts an edge off the cheese.

Caroline leans her head to one side and gives Mary the strangest of looks, as if she's weighing something up. She says, 'Have you found Chris a handful?'

Mary feels a soft wave of sorrow flood her body. 'He's a beautiful child, but I see how he could wear you down.'

'He doesn't sleep much, does he?'

'No.' Mary smiles, wants her daughter to know she understands. The boy wakes several times a night. He also has to be coaxed to eat, can't bear to be left alone, cries at nothing.

'An undiagnosed disorder,' Caroline says.

'Yes, Steve told me. I wish I'd known.'

'And what would you have done?'

'Anything you asked of me.'

Silence. Mary thinks Caroline is about to dispute this, and for a second she wishes she'd kept quiet. A retrospective offer to help sounds just like a lie.

Caroline says, 'Steve thought I was too old to have a second baby. Anyone over thirty-five is technically an "older mother", did you know?' She laughs, a soft sound. 'I was way beyond that when I had Katie and Chris came along nearly three years later, totally unplanned. I was so proud to be fertile in my mid-forties. It was like it closed the age gap between me and Steve, made us the same.' She leans her head against the back of the chair. 'It sounds ridiculous now.'

'No,' Mary says, 'it doesn't. It sounds perfectly understandable.'

'We had all the tests and they came back clear, but he had a seizure thirty minutes after he was born, and he kept having them for weeks. No one could tell us why. He had feeding and weight problems, he cried for hours on end. He was so different from Katie, absent somehow. And I could tell Steve blamed me. He's never said anything, but I feel it. He kept asking me stuff about those boys who died, your mother's sons, you know?'

Mary nods. Of course she knows.

'I told the doctors about that, but they didn't think it was significant. Anyway, Steve had been so hands-on with Katie, and it was like he couldn't bear to be Chris's father. He started staying at work later and later, and even when he was home he always seemed to be creeping towards the door.'

'I'm sorry,' Mary says. 'I had no idea.'

Caroline tops both glasses up. 'We appear to be getting drunk together.'

The fox barks again, further away now, a few gardens along. Cold air shivers its way into the kitchen.

Caroline picks up her wine glass and knocks half of it back. 'I was very depressed, very lonely and I blamed Chris. I wanted to shake him into making sense. It was like there was something wrong with his wiring and if only I could find a way to make him work, to rejig him, we could all go back to normal. I didn't ever hurt him, of course I didn't, but I got close a couple of times and it scared me so much. I felt such a bloody failure.' She closes her eyes briefly, as if she can hardly bear the thought. Mary feels her own eyes smart with tears. Caroline swigs the rest of her wine down. 'So, one morning, when Steve was at the park with the kids, I wrote a note and left it on the bedside table. It was like a dream, watching myself get in a cab and go to the airport. I kept thinking I was going to turn round and come home, but I didn't. I phoned Steve when I landed, so he wouldn't think I'd been murdered and he went absolutely nuts. He called me selfish, stupid, pathetic – all sorts. I figured the only way to survive was not to speak to him for a while, so I just sent postcards.' Caroline looks at Mary, amazed. 'I went to Spain and left my family behind. How did that happen?'

'Let me help you.'

'Don't be ridiculous.'

'I mean it. I've been here for weeks now, we've established routines and the children know me. You can take more time for yourself. Let me keep looking after them.'

Caroline shakes her head, bats Mary's hand away. 'There's something else.' Her voice sounds strained, as if it's going to hurt to say these words out loud. 'Something else for Steve to hate me for.'

And Mary knows then. She recognizes the weary guilt. 'You met someone?'

'Is it that obvious?' Caroline rubs her hands over her eyes as if trying to erase the memory. 'I'm such an idiot.'

'Are you still seeing him?'

'No, of course not! It was a few nights, that's all.' Caroline smiles – a tiny shadow of a smile. 'He was only twenty-five. He was the waiter at the hotel.' She slaps her forehead with the palm of her hand. 'Juan, the waiter!'

Mary laughs. She can't help it. It's such a wonderful cliché and she loves how life does that sometimes.

Caroline begins to chuckle too. 'I sound like I'm describing a very bad film, don't I?'

She gets up for another bottle of wine. They really are going to get drunk. Mary wonders if that's a good idea. There's a line they might tip over and where they are now – quietly laughing together – well, this is how special it gets. She doesn't want it to change.

Caroline sits down, opens the wine and slops some into both glasses. 'I felt more alive than I have for years. But every single morning when Juan left for work, I realized I hadn't thought about my husband or kids all night.' Her smile dies at the corners. She takes a slug of wine, slaps the glass back down. 'What does that say about me?'

Here we go, Mary thinks.

'Does it make me the same as you?'

How can she tell her daughter that disappearing for weeks is perhaps the most honest thing she's ever done? Foolish perhaps, definitely selfish, but certainly the most eloquent. For once in her life, Caroline has said, *I can't manage*, and it's such a relief.

'Perhaps,' Mary says, 'it makes you someone who needed a little time for themselves.'

'Is that what you needed when you dumped me with Pat? Nine years for yourself?'

'That's not fair.'

'No, it wasn't.' Caroline sighs and turns away. 'It must be strange to be you, to never think about other people, to always put yourself first.'

'I always wanted to be your mother, Caroline. I want to be a grandmother too.'

'I've often thought,' Caroline goes on, 'that you got pregnant on purpose. You knew your dad would throw you out, knew Pat would offer to look after me, knew you'd finally get the freedom you wanted. Sometimes I think you sacrificed me so you could have the life you dreamed of.'

'That's not how it was.'

'Wasn't it? Are you sure?'

'Let's not do this,' Mary says. 'Let's not rake over the past. Why don't we think about what's going to happen tomorrow when Steve gets home? How are you going to tell him?'

'Are you mad? I'm not going to tell him.' Caroline stabs a finger at Mary. 'You better not breathe a word. I swear, if you do, I'll never speak to you again. He'll divorce me. I probably won't even get custody.'

'Steve loves you, Caroline. He's not going to use the children to hurt you.'

'You know him best, do you?'

'I'm just suggesting you trust him, otherwise all that fear and resentment is going to sit there festering.'

'Please stop. I really don't need any of this hippy shit right now.'

'You'll end up blaming Steve for not understanding you, when you don't even talk to each other.'

Caroline gives her a long look. 'So, your advice is that I tell Steve I had a seedy fling with a waiter and ask him to forgive me, because if I don't, it'll eat us up like cancer?'

Mary shrugs. 'Something like that.'

'And if it breaks his heart, should I swap him for another model? That's what you told Pat, isn't it? Leave Lionel, divorce him, be happy. Well, look where that got her – walking into the sea with her pockets full of stones. So much for your good advice, eh?'

That hurts. Mary takes a breath.

'I'm nothing like you,' Caroline says, jabbing a finger across the table. 'You're the most selfish woman in the universe. You dump me, bugger off for years and then come back and steal me away. By the time I get home again, my mother's suicidal and my grandfather's a broken man. I gave up everything to look after him – *your* father. That should have been your job.'

'Not my job,' Mary says, 'and not your job either. No one asked you to do it and you didn't listen when I told you not to.' She pulls her shawl from the back of the chair. She'll go out for a cigarette. She needs to calm down. 'It's no one's fault Pat died, and yet you stayed there because you felt guilty. Chris's disability isn't your fault. Stop punishing yourself for everything.'

'Shut up,' Caroline says quietly. 'Please shut up and go away.'

'Steve might understand about Spain. He might like to get to know your fire.'

'Fire? I don't want to be someone who dumps their kids to run off to Spain to shag a waiter. I don't want to be someone who throws my guilt at my husband to make myself feel better. Stop going on about fire.'

Katie appears in the doorway shivering in her pyjamas. She's half asleep, disorientated. She looks from her mother to Mary. From Mary back to her mother. 'What fire?'

Time slows down.

Caroline holds out her hand. 'Baby, what are you doing down here?'

'I heard noises.'

'That was us. Were we loud? I'm sorry.'

'I didn't like it.'

404

'Come here and have a cuddle. Shall I take you up to bed?'

Katie sticks her thumb in her mouth. 'Why are you here?'

'I've come home.'

Mary sees the girl frown, like perhaps she's still asleep and doesn't trust this dream mother, this thin brown woman with braids in her hair who she hasn't seen for weeks.

Go to her, Mary wills.

She can't bear to see Caroline sitting at the table with her arm out to welcome a child who seems stuck in the doorway.

'I didn't like it,' Katie says again.

Caroline scrapes her chair back and stands up. She half stumbles to the door, sweeps Katie up and plants kisses on her hair. 'Let's go upstairs to bed, come on.'

'You smell funny.' Katie squirms to get down. 'I don't want to go to bed. I want sugar milk.'

'What?'

'Hot milk with a little sugar,' Mary says. 'Sometimes she wakes in the night and it soothes her.'

'I want to sit outside,' Katie says, still wriggling to get down. 'Can we do that? There might be wolves.'

Mary shakes her head. 'Not now, Katie. Mummy wants to take you to bed.'

'Wolves?' Caroline says.

'Big ones,' Katie says, holding her arms out wide. 'We ride them.'

'It's just a story,' Mary says. Which sounds ridiculous as soon as she says it, because of course Caroline knows there aren't real wolves in her garden.

Caroline stands in the doorway looking at Mary. She's thinking terrible thoughts – Mary can see them roaring behind her eyes. She's thinking her daughter is different. She's thinking it's Mary's fault. She's also thinking she's given too much away, that Mary's not to be trusted with children, husbands, secrets. But the worst, the very worst thought of all is – what if she is the same as Mary? What if abandoning children and loving the wrong men is in her blood? It cannot be. She has to make it go away.

'You need to leave,' Caroline says. 'I'll book you a taxi. There'll still be plenty of trains.'

She sounds ridiculously polite, as if cold practicality will keep the child from knowing her mother is raging. But look at the girl. She knows. She's pushing away from Caroline, reaching her arms towards Mary.

'Stop it,' Caroline says, pulling her close. 'You're going to bed.'

'I'm not. I don't want to.'

Mary takes a step forward. 'Could I take her up?'

As soon as the words fall out, Mary knows they're preposterous. As if Caroline would ever leave the two of them alone together now. They'd be climbing out of windows, shinning down drain-pipes, riding off on wolves . . .

'You need to pack your things,' Caroline says. She takes a step back, licking her lips as though something bitter is there.

Mary looks at her feet. She nods. She'd hoped for a few minutes alone with Katie, to say sorry for leaving, to promise to love her always. But she isn't going to get it. 'A goodnight kiss then?' she smiles at Katie. 'How about one of those before you go to bed?'

'Why are you getting a train?' Katie's voice is small and fearful. 'Where are you going?'

'I have to go home now, to my own house.'

'Will you come back?'

'I hope so.'

'Can I visit you?'

The question fills Mary with a dull pain. 'Of course you can. Whenever you like.'

'Don't,' Caroline breathes. 'Don't tell her that.'

She expects them to give each other up, just like that. She wants Mary to pack her stuff and vanish. She wants Katie to be obedient and stop resisting every damn thing.

Steve will have his part to play. If he wants his dutiful wife back, he needs to ask no tricky questions.

And Caroline? Instead of thrashing it out with her husband, instead of saying, *You know what? I can't do this, I need your help, I need us to be closer*, she's going to pretend everything's fine, that her absence was a never-to-be-repeated aberration. Nothing happened, nothing went wrong, nothing needs talking about. She's going to lock all her feelings in a box.

Mary feels as if she's stepped away from herself, out of her body, and is observing, watching herself as she leans in to kiss the child, to stroke that beautiful hair one last time. 'I love you,' she says and she hears how desolate she sounds and she hates it about herself, hates that Katie hears it too, is looking at her uncertainly now.

Caroline frowns, as if telling Mary not to display emotion in front of the girl when here she is, ripping them apart. 'I'm going to take her up.'

Mary watches as they go down the hallway. A mother and her daughter. At the turn of the stairs, Katie waves, her chubby hand a pale starfish in the dark.

'Goodbye,' Mary whispers. 'Goodbye, my beautiful girl.'

Forty

There it was – the heart of all that Mary was missing. Two little girls – one her daughter and one her granddaughter – had both been taken from her. And, as her memory failed, she'd only been able to recall the pain of their absence, but none of the details.

Katie drew a line under the story in the memory book. There were no pages left. The story of the photo was told, in so far as it was possible to recall it today.

She was glad Mary seemed so relieved to have the facts at last. 'That's right,' she'd said. 'Every scrap of that is true. I remember it all now.'

'I can't believe I did it,' Mum had said. 'It feels like something I heard once or something I read about. How could I have done such a thing? How could I have pushed you out into the dark after you'd looked after my children for weeks?' She'd looked around the room bemused, as if expecting answers from the furniture or the walls.

Mary had reached out a hand and smoothed Mum's hair. 'You needed me to be the bad one. It's all right. I don't mind.'

Mum had turned her head to look at her. 'Mum,' she'd whispered to Mary. 'I'm so sorry.'

No one died because Mum threw Mary out. Mary went to live with Jack. Dad came home. Chris got back into a routine. Katie started nursery. Letters were never written (both women agreed this was the case) because Mary didn't want to interfere and Mum was trying to be the good one all over again.

And Mary slipped from Katie's memory, because eight weeks is no time in the life of a child and kids need help to hold onto memories. They need photos and videos and family stories told again and again – *Remember when Mum left? Remember when Mary came to stay?* No one was going to tell horror stories like that round the dinner table, so it became a secret – kept inside by Mum, studiously ignored by Dad, never really known of by Chris, let go of by Katie, and eventually forgotten by Mary.

Katie shut the book and placed it on the coffee table. Hopefully, the pain of Mary's blue blank would recede now she had the facts to hook it on. And when those facts slipped her mind, as they inevitably would, they existed in the book and Katie would tell her the story again.

Although, perhaps she should start a new book and transpose Mary's stuff across? Because when Mary went into a care home, she'd need her memories with her and the nursing staff were definitely not having access to the things Katie had written at the back!

She smiled at that as she stood up and gave Mary a kiss on her fuzzy sleeping cheek. She peered round the kitchen door to wave goodbye to Mum (on the phone to social services), who frowned and looked surprised.

'Where are you going?' she mouthed.

Katie pointed at the world beyond the window, then waggled her mobile to show she'd keep in touch and blew Mum a kiss.

Mum looked ridiculously pleased to be given so much.

Outside, Chris was still in goal.

'You can go back if you like,' Katie told him through the fence. 'The worst is over.'

409

'Can I stay out if I want?'

'I guess.'

One of the boys ran across and looked her up and down. 'You know Chris?'

'He's my brother.' She tried to make herself sound hard in case he was thinking of using Chris as a drugs mule, but the boy just grinned.

'Thought so, you've got the same hair.' He turned to Chris. 'You going?'

'Not yet.'

The boy nodded, as if that was good news and ran back to the game.

'Go away now,' Chris told Katie. 'You're embarrassing.'

A story, Katie decided as she crossed the courtyard to the gate, is like a bolt of material or a woollen scarf, and you might pull out a thread and look at it boldly because there it is sitting in your palm. But there are countless threads tangled together and some belong to you and some belong to other people, and incoherence and inconsistency become part of the narrative.

Mary had her version of the time she came to stay and Mum had hers. Dad would have something to add. If Katie interviewed the old neighbours, she'd get more. If Jack was alive – more still. Maybe she'd seek out the Spanish waiter and find out what he thought. All the threads bind and twist together. And every time you look it's different, because stories change in the retelling.

Even now, if Katie was challenged to repeat what she'd heard, she'd add bits, miss bits out, maybe ramp up her own role. She might accidentally sit on Mary's lap when her four-year-old self came down the stairs, or make Mum miss her in ways it sounded as if she hadn't. If she really wanted to embellish, she'd let Mary live next door with Jack, let Dad forgive Mum and not hold a grudge so deep he'd find himself attracted to another woman. Or maybe Mum could come back with the waiter (Katie secretly loved this part of the story, because it made Mum so much more human and gave Katie so much more room to trip up in her own life). Maybe they'd all live in a commune – waiter, Dad's girlfriend, Dad's baby, Jack and Mary – a happy sprawling family.

Katie laughed out loud as she crossed the road to the garage, because that was possibly stretching the realms of believability.

And this next story – the one she was walking into right now. How would that pan out?

What if she lost her nerve? What if she got arrested? What if Simona came storming out of the café and went crazy? The plot lines would all adjust, the narrative would shift and who knew what would happen next . . .

Forty-one

Katie walked over to the menu board and grabbed the little box of chalk from the shelf underneath. Simona pretended not to notice, but her shoulders tensed as Katie walked past and back out the café door.

She crossed the road to the library. It felt important to be close to the garden, as if she might rebalance what happened there. She knelt down on the pedestrianized area in front of the bike racks and shook the chalks from the box. She started with a long curved pink line on the pavement. It was supposed to be red next (she'd checked the colours on her phone) but there wasn't a red chalk, so she drew an orange line underneath and went over it with pink. Both lines looked a bit thin and nondescript, so she went back over them and fattened them up.

Katie had always tried very hard to avoid danger. Why not? Hadn't her mother always warned her? But in avoiding danger, you have to keep to yourself. To guarantee not catching Ebola or Sars or bird flu, for instance, you have to live in isolation and see no one. Viruses are transferred by bodily fluids, by intimacy. If you don't touch or kiss another person or breathe near them, you'll never catch anything. But you'll never know closeness either. Or what it is to love. Or really be alive.

Yellow was for sunlight and green for nature. Katie liked the fact that each colour had an ascribed meaning. She'd never known that before. There wasn't a turquoise chalk, so she used blue.

A little boy came over. 'That's a rainbow.'

Katie smiled at him. 'That's correct.'

'Why are you doing it?'

'Guerrilla action.'

'Can I help?'

She handed him the green chalk and he took it. He glanced at the library door where a woman was strapping a baby into a push-chair. 'What shall I do?'

'Go over the blue line and turn it turquoise. That's the colour for magic.'

He squatted next to her and began to chalk. Katie had a brief fantasy that his mother would let him stay, that other children would join in, that by the end of the afternoon this drawing would arc down the high street.

'We're doing a rainbow,' he told his mum as she came over.

'Any particular reason?'

Katie looked up at the woman's polite puzzled face and tried to remember all the meanings she'd just Googled. 'It's about being proud of your identity. It's about humanity and also sexuality.'

The boy giggled. 'You said sex.'

'No, I said sexuality.'

'OK,' the woman said, 'we have to go now.' She pulled the boy to his feet and made him give the chalk back. 'If this is to do with gay pride, then you probably shouldn't be doing it here,' she told Katie. 'You should do it somewhere else, somewhere that isn't out-side a library where there are kids about.'

Katie swallowed hard as the woman hauled the boy away. It didn't matter. It wasn't important. She was just a stupid woman. Not very many years ago, the cops would probably have been called and Katie would've been arrested. And not many years before that, she might've been put in the town stocks and pelted with rotten fish and vegetables. And before that, she'd most likely have been burned as a witch. Progress in the UK might be slow, but at least it wasn't one of the many countries in the world where loving someone of your own sex was still illegal.

There wasn't an indigo chalk for serenity, so Katie did blue again and there wasn't violet for spirit, so Katie blended pink and blue together. Now the rainbow was complete, she began the first figure. The little stick-girl reminded her of Jack's post-it note and she wished with her whole being that he wasn't dead. Imagine if he walked up right now and sat down beside her? He'd understand why she was doing this, she knew he would. She drew a second girl next to the first and another next to her. She wondered if there was a collective noun for girls. A pride of girls? A tribe?

A bloke unlocked his bike behind her. Katie didn't look up, but as he wheeled past, she heard him whistle the song from the *Wizard of Oz*.

That made her smile. That made her think Jack wasn't so far away after all. Mary was right about so much. Katie hummed the song under her breath as she drew another girl.

Mary knew that young women in nineteen-fifties England were supposed to be modest, self-deprecating and demure. They should not have too much self-confidence, not assert their sexuality or independence and never express their appetite or desire. They should be restrained, make sacrifices and put others first.

Mary knew it, but she thought it was poppycock. *Baloney*, she thought, *what a load of nonsense*, and she cocked a snook at it.

There were a whole row of girls now. They reminded Katie of a string of paper dolls her dad had cut out for her birthday years ago. She wondered where Dad was right now. In the hotel pool with his baby daughter? Drinking cocktails on some French beach?

Katie picked up the orange chalk. She'd give all the girls orange dresses. Orange was for healing.

If Mary was never a good girl, Mum went in the opposite direction. She even blamed herself for Pat's death and spent years atoning. Good girls don't come any better than that. But being good all the time makes you resentful. And the resentment leaks out as you get quietly and politely furious.

Two elderly women pulled shopping trolleys towards Katie. One of them said, 'You don't see kids using chalk any more.'

The other one said, 'Remember how we used to play hopscotch?'

Katie didn't know if they expected a response, but she smiled anyway and they waved and smiled back at her as they walked away. She wondered if they were a couple. She wondered if they'd been together for sixty years and no one had even noticed.

There were twelve girls in a row now. Like dancing princesses, or months of the year. She'd run out of rainbow, but she wasn't ready to stop. What was the point of that? She needed a witness before she could go home. Wasn't the definition of 'brave' being afraid and doing it anyway? What if she took a photo and sent Simona a Snapchat? Would that count for anything? What if she made this rainbow her Facebook picture? She made the lines neater while she thought about it, she blended colours together, drew more girls, breaking out from under the rainbow, no longer protected by its arc.

Would it be brave to text Esme? She could text, LIBRARY. URGENT. Esme wouldn't come alone, of course – she wouldn't dare. She'd bring Amy and a whole load of girls from school and they'd look like they were in a girl band with their miniskirts and brown bellies and their hair all dip-dyed and they'd stand looking at Katie as if she was an exhibit in a gallery.

Then Amy would say something hateful like, 'Oh my God, you are so entirely weird. What are you even doing?'

Because everyone needed a fall guy, someone to blame so they could keep looking good. And when Katie had dared to lean in and kiss Esme, she'd broken all the rules. Good girls mustn't be threatening or strange, or they'll be punished. They'll be left out, talked about and marginalized.

But Katie knew if she texted Esme, she'd only end up getting into a fight with Amy, and it wasn't time for that yet and it wouldn't help with what she really wanted, which was for Simona to believe in her. So she texted Simona instead: I AM UNBECOMING. Which felt very apt, because Mary's father used to say she was 'unbecoming' when she misbehaved. It meant perverse, incorrect and unseemly. Everything a girl wasn't supposed to be. Of course, it also meant unravelling, which was true of Mary in another way, but Katie wouldn't think about that now . . .

She wondered at one point if she'd gone mad, because she'd drawn about thirty girls. She wondered what would happen if she didn't stop. Would Mum come looking? And what would she say? And thinking about that, Katie felt sadness creep through her, because there were clearly so many difficult conversations still to come, so many tears still to be shed. She distracted herself by thinking of Chris playing football, of Mary's contented face when she said, 'Every word of that story was true.'

'A rainbow?'

Katie looked up, heart slamming, to see Simona frowning down at her.

Simona folded her arms. 'You think this is going to impress me?'

'Probably not.'

'Did your mum kick you out? Is that what's happened?'

416

'No. Apart from talking about herself most of the time, she was remarkably OK.'

Simona looked surprised. 'Well, that's good. I'm glad about that.'

Ah, so she did care . . .

'So,' Simona said, 'why a rainbow?'

'I wanted to show you I meant what I said. You know, about holding my hand up.'

Simona scowled down at it. 'Are they supposed to be people?'

'They're girls.'

'It looks like a queue for the toilets.'

Katie smiled and held out a stick of chalk. 'I'm not very good at drawing.'

Simona took the chalk, but didn't sit down. She said, 'I don't really believe in all this rainbow shit by the way. I'm not interested in joining a gang or a group. I'm my own person.'

'I think it's supposed to represent diversity. You know, each of us is unique?'

Simona rolled her eyes. 'Then why are all your girls wearing orange skirts? That's not very diverse, is it?'

She was so close and so gorgeous that Katie didn't know which bit of her to look at. They were only a metre apart. Katie could reach out and grab her ankle, pull her down to the pavement and hold her close.

'Please sit down, Simona. You're making me nervous.'

She looked pleased about that. 'Nervous of what?'

'I don't know. That you'll go away?'

Simona sat down and began to chalk over one of the orange skirts with blue, turning it muddy brown. 'I wish black chalk existed,' she said. 'Or gold.'

Katie loved having her this close, loved watching her beautiful hands swap the second girl's skirt for trousers and give her sandals and rub out some of her hair, so it was shorter. She was drawing herself.

Katie gave the first girl a green tea dress with pink roses and boots. She made her arms longer and gave her little chalk hands that reached out to the second girl.

'Her fingers look like fish fingers,' Simona said, but she had a smile in her voice as she allowed her girl's arms to stretch just far enough for the chalk girls to touch.

Katie drew the sun, bright orange. Simona drew clouds and the rain and they both drew birds flying high. Katie wondered what would happen when they ran out of rainbow-themed things. She started on a tree in case Simona said she had to go, because a single tree could lead to a wood, to acres of forest, to hours sitting drawing together.

'Unbecoming?' Simona said.

'Improper,' Katie said.

Simona nodded. 'I see.'

'Or like someone who can be anyone. A work in progress.'

A bloke stopped his bike right by them. 'You girls are sort of in the way there,' he said.

Simona smiled at him. 'That's sort of the point.'

'The point of what?'

'Recognition.'

He looked intrigued. 'What do you want to be recognized for?'

'Surviving,' Simona said.

'Hope and pride and diversity,' Katie said, remembering what she'd read on Google.

He got it then and looked a bit embarrassed, but he gave them both a high-five before walking round the rainbow and locking his bike up. He didn't say anything else, but he grinned as he walked away.

'That told him,' Simona said.

'What's the collective noun for girls?' Katie asked.

'A sapphist of girls?'

They both laughed. Katie's entire body felt warm, like she'd been at the cocktails again. Nowhere was better than this. Tuesday afternoon washed in warmth, chalky fingers, a slow breeze lapping at her dress.

She drew roots for the trees. She buried acorns beneath their folds, summoned worms and strata of rock. Simona set a fire with sparks of orange and yellow and pink chalk. Katie drew a tent. Simona a blanket.

'Did you know,' Simona said, 'that some bloke in America bought a house and painted it the colours of the rainbow just to piss off the preacher from the fundamentalist church opposite?'

'A house?' Katie said. 'Maybe that should be our next project?'

'Our?' Simona said. But her voice was still warm.

'I hate Amy,' Katie said.

'She's an anomaly. Don't worry about her.'

'I still hate her.'

Each girl had a different outfit now, like the paper dolls on the back of old-fashioned comics. There was a sun and a moon and countless stars. However much they wanted to carry on (and Katie definitely did) there was nothing else to draw and no room to depict it. They sat there contemplating it, occasionally leaning over to blend lines together. Cyclists walked round, like they shouldn't wheel their bike on it. One woman even tied her bike to the railing instead of using the last rack which was directly behind them.

Katie told Simona about a magician she'd seen on TV once who'd drawn a chalk circle round a five-pound note and crowds of people had walked right by and not one had dared pick it up.

'That reminds me,' Simona said. 'I forgot to tell you – my boss wants to see you. That's actually why I came over.'

'Your boss? Why?'

'You stole the chalk.'

'I was going to give it back.'

'Well, you'll just have to explain that to her then, won't you?'

'That's ridiculous.'

'Sorry, but she asked me to come and get you, so you'd better hurry up.' Simona grabbed Katie's hand and it was like a powerful jolt surged through Katie's entire body, like her hand became some kind of conductor.

'Where are we going?'

'I just told you.'

'Are you actually serious?'

'Yeah, she was really quite angry.'

Katie followed Simona back across the road and into the café and she had no idea, none at all, where they were going and Simona led her past the counter and past the customer toilets and through a door marked *staff only* and through a little steamy kitchen where a bloke in a chef's hat looked both amused and pissed off and Katie thought the door ahead must lead to the manager's office and was she really going to get bollocked for pinching chalk? But actually it led into a stockroom – shelves and boxes and packets and tubs of things and then total darkness as Simona shut the door and switched the light off and said, 'I was kidding about my boss.'

Simona smelled of hot skin and sweet cakes and that cleaning fluid they sprayed about the place. She said, 'No one's going to see us this time.'

'I don't care if they do.'

Simona laughed. 'How about a roar of girls?' And she gently pushed Katie against the closed door.

'A brazen of girls?' Katie whispered. Her eyes were adjusting to the dark. There was a tiny window way up high at the back of the stockroom and delicate light flickered in. 'I can see you now,' she said.

Simona smiled. 'Me too. I can see you.' She took Katie's hand and brought it to her mouth. She kissed each finger. Katie watched her, mesmerized.

'A goddess of girls?' Katie said.

Simona laughed. 'Lesson number four,' she said. 'And I warn you now you'll be addicted for ever. Are you ready?'

Katie nodded. *Let it come.*

'We're the most beautiful people who ever lived,' Simona whispered. 'Did you know?'

'Yes,' Katie said.

'Yes?'

Katie said it again. 'Yes.'

Simona touched Katie's belly. Up. Gently. Her fingers running over the ridges of Katie's ribcage.

Katie dared to do the same, a mirror image. Through the crackle of Simona's shirt, Katie's fingers conjured pearls.

Simona gasped. A sound Katie had never heard before, so new it made her heart leap. She felt as if the moment was held in air, suspended.

She knew then that this was how it was supposed to be.

Forty-two

Here's what happened, exactly how it went.

Three weeks after drawing the rainbow, Katie yelled, 'Stop the car!' and like someone in a movie, her mum slammed on the brakes. Also like someone in a movie – someone determined and very sure of her lines – Katie leaped from the car and ran across the street to Esme, who was walking arm in arm with her not-so-new boyfriend, Lukas. Katie skidded to a halt in front of them.

She said, 'I'm not going to keep quiet about my side of the story any more.'

Esme looked horrified.

Katie said, 'So, if you keep going around telling everyone I jumped you, then I'm going to come right out and give my version, you understand?'

Lukas put a protective arm round Esme. 'You want to just leave my girlfriend alone? She's had enough of you lot.'

But Katie wasn't interested in talking to boys about their owner-ship of girls. She looked Esme right in the eye and said, 'My version includes many salient details.'

Esme glanced nervously at Lukas. 'Please make her go away.'

As if Lukas had any power about that.

Katie said, 'You've been a bad friend to me, Esme.' Then she said, 'And Amy's dragging you down. Do yourself a favour and either educate her or stop hanging around with her.'

She'd been wanting to say that for a while.

Lukas pulled Esme closer. 'Esme asked you to go away. Did you hear her?'

Esme rested her head on his shoulder as if it was all too much for her and for a moment they looked like an elderly couple. Katie could see their lives stretching ahead for years and years.

She blew Esme a kiss. Esme, of course, did not try and catch it. It blew into her face and away over her head and into the sky. But, hey – kisses are wasted on some people.

Katie got back in the car and told her mum to step on it and the two of them giggled – even Chris, who'd moaned about the day's plans since Katie proposed them, deigned to smile. She could see him in the rear-view mirror.

'It'll be fun,' she told him, turning round. 'Trust me.'

'I wanted to play football.'

'When you could be spending the day with your three favourite women?'

He shook his head as if she was an idiot.

And now, as they drove out of Bisham, Katie imagined another story. One that hadn't happened yet.

It was the one where Simona got her A level results (only a week to go) and did brilliantly and her attention turned to the future, to Manchester and her life away from this town. And Katie got her AS results and discovered that although maths wasn't really her subject, she'd done fine, so perhaps these things had some genetic element after all. She'd stop fighting Mum over which A level to drop, and to keep her brain busy she'd keep all four subjects on.

And the story would keep going (as all stories do) and once term was in full swing and the trees were turning to autumn, Simona would invite Katie to visit Manchester. They'd be on Skype when the invitation was issued (something they were going to do at least twice a week).

'Get your mum to drive you to Cambridge,' Simona would say, 'then change at Ely and it's straight here.'

Katie would blush (some things never change). 'For the weekend?'

'Of course for the weekend.' (Simona never blushing, Simona smiling that devastating smile).

And so Katie would get on the train after school on a Friday and Simona would meet her at the station and they'd go to the student union, a place where no one knew Katie, a place crowded with strangers, with people Katie could only dream of knowing. But loads of them would know Simona and they'd give Katie admiring looks that held all sorts of possibilities.

And Simona would talk about a new world – about lectures and tutorials and her crazy social life – and Katie would recognize her all over again: her energy, her courage to be exactly herself, just like Mary. She'd remember how Simona was always fully charged and she'd wonder (as she'd wondered many times already) if she wanted to kiss her or *be* her.

And Simona would ask how life was back in North Bisham and Katie would shrug and tell her not much had changed.

'School?' Simona would say. 'They treating you right?'

'A long story,' Katie would say, because it wasn't going to be easy to dare to be herself. 'Jamie's talking to me again and I'm mates with his new girlfriend. He's got a lovely girlfriend.'

Simona would smile. '*How* lovely?'

Katie would know she was being teased and try not to blush, but it would be hopeless.

'Any ideas about uni yet?' Simona would say.

But Katie wouldn't want to relay the continuing battle about Cambridge (not all things could turn out well in imagined stories, or they wouldn't be believable) – how it was still hard for Mum to let go of old patterns, to allow Katie to have autonomy over her own destiny. 'I might take a gap year.'

'And do what?'

'Travel. I've never even been on a plane. There's a whole world out there.'

What would happen at night? Where would Katie sleep? Didn't students only have single beds? The story had many possible paths.

And maybe, at some point over the weekend, Katie would dare to ask if Simona was seeing anyone, and of course she would be – but no one special, she'd say.

And Katie would smile because Simona was leaving open a door and they both knew it.

'If you come to uni here,' Simona would say, 'we could see more of each other. I'll move into a shared house next year, so you could be the most radical fresher ever and live with a bunch of second years.'

Was she asking Katie to move in with her? Once again, the story twisted and turned . . .

Simona would, of course, be interested to hear about Mary, about how well she'd settled into the nursing home, how the staff all loved her and she was the biggest flirt in the place. 'She's got a boyfriend,' Katie would say. 'Some old bloke whose wife died years ago. She says Jack approves completely. Can you believe it?'

Simona would laugh and say she could believe anything about Mary. Anything at all.

They wouldn't talk about Katie saying, *teach me*, and how embarrassing and how painful it had been. Or about Simona saying,

We're the most beautiful people who ever lived, did you know?
which was a line Katie would remember for ever. Or about the
lessons and what number they'd got up to before Simona left. No
– they'd forge new paths, navigate new territory. Because the world
was various and unfolding and anything was possible.

Forty-three

Katie walked arm in arm with Mary, along the corridor. As they passed the dining room Mary gave a cheery wave to some other residents who were just sitting down to their lunch.

'I'm off,' she called. 'They're taking me home!'

Mum, walking ahead with Chris, turned round and gave Mary a stern look. 'No,' she said. 'You're not going home. We're going to the beach.'

'But it's lunch time!' Mary protested. 'I'm going to miss pudding!'

'We've got food with us,' Mum said. 'You won't starve, don't worry.'

'Well, I hope you've got something I like. I hope you haven't just brought rubbish.'

'Definitely something you'll like,' Katie told her as they passed through the lobby and waved to the staff at the reception desk. 'Mum's gone to loads of trouble.'

But Mary wasn't listening. She was pointing a finger across the car park. 'Look,' she whispered in awe. 'How beautiful everything is.'

Katie looked. It was dazzling – the sea, the grey rolling clouds, the faraway stones on the beach shimmering.

'I'll just get the stuff out the car,' Mum said. 'Then let's get down there before it rains.'

They made their way through the car park and across the road to the sea wall. The beach was almost empty. The few families braving it had their windbreaks up and were huddled into deck-chairs staring gloomily at the sea. A couple of children played in the shallows with fishing nets and buckets.

'I love all this water,' Mary said, as they made their way down the wooden steps. 'It's never far away.'

It was true. She could even see it from her bed. She'd only been at St Catherine's a fortnight and Mum had already procured her a room with a view. She'd helped Mary recreate the memory wall too (including some previously hidden away photos) and hired a van to bring Jack's G plan chair and the Welsh dresser from the old house. Mum was a much more thoughtful daughter now she didn't have to live with Mary.

When they got to the sand, Katie flapped the blanket open and Chris put up the deckchair. Mum put the ice box down and took off her shoes.

Seeing Mum do that, Mary kicked her own shoes off. 'I'm going to dip my toes in the sea,' she said. 'I haven't done it for years and you're not stopping me.'

Mum smiled. 'You do it every day. You come down here with Charlie, your key worker.'

'I do not. What rubbish you talk.'

Mum linked arms with Mary and they walked together down to the water's edge. Chris and Katie wandered down behind them.

There were small blue mussels left stranded on the sand, scallop shells, lumpy black seaweed and the occasional dead crab, over-ripe, legs askew. Katie picked up two shells and handed one to Chris.

'Here. Mother of pearl.'

He smiled, put it in his pocket. 'I'll give it to the baby.'

428

'She won't want it. You should get her a proper present.'

He nodded. 'I'll ask Dad.'

'Have you emailed him? Is everything sorted?'

'Next weekend for a sleepover.' He gave her a look. 'You should come.'

What would she talk about if she did? *Dad, I have something to tell you . . . Dad, there's this girl . . . Dad, will you still love me if . . . ?* So many painful discussions ahead. 'I miss him too,' she said. 'If I don't come with you this time, it doesn't mean I never will.'

'Yes,' Chris said. 'I know.'

Across the water, clouds were brooding and there was the low rumble of thunder far away, but that wasn't stopping Mary. She'd tucked her skirt in her knickers and was wading into the shallows. Mum held onto her arm, clearly convinced Mary would swim off if she let go.

Katie crouched down to untie her boots. Chris did the same with his trainers and they went to join them. They stood in the water, the four of them in a row.

'Isn't this lovely?' Mary said. 'So much water just for us.'

The sea was freezing, but it felt exactly right. The roar and rush of it, the tang of salt in the air, the tumble of foam.

Teenage Mary had walked to the beach near her father's house every day. Trapped in a town that was too small for her, she'd gazed longingly at the horizon and imagined a future for herself. As the cold bit into Katie's legs, she made a silent pledge to bring Mary here every time she visited and remind her of that teenage girl. And if Mary forgot how to walk (as one day she might), Katie would bring her in a wheelchair.

'Look!' Mary said. 'Over there.'

She pointed to the place where the bay ended. Beyond it, the coastline curved again, and again beyond that. A series of curves, stretching away.

'See up there? On top of that cliff? That's where Robert keeps his caravan.'

'Ah, Robert Gibson,' Mum said. 'Whatever happened to him, I wonder?'

'You know him?' Mary looked pleased. 'He's a particular friend of mine.' She smiled shyly as if entrusting Mum with a secret. 'We lie together listening to the waves. Sometimes, when the tide's in, it's like a great storm and us all cosy inside.'

Mum patted her hand. 'That sounds romantic.'

'He's got a wife,' Mary said, still looking over at the cliff top as if Robert and his wife and a ghostly caravan might materialize.

'Yes,' Mum said. 'I wonder how things would have worked out if he hadn't?'

'Oh, not much different,' Mary said breezily. 'I'm not a fan of marriage.'

Mum shook her head. 'Well, at least you loved him. I'm glad you did. I find it comforting.'

Mary looked at her amazed. 'I loved all of them. Every single one.'

Poor Mum – a father she never knew, an adoptive father who gave up on her and a string of 'uncles' after that. A mother who left her, and an adoptive mother who killed herself. Whenever Katie really considered what Mum had to put up with in her childhood, she was stunned that Mum managed to parent her and Chris with any warmth at all. She took Mum's arm, linked her own through it and gave her a squeeze.

'All right?' Mum said. She leaned in and gave Katie a quick kiss on the side of her head. It felt awkward, but Katie appreciated it.

Chris scooped up a handful of water and threw it back into the

430

sea in an arc. There was no sun, just a vague glare, but it made a rainbow. A tiny perfect rainbow. He reached down to do it again.

'I've decided,' Mary said. 'I don't want to be buried. Burn me instead and scatter me over the sea. Right here would be fine.'

Mum nodded very seriously. 'All right.'

Katie didn't want to imagine it. But it would come. The day they carried Mary in an urn across the sand. They'd wade into the shallows to tip her into the water. She'd spread everywhere. She'd be washed up on the beach, swooped at by gulls, eaten by sharks. She'd sink to the bottom and lie there with all the treasure ships and mermaids. She'd wash away to Scandinavia and lap along the fjords to the mountains. Mary's adventures would go on and on.

'Right,' Mum said, 'let's get some food down us. We've got a special treat for you, Mum, and I don't want it raining before we get to it.'

'Is it sandcastles?' Mary said. 'Because I haven't got my bucket.'

Mum laughed. 'I should've thought of that. Next time, we'll bring one.'

Mary looked thrilled. 'You will? And a spade?'

Mary was encouraged into the deckchair and Mum spread a shawl round her shoulders. The rest of them sat on the blanket. Paper plates were handed out, Tupperware dishes of jerk chicken, rice and peas, curried lamb and samosa were passed round. Katie had been cross-examined about Mary's dietary preferences so Mum could pass details on to the care home, but she'd clearly made a mental note for herself.

'You certainly have eclectic taste,' Mum said. 'Pat would have hated every bite. It would've been fish paste sandwiches followed by an apple if she'd had anything to do with it.'

'Ahh,' Mary said. 'Poor Pat. She walked into the sea, you know,

431

weighed herself down with rocks. Never dared go in the water her entire life and then she finally took the plunge.' She smiled sadly. 'There's a word for that, I expect.'

Sacrifice might be the word, Katie thought. Or *fury*.

'Let's not get the ghosts out,' Mum said. 'We're supposed to be having fun.'

'Aren't they already out?' Mary asked, puzzled.

Because for her, the dead were everywhere. Pat had already been spotted preparing vegetables in the kitchen at the care home. Her father had been spied shuffling round the corridor in his overcoat. Jack was probably strolling along the beach this very moment, about to reach for a stone to skim across the waves.

It wasn't just the dead Mary saw either, but the living in other phases of their lives. Time was fluid in Mary's head. Mum might be a teenager, slamming doors at St Catherine's and throwing Mary's things about. But she could also be a sturdy girl with pigtails and ribbons, sitting contentedly in the garden, making daisy chains with four-year-old Katie – two little girls together.

As they ate their way through the picnic, the clouds darkened. Seabirds occasionally lifted from the water, unnerved, it seemed, by the swelling waves. The windbreak along the beach billowed and flapped.

'Summer in England,' Mum said with a wry smile.

Katie liked it. It felt as if the elements were pressing in on them. There was an absence of restraint.

'We better get on with it,' Mum said, collecting up the dirty plates and napkins. 'Everybody ready for the *pièce de resistance*?'

They'd practised at home and each had their assigned role. Katie unpacked the glasses (borrowed from the café along with four long-handled spoons) and Chris opened the tub of fruit they'd prepared together earlier – strawberries, raspberries and crushed pineapple (Mum had insisted on a particularly posh recipe). Mum clicked open the ice box, pulled out the tub of ice cream and cautiously peeled off the lid.

'Not too bad,' she said, 'considering it's been out of the freezer for nearly two hours.'

'What is it?' Mary asked.

Mum angled it so Mary could see. 'Neapolitan.'

Mary laughed. 'If you say so.'

Katie held the first glass out and Chris spooned fruit into the bottom. The glass was passed to Mum for a scoop of vanilla, to Katie for a dash of melba sauce and back to Chris for more fruit. Round it went until there was strawberry and chocolate ice cream, several layers of fruit and a squirt of spray cream (courtesy of Chris, who'd solemnly pledged not to squirt any in his mouth). Finally, it went to Katie for decoration. She had the best job and she'd had to fight Chris for it. She carefully manoeuvred a wafer down the side of the glass, drizzled melba sauce over the cream, shook sprinkles on top and lastly (and best of all), placed a fresh cherry in the centre.

'Goodness,' Mary said, as she accepted a tea towel across her knees, a spoon and the first complete sundae. 'That's the best knickerbocker glory I ever saw in my life.'

Mum laughed. 'Let's get three more together quick, before we get rained on.'

In honour of one of their favourite customers, 'Mary's knicker-bocker glory' was on the menu at the café now. Mary had been told twice, but Katie wasn't sure it had sunk in. As she ate her way through her own sundae, she decided that tomorrow, when she was at the café, she'd take photos – of the boxes of cocktail umbrellas and wafers that were stored in the stock cupboard, of the chalkboard and the way Simona had taken such care over the

433

lettering – it was all curlicued and every colour of the rainbow. Next time Katie visited the care home, she'd bring Mary printouts for her wall.

'That tide's turning,' Mum said. 'I'd say that water's definitely coming in now.'

Chris stood up to look, maybe expecting to see the ocean coming to a halt before shifting gear and changing direction. But all there was to see were a few waves lap-lapping up the sand. He sat down, clearly disappointed.

'It's freezing,' he said. 'Can we go?'

'Soon,' Mum said. 'When we've all finished.'

It was definitely colder, although maybe that was something to do with the ice cream. The kids with the nets had gone and the family with the windbreak were packing up. Katie's teeth chattered as she scraped syrup from the bottom of her glass.

Mary had saved her cherry until last, resting it on her knee while she savoured each mouthful of sundae. Now she'd finished, she popped the cherry in her mouth.

'I know someone,' Katie said, 'who can fit five cherries in her mouth at once. She spits the stones across the garden.'

Mary turned to Katie, delighted. 'I know her!'

Chris frowned. 'Who are you talking about?'

'Mary,' Mum told him.

As if to prove it, Mary spat the cherry stone metres across the sand. 'There was a tree,' she said, 'and a boy polishing his bike saddle.'

'Norman,' Katie said.

Mary clapped her hands. 'That's it. It starts with "N" and ends in "N" and it's got six letters. I told him, if it's Nelson, you can forget it!'

'Forget what?' Chris said.

'Kissing!' Katie and Mum said in unison.

Mary hooted with delight. Mum and Katie laughed with her. Even Chris joined in. It was wonderful, the sound of them all laughing.

Mum said, 'It wasn't funny when you got dragged up the path by your dad though. He made you scrub your face at the sink.'

'That was because of the lipstick,' Katie said. 'You didn't tell Norman you'd left the shape of a kiss on his face. And because he didn't know it was there, he didn't wipe it off. And that's how you got caught.'

'And the lipstick was your mother's,' Mum said, 'which probably made it worse in your dad's eyes. You found it in the wardrobe on the night of an air raid and kept it with you for good luck.'

Chris looked utterly bemused, but Mary gazed at Katie and Mum in amazement. 'You two know a lot of things,' she said. 'I have to say, it's absolutely magical sitting with you.'

'It's all in your memory book,' Katie said. 'You told me everything in the first place.'

'Did I? Well, that doesn't surprise me. I've always been very good with words.'

The sky had turned the colour of ink. Mary laughed as her skirt lifted in the breeze.

'We should get going,' Mum said. 'It's going to rain any minute.'

'And what if I want to stay?' Mary looked at Mum, expecting something from her, but Mum only smiled.

'Then I guess we'll get wet.'

Chris groaned and huddled himself into his jumper. 'I won't. I'll go and sit in the car.'

'And what about you?' Mary asked Katie. 'What will you do if the sky opens up?'

435

'Brave it out with you, of course.'

'Although really,' Mum said, 'it'd be much better if we went inside and got a nice cup of tea together, don't you think?'

Mary considered that. 'Will they have biscuits?'

Mum laughed, a soft noise through her nose. 'If you've got room for biscuits after all that ice cream, I'll be very surprised. But they've definitely got some. Shall we go and see what kind?'

Katie helped Mary to her feet. They stood shoulder to shoulder as Chris folded the deckchair and Mum packed the ice box.

'You know,' Mary said, her eyes lit with amusement, 'I'm sure they just did all that.'

'That was when we arrived,' Katie said. 'Now they're doing it in reverse.'

Mum whisked up the blanket, gave it a shake and passed it to Katie to carry. 'You'll be all right seeing Mary up the stairs?'

'Sure, don't worry about us.'

'What's happening next?' Mary asked as Katie linked arms with her.

'Anything you want. What would you like to happen?'

'Well, I don't want to go to bed.'

'It's not bedtime,' Mum called over her shoulder. 'It's cup of tea time.'

'But after that,' Mary insisted.

'After that, you're going to stay awake all night,' Katie said. 'You're going to wait until everyone's asleep and then you're going to watch a movie in the TV room and steal cakes from the kitchen.'

'Don't,' Mum said. 'You'll give her ideas.'

But Katie wanted to give Mary ideas. Hundreds of them. Resistant, demanding ideas. Indecorous and unseemly ideas.

Chris stood with Mum at the top of the steps and looked down at Katie and Mary as they made their way up. 'You could have a party.'

'Great idea,' Katie said. 'You could borrow a radio and invite everyone to your room.'

'I do like a bit of dancing,' Mary said, pulling herself up by the rail. 'And I know where they hide the cigarettes.'

Katie laughed. 'Sounds like a plan.'

Mum shook her head. 'I clearly have no control over anyone.'

The first fat drops of rain began to fall, changing the smell of the air. Chris yelped and ran across the car park, banging the ice box against his leg. Mum hurried after him.

'And tomorrow?' Mary said, pausing on the step to gaze back at the waves. 'What will I do then?'

Outlined against cloud, birds appeared – autumn migrants streaming out to sea.

'Beautiful,' Mary breathed.

Katie drew Mary close and linked their arms more securely. 'You'll have more adventures.'

'What kind?'

'All kinds. You're a work in progress.'

Mary jigged her feet in delight. 'That'll do me.'

It would do Katie too.

She was bound to stumble, but if she did – she'd pick herself up and try again. She'd falter, resolve, lapse, have another go. Her whole life over. On and on.

Just like Mary. Just like Mum and Chris and everyone else.

Works in progress, all of them.

Acknowledgements

Thanks to Nathalie Abi-Ezzi, Katherine Davey, Patrice Lawrence, Sarah Lerner, Anna Owen, Aisha Phoenix and Elly Shepherd for their camaraderie and encouragement.

Thanks to Louis Hill and Archie Hill for their patience, wisdom and general brilliance.

Thanks to Andrew St John for braving the storm.

Thanks to Catherine Clarke, Bella Pearson and all at David Fickling Books for their unfaltering belief and many kindnesses.